# PART OF THE GAME

To: Zoe

Thanks for the love and support

J.K. Vereen

ISBN: 978-1-5136-6577-1

Published by Pen 2 Pen Publishing
2261 Talmadge Rd.
Suite #71
Lovejoy, GA 30250

www.pen2penpublishing.com

Printed in the U.S.A.

This is a work of fiction. Names, characters, places, and incidents are products of the author's imagination or are used fictitiously. Any resemblance to actual events or locales or persons, living or dead, is entirely coincidental.

# PART OF THE GAME

By J.K. Vereen

# Chapter 1

Another scorching summer in the Magic City was coming to an end. The year was ninety-eight, and, like most hustlers in the south, Crow was pumping the Trick Daddy Dollars classic 'You Don't Know Nann' out of his Pioneer stereo. Sitting at the dinner table, Crow bopped his head to the beat as he did his daily ritual, counting his tax-free money.

Crow wrapped a small black rubber band around his last stack, then looked down at his Movado timepiece. He began wondering what was taking his sister so long to return from the Arab convenience store. Although he didn't mind staying home with his twelve-year-old nephew P-Rock, Crow had other things to do.

Crow and Victoria shared a duplex their father had left them. Sadly, even without a mortgage, they struggled to make ends meet. After several failed attempts to maintain employment, Crow had returned to his old ways and followed in his father's footsteps, hustling and grinding full-time in Miami's notorious Liberty City. The nickname Crow was given to him because his shiny jet-black complexation resembled the glossy black bird.

While the bass from the stereo vibrated the sheetrock walls, Crow mimicked the lyrics word for word. Suddenly a sharp knock on the kitchen door interrupted his rap session. Assuming it was his sister, Crow swung the door open without asking. To his surprise, his visitor was one of the neighborhood's crackheads, Carwash. And despite Miami's typical 80-degree nighttime temperature, Carwash wore three layers of clothing. Thanks to Carwash's lack of hygiene, along with his wanton consumption of Wild Irish Rose wine, his body gave off a stench that Crow could barely tolerate.

Rubbing his hands together, Carwash said, "Ooooh wee, I'm so glad you home."

"Wuz up?" Crow asked, breathing through his mouth to avoid Carwash's reek.

With only one reason for Carwash to be standing in his doorway, Crow reached in his crotch and pulled out a small brown bag filled with ten-dollar and twenty-dollar pieces of crack.

"Lem'me get a wake-up for three dollars," Carwash said, holding out one dollar bill and eight quarters.

Crow looked down, and slapped Carwash's hand away, sending the loose change flying. "Muthafucka, how many time I gotta tell yo ass bout' dis unnecessary traffic! It's nine o'clock at night and you gon' come round' here wit three muthafuckin dollars. Man… get da fuck on through!"

As most fiends do, Carwash felt obligated to give it another shot. With a pitiful expression on his face, he began begging.

"C'mon, Crow, all da clientele I bring you, don't do yo boy like dat. You know my birthday today," Carwash lied with a straight face. "Bless me at least for my birthday."

The birthday game was a junkie's favorite line to use in hopes of receiving a little sympathy from dealers. Crow heard this same line numerous times, and actually Carwash's third birthday in five months. With all the yelling Crow had been doing, P-Rock walked into the kitchen to investigate the commotion. P-Rock's presence drew Crow and Carwash's attention.

P-Rock asked Crow, "Is my mama back?"

"Nah, P-Rock, gone back in da're and finish playing yo videogame," Crow said. As Crow spoke with P-Rock, he was completely unaware of Carwash's eyes illuminating when he spotted the stacks of money on the kitchen table. Crow swung back to face Carwash and immediately noticed that his facial expression was different. Crow dismissed any meaning behind his look and simply considered it ordinary addict behavior.

"Carwash, let 'dis be my last time telling you, don't come here wit' no muthafuckin three dollars!" Crow slammed the door in Carwash's face.

Still holding onto a glimmer of hope, Carwash stood at the door for a brief moment, praying Crow would reconsider and have the compassion to at least throw him a crumb. It took five minutes for Carwash to grasp that he wasn't going to get high standing there. Without the effect of crack to guide his next move, Carwash did something he was seldom sober enough to do: he turned and headed up the sidewalk, collecting his thoughts.

Walking quickly towards oncoming traffic, Carwash began talking to himself.

"Fuck Crow! Punk ass muthafucka gon' play me like I don't know people. I'ma make him wish he did serve me for my three dollars. I can't wait to holla at my cuz Big Tank!" Carwash said to himself with a smile.

Tank was a well-known and well-respected Jack Boy. At a chiseled 6'1" and 185 pounds, it definitely wasn't his weight that established his name. Tank had earned it by his signature manner of holding his pistol-grip Mossberg pump. Most of Tank's victims that were lucky enough not to get shot were ordered to strip and give up all their belongings, including their boxers and socks. Any time Tank used his 12 gauge, he aimed directly at his victim's face. And from the receiving end of the barrel, with his block-shaped head, he bore resemblance to an army tank. He earned the big title out of fear and respect.

Parked in his '74 Chevy Caprice with his partner in crime, Crunch, Tank was in the middle of sprinkling a D.P., or dime bag of powder, onto some weed he had inside of a five-dollar bill. They sat in a secluded spot in the rear of Arcola Lake Park. Tank chose Arcola Lake because the park had limited lighting at night and minimum police presence.

Tank rolled up the weed and lit the end. Once he exhaled, he continued strategizing the home invasion with Crunch. They had a mutual respect for one another. Each had been in the stick-up game for years and both were the definition of stone-cold killers.

Tank leaned back in his peanut butter ostrich-covered seat, making himself comfortable. With the engine off and windows up, the unique scent of weed laced with coke filled the interior.

"Peep game, we need to splack two cars. Both of them gotta be late models, because all up da're in Doral is new shit," Tank explained, laying down the foundation of his plan. "We need a couple of knives, and don't forget we gotta buy some more duct tape. Best believe dem knives gonna make a muthafucka cooperate real quick."

While Tank and Crunch discussed their tactics, Carwash slunk his way to the driver's side window, camouflaged by the night. He startled both of them with a knock on the glass.

With cat-like reflexes, Tank gripped the handle of his .45 cal. "Goddamn, Carwash!" Tank shouted. "Yo stupid ass almost got shot. What da fuck you sneaking up on me fo'?"

As Carwash spoke, he rapidly moved his hands like a rapper freestyling. "Yo, cuz, I know where grands at right now. It gotta be like $100,000 up in da're." Carwash overzealously exaggerated, knowing the sound of a six-digit pay would intrigue Tank. He explained what he'd just witnessed inside Crow's place. "So how much y'all 'gon give me for the lick?"

"Slow down, cuz. How many people up in da're?"

"Crow and a kid."

"You sho?" Tank inquired, wanting all the details.

"Does a cow shit manure? Hell yeah, I'm sure. As soon as Crow opens the back door, you'll see the cash like a mountain just sitting on the kitchen table."

Tank rubbed his chin twice, then opened his door. "A'ight, get in, cuz," Tank commanded Carwash, cranking up his car. He turned toward Crunch and smiled. "Dawg, you already know what time it is."

Watching Crunch nod in agreement, Tank dropped the gear into Drive and mashed the accelerator, bringing the grumbling sound of the Flowmaster exhaust pipes to life.

****

Victoria struggled to unlock the front door to the duplex. Holding her 14-month-old son Victor and three plastic bags of groceries, she twisted the doorknob. Suddenly Crow snatched the door open. "Damn, gurl, 'bout time you got back! I told you I needed to go to my baby mama's house." He frowned at his sister.

"Do you see me with a damn car? Boy, don't start with me. That juice you gave Victor ran right through him and gave him the runs, and shit leaked all down my arm. I am not in the mood. Anyway, where's P-Rock?"

On cue, P-Rock came running from the living room to impatiently go through the grocery bags. "Ma, what did you buy me?"

"I ain't have no extra money for nothing else. Look at that money your uncle got over there on the table." She said pointing at the stacks. "Ask him for some money."

Victoria put Victor down so she could change his pull-up diaper. She told P-Rock to bring Victor's diaper bag, and Crow told him to bring his Nike shoebox from under his dresser while he was at it. P-Rock went straight into Crow's bedroom, kneeled, and pulled out the shoebox Crow used for stashing his money. He quickly returned with the shoebox and diaper bag.

"Thank you, baby," Victoria said.

Crow took the shoe box from P-Rock and gave him a ten-dollar bill, smiling. "A'ight, youngin, don't never say I didn't give you anything."

After throwing the stacks in his shoebox, eight grand in total, Crow gave it back to P-Rock to return to its hiding spot

"He needs a good example from you, not just money," Victoria complained, and Crow rolled his eyes. Victoria was Crow's only sibling, and growing up in Liberty City hadn't been easy for either of them. Like many people in the world, they hadn't been born with a silver spoon, but their father did what was necessary to give them comfort. They both had his dark complexion, and Crow was the spitting image of his father at a younger age. Sadly, because Congress had passed the Anti-Drug Abuse Act, their father was doing life without parole at Atlanta's U.S.P. He had been convicted in trial on multiple drug charges, which occurred as a result of a simple traffic stop where a low-level hustler turned informant led one of Miami's most legendary conspiracy cases of the late 80's. Their father's conviction had brought the fury of the government upon him, and he learned what happened when you were convicted of running a C.C.E.—a Continuing Criminal Enterprise.

Before and after their father's incarceration, their mother had fought a brutal battle with breast cancer. She fought with every ounce of strength she had until sadly, in the winter of '92, she passed away.

Tonight, Crow was on his way to take his daughter, Raven, and her mother out to dinner, and afterwards they were going to the theater to watch the new Disney movie.

"It's 'bout time you spend some time with your child. If you spent half the time with your daughter that you do wit' dem hoes, maybe Raven would respect you and call you Daddy instead of Crow," Victoria scornfully said.

"Gurl, what you talking 'bout? Raven be over here almost every day. Shit… the only reason she call me Crow is because she grew up hearing everybody else say it. Damn, Victoria, that shit don't bother me. Raven knows who her ol' boy is. Ask her who buy her shoes and clothes, you know what she go say? My daddy," Crow said, impersonating his daughter's voice.

Victoria sucked her teeth and rolled her eyes at Crow. "Boy, pleeese… That's your fault Raven don't call you Daddy. When she first started that, you should've corrected her, but noooooo… You and her trifling mama thought it was cute that her first word was Crow."

Knowing he'd never win a debate with Victoria, Crow surrendered. His point was falling on deaf ears. To even the odds, he began letting her words go in one ear and out the other.

As always, Victoria didn't let Crow off the hook. Relentlessly, she kept going about Crow's lack of responsibility while she finished changing Victor's diaper. Once she was done, she wrapped Victor up in his powder blue blanket. She only eased off of Crow when someone knocked on the kitchen door.

"Who dat?" Crow loudly asked, relieved that the knock had shut Victoria up.

"It's me, man, this Carwash!"

Crow stormed to the door, unlocked it, and flung it open with rage in his eyes. He was prepared to literally kick Carwash's ass. Before Crow could get a word out, Carwash held up five $20 bills. The sight immediately soothed Crow's rage.

"Bless me for 100 dollars," Carwash said with anticipation.

Crow stuck his head out the door and looked past Carwash. He looked left, right, then looked Carwash up and down. Crow's thoughts quickly shifted to wondering where Carwash got $100 from, when earlier, he'd barely had three. Crow initially suspected a trick by the Narcs, but swiftly dismissed that thought because of Carwash's reputation for hating the police.

Crow stepped to the side. "Damn, Carwash, how the fuck you come-up?" he inquired before inviting him inside and double-locking the door.

Not expecting that question, Carwash came up with the fastest, most logical answer he could. Rapidly rubbing his hands together, he said, "You know me, I was walking through Amoco gas station, and, with my hawk eyes, I saw this clown drop his wallet on the ground. I hurried and snatched dat muthafucka up. I was 'bout to buy me a bottle of Wild Irish Rose, but instead I made a U-turn and came straight back here." He handed Crow the money.

Satisfied with Carwash's story, Crow proceeded to give him five small pieces of crack; each was approximately the same size as a piece of Chiclet chewing gum.

Carwash gazed at the dope in his hand. "Good lookin, Crow, damn good lookin." He noticed the kitchen table was clear. After securing the dope in his briefs, Carwash twisted the top lock, then turned the doorknob when…

*BOOM!* With the force of a hurricane, the steel door slammed into Carwash's chest, knocking him to the ground.

Tank raced inside the duplex with a menacing look enhanced by his bloodshot eyes. He aimed his gun at Crow. "Yeah, playboy, you know what it is, lay down or fall down!" Tank screamed with authority. Crow instantly dropped to his knees.

Crunch followed with his 9mm drawn, slamming the door as he entered the duplex.

"Don't play dumb, you know what we want. Where dat bread and work at?" Tank asked with his .45 cal trained at Crow's head.

Lying flat on the carpet, Victoria was petrified and shivering uncontrollably at the sight of the intruders. Despite the grave danger she faced, her biggest concern was the safety of her kids.

"Crow, pleeeese!" Tears crowded her eyes. "Give them what they want."

Tank slapped Crow on the side of his face with his gun. "Yeah, Crow, give us what we want, or your life along with it. Shit… Makes me no difference cause we not leaving without what we came here for. Now don't make me ask twice."

The powerful blow lacerated Crow deeply above his right eye. Even with a stream of blood flowing into his eye, Crow refused to show panic. Prepared for a situation like this, he was ready to give up his decoy stash, which would satisfy any Jack Boy's greed. Just as he was about to comply, all hell broke loose. *POP!* Crunch discharged a round next to Victoria to help intimidate Crow. He shot into what he assumed was merely a powder blue blanket; however, when the blanket turned from powder blue to maroon, it registered.

"Noooooo!" Victoria cried, snatching up Victor and bolting from the duplex.

Victoria's unforeseen escape made Crunch lose focus on Crow. Standing motionless, Crunch became uncertain. Either chase after Victoria or abort the robbery. He carelessly lowered his gun to his side.

Reacting without considering the consequences, Crow sprung to his feet, fiercely grabbing Crunch's wrist. With adrenaline fueling his vengeance, Crow jarred the gun from Crunch's hand. As the gun hit the floor, Crow poured all his strength into a right hook to Crunch's jaw. The blow knocked Crunch off balance. Crow dove for the gun.

*POP... POP!* Crow's body jerked twice as two bullets entered his back. Tank shot with a marksman's accuracy. The powerful rounds from his .45 were fatal. One bullet exited his chest, the other his throat.

Outside, Victoria ran towards her neighbor's house with tears in her eyes. She tightly held Victor to her chest as she screamed at the top of her lungs.

"Help me pleeease! Somebody help me!" Victoria repeated over and over, banging on the aluminum screen door. Her neighbor Mrs. Knowles peeked out of a living room window and made eye contact with Victoria. She was perplexed, trying to figure out what was going on.

"Call the paramedics! My baby's been shot," Victoria cried out, barely able to speak clearly.

Back inside the duplex, Tank and Crunch were unaware of P-Rock peeking from the living room, where he was hiding behind the sofa. As he watched his uncle lay lifeless in a pool of his own blood, tears formed in his eyes.

Pissed about the unplanned caper going horribly wrong, Tank and Crunch looked at each other, overwhelmed, with Crow's lifeless body on the floor, a child shot and no cash to show for their time. Tank stared at his cousin in disgust. Carwash was cowering under the kitchen table. Tank despised Carwash for putting him in this predicament. Following the rules he'd always lived by, Tank kneeled down and shot Carwash in the temple.

"Sorry, cuz, no weak links allowed." Tank and Crunch barely waited for Carwash's body to hit the floor before they bolted from the duplex, leaving the door wide open.

****

With sirens blaring, the police arrived on the scene several minutes after the pandemonium erupted. Exiting their vehicles with their service weapon drawn, the uniformed officers secured the scene, making clearance for the paramedics. The officers roped off the crime scene with yellow tape. Once given the greenlight, two medics raced directly to Victoria.

Sitting on Mrs. Knowles porch, Victoria rocked back and forth, numb, desperately trying to maintain her sanity.

"Ma'am are you injured?" the Hispanic female medic asked, looking at the massive amount of blood on Victoria's shirt.

The other medic, a black male, compassionately removed Victor from Victoria's arms. Fearing the worst, the paramedic was relieved to feel a slight pulse. In record time, he placed Victor on the stretcher.

Standing next to a police officer, P-Rock cried out, "Ma…!"

Mrs. Knowles ran over to P-Rock, embracing him as the medics loaded Victor into the ambulance. Victoria looked over at P-Rock and Mrs. Knowles, distraught, as she climbed into the ambulance.

Terrified, P-Rock stood still, staring at the ambulance as the double doors slammed shut and it sped away.

****

A dark green Crown Victoria arrived on the scene, and a large African American detective stepped out of the sedan. At 6'4" and 270 pounds, and with a clean-shaved head, he looked more like a Miami Dolphins lineman than a detective. He glanced at the roped-off area, then made his way over to where three officers stood with Mrs. Knowles and P-Rock.

"I'm Detective Sherman," he said to Mrs. Knowles. Then one of the officers cleared his throat to get Sherman's attention. Once they made eye contact, the officer shifted his head towards P-Rock. "Excuse me," Sherman told Mrs. Knowles. "Hey, little man, what's your name?"

"Patrick," P-Rock replied.

"How are you doing, Patrick? Did you see what happened next door?" P-Rock did not answer Sherman verbally. He simply nodded his head. "It's OK. You can tell me what you saw," Sherman said in a lenient tone.

"Them men shot my brother and uncle."

"What men? Who were the men that shot your brother and uncle?"

Once again, P-Rock did not answer Sherman. He merely shrugged his shoulders, then released more tears.

"Did you see what these men look like?"

"Yes."

Sherman glanced over and tilted his head at the officer, affirming he was speaking with an eyewitness to the shooting. "Stay here with Patrick. I'ma go check out the scene."

Sherman ducked underneath the crime scene tape. He shook hands with a few uniformed officers. After several handshakes and familiar nods, Sherman entered the duplex through the same door Tank had kicked in. Before even seeing a body, Sherman could smell the odor of blood in the air. He looked down and noticed a trail of blood that led beneath the kitchen table, where Carwash's lifeless body lay in a fetal position. Sherman squatted down to get a better view.

He stared at the hole in Carwash's head, immediately noticing skull fragments and soft grey matter scattered about on the kitchen floor. From the size of the exit wound and damage to the skull, Sherman concluded that a large-caliber weapon was used. Also, as a result of Carwash's frequent run-ins with law enforcement, Sherman knew exactly who he was. Assessing the scene, he turned and saw, about 15 feet away, Crow's body lying face down in a pool of blood.

Sherman, a senior detective, had dedicated 18 years to law enforcement; the last ten had been spent in Robbery/Homicide. He'd seen his fair share of surprises; however, he was puzzled over the reason to shoot a child, a junkie and his dealer. He began contemplating whether their murders had been a hit, or if it was in fact a very sloppy robbery.

The first officer on the scene walked up to Sherman to give his account of what he had discovered upon his arrival. "Detective, I believe there's a good chance that the victims knew their killers."

"How so?"

"Well, from the looks of the door, the locks are still intact, with no damage."

"Do we have any more witnesses?" Sherman asked.

"Yes, sir, the paramedics have already taken the other witness, Ms. Victoria Cole, and her youngest child to Jackson Memorial."

"How old was the child?"

"I'm not sure. Couldn't be no more than two years old."

"Damn, these bastards shot a toddler."

"Yes, sir."

Sherman took all his cases seriously, but the cases that involved kids he took personally. As a rookie fresh on the force, he and his ex-wife had lived in Aswan apartments in Opa-Locka with their only child. That summer, with school out, Sherman allowed his son to go swimming in the complex's pool with a few of his friends. While Sherman and his wife were watching the evening news, the thunderous sound of gunfire erupted. Overcome by a blanket of panic, Sherman ran outside to investigate and check on his son. What he saw changed his life forever. Lying on the concrete next to the pool was a teenager with a tennis ball-sized hole in his leg. Sherman then looked in the water and saw the unthinkable. There, with the same size hole in his back, floated his only child. Sherman buried his son at the age of eight years, and to this day that pain still dwelled in his heart. He vowed to one day find his son's killer and had never stopped looking.

Sherman stared at a wall portrait with P-Rock and Victor posing with big smiles. He softly grinned at the sight, then returned to analyzing the crime scene.

An officer standing on the porch stuck his head in the door and alerted Sherman. "The media just arrived."

"I don't care who's here, just keep them away from my witnesses."

The officer turned his head, then looked back at Sherman. "Ah… Sir, they're interviewing the neighbor."

"Goddammit, move!" Sherman shouted, running out the door.

Outside, in front of Mrs. Knowles's house, a cameraman was filming the entire scene. While zooming in on the station field reporter interviewing Mrs. Knowles, the cameraman was blindsided by Sherman appearing and covering the camera lens with his hand.

Instantaneously, Sherman jumped in the reporter's face. "What the fuck do you think you're doing? I'll tell you right now, you're interfering with my investigation. And turn that fucking camera off," Sherman yelled, taking two steps towards the cameraman. He then walked over to Mrs. Knowles. "Ma'am… please don't answer any more questions, and wait for me on your porch."

# Chapter 2

Jackson Memorial Hospital was known throughout Florida for having one of the best trauma centers in the state. Inside the trauma unit, Victoria ran behind the gurney that carried Victor, dried blood all over her shirt. As the nurses and assistants raced Victor to surgery, Victoria continued following them, not wanting to leave Victor's side. A nurse attempted to stop Victoria from gaining entrance to the surgery.

However, stopping Victoria was an impossible task for the 115-pound nurse. Determined to be with her son, Victoria effortlessly pushed her aside. "Lady, get the hell out my way," she said, trying to keep up with the gurney.

Two large orderlies saw Victoria's irrational behavior and rushed over.

"Ma'am, please calm down. You going back there right now will only complicate the situation. Let the doctors do their jobs," one of the orderlies said, doing his best to console her.

"Let me go!" she screamed, struggling to get out his grasp. Yet her fight was to no avail. She surrendered.

Victoria leaned into the orderly's shoulder and let out her pain in her tears.

The orderlies escorted Victoria to the waiting room, which was extremely crowded. Even though there were over fifty chairs, one of the orderlies had to bring in an extra chair for her. Nevertheless, instead of sitting, Victoria paced between the vending machines and pay phones, praying.

In the surgery, the doctors worked vigorously to reduce the critical condition Victor had arrived in. Regrettably, the bullet had entered his forearm, doing severe damage before exiting his elbow.

Victoria's anticipation seemed to have slowed down time. It had to have been well over an hour without any news on Victor's condition.

"Victoria!" someone yelled.

Victoria turned towards the voice. Heartbroken, and in drastic need of moral support, she spotted her Aunt Tara running in her direction. They immediately hugged, and Victoria let out a sob.

Behind Victoria and Tara was her younger cousin Tanika. Moments later, Crow's daughter Raven and her mother Pam showed up as well. They all gathered around Victoria and embraced.

"What did they tell you? How's Victor doing?" Tara asked, full of concern.

"I dun'no. The only thing they told me was that he's in surgery."

Raven tapped Victoria's arm. "Auntie, is my daddy OK?"

Victoria's bottom lip trembled at the answer to Raven's question. She placed her hands over her mouth, and was grateful Raven's mom intervened. Instinctively, Victoria looked up at the television and noticed the Channel 7 breaking news logo posted across the center of the screen. She and everyone else faced the TV and saw Victoria and Crow's duplex in the background of the reporter.

"This is Helen Mitchell reporting outside the residence where a child was shot and a double murder took place. At the moment, little information is available, but police sources say this tragedy was possibly the result of a drug deal gone wrong. That could be the motive behind this heinous crime, which left two men dead and one child clinging to life. With me now, one of the neighbors, Mrs. Monica Knowles. Please, Mrs. Knowles, can you shed some light on what occurred next door?"

"Well… my God! I heard three gunshots, and everything happened so fast." She paused, covering her face with her hands. "Lord… I sure hope that baby gon' be alright. He's such a…" Mrs. Knowles' words stopped mid-sentence when a hand covered the camera lens, putting an end to the interview.

After Mrs. Knowles was led away, the reporter turned and faced the camera. "We will bring you more information as it develops. This is Helen Mitchell reporting for Channel 7 News."

An additional thirty minutes passed, then finally a white female doctor entered the waiting room. "Excuse me… Ms. Cole," the doctor said, pausing for Victoria to come forth.

Victoria rushed to the doctor. "Is my baby okay?"

The doctor gave Victoria a faint smile. "Ms. Cole, your son's condition is stable. The surgery went well. Sadly, there's no easy way to say this. But I'm sorry to inform you that your son will have to undergo another surgery. Because of the severity of his injury, we're going to have to amputate his arm below the bicep. I give you my word, we used every exertion we could muster to save his arm."

Victoria pulled her own hair, hoping to wake up from this nightmare.

"Ms. Cole, I promise that your son will receive the best treatment and therapy available."

Barely able to comprehend the doctor's last words, Victoria let out a ghastly howl. Trying to fathom all the atrocities that had taken place in such a short time unsettled her equilibrium. Victoria began rocking from side to side. Emotionally exhausted from the abundance of turmoil, Victoria tilted her head up towards the fluorescent lights. Her vision became blurred, and darkness engulfed her as she fainted and collapsed on the floor.

Victoria was rushed to a room for observation. An hour later, after the doctor was satisfied that Victoria had recovered, she allowed Victoria's family members inside the room.

Sitting up in the bed, Victoria looked at her Aunt Tara as she walked in. "I thought this was all a dream, but, when I woke up in this bed, I knew this nightmare was real. My baby has to lose his arm, and my brother is dead."

Tara sat on the bed next to Victoria to comfort her. There was a knock, and the door opened.

All eyes were on the towering man that stepped in.

"Excuse me, folks, I am Detective Sherman." He approached the foot of the bed. "I need to speak with Ms. Cole."

"Do you need to do this right now?" Tara said frowning.

"I know the unbearable pain of losing a loved one. Believe me, I do. I know this very moment is a tough time, but it also is a critical time in this part of my investigation. Although my timing may seem inappropriate, it's imperative that I ask you a few questions. We need to apprehend the animals responsible for this tragedy as soon as possible. So please take your time and reiterate what happened."

Victoria took a deep breath and cooperated as best she could with Sherman. However, due to her continuous sobbing, Sherman decided to end his questioning and speak with her another time. He handed her his card and recommended she call later.

****

The following day, Sherman arrived early at the police station, making it his top priority to track down the suspects in the double murder and attempted murder of Victor. Sherman gave instructions to have all calls pertaining to the case transferred to his desk. Before he'd finished his first cup of coffee, tips began pouring in through the tip line. Sherman treated each call as the one that could break the case; unfortunately, none had any credibility. Growing impatient with the amount of irrelevant calls, he finally found relief in the next one.

"Sir, as I stated, your name will remain anonymous. Now, can you repeat the information you have?" Sherman pleaded with the caller.

"Don't I get $5,000 for the information?"

"Absolutely; that is, if your information is substantial and a conviction is made based on your tip. Then, sir, you are entitled to the reward money. Now what should I call you?"

"Uh… uh… you said I ain't gotta give you my name."

"Sir, I said your name will remain anonymous. I will still need some way of referring to you," Sherman said, becoming frustrated with the caller. "How bout this? For now, I'll just refer to you as Mr. Chance. Okay, now what can you tell me about what transpired yesterday?"

The caller went quiet for a brief moment, then explained. "One of the guys killed was my buddy. His name was Kevin Hawkins. Everyone call him Carwash."

"I'm familiar with Mr. Hawkins' alias," Sherman added.

"The news said he died over a drug deal, except Carwash don't sell no drugs. He was a stone addict, but, hell, most Americans have some form of addiction. Anyway, just before he was murdered, I seen him get into his cousin's car, and that was the last time I saw him alive."

Sherman was under the impression the caller had a few more details then he was sharing. And his presumption was correct. The next thing the caller said gave Sherman his first big break.

"Big Tank is his cousin's name."

The mere mention of the name Tank registered prime *suspect* in Sherman's head. He straightened from his slouch, giving his undivided attention to the caller.

"Give me a description of the car," Sherman said, fully aware of the answer due to an unrelated robbery he had investigated. An interracial couple was robbed and fingered Tank as their attacker. In a routine traffic stop, Tank was subsequently arrested. Drastically, following his apprehension, the couple changed their story and refused to testify.

"Tank drives an old Chevy. You know, the kind they call a Donk."

"A Donk… is that an antique Chevy?' Sherman asked, tapping his pad with his pen.

"Yeah. It has a candy tangerine paint job and chrome rims."

"Anything else?"

"Hell, yeah… When y'all arrest Tank, how long before I get my money?"

"There is a process, and, once all the procedures are done, we will contact you. I'm going to need a number where I can reach you."

Sherman wrote down the caller's information, then ended the call. Immediately, he put out an A.P.B. on Tank as a person of interest. Next, he printed a copy of Tank's mugshot and headed back to the hospital with hopes Victoria could identify him.

It only took Sherman a few minutes to drive from the station to Jackson Memorial. He found Victoria in Victor's room, along with P-Rock, Mrs. Knowles, and her Aunt Tara. At the sight of Victor's bandaged limb, Sherman became infuriated at the thought of what the child had been through. Concealing his true feelings, Sherman remained professional.

"Pardon me, Ms. Cole. May I have a word with you in private?" He tapped Tank's mug shot on his chest.

Victoria stepped into the hallway, with P-Rock and Sherman following.

"Ms. Cole, I have some photos of possible suspects for you to view." He gave Victoria a small stack of photos with Tank's picture among them.

Victoria sat down and flipped through the mug shots with P-Rock looking over her shoulder. Victoria stopped scanning the photos at the sight of Tank's unforgettable image. Instantly, she started crying; and, without any comment, she handed Sherman Tank's picture.

*Bingo,* he said to himself. "Ms. Cole, I'm not supposed to make promises, but we're going to get that bastard, and that's a promise."

****

After Crow's funeral, Tara saw the pain Victoria was going through and, as a sympathetic gesture, invited her and the kids to move in with her. Tara offered Victoria a small room she used to use as a den. Despite the uncomfortable size, Victoria was grateful.

"Victoria, I finish making breakfast. Y'all come on down and eat," Tara shouted from the kitchen.

"Boy, quit staring at your brother's arm. Gon' ahead in da're and eat," Victoria said, catching P-Rock's eyes glued to Victor's bandages.

Once P-Rock left the room, Victoria looked around at her new living conditions. There was no closet, and their clothing wouldn't fit in the dresser; therefore, Victoria had stacked most of her clothes in the corner. As Victor slept, she caught herself watching him in a daze. Though she hid her fears, Victoria was really worried by the fact Sherman had not yet notified her he'd made an arrest. She remained in constant fear of her brother's killers one day returning to finish her off.

She snapped back to reality as Victor rolled over and started crying.

"OK… Mama's here… Mama's right here." Victoria picked Victor up and rocked him on her shoulder.

Finally, after soothing the pain Victor was in, Victoria joined P-Rock for breakfast. From the aroma of beef sausages, Victoria predicted the entire meal. Tara wasn't much of a chef, or creative when it came to cooking. So, as usual, the meal was grits, scrambled eggs, and toast, along with the fried sausages.

"Victoria, I'm working a double today, so you'll have to cook dinner. There's some Hamburger Helper in the cabinet, and some ground beef in the fridge," Tara said, hanging her apron on the pantry door. "Oh, yeah! And don't forget to register P-Rock for school today."

"Aunt Tara, I thought you were going to drive me to the schoolhouse."

"Gurl, you know I work Monday through Friday. And not one, but all my bills are past due. I can't afford to miss a minute, let alone a couple of hours from work. The 32 bus runs in front of the house. It goes right down the street from the school." Tara looked down at her watch. "Shit… I'm already running late. I'll see y'all when I get off." Grabbing her car keys off the counter, Tara bustled out the door.

After Tara left, Victoria sat at the dinner table literally forcing herself to eat. She had lost her appetite the instant Tara told her to catch the city bus. When P-Rock finished eating, Victoria had him to wash up and get ready.

It took Victoria a little over an hour to get herself and Victor ready. Yet P-Rock only took twenty minutes. Like the average 12-year-old, he took minimal time getting dressed. Feeling a little stressed, Victoria took another 15 minutes to sort through various boxes in search of P-Rock's immunization records, along with a few other documents needed to enroll him in school. Finally, after finding everything, she placed Victor in his stroller, and the three of them headed to the bus stop.

During their wait, P-Rock kept busy entertaining Victor, while Victoria drifted in her own world, reminiscing about Crow. Ten minutes passed before the bus arrived.

As Victoria settled down in a seat, a teenager with a blown-out afro sat in the empty seat in front of her.

"Wuz-up, Victoria. Remember me?"

Victoria intensely studied his features, trying to put a name to his face.

"It's me, Nut." He removed his sunglasses.

"Oh, hey… Peanut! I couldn't recognize you wit' dem shades on. Damn, boy, your hair has grown since the last time I seen you. How long it been, 'bout a year, huh?"

"Yeah, that or longer. So, wut-up, Victoria, you still braiding hair?"

"No, not really."

"I need my shit done bad azz hell. I can pay you. What you charge, $30?"

It didn't take Victoria long to consider whether she would do his hair. She was unemployed, and, on top of that, she could really use all the extra money she could get. "Ok, I'll do it for you. Lem'me get your number."

Peanut wrote his number down on an old receipt and handed it to her.

"Do you still stay wit' yo brother in Liberty City?" Peanut asked, unaware of the tragic event.

"No, my brother passed" she said emotionally.

"What… Crow dead! Damn, that's fucked up. How did he die?"

Victoria did not want to go into detail, so in a low whisper she asked if he had seen the news.

Peanut nodded, then looked at Victor's limb. "Oh, shit, that was y'all?" His question was loud enough to draw the attention of several people on the bus.

The other passengers' voices could be heard in whispers. They stared, gossiping over what the news had reported, and what rumors had said. Victoria felt embarrassed and distraught by some of the remarks she heard.

"…Umm, she had them kids in a crack house," one passenger whispered.

"They were cooking dope right in front of her kids," another said.

"Chile… I heard Health Services investigating her, and word is she 'bout to lose her kids."

Each comment was loud enough to decipher, and Victoria had finally heard enough. Before they had even reached their destination, she rang the bell signaling to the bus driver that she wanted to get off at the next stop. Heartbroken and nearly in tears, Victoria gathered her boys and hurried off the bus.

"Ma, what's wrong?" P-Rock asked.

Tears began flowing down her face. Unable to give P-Rock a decent answer, she simply told him to come on. They walked the remaining two miles to Lake Stevens Middle School, and, by the time they reached the school, Victoria had her tears under control.

It didn't take long to enroll P-Rock for school. In 30 minutes, they were back at the bus stop, waiting to return home. P-Rock occupied his time reading over the literature pertaining to his new school, Victor was fast asleep in his mother's arms, and Victoria went back reminiscing. Only this time, she was trying to figure out why her life was so hard and why she suffered so much. Her thoughts drifted to the time she got pregnant with P-Rock.

****

## Part of the Game

In 1984, the crack epidemic was rapidly spreading through housing projects throughout Miami. With some help from the Cuban community, many local hustlers found refuge from their financial worries. Street-corner dealers went from chasing cars to running their own drug organizations. The same as legitimate employees, workers were given salaries, and some were even given bonuses for putting in overtime. If connected with the right team, you could be riding a bike one week and driving a Cadillac the next.

As with any profession, the limelight and the cash hustlers were making attracted young females. Victoria and her best friend Latricia were no different. At the time, both girls attended Central High School, and they were members of the cheerleading team. Victoria was a few months younger than Latricia. At 16, both had the voluptuous curves of some 25-year-old women. Victoria had been very petite at twelve, but, as the years passed, her thighs grew, and her breast reached D-cups. On the other hand, Latricia was always thick, practically a Big Mac away from being obese. However, from her early teens, Latricia always attracted older men. Some even old enough to be her father.

After each cheerleading practice, Victoria and Latricia would walk across the street to the Plaza, where several dope boys hung out, shooting dice. Down on one knee shaking the dice, Yella glanced to his right and noticed Victoria standing with Latricia. He gave the dice one last shake, then let 'em roll. He pushed the point, then made eye contact with Victoria. Immediately Victoria started blushing; she thought he was cute and admired his natural curly hair and his mouth full of gold teeth. As Yella walked over to introduce himself, infatuation was written all over her face.

"Hey, sexy. What's yo name?"

"Victoria," she answered with a smile.

"Damn, gurl, you fine as hell. I've been watching you, and this not the first time neither. Let me holla at you in private cause it seems like everybody all up in my grill."

"Talk in private where?" Victoria said, looking around.

"That's my blue DeVille over there." He pointed at his car. "Let's go sit down and get to know each other a little better."

Attraction and lust spurred her, and she followed Yella's lead. Yella's Cadillac DeVille was fully customized. He had navy blue curtains with his initials embroidered in the center, an oversize chrome grill, and, between the driver and passenger seats, a small box TV hooked to the boomerang antenna on the trunk. For its time, the DeVille was truly enough to make any woman who was fascinated by material objects weak.

While Victoria sat inside admiring the suede upholstery, Latricia was smiling and getting acquainted with Yella's right-hand man, Paul. Latricia was always known for being hot in the ass, so it was no surprise to Victoria to see Latricia and Paul holding hands as if they'd known each other for months.

Yella licked his lips and looked directly into Victoria's eyes.

"Victoria, there's this new movie everyone's talking about call The Terminator. Why don't you and yo homegirl come hang out with us? We can go get a bite to eat, catch the movie and chill. You wit' that?"

Before Victoria could reply, the back door opened, and Latricia and her new friend Paul rudely climbed into the back seat, interrupting their conversation. Without even conferring with Victoria, Latricia had already agreed to go with Paul.

"C'mon, Victoria, it's still early. Let's hang out awhile," Latricia said.

Yella quickly interjected, "See, yo gurl down. C'mon, I won't bite you."

With a little more negotiating, Victoria gave in and agreed to go. Yella put the gear in drive and headed down 95th Street, riding to Run DMC's "Hard Times."

Nodding her head to the beat, Victoria was oblivious that her cheerleading skirt exposed a little more than intended. Yella took a glance at her smooth dark chocolate thighs, then his eyes roamed up her body, resting on her well-developed breasts. Shifting his eyes to the rearview mirror, Yella gave Paul a satisfied nod, just as he turned onto 22nd Ave, heading south.

Yella drove to the Lincoln Field projects, parked, and hopped out. Paul did the same, pulling Latricia by the hand.

Victoria reluctantly climbed out as well. Walking behind Yella, Victoria carefully watched a group of guys standing in front of the apartment building. In passing, Yella gave fist bumps to most of them. The stares they gave Victoria made her feel uncomfortable. She noticed that, as Latricia passed one of the guys, he palmed Latricia's ass. Victoria felt queasy about the disrespectful act and wondered why Latricia did not retaliate, ignoring him instead.

Thankfully, after that little incident, they made it to their destination without anything else happening. Paul opened the apartment door and stepped to the side, allowing Victoria and Latricia inside. The apartment was in drastic need of some serious housecleaning. The carpet looked like it had not been vacuumed or swept in months. The walls were covered with scribbled markings from different colored crayons, and there was an extremely dusty fan in front of the living room window. The smell of urine dominated the tiny space, and came from God knew where.

The fan blowing did nothing to alleviate the stench or the Miami heat. Victoria and Latricia sat next to one another on a dingy sofa, looking at a 20-inch television sitting on top of a floor model TV. Paul walked over, crouched next to Latricia, and whispered something in her ear. Whatever he said aroused a smile from her. Seconds later, he grabbed Latricia's hand and led her to a back bedroom.

As Paul and Latricia exited the living room, Yella sat exactly where Latricia had been sitting, except he sat close enough that their legs were touching. For about thirty minutes, Yella spoke with finesse, complimenting Victoria on how beautiful she was, and telling her how he would treat her if she was his woman. Every word that came out his mouth, Victoria could feel in her heart. Leaning into Victoria, Yella whispered in her ear and snuck passionate kisses onto her neck. Victoria listened to Yella with her eyes closed, and when she opened them a pair of eyes were watching her.

"Damn, them muthafuckas peeking in the window!" she angrily screamed, making the peeping Tom jump back.

"Gurl, don't pay dem no mind, they just being nosey. Come on, let's go in the back for some privacy."

Victoria followed him down the hallway. As they passed a bedroom door, even with the radio playing, Latricia's sexual moans and the sound of the headboard banging against the wall escaped through the door crack.

The bedroom Yella went into was right next to the one Paul and Latricia occupied.

"Ahhh... Ahhh... oooh..." Latricia's moans could be heard through the walls.

The sound of another woman's sexual fulfillment and the sight of Victoria's cheerleading outfit gave Yella an instant erection. Hoping for the same kind of luck as Paul, Yella sat next to Victoria and placed his right hand on the inner part of her thigh.

Feeling uncomfortable, Victoria moved his hand and closed her legs tightly. Her refusal did not deter Yella's advances. Slowly, he eased his hand under her skirt, giving her second thoughts about coming with him.

"Stop teasing, gurl. Your homegirl ain't tripping. Relax." He slid his hand up a little further.

Victoria put her hand on top of his to prevent him from sliding her panties to the side.

"Come on... look how hard you got me," he insisted, unbuckling his jeans.

"No, I'm ready to go," Victoria said in a low tone.

Perhaps her tone was too low, because he took her faint resistance as a sign to proceed. Without warning, he forced himself on top of her, pressing his erection against her. He began slowly grinding her midsection and kissing her neck. Suddenly, he raised her skirt, exposing her panties. He yanked his boxers down, and, when he felt Victoria's skin against his manhood, he became aggressive. Out of fear, Victoria gave in.

Pulling her panties off, he wasted no time penetrating her. Victoria wasn't a virgin, but Yella was only the second man she'd ever been with. Though Yella was aggressive before feeling her insides, he delivered delicate strokes as if they were making love. Pulling in and out spontaneously until he found a rhythm, he went from gentle strokes to rough pounding. He began grudge-fucking like it was more for punishment than pleasure. The more she complained about him hurting her, the harder he thrust.

As Yella thrust his manhood faster and faster, Victoria yearned for him to finish. Finally, his body did a triple jerk, then collapsed on top of her.

Easing out of Victoria, Yella kissed her breast. "I'll be right back," he said, climbing out of the bed.

Once Yella left the room, Victoria jumped up and immediately put her panties back on. Standing in the center of the room, she looked at her surroundings and heard indistinct moans coming through the wall. Shocked, she couldn't believe Latricia and Paul were still going at it. Curious, Victoria walked over and pressed her ear against the wall.

"…Y'all stop!"

Victoria pressed her ear harder to the wall to see if she had misheard. Indeed, there was no doubt: not only was Latricia saying stop, someone was laughing, and another person was saying hurry up. Victoria was troubled by what she heard and ran to Latricia's aid. But when Victoria opened the door of her room, the same guy that had grabbed Latricia's ass outside was standing in front of her in the hallway with nothing on except his boxers.

"Boy, move!" Victoria yelled, trying to get out the door.

Just as she passed him, he hugged her from the back, dry-humping her ass and squeezing her breast. Victoria spun around to fend off her violator, but his hormones would not be denied. She struggled to escape his grasp, and in her attempt they both lost their balance and fell on the floor. She landed on her back, making it easy for him to mount her. She kicked and screamed for him to get off her. He pulled her panties to the side and raped her. With him inside her, Victoria cried as she deplored that she'd put herself in this situation. She closed her eyes to avoid seeing the painful ordeal.

With no remorse, from beginning to end he thrusted as fast as he could. And within five minutes, he shot off his sticky load.

Feeling dirty, sick and disgusting, Victoria slowly opened her eyes, only to see her ordeal was far from over. Standing in the doorway was another guy, smiling as he massaged his erection.

After they ran a train on Victoria and Latricia, all the guys left with Yella and Paul, leaving them in the apartment with Paul's eight-year-old brother. Hurt and violated, instead of going home, Victoria spent the night at Latricia's house. Both were afraid to call the police or tell their parents what had happened because neither of them could come up with any valid reason for being in Lincoln Field.

The following day, Latricia gave Victoria an outfit to wear to school. On their way, they bumped into Victoria's brother Crow.

"Victoria, where the fuck you been? Momma got da police to the house. She done told dem yo ass been kidnapped," Crow said.

Victoria was speechless. The more questions Crow asked, the quieter she got.

"I fell asleep over Latricia's. We were watching TV and I dozed off. When I woke up, it was one in the morning. I knew everybody was asleep. So, I figured I'd just call home in the morning."

"Shhhit… Don't tell me. You betta tell Ma. What you need to do is call her right now to stop her from worrying."

Victoria assured Crow she would call. However, there was no need because, after leaving Crow and crossing the street, Victoria's mom drove up beside them. Her mother was relieved to see Victoria unhurt, but the next moment her mom's delighted look transformed to anger.

"Victoria, where the hell yo ass been? Get yo behind in this damn car right now!" her mother said, scolding Victoria once she got inside. "Your fast ass going straight to the police station to explain where you were last night."

Latricia had the most pathetic look on her face. She did not dare interfere or come to Victoria's defense, so she simply watched as they drove away.

Seven weeks later, Victoria found herself nauseated. Her mother walked into the bathroom and caught her kneeling and vomiting in the toilet.

"Heffa, I know yo ass ain't pregnant!"

"No, Mama, that shrimp I ate last night tasted funny."

"Shrimp my ass, we going to buy a pregnancy test right now."

Victoria's mom was accurate with her speculation. Victoria was pregnant and going through it alone. On top of the stress associated with a pregnancy, Victoria's mom walked around the house calling her a whore, slut, bitch, and whatever other insult she saw fit to hurl. And her inability to tell her mom who the child's father was made matters worse. Throughout Victoria's pregnancy, her mother was unsupportive and classified her as just another statistic.

****

"Ma… Ma…" P-rock called out to Victoria, ending her deep daydream. Startled, she jumped, breaking her train of thought. "What, baby! What?"

"The bus coming."

# Chapter 3

Desperate and broke, Victoria saw her living situation take a turn for the worse. Her Aunt Tara became aggravated at being the only one in her household paying the bills. To ease the tension, Victoria began doing hair in Tara's garage. Initially, Tara was cool with Victoria's side hustle—the extra income was greatly needed—all until one day Tara returned from work and the police had her house surrounded. She quickly parked and raced to find out what was going on. Two black males were seated on her lawn in handcuffs while their car was being searched.

Tara marched past the plain-clothes narcotics officers and stormed inside her house. "Victoria!" she shouted. "Why the hell is the police in front of my house?"

"I don't know. I was supposed to braid those guys' dreads. All they were doing was sitting in their car, waiting on me to finish with Tanika's hair. When I went to tell them I was ready, the police was handcuffing 'em."

Tara listened to Victoria, then, to cure her curiosity, she walked outside. As she stood on her front porch, the officer in charge came over to have a word with her.

"Good evening, ma'am. Do you live in this residence?"

"Yes, I do, officer. What's going on?"

"Do you always let thugs sell their drugs in front of your home?"

"Excuse me?" she sternly replied.

"Look, ma'am, concerned neighbors have been reporting about a high volume of traffic in and out of this residence. Today me and my team monitored three hand-to-hand transactions. The two suspects in custody are under arrest for possession of marijuana and possession of a concealed weapon."

Tara put her hands on her forehead, trying to massage the stress away.

The officer studied Tara's expression. "I'll take it from your dumbfounded look that you're clueless about their activities, but, ma'am, I'm warning you. If we receive one more call, I promise you we'll return with a search warrant and a tow truck. If we find a gram of dope, I will confiscate your vehicle. Now you have a nice day."

Tara rushed back inside, slamming the door behind herself.

"Victoria, you got muthafuckas selling drugs in front of my house? Girl, you done lost yo damn mind."

"Aunt Tara, they weren't selling no drugs. They were just waiting to get their hair done."

"Don't be stupid all your life. You see they ass in the backseat of that police car? They're on the way to jail. Since when do you go to jail for getting your hair done?" Tara sucked her teeth. "Matter of fact, from now on, don't have nothing but females up in here. I ain't got time for the police kicking in my door over your nonsense!"

Victoria hesitated to respond. It would be best not to open a can of worms she couldn't close, so she kept her mouth shut.

The majority of Victoria's customers were guys either getting braids or having their dreads retwisted, but Victoria respected Tara's wishes and abided by her rules. Every day, some guy would call and beg Victoria to make an exception, but they always got rejected.

Three weeks later, while Tara was at work, Victoria had a couple of female clients over. One was an older woman in her early 40's. She wanted her hair dyed and cut. The other was much younger and wanted a simple bun. Victoria decided to do the bun first since it would take less time. While she worked on the bun, the two gossiped about shops, hair products and who sold the cheapest weave.

"Hey, Victoria, can I use your bathroom?" the older woman asked.

"Sure. It's upstairs, second door on your right."

The older woman went upstairs and slowly walked past the first door on the right. The bedroom door was open wide enough that she could see some jewelry on the dresser. Pausing, she then took a few steps back and peeked downstairs to ensure the coast was clear. Convinced Victoria was still busy, in a swift stealthy motion, she hurried inside the room and grabbed a small Cuban link chain and matching bracelet. Rushing to leave undetected, she left untouched a pair of diamond earrings and two gold rings. She returned downstairs, doing her best to look calm.

After Victoria completed the bun, the older woman stood up and said, "I don't know what's wrong with my stomach. It has been bothering me all day. I'ma have to reschedule my appointment. Is that OK?"

"Yeah, that's fine. Just come around the same time tomorrow."

Both women thanked Victoria and left. Around 5:30 that evening, Tara came home exhausted and relieved to be home after a hard day of work. She plunked down on her plush dual recliner.

"My feet are killing me. I sure need Mr. Right to come give me a foot massage A.S.A.P., Victoria. You think L.L. or Will Smith make house calls?" Tara said, laughing at her own humor.

Tara kicked off her Reebok sneakers, eventually massaging her own sore feet. Then she trudged upstairs to take a hot shower. In the meantime, Victoria was making dinner. Suddenly Tara stormed back downstairs.

"Bitch, I want my shit, and I ain't muthafuckin playing!"

"What shit?"

"This ain't no time to play dumb. Yo ass best to be coming up wit' my shit." Tara came all the way into the kitchen and stood inches from Victoria's face. Pointing her index finger, she yelled, "I don't care if you pawned it, sold it, or yo trifling ass stashed it, my jewelry betta come back up. Here I am letting yo sorry ass stay up in here, and you go steal from me."

"What are you talking 'bout?" Victoria asked, puzzled by Tara's accusations.

"You thirty years old, and around here playing childish games. You might as well go pack yo shit, because yo ass gotta get the hell up outta here. I'm tired of playing this sympathy role anyway. I'm sorry Crow died, and I hate what happen to yo child. That was tragic, but if you think you're going to sit up in here and make a fool out of me, you got another thing coming!"

Tara spit her venom with deadly delivery, crushing Victoria's spirits. She dug deeper and deeper, penetrating the core of Victoria's feelings.

Victoria was so outdone, she made up in her mind that, even if Tara found her jewelry, an apology could never heal the mental scars she'd given her.

****

With no other choice, Victoria moved back to where her nightmares dwelled… the duplex. Tara did not only put Victoria and her kids out. She even refused to drop them off, making her catch a cab.

The metro taxi pulled into the duplex driveway, and a chill went through Victoria's spine. The driver helped her unload her boxes and garbage bags full of clothes. Prior to his departure, Victoria gave him a five-dollar tip.

Standing on the porch with her kids and their belongings, Victoria closed her eyes momentarily, taking a deep breath before unlocking the front door. As soon as she twisted the knob and opened the door, she was greeted by the offensive odor of spoiled food and trash. The duplex hadn't been cleaned since Crow's murder. A few spots of dried blood were still on the floor; even Victor's soiled diaper remained in the same spot she had left it. The duplex also had a horrible stuffy odor, a result of the windows being tightly shut, and the power being disconnected.

Frustrated, with Victor in her arms and P-Rock following close behind, she walked next door to Mrs. Knowles house.

*Knock… Knock… Knock…*

As usual, Mrs. Knowles looked out her curtains, and was surprised to see Victoria. Swinging her screen door open, she held her arms out for a hug. "Oh my God, Victoria, it's so good to see you. How have you been doing, and how's the baby?" she asked, lightly stroking Victor's partial limb.

"We fine, Mrs. Knowles, but could be better. We're moving back next door, but the power is off. I don't have enough money to turn it back on right now." She dropped her head in shame. "I'm so embarrassed to ask you, but I'm all out of options. Mrs. Knowles, can you give me a small loan? I'll repay you 'bout two weeks."

"Lord knows I wish I could help you. Victoria, I don't get my check 'til the first, and that's another week and a half away. You all more than welcome to stay here if you like, or, if you want, I can turn the power back on. You'll just need to keep the power off during the day so the meter man don't sneak up on you."

"You really know how to turn the power back on?"

"I most certainly do." Mrs. Knowles had plenty of hands-on experience with restoring her own power. Numerous times, she had gambled on lasting until she got her check. Mrs. Knowles walked with Victoria back to the duplex, and in no more than five minutes the porch light came on. "You got power."

"I can't believe you did it that fast," Victoria said, impressed. "Thank you, Mrs. Knowles. I truly appreciate it."

Over the next two days, Victoria thoroughly cleaned the duplex, transferred P-Rock back to his original school, and was ready to start doing male and female hair again. However, if Victoria had any luck, it would be bad. Three weeks later, around seven in the morning, P-Rock opened the front door, heading to school, and noticed a police car parked out front. Unaware to the policeman's purpose, P-Rock set out for school. Once he stepped off the porch, the police officer got out of his car and approached him.

"Hey, little man, are your parents home?" the officer asked, grinning.

P-Rock nodded. "My mama's home. I'll go get her."

Victoria was making her bed when P-Rock returned.

"Boy, you betta get yo behind outa here before you be late for school."

"There's a policeman outside. He wanted me to come get you."

"Police! What do he want?" Victoria asked, more like a question to herself.

She assumed that the policeman's presence had something to do with Crow's murder. With Victor still asleep, she casually walked outside. She opened the door to greet the officer, and her mouth dropped. It was not because of the policeman staring at her; it was the white male from the power company standing beside him, smiling.

The officer stepped back as the representative introduced himself with pure enjoyment. He handed Victoria a citation, which she reluctantly accepted. The citation stated that the past due amount was $228; a $500 fine was also added.

"Ms. Cole, the full amount must be paid, as well as an additional $150 deposit, before we will restore your power. I advise you to take care of this matter promptly. I don't know why you people put yourselves in these kinds of positions. My supervisor wants to make examples out of all untrustworthy customers. Now, if you'll notice, at the bottom in red print, you'll see there's a 21-day grace period before a court order is issued."

After the representative finished clarifying the specifications, he and the officer departed in separate vehicles. Victoria closed the door, still analyzing the citation. The vertical blinds were shut, making the living room dark. Out of habit, she reached for the light switch, and of course the lights did not turn on. Shaking her head at their living conditions, Victoria began talking to herself.

"Where the hell am I going to get $878 from?"

She spoke loud enough that P-Rock heard her. He listened to his mother complain about how urgently she needed money.

"Ma, Uncle Crow's shoebox with his money is behind the dresser. I'll go get it," he said, dropping his books.

He returned with the Nike shoe box and swiftly removed the top. Much to their surprise, there was no money inside. The shoebox contained two unwrapped kilos of cocaine.

"I must've grabbed the wrong box," P-Rock said.

"How many shoeboxes are in there?"

"I seen three and his guns."

"GUNS!" she shouted. "Go in there wit your brother. I don't want you around no guns, and damn sure don't want you around this stuff."

Victoria put the top back on the shoebox and carried it back to Crow's bedroom. For the first time since Crow's death, she stepped in his room and sighed heavily, surveying all the items she remembered so well. She walked over to Crow's dresser, lay on her side and viewed all the items underneath. To the far right were two more shoeboxes, another Nike and a Reebok Classic. She slid out the Reebok box and looked inside. To her amazement, $32,000 was individually wrapped with black rubber bands. She looked in the other Nike Box, which contained $10,000 in counterfeit twenties. She stared at the funny money, then closed the top. Still on her side, she glanced at an AK-47 and a .357 Python revolver. Uninterested in the firearms, she didn't touch them. She was more focused on the small fortune she'd discovered. She looked back and forth over the money and drugs, contemplating what she should do with the two kilos. Originally, she considered destroying them by flushing them down the toilet. She pondered that for a while, then decided for now to put them back under the dresser, along with the counterfeit money.

Finally, carrying the box with the $32,000, Victoria returned to the living room. P-Rock was sitting on the sofa with Victor in his arms. She rushed over to P-Rock and gave him a kiss on the forehead. She could not hide the joy she was feeling.

"Ma, I'm gonna be late for school."

With a big smile on her face, she said, "Oh… I'm sorry baby, gone ahead and get out of here. Everything is going to be just fine now." She briskly kissed P-Rock on the cheek and sent him on his way.

As miserable as Victoria had felt mere minutes before, all she felt now was relief. She picked Victor up and danced in circles, making him laugh and giggle.

"The first thing Mama gotta do is get her driver license back, buy us some transportation, and take care of these bills," she said as if Victor could comprehend her words.

Victoria got herself and Victor dressed and out the door in half the time it normally took. She walked next door to Mrs. Knowles' house to see if she would watch Victor while she ran a few errands. Victoria and Mrs. Knowles talked a moment, and she thanked Mrs. Knowles and tried to hand her $20.

Mrs. Knowles would not accept the money, giving Victoria a dismissive wave. "Chile, you keep your money. I could never charge you to watch this baby."

Victoria thanked Mrs. Knowles again, and being seven inches taller than Mrs. Knowles, she bent down and hugged the five-one woman. She called a taxicab, and they chatted while she waited, but Victoria never revealed any information about the money she had discovered.

After the cab arrived, the first stop Victoria made was the DMV. The wait there was intolerable. The DMV was extremely crowded, mostly with Hispanics and Haitians applying for the privilege to drive. The line was out the door. Victoria stood in the scorching sun for over two hours; by the time she made it inside, all the chairs were occupied. Victoria was not going to let the misery of the wait steal her joy. Being able to handle her financial crises liberated her from her worries.

Victoria looked around at the many different faces in the DMV and noticed a familiar figure standing next to the water fountain. "Latricia!"

Latricia spotted Victoria and rushed over with her arms out. "Heeey, gurl, look at you. How you been, Victoria?" Latricia asked, hugging her. "I've been by your house a couple times. I even peeked in the window to see if the furniture was still inside. I thought you moved."

"I did for a while, trying to get my mind right, but I'm back now."

Victoria and Latricia caught up on old times, then had an emotional conversation about what happened the night of Crow's death. It seemed like their conversation sped up the line because, before they knew it, Latricia was next in line. Latricia was only renewing her license. Half an hour after she finished, Victoria was done.

"Do you have a ride?" Latricia asked as they walked through the parking lot.

"No, but I'm on my way to get one."

"Ooooh… car shopping, you go, gurl. Sounds like somebody's man knows how to treat his woman."

Victoria frowned. "Man! Sorry, I don't have one of those."

"Yeah, right! Man, boyfriend, boy toy, sugar daddy, whatever you call 'em, he on his job. Come on. I'm parked over there." Latricia pointed at a Mazda Millenia. As they got closer, she deactivated the alarm, allowing Victoria in on the passenger side.

Victoria admired the wood grain and soft leather seats. "This car is nice, Latricia. How much did you pay for it?"

"I don't know how much this cost. Tray bought it as a gift for me not to leave his dog ass. Let me tell you. One day I caught his ass with some hoe. Gurrrrl… I was at the red light on 135 St. and 17 Ave., and this muthafucka pulls up in the next lane smiling. I honked my horn and waved, just to get his attention, he looked at me like I was a ghost. Next thing I know, some bitch lifted her head up from his lap."

"No, he didn't," Victoria cut in.

"Yeah, gurl, he driving around with another bitch sucking his dick. We turned 135 St. into the Daytona 500!"

"Damn, and y'all still together? I know that's rare for you. Ain't you the same person that said change ya man by the seasons, cause those are the best days of a relationship?"

"You still remember that?" Latricia burst out laughing. "A'ight, you got me, but there's an exception when he can fuck good, and puts a ring on your finger like this." She extended her hand so Victoria could view the princess cut diamonds in her wedding ring.

"Uh… uh… bitch, you got married and didn't invite me to yo wedding."

"Gurl, we didn't even have a wedding. Tray kept procrastinating and postponing the date. I just said fuck it, and drove his ass to the courthouse. I wrote my vows in vain 'cause I never got to say them. Anyway… enough about me. Where do you want to go?"

"The Auto Mall."

"Ooooh, the Auto Mall… here we come," Latricia said, turning the radio up.

Once they arrived at the Auto Mall, Victoria and Latricia went from lot to lot until they came across a three-year-old Acura R.L.; unfortunately, the $27,000 price tag would use up practically all the money Victoria had.

Scanning the lot for potential customers, a young black salesman noticed Victoria looking through the driver's-side window of the Acura. He rushed to Victoria before any other salesman could beat him and make the commission.

"Good evening, ladies. This vehicle right here is an excellent choice. I can guarantee you won't go wrong with an Acura. If you're interested, a test drive is what you need to appreciate the quality and luxury the Acura R.L. delivers."

"This is a lovely car, but it is out of my price range," Victoria explained.

"That's nonsense. Here at the Auto Mall, if there's a will, there's a way. Sometimes it's not about the price, but what you can do to the price." He laughed. "Ok, corny phrase. Tell me, can you afford $450 a month?"

"How 'bout $400?" Victoria replied, folding her arms.

"I won't kid you, but, if you could come up with a five grand down payment, we can make it happen."

Victoria's credit was beyond horrible. The salesman pulled a few strings, made a couple of calls, and in 90 minutes Victoria drove off the lot in her forest green Acura, along with a new 710 credit score.

Latricia followed Victoria to the jerk machine restaurant for some spicy jerk chicken. They chose to eat inside, and Latricia couldn't wait to dive into Victoria's world.

"OK, Victoria, what's really going on? Here I am with a man and a job, I can barely keep $100 in my purse. You got neither and could drop five grand on a car and two grand to fix your credit. Goddamn! Maybe I need to start braiding hair." Latricia took a bite of her chicken wing. With a full mouth, she continued, "Tray hustle and work, I damn near gotta sell him some pussy for a few dollars to buy groceries. Now, what's up?"

"If you only knew the turmoil in my life. Things have been so hard, especially with the death of my brother. I prayed and prayed for things to get better, and I know the Lord answers prayers, but I'm sure he don't give you two kilos of coke."

"What! Gurl, you slanging?" Latricia whispered.

Replying in the same low tone, Victoria said, "No… well, yeah, at least I'm thinking about it."

"Which is it, yeah or no? You know, Tray'll probably buy what you got." Latricia paused a second, arching her left eyebrow. "Hold up. Where the hell you got two kilos from?"

"Now, there you go, trying to get all up in my business. Let's just say I ain't trying to make this a career."

# Chapter 4

Later that evening, Detective Sherman and his partner, Detective Menendez, had Tank's ex-girlfriend, Tia Williams's apartment staked out. For the past three days, surveillance had been in place in hopes of finding Tank.

"Think he'll show?" Menendez asked.

"Hypothetically speaking, criminals always seem to find refuge at their girlfriend's place. No sense in this one breaking tradition," Sherman deadpanned while looking through his binoculars. "Hang on… what do we have here? We got movement, looks like the girlfriend. That's her getting in the red Dodge Neon."

"Are we gonna tail her?"

"With flip flops on and no purse, she'll be back. We'll wait."

Sherman and Menendez maintained their surveillance. No more than ten minutes passed before the Dodge Neon returned. They watched as Tia got out of her car with a small brown bag in her hand. The moment she reached the front door, it opened from the inside. Sherman caught a glimpse of a male's silhouette. Positive I.D. could not be made; still, Sherman decided to radio for back-up.

Marked and unmarked patrol cars sped through the apartment complex's parking lot, racing to Sherman's location with their sirens off. Once a sufficient number of officers had arrived, Sherman instructed them to set up perimeters in the front and rear of the premises.

As the officers surrounded the apartment building, Sherman, Menendez, and three plain-clothes officers proceeded to the front door to serve the arrest warrant.

*Boom… Boom… Boom!*" Sherman pounded on the door with his fist. "Police, open up!"

Inside the apartment, the loud banging startled Tank's ex-girlfriend. She jumped, assuming only one person would knock on her door like a wild man. "Oh, shit… Tank!" she screamed, running from the bedroom in a panic.

Tank's ex lived in constant fear of her abusive ex-boyfriend. After recently discovering that Tank had moved out of town, she had felt comfortable enough to get intimately involved with an old acquaintance of Tank's name Leon.

Throwing on his clothes, Leon cowered in the bedroom. He heard the banging on the door once again. Shaking and disoriented, Leon put his Timberland boots on the wrong feet. Shirtless and petrified, Leon was convinced his old homeboy, the infamous Tank, was at the front door. In an attempt to flee the scene, he grabbed his hat off the bed and bolted from the rear sliding glass door.

"Freeze, don't you move, mother…!" an unknown voice shouted.

*Tat… tat… tat… tat… tat… tat.*

Those were the last sounds Leon heard. The black 305 baseball cap in his hand hit the pavement a tenth of a second before his body.

"Shots fired – shots fired!" Sherman yelled, retreating with Menendez and the other officers behind a white Chevy Tahoe. Kneeling beside the fender, he shouted into his radio. "Somebody talk to me!"

"Suspect down. We need paramedics," Officer Gonzalez replied.

Gonzalez was the officer who had prematurely discharged the first shot. Sherman and the rest of the officers raced to the rear of the apartment. Immediately upon coming around the corner, Sherman spotted Gonzalez squatting next to Leon's lifeless body. Gonzalez was vigilant and instantaneously jumped to his feet upon catching sight of Sherman in his peripheral vision.

With his gun in hand, Sherman looked down at the body. "Gonzalez, what the hell happened?"

"Jesus… it all happened so fast. We were in the process of setting up our perimeter when the suspect sprinted out the sliding door. I observed a firearm in the suspect's hand, ordered him to drop it, but instead of complying, the suspect took aim. I let off four rounds, and Adams, I believe, shot twice. The suspect finally went down. It's totally a justified shooting. Right, Adams?" Gonzalez looked to his fellow officer for support.

"That's affirmative, detective," Adams concurred.

Sherman looked down again, gazing at Leon's face. "Damn it, this is not even our suspect. I.A. is going to be all over this one."

"Well, Detective, whoever this guy is, he was armed and jeopardized the lives of myself and Adams. Internal Affairs can kiss my ass." Gonzalez pointed down at the .380 cal handgun on the ground. "Case closed."

Sherman stared at the gun, listening as Gonzalez spoke with no remorse, only malice. "Let me ask you something, Gonzalez. When I came around the corner, what were you doing?"

Gonzalez glanced at the gun, then replied, "The suspect was slurring his words. I kneeled down trying to understand what he was saying."

"And that's it? You didn't touch the firearm?"

"No."

Sherman heard sobbing inside the apartment. He looked at Tank's ex, clearly visible through the shattered sliding glass door, which two bullets had smashed. He strolled inside, stepping on thousands of square glass pellets. He unsuccessfully tried to soothe her sorrow.

"Get yo fucking hands off me!" she screamed in Sherman's face.

He quickly obliged, removing his hands from her shoulders. More officers arrived, making Silver Blue Lakes Apartments look like a police station. The ambulance sirens could be heard approaching, so Menendez jogged out front to meet the medics. Sherman continued trying to speak with the girlfriend, but she would not cooperate. Convinced he was getting nowhere with her, he stepped outside to locate a female officer, hoping a different gender would help. Looking around the parking lot, Sherman spotted Detective Lowman.

Lowman was a plain-clothes Gang Unit detective. Comforting and counseling were far from her normal activities, but, as a favor to Sherman, she entered the apartment and did her best.

"I ain't' got shit to tell none of y'all. You muthafuckas shot my man and damn near shot me."

"Ma'am, I apologize for what took place here. Look, I'm not here to give you a song and dance to justify anyone's action. The reason we're here is in reference to Sean Hawkins, also known as Tank."

"Tank!" she yelled, shaking her head. "I can't believe this. Leon lost his life because you all mistaken him for Tank. How am I suppose to tell his family Leon is dead because of me?"

****

In Columbia, South Caroline, Tank had no idea of what had transpired back in Miami. After the double murder, Tank had fled town. Unlike Crunch, he refused to take his chances on the streets of Miami. Tank maintained a low profile at his new girlfriend's place. Lying in bed, he watched the national news blast the story about the police being involved in the wrongful death of Leon. Desperately wanting the info the news didn't give, he used his burner cell phone to call Crunch.

"That pussy ass hoe was fuckin who?" Tank demanded.

"I ain't say she was fuckin nobody. I said the police killed Leon in the back of her apartment," Crunch replied.

"Leon stay in Broward. Ain't no muthafuckin coincidence he was in back of that bitch's place."

"I can't make no excuse for the man. I'm just answering yo question. Fuck 'em, the police handled that problem for you."

"You right. Anyway, what the word is on the street? The police ain't been by yo crib, have they?"

"Hell, naw. I talked to my ol' gurl, she ain't say shit 'bout no police coming by. Everythang good on this end. If anything change, you'll be the first to know. I'll holla back later." Crunch ended their call.

Tank climbed out bed enraged a so-called friend would sneak behind his back and sleep with his girl. It was thrilling to know Leon was dead—he only hated that he hadn't been able to look Leon in the eyes as he died. He began pacing back and forth, thinking of how vengeance was a known way to catch a case. But his ex's betrayal could not go unpunished. His conscience kept the death before dishonor code on his mind. A moment later, he lit a Newport, and, just as fast as he had considered returning to Miami, reality kicked in. Some codes are not to be broken, he thought to himself, smashing the cigarette butt in the ashtray.

****

Back at the Miami Police Department, Sherman and Menendez were in the middle of a conversation when their captain walked up, interrupting them.

"Sherman… in my office, pronto."

"Yes, sir," Sherman said, shrugging his shoulders at Menendez as he followed the captain.

Sherman entered the captain's office, halting as two well-dressed Internal Affairs agents stood up. They gave him a facial expression similar to the one he used on suspects, making him feel a little uneasy.

The captain stepped forward with introductions. "Sherman, this is Susan McCloy and Tony Jacobs. They're with I.A."

Sherman showed professional hospitality and shook both agents' hands. Being a veteran detective, he had predicted I.A. would speak with him. This was his second run-in with I.A. Actually, he still harbored a grudge towards them. Yet he concealed his personal feelings, kept his composure and answered their questions in a professional manner, truthful and brief.

Susan McCloy stood beside her partner and read back Sherman's initial report, confirming everything was accurate. When she finished, Sherman agreed. Minus the details of witnessing Gonzalez squatting next to Leon's body. That information was protected by the blue wall of silence. Right or wrong, the strict code of silence secured officers from prosecution.

After I.A. completed their interview, Sherman walked out of the captain's office relieved it was over. Heading back to his desk, Sherman bumped into Menendez and Gonzalez.

Gonzalez had a smile on his face and stuck his hand out to thank Sherman. Sherman tilted his head down at Gonzalez's hand and continued walking, leaving Gonzalez puzzled.

"Hey, buddy, wait up," Menendez said, catching up with Sherman. "What was that all about? You act like Gonzalez did something wrong."

"Look, that young lady said the guy barely had time to grab his car keys, let alone a gun. She said the only thing he grabbed was a hat. The same fucking hat that was on the ground. The guy died 'cause of a hat, so, yeah, Menendez, Gonzalez did do something wrong," Sherman said, feeling ashamed.

"What are you talking about? The guy wasn't Tank, but he still had a weapon. Gonzalez's actions were reasonable, and Adams confirmed it. End of story."

Sherman started to speak, then closed his mouth before the words could come out. From the direction Menendez was taking their conversation, Sherman felt he was getting nowhere. So, just as he had done to Gonzalez, he walked off on Menendez.

"Hey, Sherman!" Menendez shouted towards Sherman's back. "Lay off the coffee."

Back at his desk, Sherman was disappointed to learn no new leads had come through the tip-line. He decided to try another approach to solving his case. Instead of focusing solely on Tank, it was time to put the heat on his partner as well. He decided to go back to the duplex and speak with Victoria, only this time he'd be accompanied by the department sketch artist. Hopefully, Victoria could give a good description.

Sherman reached the duplex in twenty minutes. Once he parked, he sat in the car for a few seconds, observing the Acura and Mazda Millenia. His police intuition gave off signals, judging from the spoiler kit and chrome rims on the Millenia, that it possibly belonged to a hustler.

Clueless of Sherman's arrival, inside the duplex Victoria and Latricia were in the middle of bagging the kilos into ounces. They were interrupted by a knock at the door. Victoria walked out of Crow's bedroom and peeked out the window. She was astonished to see Sherman standing on the porch.

At that exact moment, while cleaning the kitchen of Victoria's place, Mrs. Knowles noticed Victoria's expression change to a nervous look.

Sherman saw the blinds move, then made eye contact with Victoria. She pointed her index finger up, indicating for him to wait one moment. A few seconds later, she came outside and greeted him.

"Hello, Officer Sherman."

"Detective," he corrected.

"Well, Detective, I hope you're here to tell me an arrest has been made for my brother's murder?"

"No, ma'am, sorry," he said disappointedly.

"Well, if an arrest hasn't been made, how can I help you?"

"Ms. Cole, I've brought an artist along to see if you could provide enough details on the second suspect so that we can put a name to him. I am truly sorry that we have not apprehended any suspects. That is why your cooperation is essential to our investigation. Maybe we'll have better results with tracking down the second suspect."

Sherman's timing was horrible. Victoria had Sherman and the artist wait outside while she went back inside. He figured she had male company and his presence was an inconvenience. Two minutes later, Victoria returned and allowed them inside. There was a heavy aroma of cinnamon air freshener. In Sherman's line of work, he'd smelt everything from a burnt cat to the foul odor of decomposed corpses. And, without a doubt, even masked behind air freshener, the unmistakable stench of cocaine hung in the air. Sherman took a quick glance around the room. There was no evidence of where the scent came from, and with nothing in plain view, he ignored it.

Mrs. Knowles stepped into the living room and offered Sherman and the artist something to drink.

Sherman held up his hand, "No, ma'am, we're fine."

Mrs. Knowles returned to the kitchen, and the artist sat down with Victoria, coaxing her to describe the second suspect. Victoria gave him every detail she could remember. The scratching sounds as he shaded the portrait began irritating her, and, because she was anxious to get back into the room with Latricia, her focus was not what it could have been.

The artist put down his pencil and held the portrait out. "Ms. Cole, does this resemble the suspect?"

"Yes, that looks like him, except the scar on his chin was like a check mark."

Using his eraser, the artist removed some of the shading, then added a more detailed scar. "How's this?"

Victoria studied the picture, then nodded her head. "That's identical to da bastard."

Everybody's head suddenly turned in the same direction as Latricia appeared from Crow's bedroom. She explained to Victoria that she had somewhere to go.

Sherman watched as Latricia scurried across the living room and out the front door. Returning his attention to Victoria, he asked, "Ms. Cole, let me ask you something. When the suspects were speaking with your brother, what did they say?"

"They asked him for his money."

"That's it? They weren't interested in anything else?"

"Like what?" she replied, annoyed by his question.

"Well, I'm curious. When we arrived, your brother was found with a bag of crack in his pocket. It's no secret Crow was into selling drugs. The evidence is overwhelming. Now, what's baffling me is why the scent of cocaine is so strong in the air today. Can you answer that for me?" Sherman inquired as if this was an interrogation.

Victoria was appalled by his candor, and decided not to entertain his accusation. So, instead of an explanation, she gave him a piece of her mind. "Muthafucka, you got's to be crazy, coming up in here like you're really trying to catch the people that killed my brother. And just like that, you don' ask me 'bout some drugs. Man, you and this cracka get the fuck out my house."

"Calm down, Ms. Cole," Sherman said.

"I'll calm down when you find the muthafuckas that shot my baby and killed my brother! Then I'll be delighted to answer any damn questions you have. But, until that happens, like I said, get the fuck out!" she yelled, slamming the door the second Sherman stepped outside.

"Ummm…that went well, Detective," the sketch artist said as they walked back to the car.

Victoria stood in the window and watched as Sherman drove away. Once the Crown Vic drove out of view, she let out a deep sigh of relief. Then she inhaled to see if she could smell what Sherman had smelt.

"Mrs. Knowles, if someone knocks on the door, don't answer it. Come and let me know," Victoria said, then returned to Crow's room. She sat on the bed and dialed Latricia's number.

"Gurrrl, I had to get up out of there. Them police had my skin crawling," Latricia said.

"They gone. Your scary self can come back"

"I'm on the way."

Latricia had only gone a few blocks away and was knocking on the door a couple of minutes later. Mrs. Knowles stuck her head in the bedroom, startling Victoria as she finished bagging the coke.

"Your friend is at the door."

"Thank you, Mrs. Knowles." Victoria got up and went to let Latricia in.

"I almost pissed in my clothes, hearing their voices," Latricia said.

"Gurl, they weren't worried 'bout yo ass. They were here about my brother."

After Victoria and Latricia laughed about the nervous reactions they'd both had towards the police, they went back to bagging up the ten ounces that Latricia said she could sell.

"Damn! I can't believe I'm moving work for yo ass. It's funny how life plays itself out. When my ass woke up this mornin, ain't no way in hell I would've imagined I'd be bagging this shit up with you. Victoria, you sure you don't want to sell the rest to Tray?"

"No, I need to make a helluva lot more money with what I got. I'm not trying to re-take."

"It's called re-up," Latricia said, correcting Victoria's slang.

"Re-up, re-take, it don't matter. I'm not trying to make this a career."

"A'ight, this is just a suggestion. Tray taught me how to cook. And since apparently you're striving to make every dime you can, why don't we just cool the rest?" Latricia said, emphasizing the difference.

Victoria listened to Latricia and was impressed by how acquainted she was with the fundamentals of converting cocaine to crack. The more Victoria listened to Latricia, the more she wondered what else she was capable of.

# Chapter 5

Tank was beginning to adapt to life in the Met, which was the hood's terminology for Columbia, South Carolina. He'd been maintaining a low-key lifestyle in Columbia Gardens Apartments, shacking up with an exotic dancer named Tender. Tank had met Tender at Mr. Lucky's gentlemen's club one night in search of a one-night stand. Because of the club's reputation for catering to all it's patron's desires, Tank was freaked by Tender one night and had been by her side ever since.

In the past, remaining under the radar had been far out of Tank's character. He was broke, and keeping his inner demons at bay was a challenge he refused to fight. After using his last $500 on a 9mm with a silencer, he was ready to indulge in old habits. On this particular Tuesday night, Tank trailed along with Tender to Mr. Lucky's. Inside, Tank maneuvered through the married men, drunks, and Johns, finding himself a spot in the corner next to the private dance room. After thirty minutes in the club, the D.J. called Tender to the main stage. In amazement, Tank watched as Tender mesmerized the crowd, working the pole like a gymnast. She was truly gifted and, like him, three Mexicans were highly impressed with her skills.

The three Mexicans appeared to be illegal construction workers, but by the way they were splurging on tequila and throwing twenty-dollar bills like ones, Tank thought otherwise. Nursing his drink, Tank observed the amount of cash the Mexicans wasted in an hour, then came to the conclusion that tonight was the night he put his new toy to work. He kept the Mexicans under observation throughout the night. After Tender had done a few lap dances, she came over and sat on Tank's lap the same way she did for many of her customers.

"Hey, Daddy, you miss me?"

"Yeah," he quickly lied. "Babe, I need to holla at you outside."

Tender saw the seriousness in Tank's eyes and agreed to meet him out front.

Mr. Lucky's had an all-wood patio, which was where Tank waited for Tender. When she came outside, Tank immediately explained his plan, shocking her. With some stiff negotiating, he persuaded her to perform a private party for the Mexicans. She returned inside, walked over to the group of Mexicans, and sat on the tallest one's lap. She could feel his erection instantly pressing against her thigh. Flirting was Tender's specialty. She began massaging his rod cunningly, whispering in his ear. She made him smile and nod his head, eagerly agreeing to pay for a private party. Using finesse and deception, she signaled to Tank everything was a go.

Tank subtly smiled, then casually walked outside and waited for Tender inside her Ford Contour.

After getting dressed and making one of the Mexicans pay her bar tab, she exited the club with them in tow. They were intoxicated and wobbled as they walked to their Chevy crew cab pickup truck. Tender went to the driver's side window and explained she would follow them in her car. Excited and horny, the driver tried to kiss Tender on the lips, but she turned her head, allowing him to kiss her on the cheek. He licked his lips and spoke in Spanish to the other two. She explained things again, then walked to her car. Before she could even close her door, the pickup sped off. She quickly started her car and sped after the truck.

While they traveled down Broad River Road, Tank worried that the Mexicans would get pulled over because their truck was swerving in and out of lanes. During their drive, he went over his tactics thoroughly with Tender. Fortunately for Tank, the pickup truck made it to an independent hotel called Best Way Inn. The hotel rooms could be accessed without having to enter the lobby, which was perfect for Tank's plan. He leaned his seat back as far as it could go to avoid being seen.

Tender climbed out of her car with a small rolling suitcase and followed the Mexicans to their room. Once inside, Tender surveyed her surroundings, then stripped down to her crotchless outfit. Starting off with a tease, she seductively waltzed between the double beds and bent over as she turned the clock radio to The Big D.M. radio station. Squeezing her breasts and rotating her hips, Tender moved her body to R. Kelly's "Your Body's Calling Me." She had captured the Mexicans' undivided attention. Her 34D-2-42 measurements had them hypnotized. Moving her body to the tempo of the beat, she positioned herself in front of one Mexicans, bent over, touched her toes with her left hand and spread her ass cheeks with her right. Looking back, she made sure all their eyes were in one place.

Between the radio and lamp lay the room key. Without any of them noticing, she eased the plastic key card under a napkin, then excused herself to the bathroom. Hidden by the bathroom door, which opened to conceal the room's entryway, Tender slid the key card underneath the entrance door for Tank, then darted into the bathroom. She looked at herself in the mirror, flushed the toilet, and returned to the party. When Tender walked around the corner, two of the Mexicans were shirtless and holding wads of cash in their hands. The tallest of the three sat on the bed and began taking his boots off.

"*¿Cuanto per sexo?*" one of the shirtless ones asked.

Tender frowned. "What did he just say?"

"He said, how much for sex," the one on the bed translated.

Assuming Tank would come creeping into the room any minute, Tender played her role and informed them she wanted $300 apiece. The Mexican sitting on the bed reached under the mattress and threw her a stack of twenties, fifty in all.

"That's with a tip." He laughed as he pulled his pants and briefs off, exposing his manhood.

The other two started chanting in Spanish as Tender kneeled down and began jacking his rod in front of her face.

*CLUNK... CLUNK...*

After the sound of the security latch preventing someone from gaining entry, silence filled the room. The two shirtless

Mexicans frantically dug under the mattress and retrieved twin .44 cal Desert Eagles. The one sitting on the bed reached under a pillow and pulled out a snub nose .38 cal. He aggressively grabbed Tender by her micro-braids and whispered in Spanish to the other two. With their guns drawn, they crept to the door and flung it open.

Outside, Tank pretended he was going into the next hotel room.

"*Que paso!*"

"Sorry, man. I must've had the wrong room," Tank said, peering at the guns in their hands.

They gave Tank a menacing stare and waved their guns in his direction. Tank put his hands in the air and didn't say a word. Presuming his intentions to be harmless, after the brief stare-down, they stepped back inside and attempted to close the door. Just as it was almost shut…

*BOOM!*

Tank kicked the door in and started blasting.

*Twaat... Twaat... Twaat...* He entered the room with his silenced 9mm blazing. He shot both Mexicans point-blank, hitting one in the forehead and sending two rounds into the other's chest.

"Punta, you set us up. You fucking snake."

*Pop!*

The second Tank was coming around the corner, he jumped back as the gunshot sounded. He took a quick peek around the corner and witnessed the last Mexican flinging Tender's lifeless body to the floor like dirty laundry.

The remaining Mexican noticed Tank and recklessly discharged his gun, emptying the cylinder.

*Twaat... Twaat... Twaat... Twaat...* Tank also blindly let off a barrage of rounds. Ready to make his escape, he turned to run but heard a loud thump. Taking aim, he glanced back around the corner and found, to his amazement, that he had hit his target. With no time to delay, Tank took the stack of twenties next to the clock radio, went through each of the Mexicans' pockets and got the loose bills scattered on the floor. He flipped one mattress, which had nothing underneath, but when he flipped the second, he found what he'd come for. Using a pillowcase, Tank quickly gathered all the stacks of money, then looked down directly into Tender's soulless eyes. Knowing the police were on the way, he dashed out the room.

Tender's death hadn't been part of his plan. Tank knew that, once the police found Tender's body, it would just be a matter of time before her friends described him to the police. While in South Carolina, Tank had used his nickname, having grown too accustomed to it to let it go. Unfortunately, now two states had felt the wrath of the infamous Tank.

Tank drove Tender's car back to her apartment and gathered all his belongings. Maybe a mixture of anxiety and depression caused him to view life as having no consequences. He still felt a little sympathetic for being responsible for Tender's death, yet his compassion was short-lived. His judgement was controlled by temptation, which had aroused his hatred towards his ex-girlfriend. Her betrayal began feeling like a score that it was mandatory to settle.

Back inside Tender's car, he counted the money he'd taken from the Mexicans, which totaled $17,000. Not too bad, but it definitely wasn't great for what he'd had to go through. He accepted the troubling circumstances as a steppingstone he needed in order to overcome the obstacle before him.

Tank drove to Congaree River. He hated to part with his 9mm, but keeping it would have been careless and a major violation of the street code. Certain codes were too valuable to void. Using one of his T-shirts, he wiped the gun down, removing all fingerprints, before tossing it in the river. Having rid himself of the murder weapon, Tank decided there was only one thing left to do. He parked Tender's car in the parking garage at Providence Hospital and took a Blue Ribbon Cab to the bus station.

"Can I help you?" the Greyhound attendant asked Tank.

"Yeah, I need a one-way ticket to Miami, Florida."

# Chapter 6

Victoria was used to her life taking drastic turns for the worst. Now that her life had done a 180-degree turn, she began recruiting a few of her former hair customers. After being released on bond, the two men that were arrested in front of her Aunt's house, Jay and Country, were pleased Victoria reached out to them, and glad to make money with her. The dope game became profitable to Victoria in a matter of days. She got rid of all 72 ounces in eight days, selling each for $500 apiece. Once the last one was sold, Victoria had made $36,000. It was more than enough to open her own hair salon, but not nearly enough for her dream salon.

Late that afternoon, Victoria's cell phone rang for the nineteenth time. Each call was about purchasing or collecting work on consignment. But this time, the caller I.D. displayed Latricia's number.

"Gurrrl… my phone is ringing like crazy," Latricia said.

"Mine too. I'm 'bout to just turn my ringer off."

"Off! Victoria, you tripping. I've been politicking with Tray's lug an got you the deal of a lifetime."

"Latricia, I told you I'm not trying to make this no career."

"Just listen. For a dollar and sixty-five cents."

"One sixty-five, what are you talking 'bout?" Victoria asked, confused by the lingo Latricia used.

"Fifteen-five, catch up, gurl, stay with me. They proposed an offer for 33 G's."

"Thirty-three what!" Victoria shouted. "I'm not spending 33 grand on shit."

"Damn, Victoria! If we buy two for 33, he'll front us another two for the same price. I got somebody right now ready to pay 20-5 for one. That's a $4,000 profit right there, and if we do like I said and break everything else down and cook it, you do the math." Latricia did her best to sound professional.

Victoria listened to everything Latricia had to say. They debated back and forth till the numbers made sense. Victoria finally agreed to a one-time deal. After ending their call, Victoria went into the back of her closet and pulled out the leather coat she stashed her money in. She counted out $3,000 and placed it inside her knockoff Prada handbag. Then she went to the kitchen, removed the remaining cereal from its box, and hid the $33,000 inside.

Ten minutes later, there was a knock at the door. Victoria looked outside and recognized Latricia's car in the driveway. She tossed a few canned goods into a plastic grocery bag along with the cereal box, grabbed her car keys and headed out the door.

They rode in Victoria's car. Latricia gave her the directions to the house, talking the entire way. When they arrived in a predominantly Latino community, Hialeah, Victoria felt a little uneasy with the position she had put herself in.

"This is 105 St. Make a left." Latricia instructed. "That's the place right there."

The house did not look like much for a major drug connection. The Spanish-style home was 1,100 square feet with tile roofing, and there were several chickens running around. There was no grass in the front yard; the entire yard was cemented in, making one large, distinctive driveway. Every car parked at the house was manufactured in either the 60's or the late 70's.

"Are you sure?"

"I've been here plenty of times with Tray. C'mon," Latricia said, then got out the car.

Victoria followed Latricia. They entered through a gap in the chain-link fence, sending the chickens into a frenzy. The closer they got to the front door, the stronger the mouthwatering smell of arroz con pollo grew.

Latricia took a step back after knocking on the door. The deadbolt unlocked, and a very short Cuban male opened the door.

Victoria and Latricia looked down at the five-foot man. He returned their gaze with a smile.

"Ah, Señora Tricia. Come… come…" He welcomed them into his home.

"Hey, Diaz, this is my best friend Victoria. She's the one I told you about."

"*Buenos dias*, Victoria." Diaz grabbed Victoria's hand, caressed it, and then gently kissed her knuckles. "If you're a friend of Tricia, then you're a friend of mine." Releasing Victoria's hand, Diaz turned toward Latricia. "I haven't seen Tray in a while. Is everything OK with him?"

"Tray's fine. He's in Boca Raton with his construction crew."

"Tell him to call me," Diaz said, looking Latricia in the eyes longer than necessary. He clapped his hands. "OK, ladies, let's get down to business."

Diaz led Victoria and Latricia to a formal dining room table. Once they sat down, Diaz went over the same conversation he'd had with Latricia earlier.

"How much time will we have to pay you your money?" Victoria asked.

"Señorita, we're talking about just two kilos. How much time do you need, two days, three? *Digo mi*." Tell me.

Latricia knew, from past experiences with Tray, that Diaz was impatient when it came to his money. And given the direction Victoria was steering the conversation, she felt it was time to intervene.

"Diaz, we won't be no more than five days, maybe sooner," Latricia said.

"OK, Tricia, I'll give you one week," Diaz said, then shouted in Spanish, "*Traeme cuatro kilos, Marie.*"

"Did he just say, 'Bring me four kilos'?" Victoria leaned over and whispered. Latricia nodded.

"You pay half now?"

"Yeah, *si*. Thirty-three thousand, right?" Victoria said, trying to answer in Spanish.

"Victoria, I look forward to continuing to do business with you."

Continue doing business, Victoria thought to herself, just as a young Cuban woman appeared from another room with a black shopping bag. Diaz took the bag, then handed it to Victoria. She gave him the cereal box. Diaz looked inside it and, without counting the money, gave the box to the Cuban woman.

"Thank you, Diaz. We won't let you down," Latricia said.

"I'm sure you won't," he replied, walking them to the front door.

As soon as they were in the car, Latricia looked at her cell phone and found she had missed calls. "Shit, Tray done called me six times. I know his ass gon' be trippin." She dialed Tray's phone, and he answered on the second ring.

"Where da fuck you at?"

"I'm wit' Victoria. We just left Diaz's house."

"Diaz's house! What the fuck your ass doing over da're?"

"Baby, calm down. Victoria was getting straight."

"Why the hell you didn't call me? I don't want people meeting Diaz. You wouldn't know that, because you too busy playing middleman. Hurry up and get yo ass home," Tray yelled, then hung up the phone in Latricia's ear.

Victoria looked over at Latricia and could tell her call hadn't gone well. "You aight?"

"I'm good. My man just tripping. Anyway, when we get back, I'ma go home and deal with his bullshit. I'll call you later tonight."

****

Latricia tensed up as she slowly parked next to Tray's massive black Dodge 3500 Dually. She casually walked into the house, expecting Tray to greet her at the door. She found him sitting in the den, changing the batteries in his digital scale. Latricia didn't say a word. She stood in the doorway, waiting for him to acknowledge her.

Tray looked up at her and went back to what he was doing.

"So, what, you suppose to be mad at me?" she asked, sliding her shoes off just in case he was in the mood for violence. He had been abusive in the past, but lately he'd only become physical when she caused him a financial loss.

Replacing the battery cover on his digital scale, he looked at Latricia again. "I should slap da shit out yo ass, but I don't feel like fucking you up tonight."

Tray's comment de-escalated the tension. Latricia felt comfortable enough to let her guard down, knowing they weren't going to fight.

"So, wuz up, what you and yo gurl got going on?"

"Victoria trying to make some extra money. She wants to open a hair and nail shop."

"Oh, yeah… Shit, that's what yo ass need to be doing. So, what did she get from Diaz?"

"She bought two and Diaz fronted her two."

Tray arched his eyebrows. "Ounces?"

"No, keys."

*SMACK!* Without warning, Tray slapped Latricia across the left cheek.

"Keys… y'all went over there copping keys!" Tray screamed, slapping Latricia a second time, this time knocking her to the ground. As she tried to crawl away, he stalked her every move, fuming. "Bitch, I owe Diaz $180,000 and yo dumb ass go over playing like you know what the fuck you doing. Diaz probably think that shit for me and I'm dodging him." Tray stood hunched over Latricia.

Latricia stopped crawling, tears pouring from her eyes. The sadness in her face instantly made Tray regret his actions. Deep down, he knew Latricia's explanation was reasonable and he had overreacted.

He slapped his forehead, extended his hand to her, and said in a compassionate tone, "Damn, baby, see what you make me do? You gotta realize there's a reason I keep you out the game. What if Diaz thinks I'm playing with his money, and decides to keep Victoria's money? Believe me, he'll do it and won't give y'all shit but a smile, or the option to live or die. Diaz may be a short funny-looking muthafucka, make no mistake about it, he's a notorious gangsta with stone cold killers on speed dial. Now, look, baby, I'm sorry for putting my hands on you. You're my better half, so stop trying to be my burden." He helped her off the ground.

"I'm sorry," Latricia said.

"Me too. Baby, right now I'm just so stressed. We're behind schedule wit' this house we building, I don't have all Diaz's money, and the extra money I got tied up in this project until we complete it."

Latricia was hurt Tray had slapped her, but, after hearing about his tribulations, she embraced him and pressed her head to his chest. He held her tight in his arms and gave her light kisses on her forehead. She tilted her head up, and Tray's kisses became more passionate as his lips met hers. He gently glided his tongue along hers.

"I love you, baby," Tray whispered.

"I love you too."

Tray was a perfectionist when it came to Latricia's body; he knew all her hot spots. As if they were back on their honeymoon, Tray scooped Latricia off her feet and carried her to their leather sofa. Slowly, he pulled off her shirt, revealing her curvaceous breasts. He began licking and nibbling on her nipples. He made Latricia writhe and moan with pleasure.

"Oooooh… Baby, you know that's my spot," she seductively said.

Ready to feel the inside of his wife, Tray removed her shorts, revealing her lime green panties. Latricia lifted her hips, allowing Tray easy access. Pulsating, he paused and stared at her clean-shaven treasure. He licked his lips and dove between her legs head-first. He focused on sucking her clitoris, and slid his index and middle fingers inside her treasure box.

"Ummm… uh… uhhh… damn, baby… ummmm…" Latricia wailed, grinding her hips to the same tempo as Tray's fingers.

Tray lifted his head, his mustache soaked in Latricia's natural juices.

"Ummmm… Baby, don't make love to me tonight. I want you to fuck me, Daddy," she begged, unbuckling his belt.

Tray loved when Latricia called him Daddy. That was his signal that she was in the mood to try any position imaginable. Latricia lay flat on her back, caressing her breasts and allowing Tray to squat over her face and dip his testicles in and out of her mouth. With his erection at its peak, he was unable to resist any longer. He eased between her legs and penetrated her. Giving her long hard thrusts, Tray placed one of her legs on his shoulder. He humped like, with every stroke, he was on the verge of releasing his proteins.

"Oooh… fuck me, baby… ummmm… fuck meee!" she screamed over and over.

Tray pulled his rod out and maneuvered Latricia unto her stomach. With his rod naturally lubricated with Latricia's juices, he spread her ass cheeks and with minimum force slid into her rectum.

"Ahhh… Daddy, it hurt," she cried out, burying her face in the sofa cushion.

Through the pleasurable pain, Latricia was still able to find ecstasy, climaxing multiple times. Tray felt her body shiver and started stroking as fast as he could, reaching his climax as well. The stench of their wild sexual escapade filled the living room. Latricia got up and slowly walked to the thermostat, turning up the A/C. Tray smiled at her rear, noticing she walked with a slight limp.

****

Four days passed, and, just as Latricia had predicted, they had Diaz's money. Victoria and Latricia double-counted the money at the duplex, placing each grand in an individual stack. After making sure the amount was correct, they headed to Diaz's.

"Ah, señoritas… *Hola*," Diaz greeted them as he opened the door.

"Just like we said, here's your money." Latricia passed Diaz a handbag as they entered.

"This I like. When conducting business, your word has more value than your cash. Tricia, Tray needs to learn some business skills from you two," Diaz suggested.

"Diaz, Tray told me to tell you he'll holla at you this week," Latricia clarified.

"This week? And this he could not tell me himself. What kind of man has his woman handle his business? Tricia, relay this message to him: I hate chasing my money, and the clock is ticking." He paused and let the silence deliver the true message. "Okay. So, Victoria, you buy more, yes?"

"Actually, I still have a few ounces left. I just wanted to bring you your money."

"I admire that. You're a true businesswoman. Come, sit." Diaz led them to the dining room table.

Diaz was not a gambler; however, he was a good judge of character and liked what he saw in Victoria. So, without hesitation, he decided to offer her a lucrative opportunity.

"Victoria, how long have you been in business?"

"Two weeks."

"Ha… ha… ha… Keeping your novelty a secret."

Victoria was puzzled by Diaz's humor at her answer.

"What if I give you ten kilos? Can you move them in, let's say, two weeks?"

Victoria could not believe Diaz was offering her ten kilos. Though she had no intention of continuing along the paths of the game, nor was she foolish enough to give up a beneficial proposition. She nodded her head in agreement with his deal, taking another step deeper into the game.

****

Immediately after returning home, Victoria brainstormed with Latricia, and they put together a team of distributors that consisted of five people with potential. Victoria called each person, explaining she had good news. Surprisingly, Peanut was the first to arrive at the duplex. And with his means of transportation being the city bus, she was impressed by his dedication.

Next to arrive was one of Crow's homeboys, Black. He parked his chrome and gray Suzuki Hayabusa behind Victoria's Acura. His name matched his complexion, and in the streets, he was known as a true paper chaser. Black had practically grown up with Victoria. They were only a couple of years apart, and they had attended Central High together.

The next two to arrive, Jay and Country, were Victoria's two male clients who'd been arrested in front of her Aunt Tara's house. They were also first cousins. Jay was originally from Miami; Country had been raised in Macon, Georgia. Jay had used to hustle with his cousin in Macon, until a club shooting he was involved in with members of a local gang jumped off. Jay had returned to Miami and Country had followed to escape the easily foreseeable retaliation.

Finally, Taj made his appearance. Taj was known as a pretty boy because of his wavy hair, light complexion, and hazel eyes. On occasion, he would creep around with Latricia when Tray left home for several days. Unlike the others, Taj was more middleman than hustler. When his uncle and cousins searched for work, Taj always came through after adding his on number to the price.

With the entire team present, Victoria began. "I called everyone here because it's no secret everybody in this room is about making them tax-free dollars."

Victoria scanned the room, ensuring she had their attention. She had each person explain their capabilities and was shocked by the outrageous numbers Black, Jay and Country said they could move. Black claimed he was able to run through five to ten kilos every other day. Jay and Country snickered at Black's numbers.

"Yo, Vee, between Miami and West Palm Beach, we can get rid of at least 15 in a day, especially if it's clean," Jay explained.

Peanut and Taj sat on the couch and stayed out the conversation until Victoria turned and faced them.

"So, what's up, Peanut? What you do?"

"I flow with the demand. If I can put my hands on what a muthafucka lookin for, then I'ma make dat bread."

"Same here," Taj cut in. "When my folks need something, I make sure I can handle the number."

Victoria replied, "Right now, help me help y'all, and I believe we can make a lot of money together."

"I know I'm ready. What you trying to get rid of?" Black asked.

"Five keys."

Black glanced over at Jay and Country, then smirked at Victoria. "That's it?" He got to his feet. "You got us all amp up for five keys. Shit, I'll buy all dem muthafuckas myself."

"Okay, big timer, then buy 'em. I want twenty apiece."

"And I want a real plug," Black sarcastically said. "Let me get 'em for 18-5, you got a deal."

"Nineteen-five."

"Nineteen."

"Black, 19-5, and don't tell me you writing checks you can't cash."

Everyone laughed, making Black feel beneath the caliber hustler he was.

"Victoria, now, you know how I get down. Fuck it, let me get all that shit. I'll be back in a half hour." Black walked out the door.

Jay told Victoria, "If Black wasn't going to cop them five, I could make one phone call and get rid of them."

"You ain't said nothing. Make the call. First come, first served."

Jay pulled out his phone, and in less than two minutes he had a sell for five kilos. Victoria was skeptical at first about fronting Jay the kilos. Nevertheless, she took a chance and had Latricia ride with Jay and Country.

Forty minutes passed, and Victoria heard Black's motorcycle pull into the driveway. With everybody gone, she quickly retrieved the last five of the ten kilos, then let Black inside.

Black shrugged a brown book bag off his back and dumped $95,000 on the floor. "I told you that shit ain't nothing."

Victoria couldn't believe that, in less than an hour, half her work was sold. She wondered whether, if she had told Black it was ten in all, he would have bought the other five too.

Black put the kilos in his book bag. Just as he strapped it on his back, Jay's car pulled up.

"I'ma get out of here, Victoria. Next time you call me, impress me. I'm not like ya lil' flunkies you got outside." Heading out the door, Black smiled at Jay.

In passing, Jay returned the gesture and tapped the side of the gym bag in his hand. As Black sped off on his bike, Jay gave the bag to Victoria.

"I told you, Vee, I got you. All you gotta do is let us know when things poppin. And word to the wise, next time don't ever show yo hand like that. Not everybody good peoples."

The commitment they had all displayed to Victoria built a level of trust with her. She also made sure Latricia was straight. Throughout the next several weeks, Diaz became even more impressed with Victoria. The ten kilos turned to twenty, the twenty turned to thirty, and, before she realized it, Victoria was neck-deep in the game. She transformed from a struggling single mom to a successful diva. Victoria's growing relationship with Diaz became so lucrative, Latricia even managed to help Tray pay off his debt. It was official, Victoria had finally got a sample of the good life. And she liked the taste.

****

One afternoon, Victoria was home alone, lying on her sofa, enjoying the peace and quiet, when her cell phone rang.

"Hello."

"Hey, gurl, you busy?" Latricia asked.

"Now wuz up?"

"I need you. Gurrrl… I got a fish on the hook willing to pay 20 apiece for four postcards," Latricia said, speaking in code.

"Well, c'mon over and get them. You have to hurry up because I got to pick P-Rock up from school."

"I'm on my way."

Victoria went back to relaxing on the sofa. She stayed in the same position until she heard a knock at the door. Looking out the window, Victoria recognized Latricia's car. Without seeing Latricia, she opened the front door and was shocked the first person she saw was Tray, with Latricia next to him.

This was the first time Tray had accompanied Latricia to a transaction with Victoria.

"Hey, y'all, come on in."

"What dey do, Victoria?" Tray gave his typical greeting.

"How you doing, Tray? Latricia, I thought you were by yourself. Y'all give me a minute. I'll be right back."

Tray watched Victoria until she vanished into the bedroom, then surreptitiously coached Latricia one last time about the scheme he had planned.

"Listen, baby, we gon' pay her back. I just want to flip them thangs a couple of times, and then pay her after we make a little change for ourselves." Tray massaged Latricia's hand as he spoke.

"Yeah, but how long will that take? You know she be on a deadline."

"Four days tops."

Tray stopped talking when he heard the bedroom door open.

Victoria walked in, sensing a suspicious silence between Tray and Latricia. Holding a black duffel bag, Victoria addressed Latricia. "What time are you coming back? I gotta get my kids and run a few errands." She gave Latricia the duffel bag.

"We won't be that long," Tray said, responding for Latricia. "We'll call you when we're on our way to drop off your money."

Victoria had expected Latricia to answer, not Tray, because the package was her responsibility, not his. Her woman's intuition alerted her that this was a bad move, but Victoria second-guessed herself, hoping she was just overreacting.

# Chapter 7

The next day, Victoria walked over to Mrs. Knowles' house to pick up Victor. As usual, Mrs. Knowles' front door was unlocked. Victoria went straight inside, following the scent of fresh-baked cookies.

"Heeey, Mrs. Knowles," Victoria said, finding her in the kitchen pouring herself a glass of milk. "Where's my little man?"

"Chile, that boy back there in the bed. He ran himself to sleep. Before you go back there and wake him, sit down here with me a moment. We need to talk."

Victoria grew concerned at Mrs. Knowles' tone.

"Now, Victoria, you've known me long enough to know I'm no saint. Your business is your business. I just want to share a little wisdom with you. Victor may be too young to understand what's going on, but that P-Rock is far from dumb. If you're gon' continue doing yo dirt, then you need to conceal what you do in front of that boy."

"What are you talking about, Mrs. Knowles?"

"Don't you be mad at P-Rock, cause I kinda manipulated some disturbing information out of him. Believe me, he sees more than you think he do. Lately, you've been dropping them kids off here, and been too busy to even notice how much they miss you. Victoria, you all just experience a very tragic family incident. Your babies want to spend more time with their mama."

"Mrs. Knowles, I appreciate your concern, but this is temporary. Matter of fact, I'm on my way to take them to the mall so we can do some shopping."

"That's nice, but, babe, let me tell you something. The game is cold as ice. It don't matter if you a good-hearted single mother or a backstabbing muthafucka, the game love nobody. I've seen too many people sell their souls and lose their lives behind that same fast living you doing. Victoria, don't take that same road so many others took. That road got three exits: the hospital, prison or the grave. Your baby already been to the hospital, what's next? My husband and your father traveled that road, and you see which exit both of them took. How far are you willing to go before you reach your exit?" Mrs. Knowles let that sink in. "Now, gone ahead, shower them kids with gifts. Just remember, material objects will never substitute quality time."

After Mrs. Knowles' last sentence, a tear trickled down Victoria's check. The comment brought back the last conversation she'd had with Crow. As if it had happened just yesterday, she had a vision of preaching the same words that were now being preached to her.

Victoria took a deep breath as she left Mrs. Knowles' home with Victor in her arms. Talking with Mrs. Knowles, she had realized certain commitments held too much value to be denied.

Once Victoria picked P-Rock up from school, they headed to Aventura Mall. This being the second week of December, the mall was jammed. Finding a close parking spot was virtually impossible. Tired of driving in circles, Victoria took a risk and parked in a handicap space.

"Ma, the new black and red Jordans came out. Will you buy me a pair?"

"Didn't I just buy you a new pair?"

"Yeah, but these the new ones. Please, Ma..." P-Rock said, sounding like a spoiled child.

"I tell you what, you want them, then you buy them wit' some of that allowance money you got saved up."

In truth, P-Rock had no problem spending $150 on the high-priced Jordans. He'd already saved close to $800. As they entered the mall, Victoria decided to get the kids' shopping out of the way first. They went to Kids Foot Locker, and Victoria purchased the latest Air Max with two matching outfits for Victor. P-Rock placed a pair of the new red and black Jordans on the counter with the other items, then stepped back. Victoria looked at the sneakers, shook her head and smiled.

With the kids' athletic gear out of the way, Victoria headed towards Macy's to do a little spending on herself. On the way, she did a double-take at a couple holding hands while browsing inside Kay's Jewelers. The female was not familiar to her, but the male undeniably was. Under her breath, Victoria called him a cheating dog. And once she watched him try a ring on the woman's finger, temptation prodded Victoria to tap him on the shoulder.

"Hey, Tray," Victoria said with her mouth twisted to the side.

Stunned, he tried speaking nonchalantly. "Oh, what dey do, Victoria?"

"I been calling your wife, but I keep getting her voicemail. Where is yo wife?" she said, emphasizing *wife*. She turned towards the woman with Tray. "Yes, he's married to my home girl. He didn't tell you, but then again some hoes don't give a damn no way."

Tray's illuminating expression said it all: busted… Victoria looked Tray's mistress up and down, then rolled her eyes as she walked off. Seeing Tray cheating on Latricia killed her mood for shopping. As she walked out of the mall, Victoria dialed Latricia's number. She anxiously wanted to tell Latricia that Tray was out entertaining another woman, but the call went straight to voicemail once again.

The sight of Tray's infidelity had distracted Victoria from finding out if they had her money. Instead of returning to the jewelry shop to confront Tray, she decided to swing by Latricia's house and ask her after telling her about Tray's betrayal. Victoria hurried to her car just in time to witness a public service officer placing a ticket on her windshield.

"Shit…" she mumbled.

While driving twenty miles above the 45-mile-per-hour speed limit, Victoria received a call from Jay.

"Yo, Vee, we hungry as hell. You cooking dinner tonight?" Jay asked, hiding his real question in code.

"Y'all ain't got nothing to eat?"

"Naw, we starving. Wuz up?"

"I'm not cooking dinner, but I'll make breakfast in the morning."

"Damn, you fuckin a brother's stomach up. A'ight, I'ma holla at you in the A.M.," he said, sucking his teeth.

Victoria finally arrived at Latricia's. She pulled in the driveway and parked next to Latricia's Millenia. She called her phone one last time before getting out of her car.

"P-Rock, wait here with your brother. I'll be right back."

Victoria rang the doorbell over and over. There was no answer. She looked through the window for any movement. Everything was still. Latricia's strange disappearance made Victoria worry. With no signs of Latricia besides her car, Victoria concluded no one was inside. She turned and headed back to her car.

Meanwhile, kneeling inside her home, Latricia peeped through the bottom of her blinds, watching Victoria drive away. For the rest of the day, Latricia sat on her bed praying Tray would hurry home with Victoria's money. She felt bad dodging her, and felt worse that Tray hadn't been home in all night

The next morning, Victoria sprung from her bed when she heard her cell phone ring. Without hesitation, she answered. "Latricia!" she reflexively said.

"Naw, Vee, dis Jay. Where you want us to meet you at?"

"Hold on, ahhhh…" After yawning, Victoria got back on the phone. "Jay, I'm not ready yet. Give me 'bout two hours."

"Early bird gets the worm, Vee. You killing us. I'ma hit you back in two hours. I hope you ready by then."

Ending their call, Victoria stretched and thought about Tray's infidelity. She gave Latricia another call, but still her efforts were to no avail.

"Now, I know this gurl ain't… Naw, I know her ass better than that," Victoria said out loud to herself.

To be able to supply Jay and Country, Victoria needed to make a trip to see Diaz. And because she'd fronted Latricia the four kilos, she now had to go into her stash and use her own money to make up the difference. She removed several pairs of shoes from her closet, pulled the carpet back, and removed the one of floorboards. She pulled her stash from the hole and counted out $64,000. Of course, the money wasn't much for her to scrape up; she just hated touching her stash. To Victoria, that was a clear sign of hustling backwards.

After returning the shoes to the closet, Victoria got dressed. Nothing extravagant; she simply threw on a pink Nike sweat suit with some white and pink Air Max. Once she'd gathered her things, she walked P-Rock and Victor next door to Mrs. Knowles' house, then drove to Diaz's. Before she even knocked on the door, Diaz swung it open with a big smile.

"Ah, Victoria, *¿cómo estas?*"

"*Todo bien*" she replied, recalling the little Spanish Diaz had taught her during a few of their business meetings.

"Today is a good day for you. Very good news I have."

Victoria could barely conceal her baffled expression. She became curious about Diaz's uncanny excitement.

"Good news for me is good news for you. I'm dropping the price for you. Sixteen was good, yes? Well, how does 12 sound… even better, right?" Diaz clapped his hands and laughed with excitement.

Victoria couldn't believe it. "Twelve definitely sounds good to me."

"Good. With the shipment I just received, I'm supplying you with 75 kilos."

Diaz's proposal caught Victoria off guard. Her eyes almost rolled back in her head. Even without doing the math, Victoria knew she was heading toward the point of no return. If there was any man who could give her proper knowledge, it was time to seek his guidance.

It had been a very long seven years since Victoria had last set foot in the U.S. Penitentiary in Atlanta, Georgia. She hadn't seen the castle-like prison since her last visit with her mother before her death. They had, however, recently spoken briefly, thanks to an emergency family call the prison chaplain had arranged after Crow's death. Besides that call, they kept a very distant relationship.

# Part of the Game

Victoria took a flight from Miami to Atlanta. She rented a Ford Explorer and checked into a nearby hotel. After freshening up and changing into an appropriate outfit for visitation, she took McDonough Blvd. to U.S.P. Atlanta. The visitation process was just as she remembered it: an unreasonably long wait, and the correction officers treating visitors as if they were inmates as well.

Standing in line, she watched as certain visitors were randomly searched for contraband. Other visitors looked on at the humiliating procedure. Waiting in line alone was enough to make Victoria know prison wasn't for her. She was finally escorted into the visitation room and assigned a seat. The visitation room had rows of seats connected to one another, and a row of vending machines on the back wall. Once a loved one arrived, by policy they were instructed to embrace appropriately, then sit across from one another. Before her father arrived, Victoria walked to the vending machines and purchased two sodas and some snacks for him.

Several inmates passed Victoria; some took quick peeks at her as they sat with their families. A few more minutes went by, and another crowd of inmates entered the visitation room. She smiled as she spotted her father strolling in. As if it had only been a month, her father's appearance was nearly the same. He was well-groomed, and his tan institution khakis were pressed as if they were heavily starched and not an hour out of the cleaners. Besides his salt-and-pepper goatee, the penitentiary had preserved him from the changes associated with age. Victoria stood up as he got close and received the kind of hug that only a loving father could give.

"Well, look at you. I don't care how big you get, you're still my baby girl."

"How've you been, Dad?"

"I could be fifty times betta, but under the circumstances all is well. I'm striving one day at a time. How 'bout yourself?"

"Actually, Dad, I'm stressed," Victoria replied as they both sat down.

"The world gives you a dose of stress from time to time. Believe it or not, sometimes stress is a necessity in life. It helps you avoid repeating detrimental choices. Now, are you telling me I haven't seen my baby girl in seven years, and stress is responsible for this visit?"

"Dad, you know I didn't have any transportation, and definitely no money. After Crow died, I moved in with Aunt Tara, and, for something I had nothing to do with, your sister threw me and my kids out. When I moved back in the duplex, I was practically living in the dark." She dropped her head and spoke in a low tone. "So, to make ends meet, I started hustling to put food on the table."

Her father listened without interrupting. He didn't blink, just stared into Victoria's eyes, hating to hear of her involvement in the game.

"Victoria, you know I'm a fashion connoisseur. People trying to put food on the table and struggling with financial problems don't casually throw on Dolce and Gabbana." He paused, opened a bag of chips she bought, and put a couple in his mouth. "So why don't you start over from the beginning?"

This was the conversation she had come to Atlanta to have. Butterflies swarmed in her stomach. She took a deep breath, looked her father in the eyes, and let it all out, from the two kilos in Crow's room to the seventy-five she'd just received.

"Sounds to me like you're doing a little more than putting food on the table. Victoria, take a look at me, take a real good look. Do you know what you're looking at? You're not just looking at your father. You're looking at a man with a natural life sentence, and this is the results of being naïve to the game. Making the money, that's nothing. Dope sells itself. The pros and cons of the legal aspects is what so many of us lack. We in a war we didn't even know we was fighting, and the war been going on since 1985."

"Dad, what are you talking about?"

"The war on drugs is the title it hide behind, but those that aren't blind can see the true war is with us, and we're being kidnapped and slaughtered by the Feds. When they get us in their system, by the time most hustlers get the legal knowledge to properly fight their case, they've exhausted all their avenues to get back in court. Then they become like so many others, hoping some mythical case pass. So they can get some sort of relief. Victoria, I'm going to die in prison. Do you know why?"

"Because you have a life sentence."

He smiled at her. "That's true, but the real reason is because I didn't take the time to learn and understand about what I was getting myself involved in. Listen to me, at the level you on, before you even accepted this package, if two people snitched on you, not only would you be facing a conspiracy charge, you could also receive a manager enhancement. That would start your sentence at a mandatory twenty years to life, and that's just with two statements. Four or more will get you another four-level enhancement."

"I don't understand. What's that?"

"That, baby girl… is part of the game!"

Victoria's mind was like a sponge; she soaked up the wisdom and proper street knowledge her father was giving her. To her left, there were several kids running in circles around an empty set of chairs, and, spaced out around the visitation room, girlfriends and wives were mourning their loved ones' incarcerations. However, Victoria let nothing distract her from hearing her father's philosophy.

"Do any of these people you deal with know where you and my grandkids rest y'all head at?"

She nodded.

"Move! A.S.A.P. Don't tell no one where you move to, not even your best friend. I bet you conduct business on one of them cell phones too, don't ya?"

"It's not in my name," she replied, feeling slightly ashamed.

She saw anger in her father's eyes at her answer. "That's the shit I'm talking about. People quick to chase the money, and while doing it they make the Feds' job easy. Don't you know, by using that cell phone, an indictment could have your name on it as we speak? Damn, Victoria, I hope you not cooking that shit?"

With pure confusion plastered on her face, she replied, "Sometimes."

"Hundred to one ratio, you ever heard of it? Of course not. That will have you regretting you ever bought a 49-cent of baking soda. If you get caught with one ounce of crack, it's equivalent to approximately two kilos of coke. Victoria, wake up. Get your mind right. The system don't give a damn if you male or female, first-time offender or career offender. What rhyme with crack dealer? Black dealer, and there's no sympathy, only the max of what the guideline call for. I thought you was out there doing hair?"

"I'm trying to open a unisex beauty salon."

"If that's your goal, why are you out there still throwing rocks at the penitentiary? From what you told me, you have more than enough to open a shop. Don't let greed be your downfall. Greed can cause you to lose everything you got, including your freedom. Stay ahead of the game. Get what you need, not what you want. Distinguish your needs from your wants. Believe me, when them indictments started rolling, people started folding. Your friends become your co-defendants, and, before they become your enemies, they transform to solid government witnesses. I've seen older brothers get their little brothers life sentences. And don't rely on loyalty—that shit overrated."

As if there was no other sound in the visitation room, all Victoria could hear was her father's voice as he continued giving her the game.

"I'm not going to chastise you over your choices. I want what any father wants for his daughter, and that's the best. I can't give you gifts, but I can give you what nobody gave me. Victoria, in this game, you gotta take heed to any and all remarks that trigger negative vibes. Ain't no parole back here. What these folks give you is what you'll be taking to the doe. This game ain't for everybody. If you got a family, then you already got too much to lose. Now, no matter what, you'll always be my baby girl, and I have to give it to you blood-raw. If you not willing to lie, kill or do whatever it takes to survive, then the game ain't for you. The next time you look in the mirror, if it don't reflect a cutthroat heartless muthafucka, this ain't for you. And sitting here looking at you, if I never tell you nothing else, Victoria, this game not for you."

"Visitation will be over in ten minutes," an officer announced over the intercom.

Several inmates and their loved ones began hugging, kissing, and shedding tears. Victoria and her father stood, then hugged one last time. He watched as she walked out with the rest of the crowd. He felt that, as her father, he'd done his part. To the best of his ability, he'd planted the seed. It was now up to her to nourish it and let it grow.

Victoria made it back to her rental, looked at herself in the rearview mirror, and questioned herself. "Are you a cutthroat heartless muthafucka?"

She stared in the mirror a few seconds, finally shaking her head. She knew the answer to her question before she even asked herself. Although her purpose for visiting her father had been to get advice on a profitable method of distributing the package she'd got from Diaz, she was satisfied instead to have received some jewels of life.

During her flight back to Miami, Victoria thought about everything her father had said. With all the information he had given her, by the time she was able to think about anything else, her plane was landing. Once she made it home, she went to Mrs. Knowles' house and picked up P-Rock and Victor. Even though she wasn't experiencing jet lag, the trip had exhausted her, and after a hot shower she went straight to sleep.

The following day, on her own discretion, she began distributing the kilos she'd got from Diaz. First, she advised everyone the price had dropped to 15-5 per kilo. This was music to their ears. Jay and Country took ten kilos to their new spot in Belle Glade. With the new price, Taj orchestrated several transactions with his kinfolk, moving a total of 14 kilos. Peanut was still up and coming; he'd gone from pushing dimes and nicks to eights and quarter-keys. So Victoria fronted him one kilo, and he was glad to accept.

Black turned out to be Victoria's true bread-maker. He could easily move ten kilos in two days, and to give him anything under twenty was an insult. With over half her supply gone, it was time to take her father's advice and find a new home. She contemplated selling the duplex, then concluded that was a decision to discuss with her father.

Early Monday morning, Victoria drove to Broward County to meet with a real estate agent she'd contacted. She had no problem finding the agency. The realtor had Victoria follow her to Pembroke Pines, which had a luxurious selection of modern homes. Each house they passed had immaculate landscaping. The realtor pulled into the driveway of an elegant home.

The realtor climbed out her car and waved to Victoria. "Come on, Mrs. Cole. Let me show you around."

Victoria got out and walked behind her, looking at her blonde hair. She thought of the hairstyles she might do if the realtor was one of her clients. She snapped out her brief daydream as they entered the very spacious four-bedroom home. The realtor led Victoria into the gourmet kitchen, which had a fantastic view of the entire front yard. Dying to see more of the house, Victoria was delighted when she was shown the master bedroom. She couldn't believe how big it was, and the fact it had a balcony convinced her this was the home for her. The realtor opened the double doors that led out to the balcony, and Victoria was awed by the heated swimming pool in the backyard. Last but not least, she was shown how to operate the electric built-in storm shutters. The house was more than she had ever dreamed of owning. And thankfully, by taking advantage of her repaired credit, she was in her new home by the end of the week.

Victoria packed nothing but clothes, leaving all the old furniture in the duplex, and fully outfitted her new home with brand new European furniture. Even with no one to share her bed, Victoria bought an Italian bedroom set with a deluxe king size bed. P-Rock loved their new home, especially the basketball hoop over the two-car garage. Victoria even had a secret floor safe installed. After settling in, she counted her stash and placed her money in the safe.

Everything was looking up for Victoria. She decided that, after all she'd been through and accomplished, she deserved to spoil herself for a day. Taking the kids to Mrs. Knowles' house, she got her Acura detailed, then, for the first time, she drove to Bal Harbor to do some shopping. She bought a pair of Gucci frames that she had always wanted, some Chanel boots to complement her Chanel outfit, and even an authentic Prada handbag to rid herself of her old knockoff.

She walked out of Bal Harbor, her hands full of shopping bags. Struggling with her remote, she had to place a couple of bags on the ground to push the trunk release button. The immediate sight of her jam-packed trunk made Victoria realize she needed a bigger ride.

"Do I want a new car or need one?" she asked herself, and smiled at the answer. "Hell, yeah, I need one!"

She shut the trunk and threw her shopping bags in the backseat, on top of Victor's car seat, and wherever else they fit. She drove to the same dealership she'd purchased her Acura from. Driving in circles, she finally spotted the salesman that she had dealt with the last time. He was standing on the stairs with a couple of other salesmen.

Monitoring the car lot like a predator does his prey, once he noticed Victoria parking her car, he rushed over to assist her. "Good evening, Ms. Cole. How can I help you?"

"I need to upgrade. Can you help me with that?"

"Yes, ma'am! Do you have anything particular in mind?"

Victoria didn't say a word, but pointed at a canary yellow Lexus 470 SUV.

The salesman turned in the direction she pointed, then faced her with a smile. "Let's go do some paperwork."

****

*Boom... Boom... Boom...*

Inside his girlfriend's apartment, Crunch jumped off the sofa, startled by the pounding on the front door. He rushed to peep out the window, looking down at the parking lot. He was relieved to see the usual cars parked, with no sign of any police cars.

*Boom... Boom... Boom...*

"Who da fuck dat is?" Crunch screamed through the door.

"Yo worst nightmare. Can I come in?"

"Man… I know dat ain't my dog." Crunch said, swinging the door open. "Wuz up, Tank? Why you ain't call and let me know you was coming?"

"Tighten-up. You know I never give my location or destination over the wire," Tank said, stepping through the doorway.

Crunch closed and double-locked the door. "Damn, I'm glad to see you, Fam. Come on in the back and check dis shit out."

Fortunately for Tank, he'd come at the right time. Prior to his arrival, Crunch had been in the middle of a discussion with another of his homeboys, Pig. Pig had grown up in the same neighborhood as Crunch. Before becoming a Jack Boy, Crunch had used to break inside tourist vehicles parked at hotels with Pig. Then Pig had been sent to state prison in Vero Beach, Florida. Speed was never one of Pig's traits. His 5'5", 250-pound body was his curse and had allowed the police to easily apprehend him.

Back in Crunch's self-made man cave, he sat down in his Miami Hurricanes lazy-boy, and introduced Tank to Pig. The two dapped, and Pig passed an already lit blunt to Crunch.

"So this yo partner in crime, the legendary Big Tank. Man, I've heard a lot about you," Pig said.

"I hope not too much, cause then I'd have to kill you." There was an eerie silence. Tank burst out in laughter. "I'm just fuckin with ya. Crunch, this muthafucka looked scared as hell."

Crunch joined Tank in laughter, then said, "Pig, go ahead and finish explaining about the lick."

"Like I said, my cousin told me the busta be making big-boy deals on the phone."

"What do you call big-boy deal?" Tank gazed doubtfully at Pig.

"Bricks, that's what I'm talking 'bout. Ole boy got dat work, you feel me?" Pig replied with a touch of sarcasm. He did not like the vibe Tank gave off when he started asking about details. Animosity began forming in Pig's heart because of Tank's uninvited bid to participate in the robbery they were planning.

"So wuz up, when you two plan on making this happen?" Tank asked.

Crunch faced Pig. "What you think, this week or next week?"

"I gotta wait on my cuz. She said ole boy took her shopping. He bought her a big ass diamond ring an all. We're gonna wait until she say he re-up."

Tank rubbed his hands together. "Damn! I need a lick to come up on. Shit… I'll lay his bitch ass down tonight. Just say the word." He cracked his knuckles.

Every word that came out Tank's mouth created envy in the atmosphere, as far as Pig was concerned. Pig despised the fact that Crunch would take it upon himself to dictate who would be involved with his caper. He was expecting a two-way split from the robbery he'd orchestrated. Now, with Tank in on it, one thing was for sure: their share had just got smaller.

# Chapter 8

Inside the Miami Police Department, Sherman, bent to drink from the water fountain, sensed someone standing behind him. He stood, turned, and frowned at the sight of Internal Affairs agent Susan McCloy.

"Detective Sherman, can I have a word with you?"

"Do I have a choice?" Before she could answer, he said, "Look, I'm in the middle of investigating a lead on a double murder. Can it wait?"

"I will only take a few minutes of your time. Forensics sent back the results off the weapon found on the scene of the police shooting you were involved in."

As an officer, Sherman hated speaking with I.A. To be seen causally conversing with Susan McCloy would immediately spark red flags with his comrades. Considering what she had to say, Sherman decided it would be best to continue their conversation in private. He led McCloy to the west-end corridor. Since that part of the department was under construction, he presumed the area would have limited traffic.

"OK, McCloy, where are you going with this?"

"Detective, if your record reflects your ethics, then you know, just as well as I know, that crime scene was tampered with. We've done all the necessary fieldwork to prove our case. As we speak, my partner is debriefing the commissioner. We have statements from you as well as all the officers that were present on the scene." McCloy folded her arms across her chest. "It's strange, each of you guys' statements coincides. But nobody mentioned the prints being wiped off the gun."

Sherman's mouth opened, but the bombshell McCloy had just dropped had him speechless.

"Look, I don't believe you had anything to do with tampering with the evidence. Right now, I want to give you the chance to change your deposition before it's too late," she said, giving him an ultimatum.

He took a step closer to McCloy, "My report was accurate to the events that transpired."

"Detective, this is off the record and strictly confidential. Not only was the weapon the victim allegedly possessed wiped clean of any prints, but the bullets in the magazine as well. Speaking of the magazine, we were able to pull an excellent set of prints off it. Guess whose they are? I'll give you a hint, they weren't the victims. So, let's start over. Take your time and tell me what Officer Gonzalez really did. Yes, detective, he's fucked."

Sherman was confident McCloy could never prove he had witnessed Gonzalez kneeling next to the body and gun. Helping I.A. build a case against one of his comrades would be frowned upon by every officer in the department. However, ever since the incident, his conscience had troubled him over Gonzalez's deceit.

"Alright, McCloy, you got my attention. I have no knowledge of Gonzalez doing anything inappropriate. He gave me his account as to what took place, and I also read his report. I can only go by what he said. I'm a detective, not a polygraph. If you have evidence on Gonzalez, then I suggest you do your job and prosecute. Now, if you will excuse me, I need to do mine." Sherman walked away from her.

"We'll be in touch Detective!" McCloy shouted in an attempt to irritate him.

Sherman returned to his desk to follow up on a lead for his case. He retrieved the yellow sticky memo Detective Menendez had left on his computer monitor. It read, "Significant tip (305) 555-1999, Jarvis." Sherman dialed the number, then leaned back in his chair.

"Hello… Yes, this is Detective Sherman with the Miami Police Department. Can I speak with Jarvis?"

"Dis him!"

"I understand you have some information pertaining to a double murder I'm investigating."

"Yeah I know about that, and a string of robberies," Jarvis said.

Sherman sat up straight in his chair, engrossed by the anticipation of more detail. "The man you're speaking of, what's his name?"

"Hang on, first thing first, I understand there's a cash reward for information that leads to a conviction. I don't care about no cash reward."

"What is it that you're looking for?"

"I want my little brother prison sentence terminated or at least reduced. Can you manage that?"

"That's not my call. Only the prosecutor over his case can make that decision. But I'm sure we could work something out."

"Naw, there's nothing to work out. I know how this shit works. Make some calls. Whoever it is that can make it happen, you need to be on the phone with them. And here's something to motivate you: I know the name, where he hang out, and his partner. Oh yeah, my brother's name is Corey Harris. Make your calls, then hit me when we got a deal." Jarvis ended the call.

Sherman slammed the phone down. He was fuming that the caller knew so much and had given so little. He contemplated bringing up charges against Jarvis as an accessory after the fact in the near future. But from having brokered similar deals, Sherman was well aware there would be a clause to prevent self-incrimination. After writing down Jarvis's information and demands, he got up and went to talk to the one man with enough juice to negotiate with the state attorney.

Hating to just storm into his office, Sherman knocked, then stuck his head in. "Captain, I need a favor."

"If it has anything to do with department budget, don't ask."

"No, sir, it doesn't. I need for you to set up a conference with the state attorney," Sherman said

"Oh, sure, that's all. I'll serve coffee and doughnuts too," The captain sarcastically said. "Give me what you got, not some damn orders, and I'll think about it."

Sherman looked at the captain, baffled.

The captain was holding a pen in his hand, and he tossed it down on his desk. "What, are you lost for words…? Come on, I don't have all day. Spit it out."

Sherman handed the captain his notes and began explaining what he'd heard from Jarvis. As the captain read the notes, he concurred with Sherman and agreed to put in a call to the state attorney. With his arms folded, Sherman stood in front of the captain's desk, listening to him haggle over the deal.

"That'll be fine… Monday, 9:30 sharp… Sure, see you then." The captain hung up and wiped a bead of sweat off his forehead. "Did you know Corey Harris is serving a 25-year sentence on drugs and weapon charges? He don't even have four years under his belt. The D.A. that prosecuted him is not too ecstatic about the terms of this deal. But, under the circumstances, conviction on a double homicide, along with a couple of unsolved robberies, those are some powerful bargaining chips. This Jarvis character better damn sure deliver." He pounded his fist on his desk.

****

From the window of her kitchen, Victoria watched as P-Rock played with his little brother. Pembroke Pines was a beautiful town, and the community was a reflection of the American dream. As a single mother, this was the perfect place to raise her sons.

Outside in the front yard, P-Rock dipped a plastic wand in a bottle of soap solution and blew bubbles, and Victor chased them. Victor was barely able to keep his balance as he ran through the thick, plush lawn. Victor giggled and laughed as each bubble he caught disappeared at his touch.

Three neighborhood kids passing by on their bicycles caught a glimpse of Victor's amputated limp. Skidding to a stop on the sidewalk, they stared in silence.

"Look at that freaky-looking kid," one said, pointing at Victor.

"Yuck! That kid give me the creeps," another said, loud enough to catch P-Rock's attention.

P-Rock, offended, put his hands up in the air, wanting to know what their problem was. Too young to comprehend to what was going on, Victor simply continued laughing and chasing the remaining bubbles floating in the air.

"Hey, what happened to his arm?"

"None of yo business," P-Rock replied, walking towards the three boys.

The biggest of the three, obviously the instigator and the ringleader of the name-calling, seemed unfazed by P-Rock's fearless approach. To add insult to injury, he continued his verbal assault.

"That one-armed kid should be in the circus. He's disgusting. People would pa—" His sentence was cut short as P-Rock threw the soapy bubble solution in his eyes. He instantly let out a girlish scream.

With the soap stinging the loudmouth's eyes, P-Rock rushed and pushed him off his bike. The other two kids quickly jumped off their bikes to attack P-Rock. Focusing on the bigger of the two, P-Rock unleashed an explosive barrage of punches with such hatred and rage, the kid never stood a chance. The smallest one froze, seeing blood gush from his friend's nose, then picked up his bicycle and peddled away as fast as he could. The initial instigator was still screaming horribly, rolling around on the ground, trying to wipe the pain out of his eyes.

Seeing his big brother fighting, Victor dropped to the ground and started crying. Inside the house, Victoria was just putting some ice cubes in a glass when she heard Victor cry. She looked out at him, then glanced in the direction he was facing. Outraged, she inhaled a quick breath as she witnessed P-Rock kicking another child in the ribs. She bolted out of the front door, sprinting past Victor. Just in time, she yanked P-Rock back before he could deliver an additional kick to the kid's face.

"P-Rock, STOP IT!" she yelled, nearly tripping over one of the kids' bikes.

The entire scene was chaotic. She gazed around, analyzing the devastation P-Rock had caused.

"Boy, what the hell has gotten into you?" she loudly asked, shaking P-Rock by the shoulders.

"I'm not gonna let nobody pick on my brother. Fuck dem crackas." He was breathing heavily.

*Smack!* Victoria slapped P-rock across the face. "I ain't raise you to talk disrespectful to me. What is your problem?" She shook him again, searching for some form of understanding.

With P-rock preoccupied while Victoria chastised him, the two remaining kids hurried to pick up their bikes and rapidly cleared the scene. Victor came running towards his mother with his hands raised to be picked up. Victoria scooped him into her arms and gave P-Rock a light push towards the front door.

When they stepped inside, Victoria said, "P-Rock, no words in history ever physically hurt somebody. The world is full of insensitive people, and they're going to say things you don't like. Just let 'em talk, until they put their hands on you, but before they do, ignore 'em."

Victoria spent nearly 30 minutes speaking with P-Rock. She was sincerely doing her best to bring him up with decent morals that would take him a long way in life. But despite her efforts, every word she was saying went in one ear and out the other.

****

Meanwhile, across town, Latricia and Tray were in the middle of one of their monthly arguments. Latricia was frustrated with Tray not coming home for days and for making her dodge Victoria over the money they owed her for the four kilos.

"I'm sick of yo ass. What, you think I can't smell female body lotion on you? I know I don't wear no shit smell like that. Who you fuckin?"

Tray smirked and didn't answer her question.

"Then you got me around here dodging my girl and screening her calls. You've had the money and done flipped that shit Victoria gave us five times. Yo ass need to pay her the money you owe. Damn Tray, you always burning bridges. Now I see why people always say your word ain't shit. It's not them, it's yo no good ass, then coming up in here smelling like fish."

"You tripping, and fuck everybody else, you got my back, right?"

"Don't ask me no stupid question. You know I do. But, damn, how you expect a bitch to ride for you, when you draggin me in the mud like some random chick?"

Tray stepped close to Latricia and put both his hands on her shoulders. "Dis shit ain't for me. Everything I do, I do for us. I'm getting this bread up so we can live comfortable. Shit… you around here trippin, I can take care of myself just fine."

"What's that suppose to mean?" Latricia asked with a tear forming in her eye.

"Just what the fuck it sound like. If you not wit' me, then you against me. If you against me, you don't trust me, and a bitch that don't trust me, then I can't love. And if I don't love you—" He paused and removed his hands from her shoulders. "—what the fuck do I need with you?" He added a cocky demeanor to his words. Latricia was overcome by a psychotic reaction to Tray's blunt, unaffectionate ways. She charged at him, releasing a grisly howl, punching and clawing at his face. Tray blocked the majority of her punches with his forearms, then mashed her in the face, shifting her momentum.

She lost her balance and braced herself against the wall. "Muthafucka, I hate you. After all I've done for your sorry ass, and all them fucked up predicaments you put me through, you gon' handle me like this. The sad thing is that I keep sticking by you through the bullshit. Last year, yo trifflin ass paid for that bitch abortion, and I stayed wit' yo dog ass. Now you want to leave cause you ain't got no hustle, and always fucking up people shit. It ain't my fault somebody gon' fuck you up behind their money. And when somebody kill yo sorry ass, I'll get a pedicure before I go to yo stanking ass funeral. Punk, kick rocks. I need a real man, not a little boy with no hustle. Just leave my gurl shit on your way out!"

"Psssst… Tell that bitch to get it in blood!" Tray yelled back.

Latricia rushed at Tray, swinging wildly. She fought him with pure rage, drawing blood from his left cheek. She sunk her nails into his flesh, gouging divots of skin with each scratch. They tussled in the living room, knocking over lamps, crashing into their television and anything else in their path. Latricia's adrenaline-fueled assault was exhausting Tray. His pushes and slaps had no effect on her. At the peak of his frustration, Tray blocked one of Latricia's blows and caught her with a hard right jab to the chin knocking her unconscious.

Out of breath and tired, Tray stood over Latricia, looking down at her laid out cold. With Latricia not a problem for the moment, Tray dashed to the garage and gathered the seven kilos he'd got from his Haitian connect. He then went into their bedroom to grab his stash and car keys. On his way out, he heard Latricia moaning on the floor. In passing, with no compassion for her condition, Tray spit down into her face just before walking out the door.

Latricia slowly rose to her knees and hunched over the sofa. She heard Tray's truck roar as he sped away. She wiped his spit off her forehead and began sobbing uncontrollably. Desperately needing someone to talk to, she determined that it was time to call Victoria and explain everything that had happened. She got up and dialed Victoria's number, pausing a brief moment before pressing the last number, then closed her eyes.

"Hello."

"Hey, Victoria."

"Latricia! Gurl, where are you? Is everything alright?"

"I'm sorry… fo… for calling youuuu…" Latricia cried.

"What's wrong? I can't understand what you're saying."

"He made… he made me not call you."

"Who? You're not making any sense. Where are you? Do you need me to come and pick you up?"

"I need to come talk with you. Are you home?" Latricia asked.

"I gotta meet Black at the duplex in thirty minutes. Meet me there, alright?"

"OK." Latricia said, sniffling.

Twenty minutes later, Victoria pulled up to the duplex and called Mrs. Knowles over to clean up. As soon as Mrs. Knowles walked over, Latricia arrived. Her eyes widened in amazement, seeing Victoria's new ride for the first time.

Latricia climbed out her car and greeted Victoria. "Hey, gurl."

"I thought something done happen to you," Victoria said, giving Latricia a mediocre embrace.

As Victoria and Latricia hugged, Black turned the corner in his platinum Jaguar XK8. He exited his sleek auto, swaggering confidently.

"Wuz up, Victoria?" He looked over at Latricia. "Damn, where you been?"

Latricia didn't answer. They all went inside, then she began explaining and pleading for Victoria to understand the dilemma Tray had put her in.

"I swear to god, I had no idea Tray was going to play you. I felt so bad not being able to tell you what was going on. Every time I got ready to call you, Tray would say he almost finished, or he just waiting on one more person to come through. Most nights, his ass didn't even stay home."

Victoria put her hands on her hips and sucked her teeth. "Latricia, Tray ain't stay home because he was busy spending my money on another bitch in Aventura Mall. If you wasn't so busy dodging me, you would've known that when I tried to call you."

Mrs. Knowles was wiping out the refrigerator; she looked up, surprised at the tone Victoria was using with her friend.

"Huh! What? When did he…" Latricia stopped talking and started crying. "I hate him." She had initially concealed the threat Tray had made toward Victoria, but, after hearing about his infidelity, she disregarded his wishes. "I told Tray to leave your money, and he told me to tell you to get it in blood."

"What!" Black shouted, lifting his Coogi sweater to expose the handle of his Glock 40. "I say we take him up on his offer. That shit ain't nothing but a word."

Victoria shook her head. "Naw, he gon' get his. Every dog has his day."

"I don't know if you are aware, but this shit ain't no muthafuckin Parker Brother board game. This da dope game, and experience is the best teacher. If you don't want to get your hands dirty, then maybe you shouldn't play the game. Don't tell me you believe karma will catch him, or you gon' sit around and wait for a mystery god to have vengeance. On the real, his punk ass want to turn gangsta, then I say we need to endorse that check he wrote with his own muthafuckin blood," Black said, riled up.

At that very moment, Latricia began regretting she'd told Victoria what Tray had said. She hated what he'd done, but not enough to agree with Black. Deep down, she still had a spot in her heart reserved for Tray. Despite the current change of circumstances, they had history, and she still loved him. So, instead of voicing her opinion in Victoria and Black's conversation, she simply sat at the kitchen table, hoping the situation would not escalate.

"Fuck that, Victoria, just give me a nod, I'll body his ass. Dat's some real bullshit he let come out his mouth. If Tray taking food out yo mouth, then he's taking out of mine. It's people like him that turn a good thing sour. Victoria, you got a sweet connect, and keeping your connect happy is what makes you money. Then there's killers like me that help you keep dat money. Eventually you're gonna have to choose to make an example out of someone. If not, this is just a small taste of the bullshit that goes with the game. So, before you get a reputation for being soft, are you going to make an executive decision, or you want me to?" Black waited on her answer.

Victoria refuse to let the violence associated with the drug trade corrupt her. She shook her head, which relieved Latricia. The last thing she wanted was something serious to happen to Tray. She believed that, once he cooled down, they would be able to work everything out.

"If you change your mind, Victoria, let me know," Black said, looking at Latricia from the corner of his eye.

"I'm sorry. Victoria. I shouldn't have come here with my household problems."

Victoria faced Latricia with a frown. "These are beyond yo household problems. I had to pay Diaz out of my pocket. That was an unnecessary loss that could've been avoided had I not trusted in you. Latricia, that work was your responsibility, not Tray's. Now, the real question is, how are you gonna pay me back?"

Latricia's facial expression was sad as she spoke. "The money I had, Tray took it when he left."

"Exactly, so this is far from a damn household problem."

*Ring... ring... ring...*

Victoria was interrupted by the ringing of the cordless house phone. She walked over to the coffee table and answered.

"Hello." Victoria held the phone to her ear, then pushed the number 5, and her father came on the phone. She walked into her old bedroom to talk in private, leaving Black and Latricia.

"I can't believe it. I finally caught you. You never stay home, do you?" her father asked.

"Yeah, I do. I just took your advice and moved. I don't have a house phone at my new house, so do you want my cell number?"

"No, I'll just write you or catch you when I can. I was calling to let you know I'm being transferred to a new facility. They're sending me to U.S.P. Coleman. It's not too far from Ocala. So, if you decide to surprise me again, check to make sure where I'm at."

"OK, I will. Dad, did you get the money I sent you?"

"I haven't check my account, but if you sent it, then it's there, and I appreciate it. I hope you thought about everything we talked about?"

"I did."

"You betta, cause let me tell you what my old celly did. Me and this man been cellmates for three years, and in my eyes, he always carried himself as a bonafide soldier. At least, I was under the presumption he did. Anyway, he had a sister on the outside handling business for him, and by that, I mean doing a third party."

"Dad, you know I'm not familiar with them terms you be using."

"Well, you betta start learning them, and many more before it's too late. Pick up a book sometime and read."

"Dad, please, I'm really not in the mood for a lecture."

"Like I was saying, the guy sister did a third party, and to enlighten what that is, it's a strategy the D.E.A. use to conduct a control buy. Under their supervision, she participated in drug deals. And in return, her brother's sentence was drastically reduced, and now he's a free man. Victoria, the moral to that story, it's not just the people on the streets you have to worry about. You got muthafuckas back here trying to get home by all means necessary. Plenty of 'em just dying to hear the right story to jump on somebody case. It don't take a person to get caught with drugs to get convicted. All the prosecutor need is someone to take the stand and point their finger."

*BEEP*... The alert chimed, indicating the call was ending in 30 seconds.

"Damn, them 15 minutes went fast. Well the phone is about to hang up. Remember what I said at Visitation. And never mistake knowledge for a lecture." The phone beeped again… "I'm only giving you what no one ever gave—"

Victoria held the phone to her ear, listening to silence. She didn't realize the call had disconnected. She finally hung up and returned to the living room. By the look on Latricia's face, and the menacing gaze in Black's eyes, they had obviously exchanged a few unpleasant words.

"I forgot where I left off, but Latricia, you owe me for this," Victoria said.

Latricia held her head down as Victoria spoke, which was a childhood habit she had never outgrown. She sat quietly on the couch, looking disappointed, yet Victoria had little understanding for her.

****

The next day, Victoria was awoken by the morning sunlight. She stretched and yawned, then her mind drifted to the words her father had said. Looking into the mirror while she brushed her teeth, she decided it was time to get serious and invest in her dreams. Owning an upscale unisex salon was something she had wanted to do since childhood. Her overall business plan was to cater to all respectable needs pertaining to the body, from head to toe. Whether a client wanted a hairdo, facial, pedicure, or manicure, her salon was going to be a one-stop shop. Even a full-body massage could be acquired in the type of establishment she desired to open.

The same afternoon, Victoria met with a white male realtor, searching for the perfect location for her business. North Miami Beach would have been ideal, but every available property was either too small or hidden from traffic; so, after driving around for a couple hours, she was forced to reconsider location.

Before leaving the last plaza, the realtor explained that his company owned several properties in the city of Miramar. Victoria immediately agreed to follow him there, especially with Miramar being next to Pembroke Pines. The realtor took her to different properties on University Drive, then to Miramar Parkway. Sadly, she ran into the same problems that had arisen in North Miami Beach.

They parked in a Publix Super Market parking lot. The realtor walked over to Victoria.

"Ms. Cole, I apologize you were unsatisfied, but I assure you tomorrow we will find the perfect building for your business. We still have properties in Hollywood and Fort Lauderdale, if you're interested."

Victoria told him she would give his office a call in the morning. On her way to pick up P-Rock and Victor from Mrs. Knowles, she drove through Carol City. While passing the 183 St. Flea Market, she noticed a For Sale sign on the side of a building in the plaza. It was a 3,000-square-foot clothing store in the process of having a going-out-of-business sale. The building sat in a perfect spot on 27$^{th}$ Ave, which was one of the busiest streets in Miami. Victoria did not hesitate at this opportunity. She made a U-turn and parked directly in front of the building.

As Victoria entered, the young woman behind the register took in her appearance and stereotyped Victoria as simply a customer hoping to take advantage of their liquidation sale.

"Good evening. As you can see, everything we have is on sale. We still have an excellent choice of kids' clothes to your left and women's clothing to your right. If you're looking to give that special man in your life some of the latest fashions, there's still several brand names to choose from."

"No… No… No… I'm not interested in buying any clothing. I'd like to speak with the owner. I'm interested in buying the building."

"Oh… Fo' real, just wait one minute. I'll get him on the phone." The woman picked up the store phone. "Hey, baby, there's a woman here interested in the store… No, she don't look like a real estate age— OK, I'll tell her." She hung up and returned her attention to Victoria. "My fiancé will be here in ten minutes. Please, why don't you look around until he gets here? You may see something you like. If you do see something, I'll give you a great deal."

In exactly nine minutes, the owner drove up and parked behind Victoria's Lexus. To own that exact SUV was a dream of his. But, unfortunately, for every step he took forward, his next move was two steps back. Bad money management was the cause of his debt, and also the reason he was forced to sell his store.

"Heeey, honey!" The woman said, running to her fiancé and greeting him with a hug.

Victoria was in the kids' section, sorting through the display rack. All of a sudden, a chill crept up her spine as she heard a voice that was all too familiar to her. Never in a million years would she have thought that, out of all the businesses in Miami, she'd be standing in the same one as Victor's father. Victoria stared at the couple hugging. The world seemed to have stopped, and nothing existed but the three of them stuck in a moment of time.

"Honey, that's the woman I told you about," the owner's fiancée said, and, as she turned in the direction of Victoria, she caught her staring at them in a trance-like state. "Are you alright?"

Breaking her silence, Victoria said, "Your no-good fiancé could answer that better than I can. Aren't you a registered sex offender, David?"

Victoria's question took David's breath away.

His fiancée sensed the negative energy through his fingers intertwined with hers. "You two know each other? What the hell is she talking 'bout, asking if you a sex offender?" She snatched her hand from his grip.

"We knew each other at one time," he replied.

"Yeah, we knew one another in the past. Why don't you tell your fiancée how we know each other, David?" Better yet, I'll do the honors since I know yo ass just gonna say a bunch of lies like you always do."

"Get the fuck out my store!" David yelled.

"Please believe I'm 'bout to. Gurl, if you want to know what you're getting yourself into, and yo loving fiancé's deep dark secrets, give me a call. My name is Victoria. Here's my number." Victoria wrote down her number and handed it to David's fiancée. "I believe you have a lot to talk about. And David, as for this store, I wouldn't buy water in the desert from your muthafuckin ass," she shouted, storming out of the store.

Victoria got back in her Lexus and sped away from the store, keeping a promise she'd made to herself. Never to shed a tear over another man, especially after the pain David had put her through. She stopped at the red traffic light, and thought back to how their relationship started.

****

In 1996, Victoria and Pam, Crow's daughter's mother, went out to the Martin Luther King Parade. Because of the beautiful weather in Miami, even in January Miamians celebrated the historical holiday dressed like it was summertime. All the hustlers and paper chasers pulled out their customized toys. A variety of candy-painted convertible classic automobiles slowly drove up and down 62nd street, along with the exotic luxury whips and Banshee four-wheelers. Besides the vehicles, the street was filled with tens of thousands of people.

The smell of barbecue was in the atmosphere everywhere. And while most of the men drank Hennessy or beer, the woman sipped differently flavored wine coolers.

Victoria and Pam were hanging in a convenience store parking lot as Sugar Hill DJs set up a colossal wall of speakers. A light-skinned brother—6'2", muscular build, and hazel eyes—walked up to Victoria with a wine cooler in his hands.

"Here you go, beautiful," he said, offering the bottle.

"No, thank you. I'm straight."

"You're sexy as hell, too."

"Thanks."

"My name's David, and, besides beautiful, you are…?"

"Victoria," she answered, blushing.

Still infatuated with light-skinned brothers, Victoria almost melted at David's charm. He was definitely smooth, complimenting her throughout their conversation. He offered her the wine cooler again, this time getting her to accept his generosity.

Meanwhile, as Victoria and David chatted, Pam observed Crow and his homeboys entertaining a group of females. That was Pam's cue to intervene and put a damper on Crow's personal time at the parade.

David had the persona of a dope boy, but he didn't earn his money the tax-free way. He worked at the Port of Miami, making $48 an hour. Soon after they met, Victoria and David dated for several weeks. During that time, their mutual attraction and lust drew them together. David decided to allow Victoria and P-Rock to move into his three-bedroom home. Those moments of their relationship were flawless. There was a magnetic force between them, making them practically inseparable. David took Victoria on her first cruise and on shopping sprees, and he even took P-Rock to Disney World.

Months later, David began coming home after 5 a.m.. He'd always claim to have been working overtime, or that he had to take the place of a co-worker who hadn't shown up for work. The excuses became repetitive, and their intimacy turned distant. Victoria continued trying to please David by keeping the house spotless, satisfying his sexual appetite whenever the time came, and never nagging him during the time they spent together.

Then, one dreadful morning, while Victoria was attending Miami Dade Community College, thirty minutes into class, she experienced a familiar nausea. Excusing herself, she went to the ladies bathroom and vomited. Feeling no better, she decided to return home. She was immediately surprised to see David's BMW in the driveway. Her upset stomach forced her to walk slowly. She entered the house, and it was extremely quiet. Just as she was about to call out David's name, her eyes landed on a Dooney purse lying on the dinner table. Now moving stealthily, Victoria tiptoed to investigate the contents of the purse.

"Tonya Wilson, 1981," Victoria mumbled to herself, examining the Florida State I.D.

Quietly, she eased toward the bedroom she shared with David. The closer she got, the clearer a sound could be heard. There was no need for Victoria to put her ear to the door; the moans and screams coming from the young female sounded more painful than pleasurable. Victoria threw the bedroom door open, catching David in mid-stroke as he rammed the young girl doggy style.

"Oh, shit!" he screamed, yanking his rod out of the girl and throwing his hands in the air as though innocent. "Baby, let me explain."

His young mistress scurried off the bed nude and desperately grabbed her clothes off the floor.

Despite her stomach pains, Victoria's initial reaction was to charge and beat the hell out of his mistress. But the girl's pleas, age, and constant cries of apology kept Victoria from making a move towards her.

"I'm sorry… I'm so sorry…"

The young girl's cries made Victoria channel her anger directly towards David. Victoria looked down on the bed and noticed bloodstains on the sheets. And once her eyes focused on his rod and saw it coated in blood, she lost it.

"What the fuck! I'm too much woman for you? Yo ass got to go fuck a child? You sick son-of-a-bitch, she's 15!" Victoria screamed, then attacked David with a flurry of punches.

David tried to prevent Victoria from connecting with his jaw. "Bitch, hit me again!" he said, holding both of her arms. Unable to free herself from his grasp, she bit into his forearm, piercing his flesh and drawing blood.

"Bitch, calm down or get the fuck out my house, you and your bastard son," he sternly said.

"Muthafucka, you go fix yo mouth to call my son a bastard. I tell you what, I might be pregnant right now with your child. And I swear to God, if I am, guess what? This child will be a bastard too, because your ass will be in jail for statutory rape, and that's a promise!"

Victoria moved out of David's house the same night, but not before keeping her promise. She called the police and gave them the name and address on the I.D. of the girl who David had taken advantage of. The sight of him in handcuffs was the last she'd seen of him until today. David may have owned the building she wanted, but Victoria vowed never to have any dealings with him, even if it affected her dreams.

# Chapter 9

Tank, Crunch, and Pig pulled into the parking lot of a Super Wal-Mart to buy supplies for the heist. Prior to their arrival, Pig had remained quiet for the duration of the ride, unless someone asked him a question. Crunch sensed the tension, and so did Tank. But unlike Crunch, Tank didn't give a fuck.

Tank opened the glovebox, removed his gun and armed himself. "Crunch, you and fat boy chill. No need for all us going up in there. I know everything we need." He slammed the passenger door after he exited the van.

Pig took this opportunity to reason with Crunch about eliminating a third man. "…fo' real, Crunch, we don't need another man. I put you down with the lick cause we go way back. I know Tank yo boy and all, but we don't even know how much up in there, or what's going to be the split. Shit, I could've done this lick by myself."

Crunch turned to the rear so he could face Pig. "What the fuck you talking about? You said it's bricks up in there. What you think, this cat going to give us his work with a smile? We need a gangsta to go up in there wit."

"I'm not questioning Tank's gangsta, you told me y'all history. The point is, my cousin said ol' boy goes out of town a lot. All me and you gotta do is make it look like a B&E. We can take the TV and stereo, you know, make it look like some junkies did it. My cousin gon' let me know when he got the work up in there."

Crunch pounded his palm on the steering wheel a couple of times. "Goddamn, Pig, quit being so muthafuckin money-hungry. I'd rather be safe than sorry. What da fuck you gon' do if shit go wrong and he start blasting, huh?"

"What you think this for?" Pig said, brandishing a Ruger 9mm.

"Psssst! You trippin. That shit don't make you bulletproof. So, what, now you got eyes in the back of yo head?"

Pig persistently tried to get Crunch to understand his logic. But Crunch remained firm about Tank being a part of the robbery. Seconds later, the passenger door opened. Tank hopped in, and his presence killed their conversation. Tank tossed the plastic bags down between the passenger and driver's seats. He ignored the tension circulating in the van, assuming the negative vibe was nervousness.

Pig spied a cordless iron and a bottle of ammonia sticking out of one of the bags. "What you bout' to do, iron some clothes and mop?" he jokingly asked.

Tank did not respond to Pig's lame humor. Instead, he gave Pig an envious stare. "Y'all ready to make this happen?"

Crunch and Pig both nodded their heads.

"So, what's the iron for? Pig asked, skeptical.

Tank let out a sinister laugh, "A pistol ain't the only iron that can make a man give it up."

The three of them proceeded to Pig's cousin's place to get a feel for the scenery. It was dark outside. The Bayview apartment complex in North Miami had nightlights, but visibility was limited in the parking lot. Crunch drove slowly, creeping through the complex.

"What kind of car he drive?"

"Huh?" Pig replied.

"Huh! Man, you can huh, you can hear. What the fuck he drive?" Tank asked again, frustrated this time.

"He drive a big ass pickup truck. I don't know what kind it is, but I do know it's either black or dark blue."

Crunch scanned the parking lot, looking left and right. "Do you see his truck now?"

"Naw, it's not here. He usual park right in front of my cousin's door."

"So wuz up, Pig? You still want to break in today?" Crunch waited for Pig to answer and noticed his facial expression change in the rearview mirror.

"Yeah, we could, but I got to holla at my cousin and—"

Tank cut Pig short. "Fuck that burglary shit. We sticking to the initial plan," Tank decided, taking control of the operation. "Either we lay on this spot and wait until he comes, or we come back tomorrow. What's this muthafucka's name, anyway?"

"Tray," Pig answered, just as his cell phone vibrated.

****

At 9:40 Monday morning, Sherman, his captain, and the District Attorney, Chip Gibson, were inside the captain's office going over the stipulations in the cooperation agreement drafted for Jarvis.

"Detective Sherman, once this agreement is signed by your witness, he is obligated to be debriefed, and the suspects need to be arrested promptly. Judging from the diabolical carnage committed by these animals, their arrest should bring peace to the victims and families affected," the D.A. said, then held the agreement out to Sherman. Before releasing it, he tightly held onto the documents and stared sternly at Sherman, delivering the unspoken message that his neck was on the line.

After the D.A. stood and excused himself, Sherman called Jarvis. He angrily hung up when he got voicemail.

"Damn it, this was my fifth time calling him!" Sherman said to the captain. "This maggot gots the balls to bargain with vital information, then screen my damn calls. If he keeps this shit up, his brother isn't going to be the only one behind bars."

"Sherman, find this Jarvis character, find him now! We're going out on a limb with this one, including the D.A. Believe me, he's not thrilled one damn bit about this deal. But, hey, it's your ass on the line. The last cop that made a fool out of Gibson, he made a few calls, now that cop directs traffic in front of the courthouse, and he's been doing that for the past three years."

"Take it easy, Cap, nobody is going to be directing traffic. I can assure you of that. This deal is just a shortcut to solving my case. Let the truth be told, with or without Jarvis, I will close this case."

"Sherman you've yet to let me down. I have faith in you, which is the only reason I co-signed on this one. Now, what's going on with I.A.? Have they spoken to you again?"

"Briefly. Why you ask?"

"The department is catching a whole lot of shit from I.A., the media, and all these Al Sharpton-type activists making the public think Gonzalez and Adams are a couple of racist cops," the captain said. "As you know, they're both suspended with pay. But, according to Susan McCloy, within the next two weeks there's no doubt they'll be brought up on multiple charges."

Sherman was not surprised about Gonzalez; he was, however, startled that Adams would be indicted. Officer Adams was known as a strictly by-the-book cop. He had a wife, three kids, and fourteen years dedicated to the force.

"Why Adams, Captain?"

"The department is just catching too much heat from this shooting. The problem is, if this guy they shot had at least had some violence on his record, or a few drug convictions, the media could have painted him as another rebellious street thug. But, can you believe it, the friggin guy didn't even have a parking ticket. I tell you, Sherman, I.A. is coming down hard on this mythical blue wall of silence. I've seen the report, and, with the evidence they have on Gonzalez, he's going to need a dream team because they're planning on setting an example at his expense. Adams helped cover up Gonzalez's actions. God forbid Gonzalez gets convicted. If that happens, it'll practically guarantee that Adams will lose his badge and pension."

Sherman left the captain's office feeling sympathetic for Adams. Not only was Adams a fellow officer, he was a good friend that had been dragged down by the code of silence. This was the same code which was supposed to protect officers, but now it was under scrutiny, and Adams was the sacrificial lamb.

Sherman met Menendez in Booking and filled him in on the Gonzalez and Adams situation, along with the deal for Jarvis. Afterwards, he dialed Jarvis's number, and this time he answered.

"You've been wasting my time," Sherman said as soon as Jarvis picked up.

Jarvis whispered, "Is this Detective Sherman?"

"You know damn well who the hell this is. You've been ignoring my calls. Now, you want your brother out of prison or not? I've held up my end of the bargain. It's time for you to deliver. Jarvis, I need for you to come in so we can go over the provisions." Sherman stopped talking to give Jarvis a chance to respond. "Jarvis… Jarvis, you there?"

Jarvis was unresponsive. Just as Sherman was about to ask again, the call ended. He assumed the phone had lost its signal, so he called back, only to hear "Can't Knock the Hustle," the same Jay-Z song that he'd heard many times earlier on Jarvis's voicemail. Fuming, Sherman flung his desk phone, smashing it into his filing cabinet. Several officers around his cubicle stood up, investigating the sound.

Menendez waved his hand at them. "It's OK. Just had a weak cup of coffee."

"I'm through fucking around with this guy. He's really pissing me off. I need to know what he know, and too much goddamn time has been wasted." Sherman pointed his finger at Menendez. "Get that D.E.A. agent Finzi on the line. Tell him I need a favor."

"Sherman, line two!"

He first had to pick his phone up off the floor and pray it still worked. It did.

"Sherman here."

"Well, well, well, big-time robbery-homicide detective Michael Sherman. Tell me, is it true that you need a favor from little ole me? Or the bureau?" Agent Finzi teased.

"A little of both. And don't forget you owe me. Remember, I let you take all the credit for that airport bust."

"Yeah… yeah… yeah… for the tenth time, I remember. Talk to me. What do you need?"

"I need a location trace on a cell phone, A.S.A.P.," Sherman said.

"Please tell me you got a court order, or you're at least in the process of getting one."

"Since when do I need a court order for a favor? This is Special Agent 'against the grain' Finzi?"

Special Agent Finzi was no stranger to violating protocol to secure a conviction. In most cases, with a 98% conviction rate, technicalities hardly ever mattered. Since Sherman did help bring down a major drug trafficking ring, Finzi agreed to help.

"OK, what's the number?"

"(305) 555-1999. When you pinpoint the whereabouts of this asshole, give me a call."

"No problem. And, Sherman, next favor's on you."

****

Victoria lost her motivation for finding a building. Also, with all the coke Diaz had entrusted her with, it was time to get her grind on. She'd set-up a meeting with each of her distributors on an individual basis. Even Latricia was given the chance to repay her debt. Time was of the essence, and Victoria, waiting on Taj to pick a package up at the duplex, had her running late for a meeting with Black.

*Ring... ring... ring...*

"Wuz up, you ready?" Black immediately asked.

"No, not yet. I'm still waiting on Taj."

"Come on, Victoria, you fucking my money up. I needed to hit the road yesterday. You do know making people wait is bad for business."

"Just give me another thirty minutes, alright? Then I'll come to your house."

"A'ight, thirty minutes! Damn, you need to hurry up."

Another twenty minutes passed, and Taj still had not made it. She gave him a call, but his phone just rang five times, then went to voicemail. She decided to go ahead and meet Black.

Around one p.m., Victoria pulled up at Black's house. She stayed in her SUV to avoid Black's enormous bull mastiffs and called again to let him know she was outside. With a duffel bag in hand, Black emerged from his garage. He jumped into the passenger seat and got straight down to business.

"Victoria, you act like you ain't trying to get this money." He tapped the duffel bag. "I'm not even gon' stress how much money I missed."

"I'll make it up to you on the next package."

"Shit, you ain't got to look out on a package. Just give me an answer to why you be faking. It's no secret everybody know you ain't got a man."

"And I'm not looking for one neither," she fired back with attitude.

Black arched his eyebrows. "Goddamn! I see why you don't have one. You sound like I offended you."

"Let's get something clear. Don't try to enter my personal life. You're in my business life, and that's where it stops," she said, highly aggravated.

"I'm cool wit' that, but ya need to use your third eye, cause you letting that clouded mind of yours sleep on me. And obviously you don't recognize a good man when you see 'em. You know, behind every good solder is a good heart."

Black changed the subject by unzipping the duffel bag, showing her the stacks of money inside. Victoria reached into the back seat and grabbed an identical style of duffel bag, except hers was filled with 15 kilos. While she reached back, Black couldn't help but sneak a peek at the tight jeans hugging her curves.

Unaware of Black's wandering eyes, she passed him the bag. "Here, I got you next time."

"Naw, next time I'll just be waiting on my answer," he replied with a smile, showing off his pearly whites.

"You gon' keep waiting then," Victoria said, then she too smiled.

After leaving Black's house, Victoria drove back to the duplex. As she turned onto the street, she was surprised to see Latricia's car parked in the driveway. Victoria parked behind it, walked to the driver's side, and was shocked to see Latricia smoking a cigarette inside. She knocked on the window, snapping Latricia out of her daydream.

When Latricia opened the door, Victoria said, "Gurl, I didn't know you smoke?"

"Me neither, until about two hours ago." Latricia exhaled a cloud of smoke. "I needed something to try and calm my nerves. I'm so stressed, I don't know what the hell to do. It all started this morning when I tried to use my phone. I made a call and the fucking computer operator tells me my phone is off. But that's not the worse part. When I get to work, me and this white bitch get in an argument and the manager fired my ass. And guess what, ain't shit happen to her. Gurl... When he said I'm fired, I started to go postal up in there."

"Are you going to be alright?"

"Victoria, I lost my man, my job, I even lost my phone service. Shit, I lost my mind twice and found it once," Latricia said with a laugh that sounded more like a cry.

"C'mon inside. You didn't lose your friend."

Inside, Latricia let all her emotions go. She sat on the couch and broke down in tears. "With Tray gon', it's just a matter of time before the bank start calling about our mortgage payments. I need to make some serious money. I appreciate the ounces you've been giving me, but the guys I've been dealing with need more."

"You know I got you. Latricia, that's all you got to do, just talk to me. I love you like a sister," Victoria said, giving her a hug.

"Thank you, Victoria."

Victoria got up and walked to Crow's old bedroom. She returned with half a kilo.

"Give me back $6,000. I'm not making nothing on that." She handed the half to Latricia. "This is strictly a look-out for you. I gotta go pick up P-Rock from detention, and I'm running late. Just lock up when you leave." Victoria rushed out the door.

Latricia placed the coke on the kitchen table, then went to the window and watched Victoria drive away. Her conscience pleaded for her to be grateful, but her stubborn inner demons were not satisfied with the little Victoria had done for her. Once

Victoria's SUV turned the corner, Latricia hurried into Crow's room and searched around. She looked through the closet, under the bed, and in the dresser drawers, before finally searching under the dresser. She first noticed the guns, then a shoebox.

She took the top off of the box and said to herself, "Jackpot."

What Latricia saw inside the Reebok shoebox kicked her greed into high gear. Her eyes lit up at the stacks of money, and, instead of taking a little of the cash, she took the entire box. Fueled by greed, she rushed into the kitchen and pulled a trash bag from under the sink. She put both the shoebox and the half-kilo in it. Through being married to Tray, Latricia learned how to conceal and deceive. She hurried into the bathroom, removed the window screen and opened it as wide as it could go. Rapidly looking around, she decided to do one last thing. Returning to Crow's bedroom, she flipped over the mattress, pulled out a few dresser drawers, and shook the contents onto the floor. Satisfied the place appeared ransacked, she walked out of the house, leaving the front door cracked open.

As she drove away from the duplex, she looked at herself in the rearview mirror and did not like the person she saw. "What have I done?" she said to herself, then she had an idea and made a call.

****

"Boy, I don't know what has gotten into you. If it ain't one thang, it's another," Victoria said as P-Rock climbed into the passenger seat.

P-Rock didn't ignore his mother, but he felt her comment did not deserve an answer, and, while Victoria continued to reprimand him, he simply stared out the window.

"You hear me talking to you? Why did you get put in detention for the second time this month?"

"Ma, it wasn't my fault. This girl stole my book bag and tried to hide in the girl's locker room. When I found out, I went in there and snatched my book bag out of her hand. She screamed, and Coach Reed punished me for being in the girl's locker room. She tried to steal my shit… I mean, stuff," he quickly corrected. "I don't know why I'm the only one got punished."

"P-Rock, lately you've been acting violent, disrespectful, and with that attitude you remind me of your granddaddy. I'm gon' tear yo ass up if you join a gang, you hear me?" she said, recalling that her father had been a legendary member of the Two-Two Ave Boys.

For the remainder of the ride, they rode in silence. Victoria's first thought was not to blame herself for P-Rock's repeated unexplainable conduct. But by buying him a $1,310 Gucci book bag, she'd created an easy way for trouble to find him. Her thoughts were interrupted by her cell phone ringing. She looked at the number and saw it was Taj calling.

"Now he want to call, wasting all my time earlier," she said to herself and ignored his call.

As Victoria turned in at Victor's daycare center, her phone rang again. Assuming Taj was calling again, she quickly answered this time, ready to put him in his place for wasting her time.

"Victoria… Hello… You there, Victoria?"

She found herself about to explode at the wrong person, and had to catch herself and change her tone. "Hey, Mrs. Knowles. How you doing?"

"Victoria, I called the police to go over to your house."

"You did what!" Victoria shouted.

"I saw some bad ass kids inside your place. They broke in!"

"I can't believe that. I just left, not even an hour ago."

"Well, chile, you need to get here. They caught one of them and got his ass in the backseat of a police car. It's dogs and helicopters all over the place."

"I'm on my way."

One proven fact about the Lexus 470: it had superb road handling. Victoria took tire-screeching turns at reckless speeds. She pushed the SUV as if it was a Corvette. Racing to the duplex two blocks away, she noticed the City of Miami police helicopter circling low. She turned onto her street, and, just as Mrs. Knowles had described, police were everywhere.

Victoria parked as close as she could, which was three houses down from Mrs. Knowles' home. She told P-Rock to stay in the truck with Victor, then jumped out and jogged over to Mrs. Knowles'. A black female officer approached Victoria, asking if she was the owner of the duplex.

"Yes, I am. What is going on?"

"Well your neighbor here reported a burglary in progress, and on our arrival we saw two suspects coming out your place. One of them we apprehended. The other one is still on the loose, but don't worry, we'll catch 'em."

Victoria could not believe what was happening. She felt luck was on her side because at least the only drugs that had been in the house were what she'd given Latricia.

# Chapter 10

At 3:30 in the morning, the Bayview Apartments parking lot was extremely quiet. Parked next to a Chevy Blazer in a stolen utility van, Tank, Crunch, and Pig were patiently waiting for Tray's truck to pull in. Pig's cousin had informed him Tray was coming in from Lakeland early in the morning. With that information, Tank had come to the conclusion that, after a long drive, the element of surprise would have Tray completely off balance and submissive. And if not, Tank had the proper tools to make him comply.

A bright pair of headlights slowly drove towards their van.

"Heads up! Yo, Pig, is that him?" Crunch asked

"I can't tell," Pig said, then sat up, looking closer. "Oh, shit, dat's him."

"Put your head down," Tank ordered, slouching down in the passenger seat. He carefully watched the brake lights as the pickup passed.

Tank pulled back the slide on his .45 cal, chambering a round, then pulled down his ski mask. Crunch put on his gloves, then did the same. Once Pig heard the clicks from the deadly mechanisms, butterflies arose his gut. Still, on command, he was ready to go. Tank watched as the pickup's lights turned off, and, when the driver's side door open, adrenaline began pumping through his veins.

"Y'all ready?" Crunch and Pig nodded. "As soon as he close the door I'ma kick that muthafucka off the hinges. A'ight, let's move." They all climbed out of the van.

Tray was oblivious to the three gunmen closing in on him. Tired from his four-hour drive, his movements were sluggish, and he carelessly failed to observe his surroundings. A cricket chirping was the only sound he heard while unlocking the front door. He took his time entering the apartment. Unfortunately, his instincts were a second too late to prevent the powerful kick.

*BOOM!*" Tank's size-12 foot crashed the door into Tray's chest.

"Don't move, Playboy," Tank said, aiming his gun at Tray's head.

Crunch and Pig charged inside, locking the door behind themselves.

Tray put his hands up and nervously asked, "What y'all want?"

"Everything," Tank responded.

"Look, man, my money is in the back pocket, and this is all my jewelry I got on. Take it. Shit, here's my wedding ring." Tray took his wedding band off and tried to pass it to Tank.

"Oh, you got muthafuckin jokes. Tape his bitch ass up," Tank instructed his crew. "Make sure that duct tape is tight too."

Crunch and Pig grabbed Tray and taped him to a dining room chair. The commotion woke Pig's cousin. Ignorant of the situation, she walked out of her bedroom and unknowingly entered a world of trouble. The moment he saw her, Crunch rushed and slammed her to the floor.

"Heeeel—!" she began to yell, but Crunch put his hand over her mouth, muzzling her screams.

"Gag dat bitch!" Tank said, and Crunch happily obliged him.

Her betrayal of Tray had backfired. Pig had assured her that, whenever the robbery went down, he'd make sure she wasn't home. But now, her mouth was gagged, and only time would tell her fate. Right now, her only option would be to act naïve and play her role.

Tank grabbed himself a chair and set it directly in front of Tray. He sat down and spoke calmly. "I've already told you what we want. Let me make sure you understand, because I'm gonna ask you one time and one time only. Where you keep your work, and where's the money?"

"Brother, I do construction work. The little money I got, I told you, it's in my back pocket. The rest is in the bank." Tray tried his best to sound convincing. Yet it was to no avail; his words landed on deaf ears.

Tank stood up. "OK, so you want to do it the hard way. I told you I'm only asking once. I promise you'll be begging us to take everything you got." He looked at Pig. "Pull his pants down."

"What?" Pig said, frowning at Tank's request.

This time, the calm tone he'd spoken in was gone as Tank, enraged, shouted, "PULL HIS MUTHAFUCKIN PANTS DOWN!"

Without further hesitation, Pig unbuckled Tray's pants and yanked them down to his ankles, accidentally pulling down his boxers along with them. Tank placed a piece of duct tape over Tray's mouth. Tray's eyes shifted to the left, his attention drawn to a hissing sound. Crunch walked past him and handed Tank the cordless iron. Tray knew by the look in Tank's eyes that he was no amateur. Tray rapidly shook his head, wordlessly pleading for Tank not to do what he had planned. It didn't work.

"Mmmmmm... uhhmmmm...!" Painful mumbles and grunts were the only sounds escaping the duct tape. Tray rocked violently back and forth, trying in vain to elude his captors. "Uhhhmmm... mmmhhh... uhhhmm...!" Tray's moans described the agonizing pain he was enduring from the two iron burns that Tank put on the upper part of his thigh.

"Shhhhhh...!" Tank whispered, his index finger pressed against his lips. "This is just the beginning. Brace yourself for the best part."

Tank held the iron over Tray's private parts and pressed the steam button, releasing an excruciating mist. Tray was unable to withstand any more. Suddenly, his eyes closed, and his head slumped. His body would have collapsed to the floor had it not been for the sturdy duct tape.

Tank told Crunch, "Hand me the bottle of ammonia."

Crunch twisted the cap off the bottle and passed it to Tank.

First, Tank slapped Tray across then face, then placed the bottle under his nose to revive him. It took a few seconds for Tray to groggily move his head. The reality of his living nightmare resurfaced, and tears poured down his face. Tray's body language showed he was screaming to be heard.

Tank put the iron close enough to Tray's face that he could feel the heat on his cheek. "You got something to say, huh?" He teased Tray a couple times as if he was going to burn his face. "You through playing games?"

Tray vigorously nodded, begging to be heard. Tank snatched the tape off of his mouth.

"Please… Take it. I got $175,000. Underneath the kitchen sink, pull off the back panel. It's loose. I swear dat's all I got."

"You swear, huh?" Tank teased him with the iron again. "We'll see bout that." Tank walked over to Pig's cousin and began teasing her breast with the iron.

"What you doing, Tank?" Pig incautiously asked.

Crunch slapped Pig on his shoulder for recklessly mentioning Tank's name, implicating him.

"We're going to tear this place apart. Baby gurl, we're not going to find anything else, are we?" Tank asked, still holding the iron next to her breast.

She was well aware that, if they did indeed search the apartment, the kilos stashed in the laundry hamper could easily be found. So she nodded her head, confirming Tray had lied.

Tank grabbed her by the arm. "Show me." He escorted her to the back.

She led Tank to the bathroom and kicked the dirty clothes hamper twice. Tank flipped the hamper upside down, shaking out the contents. Along with some dirty jeans and underclothes, five kilos fell out.

"Is that everything?"

"Uh… huh…" she mumbled through the tape over her mouth.

Tank brought her back to the front room. When they returned, Pig was filling a bag with the money Tray had stashed under the sink.

"You know what? You two make a beautiful couple. Tie her ass up next to her man."

Crunch complied and taped up Pig's cousin, so they were back to back.

"Let's get up out of here. Get the van, fat boy," Tank said, watching as Tray rocked in his chair, taking deep breaths. "You still crying, Playboy?" He laughed. "Don't worry, I'm not gon' blast yo ass." Tank picked up the roll of duct tape and a plastic bag. He put the bag over Tray's head and tightly taped it from the base of his neck to the bridge of his nose, suffocating Tray to death. After Tray passed away, Tank stood next to Pig's cousin. "You did good, baby gurl. Too bad yo stupid ass cousin let you know my name, cause now I gotta do this." In his hands, the terrified woman saw the roll of tape and a second plastic bag.

****

The following day, Jarvis had one hand down his pants as he talked on the phone with his on-and-off girlfriend. He was trying to persuade her to spend the day with him.

"C'mon, baby, let me make it up to you. I'm sorry… A'ight, well, let me take you shopping?" Jarvis begged. "Yeah, I bet you do. I'll pick you up around three."

Jarvis was unaware that his last call had just betrayed his whereabouts.

"Thanks Finzi. I owe you," Sherman said, ending his call.

"Patience is a virtue. Now try not to blow this one," Menendez joked.

"Very funny."

At 3:30, Jarvis waltz out his front door, glowing with a cheerful spirit. He was so excited, he was practically skipping to his unusually small Honda Civic.

"Think that's him?" Menendez asked.

"I don't know. He sure seems real happy. We'll tail him and see how we can fuck up his day. Call Finzi back and ask him did the signal move."

In a discreet Buick LeSabre, Sherman followed the Civic to the Cherry Grove development.

Menendez pushed the end button on his cell phone and told Sherman, "Finzi said the signal stopped in our vicinity. We got our man. He's a podgy guy."

Parked at the end of the street, Sherman and Menendez watched as a young light-skinned woman exited her home and got in the passenger side of the Civic. They drove directly behind Jarvis as he traveled down 37th Ave.

"Alright, Menendez, hit the lights."

The moment Jarvis saw the blue lights in his rearview mirror, his heart skipped a beat, and sweat trickled off the tip of his nose.

"Shit, what the fuck they want?" he said under his breath. A high-speed chase was an option, but not in a Honda Civic; Jarvis quickly dismissed that idea and pulled over into the post office parking lot.

Menendez walked to the driver's side. The window rolled down, and he asked for Jarvis's license and registration.

While handing Menendez his documents, Jarvis asked, "What did I do, officer?"

"Why don't you go ahead and step out your vehicle? We'll discuss the violation you committed."

Jarvis did as he was told and stood next to his trunk. Menendez observed him carefully, just in case he attempted to run.

"You look kinda nervous. You don't have anything illegal in your car, do you?"

"No, I ain't got shit."

"Good. Then you shouldn't have a problem with me searching your car."

Jarvis sucked his teeth. "You say that like I really got a choice?"

Sherman looked on from behind the steering wheel, then stepped out of his vehicle and approached Jarvis with a grim expression. "How're you doing, Jarvis? I'm Detective Sherman. It's about time we quit playing games." Sherman had Jarvis sit in the Buick with him while Menendez conducted a search of the Civic. "Jarvis, are you fucking with me? Do you think I'm here for your amusement? Either you follow me to the station, or I'll arrest your ass for obstruction of justice. The choice is yours."

Jarvis heard Sherman, but he wasn't listening. He was focused on Menendez. Jarvis prayed he wouldn't look under the backseat. Unfortunately, from Menendez's expression, he could tell it had been discovered.

Menendez waved a black nine-millimeter, showing Sherman what he'd found.

"Well, Jarvis, looks like you got the right to remain silent."

Back at the police station, Sherman left Jarvis in an interrogation room for well over an hour. Unbeknownst to Jarvis, Sherman, Menendez and their captain were watching through the two-way mirror.

"Cap, I'm gonna hold off on showing him the cooperation agreement. With that firearm in his possession, he's searching for any avenue to save his ass."

"I don't give a shit if you make him feel the yellow pages. Just get his statement."

"And getting his statement is just what I'm going to do," Sherman said, then walked into the interrogation room.

The interrogation was a small room with a desk and four metal chairs. The thermostat was purposely turned down in order to make Jarvis even more uncomfortable. Sherman stepped in and smirked as he noticed Jarvis's right leg nervously trembling.

"Alright, Jarvis, did I give you enough time to get your story together, or do you need a couple more minutes? I hope not, because if I walk out the door, the next time you see me, I'll be a government witness for the A.T.F."

"Man… the A.T.F. don't want no simple gun possession."

Sherman sat down across from Jarvis and leaned back in the chair. "You don't have a clue how this shit works. News flash, with your record, you're a perfect candidate for a federal sentence. Not only are you a career criminal, you're a felon carrying a firearm in commence of a crime. What you call a simple gun possession, prosecutors call a 924(e)-armed career criminal. That carries a mandatory sentence of 15 to life. You had marijuana in your glove compartment, and that's a felony too."

"That wasn't no felony. Shit, that was barely a quarter-ounce."

"You sure about that? I could've sworn it was a couple of ounces, maybe even a pound. We stored them in our property room, and I logged in the drug amount. You see where this going? Don't fuck with me." Sherman sprung to his feet and pointed his finger in Jarvis's face. If Sherman's tactic was to intimidate Jarvis, it was working. "Now, I'm going to turn on this tape recorder. I'm telling you right now, after I say my name and rank, it will be in your best interest to give me your full name and a detailed description of everything you know. Because if you don't, even if your mama was the judge, you'll end up with no less than 30 years."

Sherman did not wait for Jarvis to respond. He sat back down and pressed record on the tape recorder.

"This is Robbery-Homicide Detective Sherman with the City of Miami Police Department. Case number 0119, with me now is…"

There was a tense silence. Sherman didn't say a word; he simply closed his eyes, then opened them when he heard Jarvis's voice.

"My name is Jarvis Taylor."

"Do you have a nickname?"

"Pig."

Pig gave a thorough account of everything he knew pertaining to Tank and Crunch. Pig brought closure to four brutal robberies, including the double murder of Crow and Carwash.

"So, what about my brother?"

"What about 'em? You just saved your own ass. You blew our initial agreement. Your brother is not going anywhere unless you're willing to wear a wire. Then we might be able to work something out." Sherman turned and winked at the two-way mirror, aware he now had the upper hand.

The interrogation room door opened, and Menendez stuck his head inside.

"Sherman, the Captain wants you outside, pronto."

"While I'm gone, think about it, Jarvis. Your brother's freedom is in your hands." Sherman exited the room.

Outside in the hall, Menendez and the captain were standing next to a detective who Sherman wasn't familiar with. He immediately understood why when his eyes scanned the North Miami Robbery-Homicide credentials attached to his belt buckle.

"Sherman, this is Detective Becker," the captain said. "Last night, a home invasion took place at the Bayview Apartments in North Miami. One of the victims appears to have been tortured, then murdered, along with a female. There's nothing concrete pointing to our suspects besides the M.O., but maybe your guy in there heard something."

"I'll see if I can pry some info out of him," Sherman said, then returned to the interrogation room. As soon as he shut the door, Jarvis agreed to wear a wire.

"When I do this, how long before my brother get his reduction?"

"That's up to his prosecutor. But first, I need some information. Do you know what Tank and Crunch were up to last night?"

"I… I… don't know. I haven't seen them all day."

Sherman noticed that Jarvis's eyes stretched, and his leg began trembling again.

"Where were you last night?"

"Home," Pig quickly answered.

"Anybody there with you?"

"Yeah, this broad I was fucking."

"Was it the same one that was in your car when we arrested you?"

"Naw."

"OK, whoever this girl is, she can verify your alibi. I'm going to need her number. And we're going to hold you in the county jail to make sure you hold up your end of the deal this time."

# Chapter 11

Earlier the same day, Taj called Latricia and told her he had a deal set up but could not get in contact with Victoria. He explained he needed a few ounces of crack, not coke, because his customer could not cook. Taj assured Latricia that, if the product was fishscale, his friend was willing to spend plenty of money. She agreed to handle what he needed, and they decided to meet at the 163 St. Mall. After Latricia hung up with Taj, Victoria called.

"Hello."

"Latricia, why do you have a phone? You never answer it. I been calling you all night. When you left yesterday, you didn't see nobody snooping around the duplex? Cause some little thieving bastards done broke in my shit."

"Noooo… Gurl, fo' real?"

"Hell, yeah. The police caught one of them. While he was in the backseat, I tried to see if I know him, but he kept his head down."

"Damn, that's some fucked up shit."

"They came in through the bathroom window. I gotta get some security bars put in. Anyway, swing by later. Mrs. Knowles insist on cooking me and the boys dinner today."

"A'ight, after I meet with Taj, I'll be there."

"I'm through with Taj. He been blowing my phone up. Shit, after he wasted my time, I don't give a damn 'bout his ass."

"I know that's right. I'ma curse his ass out if he don't show. I'll see you later," Latricia said.

Latricia's guilty conscience had been riding her back ever since she'd stepped out of the duplex. And if Victoria ever found out she'd had Peanut break into the duplex, not only would their friendship be in shambles, but after this Black might be able to convince Victoria to let him handle it.

When she arrived at the mall, she parked in the east side parking garage. Ten minutes later, Taj called and told her he and his homeboy would be there in twenty minutes. With a little time to spare, Latricia decided to ease her mind by splurging with the cash she'd stolen from Victoria. She went into the mall and browsed through a few stores. She passed a display window at an elegant jewelry shop, where a 2 ½ carat tennis bracelet was on sale for $3,000, marked down from its original $5,200 price tag.

"Ding… Ding…" The motion sensor alerted the clerk that a customer had entered the store.

"Good evening. How can I help you?" the East Asian saleswoman asked.

"Yes, can I see the diamond bracelet on sale in the window?"

"Oh, yes, the tennis bracelet. That is a lovely choice for you… One moment." The saleswoman departed to retrieve the bracelet. She soon returned and fastened the bracelet around Latricia's wrist. "It looks very nice on you."

"It damn sho' do, I'll take it."

Latricia pulled a large wad of cash from her purse. Instead of allowing the saleswoman to place the bracelet in a box, she kept it on. Admiring the sparkles as the diamonds glimmered in the lights, Latricia began counting out the amount she wanted to negotiate for. "Can I get the bracelet for $2,800?"

Letting Latricia leave the store with $2,800 wasn't an option. "That's fine. Just promise you'll come back."

"Deal." Latricia handed the saleswoman the money.

Latricia strolled through the mall a couple of minutes longer, then headed towards the exit. As she turned the corner to the main entrance, a middle-aged Cuban man stalked her. Latricia was so preoccupied with twirling her diamonds in the sunlight, she was totally unaware he was pursuing her. In the parking garage, she deactivated her car alarm, and she was roughly grabbed from behind.

"Get yo muthafuckin hands off me!" she screamed, trying to free her right arm.

"Ma'am, I need for you to come with me," the undercover officer said, pulling his badge out from underneath his polo shirt.

All the shoppers' eyes were on Latricia as the officer physically escorted her through the mall and brought her back to the jewelry shop.

"Mrs. Chung is this the woman?" he asked the saleswoman.

"Yes, that's her."

"What's going on? Why did you bring me back here?"

Two more undercover officers entered the store, a white male and black female. The female officer studied Latricia's face, staring directly in her eyes.

"First thing first," said the Cuban officer, "you're under arrest."

"Arrest! I ain't do shit," she cried out.

"So, what are you saying? That you didn't just buy that bracelet you're wearing with counterfeit currency?" the arresting officer said. "Officer Kaye, check her purse."

The female officer grabbed the purse off Latricia's shoulder and dumped all the contents on the glass display counter.

"Bingo, I smell a conviction," Officer Kaye said, thumbing through the bulky wad of cash Latricia had had in her purse. "Sarge, looks like a couple grand here."

"Looks like we're going to have to get the Secret Service involved. Kaye, take this female scumbag to the back. We're going out to secure her vehicle."

Latricia broke down in tears as Officer Kaye placed her in handcuffs and walked her out of the jewelry store.

Out in the parking garage, both officers noticed a black guy looking through the driver's side window of Latricia's car.

"Hey, buddy, is this your car?"

"No, I'm supposed to meet a friend here."

"You don't say? How about showing us some ID."

The black guy who had been looking through the window clapped his hands and laughed. "Bravo, fellows. Do you two want to know what's so funny? Not only do you guys have perfect timing, you've ruined our operation." The undercover agent showed them his credentials. "I'm Special Agent Jerome Brown, D.E.A."

Unmarked government vehicles swarmed the parking garage, surrounding Latricia's car. Agent Brown and the rest of his team were in the middle of a domino-effect investigation. Their confidential informant had made a monitored call to Latricia and set up a control buy.

"Well, since our operation is ruin, do either of you care to enlighten us on what's going on?" Agent Brown asked.

"Fair enough. Well, we were in the process of doing an inventory search on this vehicle. We just arrested the owner. Now, before we get in a jurisdiction tug-of-war, you guys are more than welcome to assist with the search. Hell, Secret Service is going to be taking this case anyway."

After agreeing not to turn this into a pissing contest, both North Miami Beach P.D. and the D.E.A. tore Latricia's car apart. By the time they had finished, the door panels were off, and the back seat was yanked off its frame. It was all worth it once they discovered 15 ounces of crack, making Latricia's problems 22 years worse.

****

Across town in North Dade, Victoria was at Black's house, counting the money from the previous package she'd fronted him. She put a rubber band on the last stack and turned towards Black. "How long have you been hustling?"

He reclined in his La-Z-Boy. "Shit… since I was twelve. Why you ask?"

"Have you ever thought about quitting?"

"Hell, naw. I'm not trying to balance no checkbook, and I'm damn sure ain't gonna live check to check."

"You never thought about working for yourself?" Victoria asked.

"I am working for myself. Didn't you just count all that money I made?"

"You so crazy. Seriously, I'm talking 'bout owning your own business."

"Damn, Victoria, you don't remember the carwash I use to own on 182 Street?"

She sucked her teeth. "That was a carwash slash dope trap. I can't speak for you, but I'm not trying to make this a career. I'm a beautician. Sometimes I don't even know what I'm doing still selling this shit."

"Hold up. If you feel like you can't play the game, then you need to pass the ball. Put me down wit' yo connect."

Victoria listened as Black spoke, and what he said triggered the memory of her father's words: 'The game ain't for you.'

"Do you ever think about tomorrow?" she asked Black.

"I am thinking 'bout tomorrow. I'ma need 25 of dem thangs in the morning."

"You know what… Forget it. This conversation's not going nowhere. Go ahead and put the rest of the money in the bag."

By the time Victoria walked out of Black's house and hopped into her ride, her thoughts had returned once again to her father's words. Looking in her mirror, she said to herself, 'Maybe I'm not cut out for the drug game, and maybe it's time to quit.' She looked back on all her accomplishments and realized she should count her blessings. She had a lovely home in an ethical community, decent transportation, and was able to financially support her kids. For a single mother not receiving any child support or government assistance, that was a bonus in her book. The only thing missing was a steady, legitimate source of income. Never in her wildest dreams could she have imagined being this deep in the game.

While driving to Diaz's house, she contemplated how she'd tell him that she wanted to quit without it seeming like a slap in the face. Introducing Black and vouching for his credibility wasn't a bad idea, but was something to really think about.

She reached Diaz's house and sat in her SUV for a few minutes, still uncertain what to say. "Think… think… think… think… What am I going to say?" Though no closer to a decision, she climbed out from behind the wheel and knocked on the door.

It opened, and she was greeted with a smile. "Ah, Victoria, come in. I was beginning to wonder why you were just sitting outside. I did not expect you back so soon."

"I brought your money." She gave him the duffel bag she'd got from Black.

"That's my girl, a true businesswoman. So, you're ready for another package?"

"Diaz, about that, I'm thinking of opening my own beauty salon."

"Ah, yes, that's a wonderful idea. Do you have a building?"

"No, I'm still searching," she sadly said.

"Not anymore. I own a very spacious building that sits on Highway 441 right by Miami Garden drive. My daughter ran a dental clinic there. She followed her husband to New York two months ago, and the building's been abandoned ever since," Diaz said. "I tell you what, give my granddaughter a permanent staff position, and as a gift the building is yours."

Victoria could not believe what Diaz had just said. Overwhelmed with excitement, she gave him a big hug.

"Oh my God… Thank you… Thank you… Yes, your granddaughter can work with me. She has nothing to worry about. I got her." Victoria wiped tears of joy from her eyes.

"Come, I show you how it looks." Diaz grabbed his car keys off the dinner table.

Victoria headed towards her Lexus, but Diaz refused to ride in a luxury vehicle on American soil. He walked to his Chevy S-10 pickup and opened the passenger door for her.

She got in his rusty old truck, shocked that he was driving a vehicle in such poor condition. "Diaz, I'm curious as to why are you driving around in this beat-up truck?"

"Ha… Ha… Ha…" He burst into laughter and rubbed his sun-damaged dashboard. "What, you don't like my beautiful ride, señora? This is my good luck truck. I've had this truck for 12 years, and only been stopped by the police once. Why should I buy a Bentley when I drive 4-wheelers on my island?"

"Damn, Diaz, you got an island?"

"No, I have two. I could never understand you gringos' way of life."

"Who?"

"Americans, you all love your luxury vehicles with the ridiculous shiny rims. It's like no one has any guidance for economical investments. I see it all the time. As soon as they get a little money, their first investment is something that loses its value the second it drives off the lot. It's *loco*, when, for the same price, they can purchase a piece of property, which is certain to bring a profit as its value increases."

"See, Diaz, you have to understand, a lot of people are content with having just a little more than they already had."

"Are you content with your flashy Lexus SUV? Does that make you happy? Is that what you call the American Dream?"

"It's a piece of it," she replied.

"Why do you sell coke? To blow your money on useless material objects, or to obtain true stability?"

Victoria thought about Diaz's last question a moment before answering. "I got in the game to have my own salon."

"One salon? With the money you've been making, why not start with one to pave the way for a franchise of salons? When you think small, in the end all you will have is a small dream. But think big and chase it, and, by the time you catch it, you will have passed your original goal."

Diaz talked with Victoria about goals and dreams until he parked in front of the closed dental building. She followed Diaz inside and was stunned by the enormous size of the lobby. The old furniture was still there, including a large stone table with matching end tables, three sofas, and an empty 150-gallon aquarium. He led her behind the receptionist desk and through a stained-glass door.

One look and Victoria knew this place was perfect for what she planned on creating. There were eight rooms, four on each side of the hallway, which led to the main work area.

"Diaz, this is a dream come true."

"I am pleased you enjoy it. Just remember what we discussed earlier."

"Don't worry, your granddaughter will be in good hands."

"That I'm not concerned with. I'm speaking of what's next after your first salon opens," he said as they exited the building.

Victoria and Diaz returned to his home. Once he parked, Diaz put the building key in her hand.

"The building is still in my daughter's name. I will give her your number. That way, you two can arrange handling the paperwork. Now, come, Marie should have another 75 kilos ready for you."

Diaz words hit her like a brick. Her true intention had been to come clean and tell Diaz she wanted to quit, but now she was speechless and hated to bring conflict to their business relationship. After what Diaz had just given her, this was definitely an inappropriate time to mention her plans. So, instead of following her first impulse, she accepted the 75 kilos and continued to make Diaz proud.

# Chapter 12

After the robbery, Tank laid low in Overtown with Crunch. He remained indoors, poring over a map to find a small town in the Midwest or on the West Coast to reside in.

"Lawton, Oklahoma. That sound small," Tank said, pointing his finger at the area.

"Tank, you need to chill. The police don't have a clue 'bout us. You know when Channel 7 news showed what happen, they would've said who the police were looking for." Crunch said. "What'cha need to be doing is finding a country town to move this work in."

Tank waved his hand. "You gonna fuck around and catch a hundred years in one of them country ass towns."

"Fuck dat! When my day come, I'm holding court in the streets. Muthafuckas gonna film a documentary about me." Crunch made an imaginary gun with his hand and pulled the trigger multiple times.

"A'ight, gangsta. When that day come, remember them words," Tank said, then stood up. "Yo, check it, let me borrow your gurl car. I need to go handle something."

"Handle something!" Crunch arched his eyebrows. "Shit, let's just go splack a whip."

"I'm not 'bout to go steal no car, and I ain't gon make her shit hot. I'll be right back."

Reluctantly, Crunch threw Tank the car keys unaware of Tank's needs.

Tank travelled north on I-95, exiting on the 103 St. ramp. He drove west, passing his ex-girlfriend's apartment. He scanned the parking lot, immediately noticing that her Dodge Neon was in its usual spot. He made a quick right and turned into a nearby

Popeye's Chicken. He parked, then walked in the direction of his ex-girlfriend, Tia's apartment. The closer he got, the more hatred pumped through his veins. Instead of knocking on her front door, Tank took a left and walked to the rear of the complcx. Peeping around the corner, his view into the apartment was hindered by the new vertical blinds that had been installed after the police shooting. Neither the sliding door nor any of the back windows afforded him a glimpse inside.

Irritated by this, Tank walked rapidly to the front, ready to bang on the door. Practically sprinting, as he turned the corner, he bumped into a woman, knocking her backwards.

"My bad," Tank said, looking at the white woman and the way she was dressed. His eyes then rested on the white male alongside her.

The well-dressed man in his conservative two-piece suit reached up and held her shoulders. "Susan, are you alright?"

"I'm fine, Tony," Susan McCloy said, turning her attention to Tank. "Excuse me, sir. I'm Agent McCloy, and this is my partner, Agent Jacobs. We're with Internal Affairs."

Reflexively, Tank's facial expression transformed to a gloomy stare. His insides shivered, but his heart never skipped a beat.

"Sir, we're investigating the police shooting that took place here. Have you or anyone you know actually seen what transpired that day? Misteeer…" she said, waiting for Tank to fill in the blank.

"Oh… Brown, Mr. Brown," Tank quickly lied, feigning superb calmness.

"Well, Mr. Brown, did you witness the incident?"

"Naw, I wasn't around here that day."

"OK, Mr. Brown, you haven't denied hearing anything. Surely you or maybe a friend heard about what occurred?" McCloy asked.

"I saw the story on the news. I don't know what somebody else know."

Agent Jacobs was discreetly observing Tank's body language. This was one of many techniques Jacobs had learned from his years of experience in law enforcement. Reading emotions was second nature to him, and Tank he was reading like a book. Jacobs smiled at the way Tank generated a fake confidence to disguise his ulterior motive.

Jacobs took a step towards Tank. "Mr. Brown, do you live around here?"

"Naw, I'm visiting a friend."

"What's your friend's name? Maybe he saw or heard something?"

"Ronnie." Tank replied. "He live upstairs." He began mentally strategizing an escape route.

Jacobs pulled a pen and pad from his breast pocket. "Ummmm… Mr. Brown, what's your first name?"

"Kevin, Kevin Brown," Tank answered, giving Jacobs the first name that came to mind, which was his cousin Carwash's first name.

"Sorry if any of this is an inconvenience to you. This is routine during an intense investigation," Jacobs said.

Agent Jacobs walked away, leaving McCloy with Tank. He went to their Crown Victoria and radioed in the alias Tank had given him, checking if there were any warrants out for his arrest.

McCloy noticed Tank's body movements were uneasy and his fingers were jittery. Suddenly the apartment door behind McCloy opened. She instinctively peered over her shoulder, noticing Tank's ex-girlfriend exiting her apartment.

"Don't forget to call me tomorrow, Ms. Williams," McCloy said.

Tia never responded to McCloy. She was paralyzed with pure fear. Her bottom lip quivered. At the top of her lungs, she screamed, "TANK!" Dropping her purse and car keys, she raced back into her apartment, slamming the door.

McCloy quickly spun and looked Tank directly in the eyes. She swiftly reached for her firearm to order Tank to the ground, but her momentum was interrupted by a bone-crushing jab to the nose. Blood gushed out, temporarily blinding her with merciless pain.

Jacobs's head was down toward the radio when the split-second assault began. He peeped up and was appalled by what he saw.

"What the hell? Freeze…!" Jacobs yelled, storming out of the Crown Vic, aiming his gun at Tank.

Startled, Tank looked in Jacobs's direction, then took off running as fast as he could.

Jacobs ran over to check on McCloy's condition. "Susan, are you alright?" he asked in a panic.

Holding her nose with both of her hands, she said, "Go get that sonofabitch!"

As ordered, Jacobs began pursuing Tank on foot. Tank had a huge lead, but Jacobs's advantage was the fact that, while attending the University of Miami, he'd been a decent track and field athlete. Tank was near his vehicle when he saw Jacobs closing in fast. To avoid Jacobs getting a description of Crunch's girlfriend car, Tank ran through the Popeye's Chicken parking lot, hoping to backtrack to the car later.

"STOP…!" Jacobs shouted, knowing it was in vain.

Tank bolted across 103 St., darting through traffic. Several cars swerved and slammed on the brakes. Looking back to check the distance he had on Jacobs, Tank was oblivious to the Crown Vic coming straight towards him.

"Ahhhh…" Tank yelled as his body went airborne.

Agent McCloy purposely struck Tank with the fender, making his body crash on the hood. The impact caused his .45 to fly free from his waist, landing at least 13 feet away. McCloy slammed on the brakes, and Tank slid off the hood. She dashed out of the sedan with her firearm in hand.

"Don't you move!" she ordered as the blood pouring from her nose continued to soak her blouse.

Tank's adrenaline and determination would not allow his escape to be denied. With Jacobs closing in less than thirty feet away, Tank manage to roll over and quickly get to his feet, and made another dash to elude them.

"Fuck…! This guy doesn't quit!" Jacobs said, running past McCloy.

McCloy hurried back to the Crown Vic and radioed for backup. After she gave dispatch Tank's description and the direction he was running, she yanked the gearshift into drive and gunned the accelerator. The tires screeched and smoked.

Even with a painful limp, Tank hurdled residential chain-link fences like an Olympic athlete. Jacobs's suit and wingtips prevented him from performing with the same grace. Using the neighborhood as his personal obstacle course, Tank looked back and was pleased he'd finally lost Jacobs. He ran onto 95th Court and saw fumes coming out of the exhaust pipe of a Toyota Camry. A black male teenager was taking some boxes out of the trunk to carry them inside his home. Tank was unconcerned with being seen. He ran to the driver's side, jumped behind the steering wheel, and sped off, leaving the teenager standing on the porch shocked as his car drove away.

****

At the North Miami Beach Police Department, Latricia was handcuffed to a metal bench, nervously wondering what would become of her. She shivered and looked down at the goosebumps on her arms. The original arresting officer appeared, uncuffed her wrist from the bench and walked her into a room where two males sat waiting for her arrival. She was seated on the opposite side of the agents.

A gray folder sat on the table between them. One of the agents opened the folder, and Latricia glimpsed a color copy of $100 bills.

"Good evening. I'm Special Agent Helton, this is Special Agent Finzi, and you, young lady, are in a world of trouble. As you've been advised, you're being charged with passing a counterfeit reserve note, as well as possession of counterfeit Federal Reserve Notes, and that's where we come in at," Helton explained, observing the skepticism and confusion on her face. "I am with the Secret Service, so you know what type of charges you're facing?"

"No, I don't understand. What's going on?"

Helton smirked. "Wait a minute. Before you say another word, you're gonna sit there and tell me that you didn't notice all those fraudulent bills that the police found in your purse? Each bill had the exact same serial number, and, even if you were naïve about the matching serial numbers, you got to be pretty dumb to not have noticed how smooth and shiny the texture of the paper was, or the fact the color was a darker green than normal. C'mon, a big drug dealer like yourself has to have dealt with thousands of authentic bills."

"I'm not a drug dealer," she said, offended.

"Oh, no? Well, this drug charge you got says otherwise." Helton was still studying her facial expression. "Ha... Ha... Ha... You don't know. Hey, Finzi, she don't have a clue that you're with the DEA and waiting to interrogate her. This is no longer a state case, we have joint jurisdiction. So smile, pretty lady. You're with the big boys."

"I need a lawyer."

"What you need to do is cooperate and save your lawyer retainer fees for your commissary account. I don't think you realize how much time you're facing."

Latricia had never experienced the type of feeling that dwelled now in the pit of her stomach. She felt nauseous, and her hands were drenched with perspiration. This was the toughest situation she'd ever been in.

"Like I said, I need a lawyer."

"That is your right, but I got news for you. He'll only make the money we don't take. You're fucked." Helton closed his folder and called for Latricia to be removed.

After exercising her right to an attorney, Latricia was transferred to the Miami Federal Detention Center. A black female C.O. around the same age as Latricia booked her in. She was photograph, fingerprinted, and strip searched, then taken to medical. Along with twelve other women, Latricia was given several tests: routine blood pressure, temperature, HIV, T.B. skin test, and eye exam. The nauseous feeling never left; twice she tried to vomit, but nothing came up.

Five hours later, she was finally placed in population. She shamefully walked to her assigned cell, placed her institution property inside, and immediately went to the wall of pay phones and made a collect call.

"This is a collect call from (Latricia). To accept, dial five," the automated operator announced.

The call was accepted. "Mama, I'm in jail!" Latricia said, following this with a flood of tears.

For the next ten minutes, Latricia explained to her mother everything that had happened, minus the fact that she had stolen money from Victoria. "Mama, things are not looking good. I'm going to need a lawyer. These people talking 'bout I'm going to prison for a long time."

"No you not, baby. We will get you a lawyer to straighten this mess out," her mother said.

Latricia's hands trembled. Controlling her tears was an impossible task, so as they formed she let them run down her cheeks.

"Baby, don't you worry. I'm gonna find you a good attorney. Me and your sister will be at the courthouse for your bond hearing. I love you," her mother said as the call ended.

At first, Latricia was embarrassed to be crying, but when she looked at a few other women scattered throughout the unit, she noticed they too were weeping over their own sorrows.

Unlike in a state case, a week passed before Latricia was finally escorted by U.S. Marshals to the federal courthouse. Her arraignment and bond hearing was scheduled for nine a.m. As the court session began, the United States District Attorney made his opening statement.

"Your Honor, this case is more than it seems. It was originally referred to us by N.M.P.D. However, the Secret Service and D.E.A. have joint jurisdiction. To shed light on this situation, I'd like to call Special Agent Helton to the stand."

Latricia nervously watched as Helton nonchalantly made his way to the stand. He wore an all-black suit, traditional white dress shirt, and black tie. He sat on the stand with perfect posture. It was quite obvious he'd done this many times before.

"Special Agent Helton, please explain to the court how you became involved in this case."

"Certainly." Helton said. He leaned forward and adjusted the microphone. "I received a call from a sergeant with North Miami Beach P.D. He asked me to come down to his department and assist in an investigation where they'd just seized several thousands of dollars in counterfeit currency from Mrs. Latricia Joyner."

Helton shared the entire incident as it transpired. After he ended his testimony, the U.S.D.A called Agent Finzi to give his recollection of what had taken place.

"On the day in question, myself and fellow team members were conducting a monitored control buy," Finzi explained to the court. "Our target was Mrs. Joyner. We were given reliable substantial assistance by a registered C.I., and a deal was arranged between Mrs. Joyner and an undercover agent. At the time we were securing all the mall's exits, Mrs. Joyner went inside the mall to commit the passing a counterfeit reserve note charge. Once we realized Mrs. Joyner had been apprehended, a decision was made to blow cover and assist in the seizure of fifteen ounces of crack cocaine Mrs. Joyner had stored in her vehicle."

"That will be all, Agent Finzi. You may step down," the U.S.D.A. said, then turned towards the judge. "So you see, Your Honor, you have just heard the significant evidence the government has accumulated against the defendant, Latricia Joyner. The government also feels that, because of the severity of the charges, the defendant is considered a flight risk, and requests that bond be denied."

"Does the defense object?" the judge asked.

Latricia's lawyer rose to his feet. "Absolutely, Your Honor. It is absurd to believe my client is a flight risk. She has lived in Miami her entire life, and, besides one adjudicated misdemeanor, Mrs. Joyner has never been involved in anything remotely close to the magnitude of this case. The defense asks to the court for a lenient bond."

The judge removed his reading glasses and looked Latricia's lawyer in his eyes. "Counselor, as the government has stated, your client faces some serious charges. She's not a pillar of the community, she's a menace. For the safety of the community, bond is denied. Mrs. Joyner is to remain in custody."

Latricia broke down and cried uncontrollably. She looked back at her mother, seeing that she too was in tears. Two U.S. Marshals approached Latricia and told her to face front as they handcuffed her.

Latricia's mother was devastated to see her youngest child treated like a hardened criminal. Her tears continued to pour as she watched Latricia struggle to exit the courtroom in leg shackles. Latricia managed to give her mother one last look before the Marshals walked her out the door.

The following day, Latricia called her mother for the fifth time with information to relay to her lawyer. For a female, Latricia stayed firm and stuck to the G-Code. She still hadn't fully adjusted to her confinement, but she was slowly adapting.

"Latricia Joyner!" the C.O. said over the intercom. "Report to the officer's desk."

Latricia assumed she was being called for an unscheduled attorney visit. She rushed to the officer's desk and was puzzled to see a nurse standing there.

"Hello, Mrs. Joyner. I'm Mrs. Estrada, the detention center's nurse. Will you please follow me? We need to talk in private." The nurse led Latricia to the multi-purpose room. Latricia sat first inside the relatively small room. The nurse went on to say, "Mrs. Joyner, you underwent several tests on the day you arrived here. Do you remember that?"

"Yeah, I remember."

"Well, Mrs. Joyner, I'm very sorry to inform you that your HIV status is positive."

The nurse's words made Latricia's insides numb. She became emotionless as well as speechless. Her breathing stopped, and her eyes refused to blink. The nurse began discussing a variety of treatments available. Every word the nurse said was unfathomable to Latricia. At that very moment, the world Latricia had once known vanished.

"Mrs. Joyner, learning something like this is never easy. We have counselors and support groups that can help you through this critical stage in your life. Today at three, and again at nine, I will announce pill call. I will have medication for you. It's mandatory for you to take this medication. You need to begin treatment as soon as possible to prevent or slow down the transformation from HIV to full-blown AIDS. Once again, I'm truly sorry," the nurse said, then walked Latricia back to the unit.

Latricia entered the unit dumbfounded, unable to grasp the condition of her health as her new reality. Instead of calling her mother or sister for support, she went up the staircase one sluggish step at a time. She walked into her cell, collected all her positive and negative thoughts, then reminisced on the most memorable moments in her life. Most of her memories were good, so she couldn't help but wonder where she had gone wrong.

"Chow... Chow time!" the C.O. hollered as the meal cart was brought into the unit.

Latricia didn't budge. Her appetite was gone. She stayed in her cell, in the same position, for over three hours. The massive amount of turmoil she had sustained was taking a mental toll. Finally, able to concentrate on her present surreal life, Latricia focused on all she had endured:

Job gone
Husband gone
Counterfeiting charges
Drug charge
Facing a lengthy prison sentence
Positive HIV status

To make matters worse, if Victoria ever put two plus two together, Latricia was sure to lose her best friend as well. Latricia's depression transformed to pure hatred toward Tray. She knew in her heart that Tray was the one who had given her the deadly virus. And since he'd ruined her life, she was going to return the favor. Latricia carefully thought about her options and concluded there was only one thing left to do. So she made a call.

"Hello, can I speak to Special Agent Finzi?"

****

Victoria and Diaz's daughter finalized all the paperwork for the building, and Victoria began renovating. The finishing touches were nearly complete, and Victoria had a one o'clock appointment to get an estimate from one of Miami's most respected interior decorators.

While she waited for the designer to arrive, Victoria invited Black to come view the shop, especially since he said he had some urgent news. By the time Black arrived, it was 12:45. He drove up in his '89 Chevy Caprice, shaking the windows in the building with his four 15-inch Vega speakers. A few of the contractors installing the marble tile floor stopped working to get a glimpse of the vehicle producing such massive bass.

Black stepped into the building, nodding his head at the workers.

"Damn, Victoria, this all you?" Black asked, turning in circles, admiring the floors and enormous chandelier.

"Yep, this here place is for me and my boys."

"Yo, Victoria, you wasn't bullshittin 'bout quitting, huh?"

She shook her head. "In due time. Black, you can deal with all the madness associated with the game. I'm about to go all the way legit."

Black froze, hoping Victoria was going to add more. He was expecting her to plug him in with her connect, but, when she did not mention it, he snapped out of his trance.

"Oh, yeah, did Peanut call you recently?" he asked her.

"You know what? I ain't talk to Peanut in a while."

"Yesterday, he called me asking if I'd give his ol' gurl $4,500 to bond him out the County. What really fucked me up was when he said don't tell nobody. Now that's a snitch move. Nobody gives a fuck if you go to jail. It's when you go and get out and nobody know you went, that's when I look at you sideways. That shit had me thinking, so I called to see what his charges were, and that petty muthafucka got a burglary charge!"

Victoria stared at Black incredulously, shocked by what he'd said.

"What kind of charge did you say?"

"Burglary. This fool slanging all that dope, and he out da're breaking in somebody house."

"Black, my house got broke in. I didn't tell anybody but Latricia. I wanted to see if the person was going to tell on themselves. The kid the police arrested kept his head down. I'ma call and find out the name of whoever they arrested."

Victoria went outside to her SUV to retrieve the business card of the investigating officer. She called and, sure enough, Peanut had been arrested for the burglary of her duplex. The officer explained he'd called her several times to ask if she wanted to come and dispute Peanut's bond, but he'd been unable to reach her at the duplex. He further explained that a court date to appear was being mailed to her, and asked if she wanted to press charges, although, whether she did or didn't, the state was going to prosecute Peanut. She thanked the officer and hung up.

"That little piece of shit," she angrily said. "Black, did you give his mom the money to bond him out?"

"No."

"Good. Let that muthafucka rot. I'm glad he paid me all my money. And I was waiting on him so I could give him another package. His ass ain't just burn a bridge, he blew that muthafucka up."

"So wuz up, what yo gonna do about his betrayal?" Black asked, anticipating her answer.

"Fuck 'em. His ass gonna sit in jail."

Black shook his head at Victoria's methods, and simply changed the subject. "Did you hear what happen to Latricia punk ass husband Troy?"

"His name's Tray."

"I don't give a fuck what his name is. Somebody bagged his bitch ass, and, when I say they bagged 'em, they really did. I seen on the news what happened. They said nobody knew him and a female was dead until their bodies start smelling. I didn't think nothing of it when they said one of the victims was an unidentified male. But this morning, they showed his truck and said it was registered to Tray Joyner."

"Oh my God. I gotta call Latricia."

"Where she at anyway? Y'all ain't been kicking for awhile?"

Victoria thought about how much time had passed since she last seen Latricia. She'd been so busy with the salon, Latricia's absence had gone unnoticed.

"I need to call my gurl," Victoria sadly said.

"Damn, you acting like you sad! Fuck that off brand. I never liked his punk ass anyway. I hope you not gon' lose sleep over him."

Black saw weakness in the way Victoria showed signs of sympathy for Tray. He also hated her passive ways of handling problems when they arose. Even after Peanut's blatant violation, she felt no physical retribution was needed. And Black felt it was time all those issues be addressed.

"Victoria, you gotta tighten up. I'm not saying you personally got to start handling shit, but you gonna have to call some shots, or this organization is gon' crumble."

"What are you talking about? My best friend's husband was murdered. I need to be there for her to show support. And what organization? I'm standing in the only organization I need. I've told you this is my goal." She held her hands out, signaling the building. "My dream is here, right here. All that street thug shit is for you. I don't want that life. You can have it."

"So, what's this, confirmation you gonna plug me into your connect?"

Victoria loudly exhaled a breath of air. "Black, when the time comes, I will let you know."

"That's wuz up. And I'll be done with that work tomorrow. Hit me in the morning."

After Black left the salon, Victoria's mind was wholly preoccupied with Latricia and Tray. Despite what Black assumed, Victoria didn't care for Tray, especially after the threat he'd had Latricia deliver. Moments later, the interior decorators arrived.

Once they discussed the overall price and Victoria agreed to the terms, she allowed them to begin working, then excused herself.

She drove to Latricia's house, and the first thing she noticed was the horribly overgrown lawn. Driving slowly, she searched for any sign of Latricia. The mailbox was crammed with junk mail, and Latricia's car was not in the driveway.

"Where the hell is she at?" Victoria wondered, mashing the gas pedal.

Victoria was concerned with Latricia's whereabouts for the rest of the day. Late in the evening, Victoria picked up P-Rock and Victor from Mrs. Knowles' home, then decided to head over to Latricia's mom's house. The drive to the Little River neighborhood took barely 15 minutes. As she passed Little River Elementary, Latricia's mother's house could be seen, and the first person Victoria saw was Latricia sitting on the porch. She parked alongside the chain-link fence in front of the house and rushed onto the porch, where Latricia, her mother, and sister greeted her.

Latricia quickly disguised her guilty expression with a look of grief, as if mourning the death of Tray.

"Hello, Mrs. Lawrence. Hey, Stacy." Victoria said, greeting Latricia's mom and sis. "I just found out about Tray. How have you been doing?" she asked, giving Latricia a hug.

"I can't believe he's dead. It's all my fault. If we never got into that fight…" Latricia paused as she got choked up. "He would've been home and still alive."

"Latricia, don't you dare blame yourself for Tray's death, because that was not your fault," her mother said. "I'm sorry he passed away, I truly am. But you went above and beyond your wifely duties. With his death, on top of our legal issues, now is the time to stay strong."

Victoria discreetly glanced at Latricia, curious as to what legal issues she had.

Latricia's mother looked at Victoria's Lexus and noticed P-Rock in the passenger seat. "Victoria, you got dem children sitting in that truck?"

"Yes, ma'am."

"Chile, let dem children c'mon inside. Stacy's boys in there playing video games." Latricia's mom walked past the fence, opened the rear door of the Lexus, and unstrapped Victor from his car seat. She looked at P-Rock. "C'mon inside. My grandbabies need some company."

She took P-Rock and Victor into the house, and Stacy followed, leaving Victoria and Latricia alone on the porch. The second the front door closed, Latricia drooped her head, put her hands over her face, and began crying.

"I know how that pain feel you're experiencing. When Crow died, piece of my soul died with him. Every single time I step foot in the duplex, I miss hearing Crow say one of his corny jokes. There's a part of me that is so empty. No matter how much time has passed, or how hard I try that, emptiness never diminishes. I just want you to know I'm here for you. You're the sister I never had," Victoria said as tears formed in her own eyes.

They both cried on each other's shoulders—although Latricia's tears were the product of her betrayal. After releasing their embrace, Victoria looked Latricia directly in the eyes.

"Do you need a lawyer?"

Like a running faucet, Latricia tears stopped. "No, I don't need a lawyer. Why you ask?"

"Your mom said, 'With Tray's death on top of your legal issues.' What issues do you got going on?"

"Nothing serious. I wrote a few bad checks," Latricia lied.

"And you're sure you don't need any help with that?"

"I'll probably have to pay some fines. It's just, wit' Tray's death, my world turned upside down."

"Well, let me know if there's anything I could do."

"Tray's funeral is tomorrow. You coming?"

"Of course, for your support."

"It's at First Baptist and starts at 11:00 a.m.," Latricia said

"I'll be there. Let me go check on P-Rock and Victor." Victoria went inside.

With everyone inside, Latricia and her thoughts were alone on the porch. In the quiet, she reflected on the conversation she'd had with Special Agents Finzi and Helton.

Two days prior, Latricia had been led out of her unit and taken downstairs to a room that was off limits to inmates without authorization. Inside the room, Finzi and Helton awaited her arrival.

"Please sit, Mrs. Joyner." Finzi said. "OK, when you called my office, you agreed to fully cooperate with us. Is that correct?"

"Yes," she answered. "I don't want to go to prison."

"Whoa… Whoa… Whoa… Before we go any further, I need for you to understand we're not making any promises, nor can I say you won't go to prison," Helton said. "You face some very serious charges. The outcome of your situation depends on the value of your information."

Finzi interrupted, sounding aggravated. "Let's get one thing straight. We're not here to negotiate. So, don't waste our time telling us where you don't want to go. You better be giving us some damn good information, or you can go back to your cell, because I got work to do."

Latricia began her debriefing. By the time she finished and signed her statement, Finzi was surprised at just how valuable her information was. Not only did Latricia implicate Tray, she went on record and gave info on Black, Taj, Jay and Country, Peanut, even Diaz. Nevertheless, Latricia spared Victoria from her venom. After all Victoria had been through, Latricia didn't want that on her conscience.

"Mrs. Joyner, are you telling me that you're affiliated with Carlos Diaz?" Finzi asked. "Besides your family, who else knows you been arrested?"

"Nobody," she first said, then thought on it. "Well, Taj might know because he was coming to the mall to meet me."

"If Taj is the only one, we're cool. He's doing the same thing you're doing, trying to save his ass. Mrs. Joyner, we're going to need you to make a control buy from Diaz and a few of his associates. The more you deal with, the better our chances on getting them to roll on each other. If you do this, we can have you out of here first thing in the morning," Finzi said. "Once we have an agreement, there's no pulling out. If you play with me, I'll paint you as Diaz's number one distributor. I know all about your dead husband's affiliation with Diaz, and dead men tell no tales. You don't come through, guess you will have to wear his title, and here it is I thought you were just an innocent girl involved with the wrong guy."

Latricia didn't hear Finzi's last comment. When he mentioned Tray's death, her mind drifted off in space. Helton had a few questions for her pertaining to the plates used for making the counterfeit bills, but she knew nothing and couldn't answer. Finzi ended the debriefing, and Latricia was taken back to her unit. However, the very next morning, as promised, Finzi pulled the right strings, and Latricia was given a low bond and released.

Victoria opened the screen door, ending Latricia's daydream and snapping her back to reality.

"Latricia, call me later. I got to get P-Rock home to do his homework," Victoria said, giving Latricia another hug before leaving.

As Victoria drove off, Agent Finzi and his surveillance team were parked at an abandon house, six houses down from Latricia's mom's, in a modified U-Haul truck. Their vehicle was equipped with state-of-the-art cameras capable of recording videos and taking digital photos.

Finzi zoomed in and took multiple still shots of Victoria, her kids, her Lexus, and her tag number. Victoria drove past the U-Haul truck unaware of the surveillance team. She happened to look directly in the camera as she passed.

"That's right, sweetheart, smile for the camera," Finzi said, taking frame-by-frame shots of Victoria.

# Chapter 13

The next day in Overtown, Tank sat on the sofa reading the *Miami Herald.* He shook his head at the media's inaccurate description of what had taken place between himself and the two Internal Affairs agents.

"These muthafuckas crazy as hell. Check out this shit they wrote," Tank said to Crunch.

Crunch was whipping some heated liquid cocaine with an electric cake mixer. He stopped and listened to Tank.

"Suspect pointed a large-caliber handgun at I.A. Agent Jacobs, when his partner heroically struck the suspect with her vehicle…"

Tank folded the newspaper on his lap. "You can't believe shit they say. If I pointed my fire at that cracka, he would've been in this weekend's obituary. Them folks only tell you shit how they want you to hear it," he said. "Crunch, what you tell yo gurl to make her leave for the week?"

"You know how I do. I told her I got some business to take care of, and she need to go chill at her mama's crib for a week or two. Shhhit… After I put dis wood on her, and threw her four stacks, her ass was glad to leave." Crunch went back to cooking the cocaine.

Tank frowned at the potent smell coming from the microwave. "Damn, that shit stank as hell. How long think it's going to take you to bump that work off?"

"I dun'no. Muthafuckas so use to me jacking, they think I'm plotting on robbing they ass, then they be actin all paranoid an' shit. But I got a couple sells lined up down south."

"I should've been out of town," Tank said. "Yo ass need to be doing the same thang, 'cause if I'm hot, you hot.'

"Them people ain't say shit about me in that paper."

Tank didn't say a word but unfolded the Metro Section of the newspaper. He put his finger on the third paragraph, where the paper gave bone-chilling details of Crow and Carwash's murder, plus the possible connection to a string of unsolved robberies.

"You see what the fuck that say. Keep fakin, you gon' have to eat yo words about holding court in the streets," Tank said with a serious look in his eyes. "Where's yo fat ass homeboy? I ain't seen him since we did the lick."

"Shit, you got the man scared to come around here. He probably somewhere buying some pussy or putting some coke up his nose."

"That fat fucka betta be glad he got $30,000. The more I think 'bout it, the more I want to go see him."

"Goddamn, Tank. You already done shortchanged the man, now you want the little change he did get. You cold, man."

"As ice." Tank maliciously smiled. "…But on the real, what was cold was that fool calling my name out. Matter of fact, call Pig and tell 'em to come through. I need to holla at him 'bout something."

"Chill out, man. Let me finish whipping up this work, so I can get rid of this shit."

Tank ignored Crunch's request. He went back to reading his newspaper.

After they had robbed Tray, had it not been for Crunch speaking up for Pig, there was a strong possibility that, instead of a cut of the take, Pig was going to get a bullet. Now Tank contemplated giving Pig a reason to hate him. Tank folded down the newspaper.

"So, Crunch, you gon' call him or what?"

****

Jarvis, aka Pig, sat motionless as the surveillance technician fastened a micro-transmitter inside a Velcro strap installed compactly in the seam of his polo shirt.

"Testing... One... Two... Testing... One... Two. Speak for me, please," the technician directed as he adjusted the volume on his headset.

"What do you want me to say?" Pig asked, tongue-tied.

"That was fine," the technician said, then nodded towards Sherman. "We're about ready here, Detective."

Sherman and Menendez stood aside while the technician finished up with Pig. At this point in the investigation, Sherman's confidence was high that this would finally close the case. He was pleased to have progressed from having sketchy leads to a vital informant.

"We're all set," the technician confirmed.

"Alright, Jarvis. Showtime. Time to prove just how much you love your brother."

As they were exiting the police station, Pig's cell phone rang. Looking at the screen, he realized it was Crunch's number. Butterflies swarmed in his stomach as he hesitated to answer.

"You gonna get that?" Sherman sarcastically asked, leaning over Pig's shoulder and sneaking a glimpse of the number.

Pig answered. "Hello."

"Wuz good, Pig? You get a little bread in your pocket and acting brand new. Come through and holla at cha'boy," Crunch said.

"I been chilling. You know how I do."

"C'mon around here, and bring some pine wit' you."

"Yeah, a'ight, I'll swing through. Give me 'bout an hour."

"That's wuz up," Crunch said. "I only got one sweet Backwood, so bring a pack with you."

Pig ended the call, and Sherman immediately started drilling Pig. He answered each question as best he could, explaining everything Crunch had said.

"...And I told him I'd bring some weed to his house in an hour," Pig finished.

"OK, so go get some weed," Sherman nonchalantly replied.

For the integrity of the investigation, Sherman allowed Pig to drive his own car himself while they followed. Trailing inconspicuously to the untrained eye, Sherman and Menendez passed Pig as he stopped at a convenience store on 15th Ave., one of the most popular streets in Miami. From 71st to 62nd street, 15th was known for its strip of Black-owned businesses. Sadly, the local businesses were not the true reason for its popularity.

Sherman slowly drove toward the traffic light at the intersection with 62nd, watching Pig in his rearview mirror until he could no longer see him. He made a right turn, and another right on 17th Ave. Giving Pig enough time to conduct his transaction, Sherman continued driving at a slow speed. He drove a complete circle, and, by the time Pig had finished his business and reached the same intersection on 62nd, Sherman was directly behind him.

"Hey, Sherman, is the cavalry on standby?" Menendez asked.

"Not this time."

"So, if this Tank character happens to be inside, what are you going to do? Are you going to go Hollywood and do your best gung-ho act?"

The traffic light turned green, and both vehicles made a left.

"Look, I'm not leaving any room for error," Sherman said. "The one thing I don't want to happen is a repeat of the last time we thought Tank was inside an apartment. If he is in there, I promise you today he's either walking out in cuffs or carried in a body bag."

"Hypothetically, if he's not in there…?"

"Then we play it safe and hold our position with Jarvis. Eventually Tank and his buddy will walk right into our trap."

Sherman turned onto I-95 behind Pig. They travelled south, exiting at the Miami Avenue ramp. Pig was following the instructions Sherman had given him back at the station. This was the last stop they were making, to finalize everything they had gone over. Pig parked at a warehouse, then jumped into the backseat of Sherman's Buick.

"Are you ready?" Sherman asked Pig.

"Not really."

"Don't worry. Just act normal. Smoke, drink, or whatever else you guys do together. Then casually strike up a conversation to get Crunch to confess his involvement in the crimes you told us about." Sherman turned around in his seat to face Pig. "Don't forget, leave your smoking paraphernalia in your car. If Tank is inside with him, the signal is for you to leave your hat in the apartment. Can you remember that?"

"Yeah, I got'cha."

"Good. Now, here, chew this piece of gum to take that nervous look off your face," Sherman insisted, handing Pig a stick of Juicy Fruit.

"Crunch. It's been over an hour. I'ma go outside and fall back in the rental. Peep game let that fat muthafucka get comfortable, then I'ma come back inside about ten minutes later," Tank said.

"Tank, you my dog, so I gotta ride wit' you, but you wrong on this one. It's not like he gon' have his money on 'em."

"Then I'ma make is ass go get it. What, you think he won't? I don't know why you hang wit' his soft ass anyway. How the hell you put fear in dope boys fucking wit' that chump?" Tank said, standing to his feet. "I'm gone. He'll be here any minute."

Tank walked downstairs and hopped in the Chevy Malibu Crunch's girlfriend had rented for them. Yesterday, Tank went against the rental company's policy and had 5% tints installed to limit visibility inside the exterior. Just as Tank leaned back in the driver's seat, he spotted Pig pulling into the parking lot. Tank watched suspiciously as Pig twisted his head side to side for several seconds.

"What the fuck his fat ass looking for?" Tank asked himself.

Tank glanced in the direction Pig's gaze was set, noticing his eyes were on a gray Buick that had entered the parking lot. Pig gave the occupants of the Buick a nod, then dashed upstairs. Tank remained squatted down in his seat, now watching the Buick. His adrenaline raised his heart rate. He was determined to uncover the identity of the occupants and the reason they had yet to get out of their vehicle. Due to the identical 5% tints on the windows, it was impossible for him to see their facial features. He then reached into the rear, twisting the two levers on the backseat to give himself access to the trunk, where his AK-47 was.

*Knock... knock... knock...*

"It's open!" Crunch yelled.

Pig took a deep breath and exhaled at the threshold.

"Wuz up, Crunch?" Pig said as he walked through the doorway. "Damn, you crazy as hell! You got yo door unlocked while you cooking that work."

Pig scanned the apartment, searching to see who else was inside. Satisfied Crunch was alone, Pig struck up a conversation about the weed he'd bought on 15th Ave.

"Yo Pig, what you did wit' your work? Did you break it down yet?" Crunch asked, referring to the kilo Pig had been given from the robbery.

"Naw, I ain't even touch it yet. I got some folks in J-ville. I might go up there and grind." Pig clapped his hands together. "I left the pack of Backwoods in my car. I'll be right back," he said with a hint of urgency in his voice.

Pig left his Polo hat on. He rushed downstairs to his car. Prior to opening the driver's side door, he glanced at Sherman's unmarked sedan, shaking his head to alert Sherman and Menendez that Tank was not inside.

From inside his vehicle, Tank viewed Pig's indiscreet signal. "What da fuck that be 'bout?" Tank said out loud, rubbing his chin. "Well, ain't this a bitch? His pussy ass is trying to set us up." Tank figured there could only be one of two kinds of people inside the Buick: Jack Boys or cops. He pulled his cell phone from his pocket and called Crunch.

"...Yeah!" Crunch answered on the first ring. "What'cha do, change your mind?"

"Fuck that! Lem'me make this quick, yo boy up to something foul. There's a gray Buick parked down here that pulled in right in back of Pig. Twice I seen that muthafucka nod at the car. I'm looking at him right now, he getting something out the front seat... Now he on his way back upstairs. I'ma try to figure out who's in this Buick. This shit crazy, them muthafuckas still ain't get out yet," Tank said, staring at Pig walking upstairs. "Crunch, watch his fat ass. Something ain't right. I swear to God, if it's some Jack Boys in that bitch, I'ma leave them stanking."

"And if it's not?" Crunch asked.

"Then I hope you hungry, because today you might have to eat your words and hold court in the streets. He almost to your door, I'll call you later." Tank watched as Pig went back inside the apartment.

Pig closed the door behind himself and threw the pack of Backwoods on the kitchen counter next to Crunch.

"You know I can't roll them Backwoods tight. You roll up." Pig looked around again. "I'm surprise your partner in crime not here. I seen Tank in the newspaper. He wild as fuck. They said he tried to kill a police officer. I told you that fool out of control."

Crunch didn't volunteer any remarks. He simply proceeded to roll the weed, as Tank's words echoed in his head: "Yo boy up to something." He listened to Pig's abnormal references to Tank and began to realize that Pig might just have some ulterior motives.  Crunch was in defense mode.

Crunch asked, "You got a lighter?"

"Here." Pig tossed his Zippo to Crunch.

"Damn, you still got this lighter? Ain't this the same lighter you shot that white dude in the ass for on the beach?" Crunch cleverly asked, anticipating the type of response Pig would give him.

Pigs was shocked at the bad timing of Crunch's incriminating comment. Numerous times, Pig had bragged about the middle-aged Caucasian male he'd robbed on South Beach. Despite the victim giving Pig his wallet and Cartier diamond-studded timepiece, he'd refused to hand over his silver lighter. The retail value of the lighter was under twenty bucks, but its sentimental value was priceless. Pig misconstrued its worth and shot the victim in his right buttock, grabbing the lighter and getting clean away.

Normally Pig would never pass an opportunity to boast about this. Nevertheless, on this occasion he changed the subject.

"The paper said Tank was going to his ex-girlfriend's place. He should've been going out of town. You need to get him to tighten up. After y'all murked them two in the city, he should've stayed out of town. The police know he back now."

"This snake muthafucka!" Crunch said under his breath.

The facts were inarguable: this sudden interest with Tank was definitely far out of character for Pig. From the way he blatantly mentioned the murders, Crunch was expecting the police to crash in his door any minute. Pig's agenda was exposed. Crunch now knew who was in the car Tank had mentioned. He took a moment to calculate his options, and considered how to get the upper hand in this situation. A bullet to the back of Pig's head was due in the near future, but at this very moment, strategic countermeasures were Crunch's only option.

"I got that new Juvenile '400 Degreez' CD. Did you hear it yet?" Crunch asked, not waiting on Pig's reply. He walked over to the mini stereo, pushed play, and cranked the volume up to the max.

Juvenile's lyrics screamed through the apartment. "…Dat's you that can't keep an ole lady cause you keep fucking her friends huh…"

"Goddamnit… I hate the rap shit. I can't hear a thing," Menendez said, snatching the headset off. "Here, Sherman, take these things. Maybe you can tolerate that racket."

Sherman placed the headset on his head and started bopping his head and jokingly mimicking the rap lyrics. "*…You a paper chaser, got yo block on fire…*"

"Don't make me shoot you," Menendez said, getting a laugh out of both of them.

"Yo, Crunch… Crunch!" Pig yelled, drastically trying to get Crunch's attention over the loud music. "Damn, turn that shit down."

Crunch exhaled a thick white cloud of smoke. He kept his back turned until Pig walked up and tapped him on his shoulders.

"WHAT!"

"Turn that shit down," Pig repeated.

"This my muthafuckin crib! Who the fuck is you to tell me what to do in my shit? Bet'ta sit yo ass down somewhere," Crunch snapped.

"A'ight, let me smoke wit' you. Damn, you babysitting the weed," Pig said with an awkward smile.

Crunch didn't say a word, just walked into the kitchen and turned on the water faucet, then flicked the joint at Pig, nearly burning him.

"Fuck!" Pig shouted, clumsily catching the joint by the fire end. He took two drags of the joint, oblivious to Crunch creeping up behind him with a big pot of water.

"Babysit this." Crunch dumped the entire pot of water on Pig's head.

"Ahhhh... Shit!" Pig screamed, jumping to his feet. "Man... you got me soaking wet."

"Quit crying. I got plenty of T-shirts in the back that can fit yo fat ass. C'mon, I got some 5X's," Crunch said, watching Pig's demeanor change before his eyes.

Pig hesitated, his chest heaving like he was hyperventilating.

Crunch slapped Pig on the back. "You alright?"

Sherman rapidly tapped the headset. He snatched out the wires, plugged them back in, but to no avail. The audio was gone.

"We got a serious problem," Sherman said.

"What, they're playing heavy metal?"

"Worse, static. We've lost audio."

"Do you want to call for backup and prepare to go in?" Menendez asked.

Before Sherman could answer, his attention was drawn to the Chevy Malibu that had just stopped in front of their vehicle, blocking them in.

"What's his problem? Don't tell me we're in his precious parking space," Menendez said, unsuccessfully trying to see through the tinted windows.

There was an intense pause. Sherman and Menendez stared at the car like it was a game of chess, waiting for the driver's next move. Then it happened: the Malibu's passenger window rolled down.

Checkmate!

# Chapter 14

Latricia had a mandatory doctor's appointment late in the afternoon. She had missed her first two appointments, unable to face the challenge alone. This time, her mother accompanied her. They arrived at the 14th Street Health Clinic and realized so many other people had health issues too. After signing in, Latricia surveyed the variety of nationalities awaiting medical attention. Of all the thoughts dancing in her head, the ones she focused on the most were whether her condition was the worst in the room, and how long would it be before her body started to look and feel sick. She kept her head down, gazing at the freshly waxed floor, to prevent others from seeing the pain on her face.

"Latricia, keep your head up. Don't let this defeat you. I don't give a damn your last name is Joyner. You're a Lawrence, and Lawrences are fighters. We're going to beat this together, you hear me? Now hold your head up," her mother firmly said.

Latricia did her best to hold her head high, but not only did she look defeated by her current trials and tribulations, it was evident that something else was seriously wrong in her life.

"Latricia Joyner," a young Hispanic female aide called out.

She slowly rose and followed the aide to the back. She was taken into a room, and another aide examined her vitals; then she was left alone. Several minutes passed, then the doctor entered. He was an older black male with a large bald spot on top of his head, and he spoke bluntly. He informed Latricia of the stage her illness had progressed to, and the consequences of not properly taking the medication he prescribed.

An hour later, Latricia rode in silence, staring out the passenger window but looking at nothing.

*Ring... Ring...* The sound of Latricia's cell phone jolted her from a daydream. "Hello."

"Mrs. Joyner, this is Agent Finzi. I'm gonna need for you to come down to our office."

"OK, but I can't right now. I'm on my way to get my prescriptions filled."

"Let me explain something to you, Mrs. Joyner. If it wasn't for me, you would be in a cell, unable to get your prescription filled. Now, keep that in mind. I expect you here in one hour. Come to the same office we brought you to, on the third floor in the downtown Federal Building. Oh yeah, and Mrs. Joyner, for your sake, don't be late." Finzi ended the call.

Tears formed in Latricia's eyes. She shook her head, trying to shake the stress away. She slapped the dashboard, and her mother looked over at her.

"Who was that?"

"That was the agent that got me out," Latricia said.

"What did he say?"

"Not now, Mama. I'm really not in the mood to talk about it."

That was the last thing Latricia said to her mother until they pulled into a Walgreens to get her prescription filled.

"Ma, after this, I need to use your car."

****

Agent Finzi sat at his desk, counting down the minutes past the hour, aware that Latricia did not know how valuable she would be in helping him get an indictment on Diaz. In the past six years, Finzi had tried on two different occasions to secure a conviction on Diaz. Each time, the informants either changed their statements or were never seen or heard from again. Latricia was the first one actually willing to make a direct buy from Diaz.

He looked at the time in the bottom right corner on his computer monitor. Latricia was 15 minutes late. He decided to give her another call. As he waited for the call to go through, he saw the elevator door open, and Latricia stepped out. He hung up the phone. The second she stepped into his office, he started berating her.

"Mrs. Joyner, you're late!"

"I'm here," she sarcastically replied.

"Yes, you are, but let's not make tardiness a habit. Time to get down to business. I need to have an undercover agent accompany you for the deal."

"Uh… un," Latricia mumbled, shaking her head. "That won't work. Diaz is not stupid. It's like he got a master degree in psychology. There's no telling what he'll do if he sense something's wrong."

Finzi twirled a pen in his fingers as he thought about what Latricia had said.

"Will you wear a wire?"

"Hell, no! A wire, what, you trying to get me killed?"

"Mrs. Joyner, don't get beside yourself! Believe me, your safety is our first priority." Finzi honestly couldn't have cared less about Latricia's safety. "I can't let you go in there while we're left in the blind. My superiors will never approve us to give you cash without some form of monitoring."

"Well, what about Black?" she asked.

"What about him?"

"I can buy from him with someone, but it has to be a woman."

"We want Diaz or at least one of his primary distributors. Is Black one?"

"Yes, he is," she convincingly lied.

Finzi thought about it, then agreed. He had the perfect female agent to go undercover.

Jada Thomas was a 29-year-old agent who could easily pass for a 19- or 20-year-old college student. She had a beautiful caramel complexion. Standing at 5'2", 125 pounds, and flawlessly beautiful, Jada had quickly been made a member of Finzi's team. Jada's youthful features were definitely an asset, but it was her high IQ and prior law enforcement experience that were most beneficial to the D.E.A.

Finzi had Jada report to his office.

As Jada approached Finzi's office, Latricia could barely see her head over the cubicle divider. Initially, Latricia was fooled, like so many others, by Jada's appearance. Her hair was in micro-braids, and she entered Finzi's office toting a North Pole backpack. She stopped just inside his entrance and blew a bubble with her gum.

Finzi introduced the two. "Jada, this is Latricia Joyner... Mrs. Joyner, this is Special Agent Jada Thomas."

Neither woman spoke to the other. Jada looked Latricia up and down. Latricia did likewise, resting her eyes on the firearm holstered on Jada's waist.

"Now that you two have met, Mrs. Joyner, make the call and set up a deal." Finzi passed Latricia his office phone.

Latricia didn't accept it. "You really are trying to get me killed. What you think he'll do when your number show up? No, thank you, I'll use my own phone.

****

In the meantime, Victoria and Black were having lunch at one of Black's favorite restaurants, Ester's. Victoria picked through her red snapper dinner, while Black devoured his ox tail, peas and rice, and dinner roll. Since their last time together, Black had proved he was persistent in pursuing a challenge.

"I can't believe you get all this food at such a low price."

"I don't see why not. Don't you get your food for the low?" Black said, referring to the kilos Victoria got from Diaz.

"Damn, Black, can one day go by without you throwing little hints at me?"

"Not really," he said, sipping on his lemonade. "You still haven't let me know if you're going to plug me in. Are you still talking 'bout getting out the game?"

"Soon."

"Victoria, I told you, you can't play wit' da game. There ain't no part-time employment in this shit. You gotta get in, get yo money, or get the fuck out the way. And don't excuse my French, cause that's how cold the game is. You around here quitting 'cause you tired of poisoning your community. You can't have no conscience hustling. Nobody give a fuck about you in the streets."

Victoria listened and wondered whether it was a sign that Black was sounding like her father.

"Alright, Black, I'ma talk to him and see if he'll meet you. There's no guarantee he will."

"There was no guarantee we would go out on a date and look at us now. So, I'll take that as—" Black cut himself short when his cell phone vibrated. He looked at the number, held up his phone so Victoria could see the number, then answered. "Wuz up?"

"Hey, Black, this Latricia. I need to holla at you. Are you busy?"

"Sump'in like that. What you want?"

"My cousin is down here from Tampa. She hungry," Latricia said, speaking in code.

"I tell you what, talk to yo gurl," Black said, passing his phone to Victoria.

"Hey, gurl, what'er you up to?"

"I'm… I'm trying to hook Black up with my cousin from Tampa."

Jada quickly became frustrated with the lack of cooperation.

"What yo people gon' do? I gotta get back on the road before my man start tripping," Jada said, loud enough to make sure she was heard on the other end of the phone.

"Which one of your cousins is that?"

"She ain't been down here since she was 12. Victoria, let me talk to Black," Latricia suggested, trying to get Victoria off the phone.

Instead of giving Black the phone, Victoria said, "You can talk to me. Wuz up?"

"Lem'me talk to him," Jada said, snatching the phone from Latricia. "Is this Black?"

"No, this who you need to be speaking wit'. You got a problem with that?"

"Oh, no, it's no problem at all. Latricia told me Black got the groceries I need. I'm in a rush 'cause my kids hungry."

As a result of growing up in Miami's Brownville area, all Jada needed was the coded language they used. Once Latricia explained the codes, she spoke their street dialect perfectly. Your *kids* were your *customers*, *grits* meant *grams*, *ounces* were *omelets*, *kilos* were *waffles*, and they all fell under *groceries*.

"No disrespect," Jada continued. "I'm just trying to put some food in my kids' mouth. Can me and Latricia meet you somewhere?"

Latricia closed her eyes.

"I'll get back wit' you in a little while," Victoria said. "Tell Latricia to stay by her phone."

Ending the call, Victoria and Black went back to their meal, discussing the conversation with Latricia's so-called cousin. Victoria's woman's intuition kicked in, but she couldn't pinpoint the negative vibe she felt. The one thought Victoria paused over was the fact Latricia had called Black instead of her.

With a mouthful of food, Black asked, "So, wuz up? What she trying to cop?"

"I didn't get that far. I told them I'll call back later."

"I still got a little work left. Tell yo gurl to meet me somewhere."

"Naw, we'll meet them."

****

Finzi ordered Latricia and Jada to report back to his office after they were unsuccessful in setting up a deal. Once there, Jada began drilling Latricia for not trying harder.

"So, who is this Victoria chick?' Jada asked.

Before Latricia could answer, Finzi interrupted. "Mrs. Joyner, I want you to keep in mind that, if you're not 100% honest with us, the deal is off the table. Not only will you face full prosecution for your original charges, I can promise you that the U.S. Attorney will use all the information you provided us to secure a superseding indictment against you. And with your signature on your statement, a conviction is guaranteed. Now, be real careful before you answer our questions. We already know the answer. I just want to hear you say it. Who's Victoria?"

Nothing but silence followed Finzi's question. He stared at Latricia, and Jada blew another bubble with her gum, popping it to break the silence.

"Look, Mrs. Joyner, if you're not comfortable with this, imagine how uncomfortable a six-by-nine cell is gonna feel for the next 22 years. I'm trying to help you, but you're making it pretty damn hard. Guess what? I know who Victoria Cole is. She drives a yellow Lexus SUV, her brother was murdered, and her child was shot. Latricia, we work for the federal government. I know much more than you think I do. I understand betraying your friend's trust is a hard thing to do, but I have a job, so don't sit here and play with my intelligence," Finzi said, using the little information he'd acquired from his surveillance photos—his trump card to manipulate her.

Faced with the toughest decision of her life, Latricia wanted to lie, but that seemed useless. Giving up information on her best friend was unbearable to her soul.

"Forget it!" Finzi said, rising to his feet. To scare Latricia, he ripped in half some irrelevant documents he had on his desk.

"ALRIGHT!" Latricia shouted. "I'll tell you what you want to know."

"That'ta girl. Now, for the last time, who is Victoria?"

****

On their way back from Ester's Restaurant, Victoria had Black drop her off at the salon. Today, she had entirely too much preparation to do for her grand opening to be running the streets all day with him. She had decided to let him handle the transaction with Latricia and her so-called cousin. She walked inside the salon and was truly amazed by the spectacular job the contractors and interior decorators had done. The entire salon was finally complete. She had taken all necessary steps to make sure her grand opening would be a success. The local radio station 99 Jamz was scheduled to do promotion and give away prizes at the grand opening. Victoria had arranged for barbecued chicken, burgers, baked beans, and chips to be served.

While watching a pair of angelfish swim around in the aquarium, Victoria noticed a pearl white E-Class Benz pulling into the parking lot. She walked to the door to see who was in the car. A very curvaceous Cuban stepped out. She wore big designer shades and was a little overdressed to be coming to the salon. The young woman walked to the door, and, before she could knock, Victoria opened it.

"Can I help you?"

"Hi. I'm Anna. Are you Victoria?" she asked, removing her shades.

"Oh, hi, Anna. Pleased to meet you. Come in… Come in." Victoria stepped to the side. "Your grandfather told me you would be here one day this week. You just caught me."

Victoria and Anna went over some of her qualifications, which was how Victoria discovered that Anna was not, as she had assumed, a beautician. Even better, Anna happened to be a certified masseuse, a trade she had picked up after graduating school. Anna's skills were a necessity to the salon. Whether she'd been related to Diaz or not, Victoria would definitely have ended up hiring her anyway. They sat on the couch in the waiting area, brainstorming ideas for the promotional radio spot.

Deep in conversation, they were interrupted by a knock on the door. Victoria looked at the unfamiliar woman, then went and unlocked the door for her.

"Sorry, we're not open yet," Victoria said.

The very attractive light-skinned woman smiled. "Hello. My name is Kimberly Hunt, and I saw your Booth For Rent sign. I stopped by earlier to see if the booths were still available. If so, I'm interested."

"Well, Kim, my name is Victoria, and yes, there's two booths still available. I am also looking for a person capable of giving pedicures and manicures."

"I can't do nails and toes, but I'm one of the baddest beauticians in Miami."

"Are you licensed?" Victoria asked.

"No, I don't have a license. I went to school, but then I got pregnant and stopped going. Victoria, I've been doing hair all my life," Kim said in a pleading tone.

Victoria saw the determination in Kim's eyes. It was the same look she had seen for many years in herself.

"Tell you what, Kim. If you promise to go back to school, graduate, and get your license, you can work the meantime under my license."

"Fo' real! I promise, the very next semester, I'll register. Thank you so much."

Victoria watched the glow of joy all over Kim's face. She felt good about being able to put a smile on her face. The satisfaction of bringing happiness made Victoria feel as if she was finally where she belonged in the world. Unlike the dope game, in the salon Victoria found peace within herself.

"The grand opening is next weekend. Kim, come by Wednesday around two p.m. so you can get a feel of the place."

"I will. Anything else?"

"That's it. Welcome aboard. We're pleased to have you as a part of the Divas and Dons."

****

The sun was shining bright as Black turned into the USA Flea Market. He dialed Latricia's number. "Where you at?" he asked, searching for her car.

"I'm parked all the way in the back, next to the car stereo shop," Latricia replied with Jada sitting beside her.

Black slowly drove his Jaguar, surveying the rear of the Flea Market for Latricia's Mazda. Unbeknownst to him, the D.E.A. had seized her car and hadn't released it, not even to make the control buy look normal.

"All units stand by. Suspect approaching in a metallic gray Jaguar," Finzi said over his radio.

Latricia kept Black on the phone until he found her location. She stood outside the driver's side of the Nissan Altima the D.E.A.

had furnished her. Jada was stationery in the passenger seat with the pouch of marked money on her lap. Latricia waved to get Black's attention. Once he saw her, he quickly reversed into the empty parking space next to the Altima.

He rolled down his window. "Wuz up, Latricia? I was looking for your car."

"We drove in my cousin's car. Mine is in the shop," she lied.

"A'ight, come on. Time is money. You got the change?" He gazed over at Jada in the passenger seat and shrugged his shoulders at her. "Latricia, let me hold the change. I got to drive around to the front of the Flea Market."

"My money is not leaving without the groceries!" Jada yelled.

"Latricia, holla at yo people. You know I don't play no muthafuckin games. Either we do this my way, or you can spend yo lil' income tax check with someone else," Black said and started rolling up his window.

Black's arrogance convinced Jada that he couldn't care less whether the deal went through or not. And with Finzi and the rest of their team on standby, Jada figured she'd play it safe and oblige Black's request. She passed the pouch containing the money to Latricia, who walked over to Black's car and handed it to him.

Black grabbed the pouch through his window.

Parked in a tinted navy-blue Ford F-150, Finzi watched their every move. "Look alive, gentlemen. The transaction is in process."

"Latricia, y'all give me two minutes. I'll be right back," Black assured her, then winked as he drove off.

"All units hold your positions. Suspect did not complete transaction. I repeat, suspect did not complete transaction," Finzi said through his radio, carefully watching Black as he drove away. "What the hell's going on?"

"Finzi, do you want us to take him?" one of Finzi's team members asked over the radio.

"No. Stand down and wait for my signal."

Finzi continued to observe Black as he unknowingly drove past his truck. Black's Jaguar crept alongside the seven-foot chain-link fence surrounding the Flea Market. Finzi was so fixated on apprehending Black, he waited to see if Black would lead them to an accomplice.

Black continued driving along the fence, then suddenly stopped near the entrance. There was a small line of traffic preventing him from going further. He waited for it to move.

Finzi began trailing Black's car, keeping a lengthy distance. He eased off the accelerator, focusing on the Jaguar's brake lights. The brake lights went off.

A motorist had left a decent-size gap. Black brought the supercharged turbo motor to life, speeding onto 79th Street. Unsuspecting of the sting Finzi had orchestrated, Black's intention the entire time had been to swindle Latricia's so-called cousin. Horns honked as Black sped away, nearly crashing into an R/V. The well-made European vehicle performed as it was built to do. Black accelerated to 27th Ave with incredible speed. He quickly turned right, the Jaguar hugging the corner with extraordinary handling.

Finzi immediately flicked on his blue lights and siren. He desperately tried to speed through the motionless traffic, but it was too congested.

"All units, the suspect is heading south on 27th," Finzi screamed.

Black made another quick right at the next turn. He sped pass the Metrorail station, then turned onto 32 Ave. He felt content Latricia and her so-called cousin were still parked at the Flea Market, clueless about the scheme he'd just pulled off.

It wasn't until Jada noticed her team scrambling through the parking lot that she realized something was wrong. "Ah, shit!" she shouted, jumping over to the driver's seat. "Latricia, get in the car, NOW!'

Finzi and his team finally made it onto 27th Ave. Racing to locate Black, they sped past the first turn he'd taken. Swerving in and out of traffic, Finzi strained his eyes searching for Black's Jaguar.

Black's swift navigating meant his scheme was a triumphant success. He drove without a hint of guilt in his heart. For the third time, he looked down and watched as Latricia's number continuously appeared on his screen. Laughing to himself at a red light, Black rolled down his window, removed his SIM card, and tossed his cell phone to the median.

"Fuck it, time for a new phone anyway," he said to himself, rolling his window back up.

The traffic light turned green, and Black proceeded home. With his left hand on the steering wheel, he unzipped the pouch with his right. Thumbing through the crispy Ben Franklins, Black was pleased with the amount he'd taken.

Finzi received a call on his radio and fumed with rage at the message.

"Goddamnit! All units, suspect is heading north. I repeat, suspect is heading north. Dispatch, we need a bird in the sky. Notify Metro-Dade and tell them we need their assistance," Finzi screamed into his radio, making a violent U-turn in the middle of the street.

The message he'd received had come from the command center. They were relaying Black's location based on his last cell phone pings. Little did Finzi know Black was safely minutes from home.

****

*Ring... Ring...* Victoria's phone rang.

"Hello."

"Victoria, Black just robbed us. My cousin wants to know where he lives," Latricia frantically said.

"He did what?"

Jada snatched the phone from Latricia. "Where the fuck do your man live?" she demanded.

"Hold up, bitch. First of all, he ain't my man, and secondly, you got me fucked up trying to check me. Bitch, you don't know me. Now what you need to do is put Latricia back on the phone so I can see what's going on."

"Yeah, I'll do that this time, but I promise you, we'll speak again real soon," Jada said, cold and confident.

Victoria offered no response, and simply waited for Latricia to return to the phone.

"Hello."

"Latricia, what the hell is wrong wit' yo people? I don't even know that bitch, and she gon' come out her mouth sideways."

"She's just mad Black played us like that," Latricia said. "Victoria, I really need to get that money back."

"Listen, when I hang up, I'll call Black and find out his problem."

"Why can't you tell us where he lives?"

"WHAT! I just told you what I'll do. Bye, Latricia!" Victoria ended the call frustrated with the entire conversation.

After she cleared her line, Victoria massaged her eyelids and recalled her father's words: 'Take heed to any remark or comments that trigger a negative vibe. This entire incident had been giving Victoria negative vibes from the beginning, and truthfully, she wanted no part of it.

Standing beside the aquarium, Anna observed how zoned out Victoria was.

"Is everything alright, Victoria?' she asked, concerned.

"Huh?"

"You OK?"

"Umm… Yeah, everything's fine."

"Victoria, I'm no shrink, but there's something heavy on your mind." Anna sat down next to her. "You want to talk about it?"

"Anna, sometimes I just get so happy seeing my dream come true. Opening something right. Then there's this dark world that I'm uncomfortable with, but, if not for this dark world, none of this would exist."

"What are you talking about, selling drugs for my grandfather?"

Victoria didn't believe Anna was naïve, but she had misjudged Anna's knowledge of her involvement with Diaz.

Victoria had thought that, since Diaz never conducted business in front of Anna, she was unaware of their business relationship.

"You look surprised. I know you don't think I'm blind and clueless to the fact my grandfather gives you drugs. My older sister is the one that put your package together. It was my sister that spoke up on your behalf."

"Marie's your sister?"

"Yep, and from the first day you came to my grandfather's house, he talked about how much he liked you, and the dedication in your eyes. My sister saw it too, unlike in your friend Latricia. If it wasn't for her husband, my grandfather never would have dealt with her.

"So, if your grandfather see dedication in my eyes, how come he couldn't see how tired I am of selling drugs? People tell me all the time I'm not cut out for this. Your grandfather is the only one see otherwise."

"Victoria, my grandfather is not stupid, nor is he generous with very many people. He took a liking to you. This building was supposed to be mine, but I didn't have a vision like you. I like spending money, not working for it. So, when you came to him with your plan, he preferred to fulfill your dream rather than just sell this building. I guess making me come here is supposed to show me work ethics."

"I want to go legit. I have two sons that I raise on my own, and I need to be here for them. Anna, eventually every good thing comes to an end, and, when that day come, I'd rather go out of business than go to prison. You understand where I'm coming from?"

"Yeah, I do, and so will my grandfather. You just need to talk to him. I'll be by your side, if you need me," Anna sincerely said.

"Thanks, Anna." Victoria hugged her. "I need to go check on something. If I'm not back by seven, go ahead and lock up."

Victoria left the salon feeling relieved she'd talked with Anna. Now she needed to see what Black's problem was. She dialed his number, but the call went to voicemail. She headed to his house. Her timing couldn't have been better. As she pulled up in front of his house, he was just about to leave on his motorcycle. She stopped her truck in his path.

Jumping out, she charged towards him, raising hell. "What the fuck you doing, Black? You need money? Why would you rob my girl?"

"What?" he said, smiling.

"You heard me… Why did you rob them?"

Still smiling, Black said, "You know how I feel about off brands, male or females. Shit… I'm starting to wonder about that bitch anyway. She suppose to be in the streets trapping. How come she copping with nothing but brand new hundred-dollar bills? That money look like it was just printed."

"That ain't got nothing to do with why you robbed them. When they call me again, what am I suppose to tell them?"

"Fuck 'em! Latricia betta keep her fuckin mouth shut, and her cousin need to get her ass out of town before she live here permanently."

Victoria slapped his shoulder. "How am I suppose to introduce you to my people when you around here doing this bullshit? Acting like you needed that money, and you know damn well you don't."

"Shhhhit… I guess she didn't need it neither. You should've seen how easy she gave up her money. I didn't even have to use a gun. See, Victoria? This the kind of shit that comes with the game. I don't make the rules, I just follow them. And as for yo people, I'll never bite the hand that feeds me." Black rubbed his hands together, smiling. "Wuz up, you plan on introducing me?"

"After this bullshit you pulled, I don't know. I was gonna speak wit' him about that the next time I see him."

"Go ahead and do that, Victoria. If you seriously ready to get out the game, pass the torch to me. You know when it comes down to real business, I don't play no games."

"I'll think about," she said, back-pedaling to her Lexus.

Black stretched his arms out. "C'mon, gurl."

"I said I'll think about. You just pray your lil' stunt don't turn around and bite you in the ass."

# Chapter 15

The Juvenile track "Gone Ride With Me" blasted in the background as Crunch carefully watched Pig's movements. They walked down the hall to a back bedroom. Pig stood in the doorway while Crunch searched in the dresser drawer for a T-shirt.

"Here, this a 5X. It may be hard, but your fat ass can squeeze in it," Crunch mocked, disguising his suspicion.

Pig caught the T-shirt in midair, then turned and headed toward the bathroom.

"Where the fuck you going?" Crunch asked.

"To the bathroom."

"My girl got all kind of shit hanging up in da're. Yo ass can change right here," Crunch said, passing Pig to go use his phone in the kitchen.

Outside in the parking lot, Tank chambered a round in his AK-47, then aimed the barrel, resting it on the passenger door panel with his finger on the trigger. Stopping in front of the Buick was a maneuver Tank intended to provoke a reaction. In spite of his challenge, neither silhouette within the Buick moved. Tank decided he had only two options: either wait for something to happen, or make something happen. On the spur of the moment, he started rolling down his window. With the window partially down, he paused when his phone rang.

In a rapid whisper, Crunch said, "Yo, dat's dem folks."

"SHIT!" Tank mashed the gas pedal and sped out from in front of the Buick. "Dat muthafucka brought da police here?"

"Is dey still out da're?"

"Is they out there. I was 'bout to leave dem da're with holes in 'em."

"Where you at?" Crunch asked.

The tires screeched as Tank made a sharp left turn. "I'm heading toward 7th Ave."

"A'ight, let me get right. I'ma hit you back." Crunch swiftly hung up, seeing Pig move in his peripheral vision. "Damn, you make dat 5X look like a medium. Throw me yo shirt. I'll throw it in the dryer."

"Don't worry bout' it, I gotta get to da crib," Pig tensely said.

"What? You just got here."

"I came to bring you some pine. I got dis animal coming over."

For every step Crunch took forward, Pig took two steps back towards the door. Sweat seeped from Pig's pores. With the apartment's temperature quite cool, Pig's sudden perspiration and apprehensive behavior made it obvious he was scared.

Crunch took another step closer. "Pig, why you actin all jittery? You took something out my room?"

"Naw!" Pig said, shaking his head. "You know I won't take nothing from you."

"What you got in yo shirt? What you hiding? Lem'me see."

Pig inched even closer to the door. His heart pounded against his chest while his soul prayed Sherman and Menendez would burst through the door any minute. Crunch took a quick peek out the front window; he was satisfied everything was normal except for the out-of-place Buick.

"Yo, Pig, you must think I'm asking you. I said, lem'me see that muthafuckin shirt."

Sherman, I still think we oughta have pursued that vehicle. Something just didn't feel right. Besides, for all we know, that could have been our suspect," Menendez said.

"You're right, but what if you're wrong? Now, what I do know for a fact is that we have a valuable informant inside that apartment, with a possible suspect just as dangerous as Tank, wearing a wire. We have no audio nor visibility inside. If something was to happen to our informant, how on earth would you explain it?" Sherman asked Menendez. They sat quiet for a few seconds, looking at one another. "That's what I thought. Did you get the tag number?"

"No."

"Well, then, let's keep our eyes on the prize, shall we?"

Pig watched as Crunch's demeanor changed from calm to belligerent. Crunch lifted the hem of his shirt over the grip of his nine millimeter to emphasize how serious he was.

"Man, you trippin!" Pig said, bolting out the front door.

Crunch began to pursue Pig, then stopped just outside the door at sight of both the Buick doors swinging open.

Observing Pig run hysterically from the apartment, Sherman and Menendez raced towards him with guns in hand. Crunch darted back inside, slamming the door and double-bolting the locks. He drew his gun, readying himself for street court to begin.

Menendez reached Pig first. Grabbing him by the back of his head, he quickly ushered him safely behind their vehicle. Sherman walked backwards, keeping his firearm aimed at Crunch's apartment door.

"Jarvis, what the hell happen in there?" Sherman shouted, reaching the rear of the Buick.

Barely able to catch his breath, Pig replied, "He knew…! He knew something was… wrong. He was in da're actin funny."

Menendez got in Pig's face. "You ran like that just cause he was acting funny, or because you was fucking paranoid?"

"Paranoid!! He threw a fuckin pot of water on my damn head, then showed me his gun, and tried to take my shirt. Do dat sound like I'm fuckin paranoid? Damn, I knew I shouldn't have done this shit."

"Quit crying and tell us, what kind of weapons did he have inside?" Sherman asked.

"I know he got a nine on 'em."

"Is anyone else inside the apartment?"

"No, just Crunch."

Sherman got on the radio and called for backup, relaying the situation to S.W.A.T. for deployment.

Crunch, in the meantime, was gathering all the cocaine and crack he had in the apartment. He threw everything into a shopping bag, moving as fast as he could. Rushing to the window, Crunch inconspicuously peeped out and saw City of Miami police officers flood the parking lot. Crunch was true to his word about holding court in the street. Yet, now that the time had come, he also wanted a realistic chance of coming out on top. Holding the bag of dope in one hand and his gun in the other, he backed away from the window when he saw one of the officers put a bullhorn to his mouth.

Several times Sherman shouted for Crunch to come outside. All of his commands went ignored.

Crunch paced back and forth, weighing his options. The more he pictured Pig, the angrier he became.

"I swear, if I get out this shit, dat fat muthafucka is a dead man."

"This is your last chance come out with your hands up," Sherman yelled.

"Fuck dat!" Crunch said to himself.

Holding court in the streets was no longer an option. Crunch was not in the mood to die. He stopped pacing, then considered maybe it was time to do as he was ordered. Still clutching his gun, Crunch looked down at the bag of dope he was carrying. Coming back to reality, he sprinted to the bathroom.

In the parking lot, the S.W.A.T. team arrived in their black armored F-550. After each member jumped out, Sherman explained the situation to the squad leader of the S.W.A.T. team. Most of the team stood listening with their arms folded, while others double-checked their MP5's. Each was dressed in black fatigues and was prepared to neutralize the threat. After Sherman confirmed no hostages were involved, S.W.AT. was ready to move in.

"Sir, we breach in five," the team leader said to Sherman.

The team stealthily moved in on Crunch's apartment from the east and west. They approached strategically in a military-like formation. The lead officer held a bulletproof shield in front of himself with the S.W.A.T. insignia in the center. The team crouched on both sides of the apartment door. The team leader held his hand counting down with each finger, until he held a closed fist.

On the opposite side of the door, Crunch turned the water on in the sink and tub. Frantically jamming piece after piece of crack down both drains, he then dumped the powder cocaine in the toilet. While flushing, he improvised a method of cramming the crack into the sink and tub simultaneously, allowing the water to drain the evidence out of the apartment.

*BOOM...!* A concussion grenade exploded in the living room, causing the walls to tremble and smoke alarm to go off.

"Down… Down… Down…!" each S.W.A.T. team member yelled upon entry. They cleared the living room. Some went to the first bedroom on the right side of the hall, two more stormed the bedroom to the left, and the rest went straight towards the bathroom.

The bathroom was kicked open. Inside, Crunch was already on his knees with his hands up high in surrender. A hulk of a S.W.A.T. officer rushed in, slamming Crunch down and securing his wrists in plastic zip-tie cuffs.

"Don't you move, you piece of shit, or I'll blow your fucking head off!" the team leader shouted, aiming his assault rifle at Crunch's head. He grabbed the radio connected to his shoulder strap and informed Sherman, "Target is in custody."

Sherman smiled and gave Menendez a pat on the back. That was the notification he'd been waiting for to enter the apartment. Casually, Sherman and Menendez walked inside. They were instantly annoyed by the beeping alarm from the kitchen's smoke detector. Menendez moved one of the dining room chairs, stood on it, and yanked the battery out.

"Thanks," Sherman said, then looked at the team leader escorting Crunch into the living room. "So, this is our suspect? Shit, he don't look like much. I'm embarrassed, we could have taken this guy down by ourself."

"Sir, we recovered one firearm so far," the team leader explained, handing Sherman the weapon.

Sherman walked up close to Crunch and looked him square in the eyes. "So, where's your buddy Tank?"

Without a word or even a blink, Crunch gave Sherman a blank stare, exercising his right to remain silent early.

"What's the matter, chump, cat got your tongue?" Menendez asked, then looked at the team leader, giving him a nod.

*Thump…!* The team leader clubbed Crunch in the back of the head with the butt of his assault rifle. "Speak up, punk. We can't hear you."

Crunch took the blow and smiled at Menendez, and still remained silent.

The team leader raised his weapon again to strike Crunch once more, but this time he was stopped.

"That'll be all, Sergeant," Sherman said, ending the brutality. "Menendez get this piece of shit out of my sight. Take him downstairs and place him in a patrol car."

Local spectators watched as Menendez led Crunch out of the apartment.

Suddenly, Crunch broke his silence. "Why don't y'all beat my azz now, so people can see how you muthafuckas really handled me?" Crunch blurted loudly so the crowd could hear. He put on a dramatic scene. "Dey pistol-whipped me. I put my hands up and got slammed, then hit in the head with a gun."

"Shut the fuck up!" Menendez said.

Residents young and old looked on in dismay as Crunch shouted accusations of police brutality over and over. And due to the City of Miami's track record on the use of excessive force, the residents watched with great scrutiny. After Crunch was placed in the backseat of a patrol car, some of the more concerned residents walked alongside the car, seeing if they could spot any bruises, while the older people warned the officers to ensure Crunch was handled appropriately.

Menendez took a couple of steps back, hoping the tension in the crowd would not escalate. Just to be on the safe side, he radioed for additional officers to maintain crowd control on the scene. He then returned upstairs to assist with the search of Crunch's apartment.

A thorough search was conducted. The accumulated evidence was an empty plastic bag with cocaine residue, a digital scale, marijuana paraphernalia, and a firearm registered to Crunch's girlfriend. With the search complete, Sherman and the rest of the officers exited the apartment. Definitely not happy with the little evidence they had, Sherman now hoped he could get Crunch talking.

Crunch was taken to the police department and placed in a holding cell. He anticipated hearing what the cops had on him, besides what they had discovered in his apartment.

Sherman and Menendez arrived on the second floor, heading to the holding cell Crunch was secured in. But when the elevator doors opened, their captain was standing in from of them.

"You two in my office, now," the captain said.

Sherman and Menendez looked at one another, then followed the captain. Neither said a word. They reached the captain's office, and he never turned to face them until he sat behind his desk.

"Shut the damn door."

Menendez obeyed.

"Is something wrong, Cap?" Sherman asked.

"Damn right something is wrong. Both of you know this department is under an Internal Affairs investigation, especially you, Sherman. You two have a major suspect brought in, and, before he even opens his mouth, we've received over 20 calls claiming police brutality, and don't give me no covering-your-ass bullshit, I seen his head. Any half-ass doctor will confirm the blow he sustained to the back of his head was caused by a blunt instrument."

"What blow to his head?" Menendez stupidly asked.

"Menendez, another word out of you, I swear to God you'll be back in a uniform, driving a golf cart. Now, do not interrogate the suspect until his attorney arrives."

"What, his attorney! Who the hell let him call his attorney?" Sherman said.

"No one. He's been in the holding cell the entire time he's been here. Nevertheless, Phil Bowlby called in reference to his client, and he'll be here any minute. It has already been established, no interview with his client until he arrives. Is that understood?"

"Yes, sir."

Phil Bowlby was one of the best criminal attorneys in Dade County. He'd built his reputation on his aggressive style of arguing and his way of filling the hearts of jurors with compassion. But most of all, Bowlby was known for winning. He specialized in lawsuits against police departments accused of brutality.

The captain pointed his finger at Sherman. "Right now, the only thing I want to hear out of you is the amount of evidence you have against this guy to guarantee a conviction."

"Cap, I won't know until I get the chance to interrogate him. I believe I can coax a confession out of—"

"That's not going to happen without his attorney present." The Captain interrupted Sherman mid-sentence. "What about physical evidence? And didn't you guys gather some audio?"

"Not much. There was some technical difficulties with the sound. The suspect threw water on our informant."

After enlightening the captain about the wire incident, Sherman laid out everything that had occurred inside the apartment. Once he finished, the captain was displeased with the entire operation.

*Knock... Knock... Knock...*

"It's open," the captain shouted.

The door swung open, and everyone looked at Phil Bowlby stepping in. He wore his usual Armani suit, classic rocker ponytail, and his signature conceited smile plastered across his face. Bowlby looked like a hippie who refuse to let go of the past. With his sandy blond hair and surfer sunglasses, the last profession anyone would have expected him in would be law.

"Good evening, gentlemen," Bowlby said, addressing everyone in the room. "Time is money, people. Without further ado, where's my client?"

No one answered Bowlby. The captain simply rose to his feet, walked from behind his desk, and led the way out of his office. While a uniformed officer went to fetch Crunch from the holding cell, the captain, Sherman, Menendez, and Bowlby all went to a conference room to wait.

A few minutes later, Crunch was led in. He walked in rubbing the back of his head and frowning as if he'd been experiencing severe pain.

Sherman shook his head, watching the pathetic theatrics Crunch was putting on. "Fuckin pansy," he said under his breath.

Phil Bowlby sprung to his feet. "What's wrong with my client's head?" he demanded.

"You'll have to ask his mother that question," Menendez said.

"Look, your client knows he's in a lot of trouble," Sherman told Bowlby. "He's a murderer, and facing a life sentence. If he knows what's good for him, he'll tell us how to locate his friend."

Bowlby stared at the blood on the back of Crunch's collar, then walked over and made a close evaluation of Crunch's wound. "I don't know anything about him being a murderer, but I do know he hasn't been charged with resisting arrest. And he definitely looks like a poor victim of police brutality."

"C'mon, Bowlby. That's not what we're here to talk about. Let's discuss armed robberies, home invasions, and murders. Then, when we get through, we'll get your client a Band-Aid for his boo-boo." Sherman said.

"I don't know shit 'bout none of dat. You muthafuckas got the wrong man," Crunch blurted out.

"Shhhh… Don't say another word," Bowlby ordered. "Please, may I see the affidavits and arrest warrant?"

"Sure. Menendez will go get them," Sherman said, then walked to the door and whispered in Menendez's ear. "While you're at it, get on the phone and try to reach Victoria Cole A.S.A.P. We need her to ID this asshole."

Menendez nodded and shut the door behind himself.

Sherman came back and stood next to Bowlby. "Counselor, your client was a major participant in a brutal home invasion that left two people dead and a child shot, nearly killing him as well. As for your client's future, he's done. He confessed the crime to one of our informants. Now, if he wants to help himself out, his accomplice is still on the loose. We need his assistance with apprehending his partner, Tank." Sherman turned and looked at Crunch. "I promise I'll personally see to it that the prosecutor shows you some leniency."

"Ha… Ha… Ha… Please don't insult my intelligence. First thing first, I need to see the arrest warrant and affidavits. And while we patiently wait, do you care to share what kind of evidence you have against my client? Surely you have enough to arrest him with force, don't you?"

"On top of everything, we have our informant and audio," Sherman confidently said.

"Detective, this is a state case, not federal. Informants do not intimidate me, but I am going to need to analyze the authenticity of this audio."

"Of course, that's not a problem. Let's say we schedule another meeting by the end of the week," Sherman suggested.

Bowlby looked at the captain, then at Sherman. "You're kidding, right? What kind of evidence did you present to the judge who issued that arrest warrant?"

Bowlby's cocky mannerisms were irritating Sherman, and it started showing in his facial expression.

"I did not hear you, Detective. You did secure an arrest warrant for this debacle? And certainly, you have legally obtained a search warrant before ransacking my client's place? Pleeeease… tell me you at least have a search warrant?" Bowlby said sarcastically. "I sure hope your partner brings back more than just an arrest report."

The captain shook his head in defeat. Sherman had secured neither an arrest nor a search warrant. Despite what Crunch was allegedly charged with, his record was unblemished. His entire criminal record consisted of one third-degree felony where adjudication was withheld.

Menendez return to the room and was greeted by silence and an atmosphere full of tension. He handed Sherman two sheets of paper. Sherman looked at them, then passed the papers to

Bowlby. As Bowlby started reading, Menendez glanced at Sherman, slowly shaking his head.

Bowlby rubbed the two sheets between his index finger and thumb. "What is this, a cosmetic affidavit? This paper is still warm, and the ink is barely dry. Detective Imbecile, why don't you run back out there and type up a search warrant too? I will need to add it to my file when I submit my motion to the court critiquing this police department's bad faith," Bowlby said, placing the documents in his briefcase.

"Listen, Bowlby, your client perfectly fits the description of a sketch our victim and eyewitness described, down to the fucking scar on his chin," Sherman said.

"We both know I eat circumstantial evidence for breakfast. Has this victim positively identified my client?"

"Just before you arranged this little soirée, we were in the process of having the victim transported down here," Sherman lied. "And when she IDs this scumbag, she will also corroborate our informant's version of what took place."

"Detective, you're entitled to your own opinion, I do understand it's a part of your job, but at this very moment what is my client being charged with?"

"Possession of drug paraphernalia and possession of a firearm. As for now," Sherman replied, coldly staring at Crunch.

"Oh, the firearm that's registered to my client's girlfriend, and the drug paraphernalia discovered during an illegal search. Righhhhhhht… We'll see you guys in court," Bowlby said, then turned to Crunch. "Don't say anything to anyone, and I'll see you at your bond hearing." He patted Crunch on his shoulder and walked towards the door. "Oh, yeah, I will be sending someone to retrieve that audio. And one more thing, Detective."

"What?" snapped Sherman.

"This interview is over. There is no need to strike my client again. He can be taken back to his cell. Matter of fact, my client should have received medical attention for the contusion on his head." Bowlby patiently waited by the door for Crunch to be escorted out of the room. As Crunch was passing him, Bowlby said, "One second, Detective."

"Now what?" Menendez spat back.

Bowlby didn't say a word. He opened his briefcase, removed a digital camera and snapped a few shots of Crunch's head.

Afterwards, Bowlby walked out of the police station and jumped into his navy-blue BMW 750. Once he was out of the parking lot, Bowlby dialed the number Tank gave him.

"Hello, Mr. Jones. This is Phil Bowlby. Well, my friend, our buddy is in quite a jam. He's looking at several capital offenses, and they're playing hard ball. The good news is, with a proper strategy, and a couple greased palms, there's a chance he can come out of this."

"How much?" Tank bluntly said.

"Well, Mr. Jones, the $5,000 in cash you provided will cover my fee for today and your pal's bond hearing tomorrow. He will get a bond, and there will probably be a few hundred bucks left from the retainer. You could put that towards your pal's bond or toward my fee for representation. The choice is yours. However, for a capital case like this, my rate is $35,000 plus expenses, such as private investigators, expert witnesses, etc. Now, minus the $5,000, there's a balance of $30,000."

"$30,000! What kind of guarantee comes with that kind of money?"

"None, but what you do get is Phil Bowlby representing your friend, and my name speaks for itself. Why get a Toyota when you can have a Ferrari? Believe me, if you get a Ferrari, it's guaranteed to perform like it's supposed to. Think on that and give me a call when you decide what you're going to do."

"Phil, there's no need. You'll have your money in the morning."

Back at the police station, Sherman, Menendez, and the captain listened as the technician played back the audio from the wire Pig had worn. When it ended with static, the captain rubbed his bald head.

"Sherman! What the hell was that? I didn't hear anything concrete to get a conviction. There's more on that audio to incriminate your informant than your suspect. And I remember that case where that poor guy was shot in his behind over his great-grandfather's lighter. Where is this informant of yours?"

"I sent him home."

"You might need to have another conversation with him, and for God's sake confiscate that lighter. Miami Beach P.D. will be interested in having a few words with your informant."

"Yes, Sir."

"And another thing. Thank God this arrest was not another police shooting, but excessive force was used. When the shit hits the fan—and, with Phil Bowlby, it will—please know that someone's going to have to wear this. I don't care who. This department's reputation is already severely tarnished, and Internal Affairs is not making things any easier." The captain crossed his arms. "Sherman, the million-dollar question is, what are you going to tell the D.A.?"

Sherman did not have an answer for the captain. He held a closed fist on top of the table, thinking of how his investigation had turned into a failure. His key informant was quickly turning to a devastating disappointment. Sherman now hoped at least Victoria could finger Crunch as one of the two who stormed inside her duplex.

Numerous times throughout the day, Sherman tried calling Victoria. Sadly, each call went unanswered. He even drove out to the duplex. Despite his efforts, locating Victoria was becoming as hard as finding Tank.

****

Later that night in the Dade County Jail, Crunch listened to inmates gossiping about whose spot got hit, who's fucking whose girl, who's snitching. But the conversation Crunch took most interest in was who was making all the money in the streets. He eavesdropped on three different conversation and could not believe what came out of the mouth of a young kid with a wild afro.

"I'm telling you, ever since Crow got murked, Victoria been eating."

The name Victoria did not ring any bells with Crunch, but the name Crow got his undivided attention. He moved closer to the kid and listened as he continued to run his mouth without knowing or caring who heard him.

"...Yeah man, funky ass Latricia put me down wit' da lick. Bitch done gassed my head, now I done burnt my bridges."

"Damn, Peanut, you fucked up a sweet connect," his friend said.

"Man… I know. I been eating good too. Da crazy shit, somebody broke in the crib before we even got there."

Crunch decided to sit at the table next to Peanut. "Wuz up, Jitt. You know Crow?"

"Who da fuck is you?" Peanut asked, staring at Crunch with a menacing gaze.

"Calm down, lil homie. You don't want dees problems," Crunch said.

Crunch's threat put Peanut on the defensive. He sprang to his feet, and his homeboy also quickly rose as reinforcement.

"Naw, homie, you da one that don't won't these problems." Peanut gave Crunch his best intimidating expression.

"Hold up, Jitt. I just heard you talking 'bout getting yo bread, right? This shit ain't dat serious. Besides, money and mayhem don't mix. So why don't you and ya boy chill? I'll rather talk about making money together."

"So talk," Peanut said, keeping his guard up.

"I know Crow from back in da day. I heard somebody killed him," Crunch convincingly lied. "You over here talking bout a lick. Word on da street, Crow been getting it." Crunch was trying to manipulate Peanut into talking.

"I don't know who put that word in the street. It wasn't shit up in there."

"Who put you down wit da lick?" Crunch asked

"Latricia. You know her?"

"Yeah, Latricia. That bitch got some good head," Crunch lied again.

"You know Latricia and Victoria like sisters."

"Who?"

"Victoria, Crow sister," Peanut replied.

"Oh, Crow sister. Yeah, I know her black ass. What she up to?" Crunch asked, desperately needing to know her whereabouts.

"She got her paper right."

"Oh, yeah."

Crunch and Peanut talked into the wee hours of the morning. Peanut didn't know it, but Crunch had an entirely different reason for inquiring about Victoria. Peanut went on, explaining the status Victoria had reached in the drug game.

"Wuz up, Jitt, when you gon' get out of here?"

"I don't know. I need somebody to pay my bond."

"Oh, yeah, I tell you what, if I get yo bond paid, I think we can help each other come up," Crunch said

"I'm wit' dat. I need $4,500. If you pay my bond, shit, I'm go all out wit'cha. I know this dude name Black. He got a nice piece of change up in his crib."

"We gon' have to look into his ass too. Go ahead and write yo info down. After I get out, Jitt, I got you."

Peanut went in search of something to write on. Scrap paper was hard to find; the rest of the inmates only had their legal work. With nothing else but a Bible, Peanut ripped out the blank back page and wrote down his legal name and case number. He slid his info across the table to Crunch.

"My bond hearing is in the morning. As long as no bullshit come up before then, when I make bail, I'ma find someone to sign your bail."

"My mama will sign for me. She just need da money. If you tell her what she need to do, she'll do it. I'll write down da address."

"I got'cha, Jitt," Crunch said, ending their discussion and calling it a night.

Crunch only got about 45 minutes' worth of sleep before the rest of the inmates were back up making noise. The breakfast cart arrived, and, though he was hungry, Crunch chose not to eat the cold oatmeal and hard biscuit. Instead he was focused on the murder charges Sherman was trying to pin on him. The thought of a victim witness being able to identify him focused his mind on one resolution: Victoria had to die.

Several hours later, Crunch was handcuffed to another inmate and walked to the Dade County Courthouse. The two corrections officers escorting the inmates, entered the courtroom, and sat Crunch and the rest of the inmates in the first row. Twenty minutes later the bailiff stepped in the courtroom.

"All rise for the Honorable Judge Davis," the bailiff shouted, notifying everyone present that court was now in session.

With Phil Bowlby's influence, his case was called first.

"Case number 50894, the State versus Curtis Hayes," the clerk called out.

Crunch sat next to his attorney as the prosecutor presented his case. The D.A. fought vigorously to paint Crunch as a menace to society. However, each time the D.A. mentioned the brutal home invasion, Bowlby jumped from his seat, objecting.

Phil Bowlby's representation was everything he had vouched it would be. By the end of the bond hearing, the D.A. said on record that he would not be charging Crunch for possession of a firearm. But, for now, he was to be charged with the possession of drug paraphernalia.

Sherman sat in the courtroom feeling like he had just been slapped. He looked at the judge in disgust as he set a $4,000 bond. And to add insult to injury, Sherman received another mental slap when the judge said Crunch would be able to be released on his own recognizance.

When Crunch made it back to the housing block, he was immediately turned around for release. It took Crunch about 50 minutes to go through the release process. As he was finally let out of the county jail, he squinted his eyes as they adjusted to the sunlight. He looked from side to side, figuring his girlfriend would be parked nearby. He did not want to hang around the jail any longer than necessary, so he began walking. He went towards the street the jitney bus passed, then suddenly stopped and spun around. Someone had called him by his legal name.

"Looks like you could use a ride."

"Fuck you!" Crunch saw that it was Sherman who had called him.

Sherman drove alongside him. "Hold that thought, 'cause after you and your buddy get a much-deserved life sentence, you're gonna want to fuck somebody."

"This shit is harassment!" Crunch barked, sprinting across the street.

Sherman slammed on the brakes and shouted, "And what you and Tank did was senseless murder. I'm coming for you!"

Crunch disappeared behind a University of Miami medical building. He'd heard everything Sherman had said and vowed never to let him make good on his word. Crunch darted inside the building and searched for Sherman's car through the large glass window. Seeing no sign of the Buick, Crunch found a pay phone and made a collect call.

"Damn, girl! Why da fuck you ain't up here yet?" Crunch shouted at his girlfriend.

"You should've called and let me now you was ready. Where you at?"

"Hurry up and get yo ass down here, I'm at the…" Crunch paused and looked around. "Shit… I don't know what's the name of the building. Oh, I'm at the University of Miami cardiovascular center."

"OK, I'm on my way."

After hanging the pay phone up, Crunch wasted a few minutes pacing back and forth, then nervously walked back outside to see if he could spot Sherman or the Buick. Relieved the coast was clear, he stood on the side of 12$^{th}$ Ave until his girlfriend pulled up.

Quickly hopping into her Nissan Maxima, Crunch exhaled a breath of relief. "'Bout time you got here. Did Tank call you?"

"Yeah, twice," she replied.

"Later on, I'ma need you to get one of yo homegurls to sign my little homeboy out."

"Boy, I don't know nobody that will sign somebody out that's not their man."

"Well, here." He passed her the paper with Peanut's mom's address. "Go get $4,500 out my bread and take it to his mama. Tell her it's her son bond money. Now let me hold your phone."

*Ring...*

"You got 'em?" Tank asked.

"This me. Where you at?"

"I done told you 'bout dat. Where you at?"

"Right now, I'm coming down 12th Ave."

"Have yo gurl drop you off at the bus stop across the street from da west."

"Northwestern High School," Crunch confirmed.

"Dat's da west, ain't it?"

Crunch instructed his girlfriend where to take him. She dropped him off at the bus stop, and he sat there roughly seven minutes before he saw the Malibu. Tank pulled over on 71st Street and surveyed his surroundings, watching every car in the vicinity. Once he felt safe, Tank gunned the Malibu and picked Crunch up. The second Crunch sat in the passenger seat, Tank sped away, checking his rearview mirror to see if he was being followed. Tank looked over at Crunch and passed him an already lit boonk joint.

"Dat's yo homeboy, huh?" Tank said with sarcasm, referring to Pig.

"You already know I'ma handle him. But on some'mo serious shit, remember that bitch dat ran out da crib wit' her baby? Man, dat bitch a problem. The police ain't talk to her yet, but dey tryin to get her to point me out. We need to have more than a word wit' her. And I stumbled on a way to make that happen. I met this Jitt in da County dat use to push work for da broad."

"Work! What the fuck, da bitch slanging?" Tank asked.

"Naw, she ain't slanging. Da bitch ballin," Crunch said vehemently. "I told Jitt I'll pay his bond, and he agreed to set something up."

Tank gave Crunch the briefest gaze as he turned onto 7th Ave. "You still puttin trust in these soft ass clowns out here. Fuck Jitt, we roll back to where she live and do what we should've been done."

"It ain't dat simple. She don't live there no'mo. That's how good she eating. She pushing a Lexus 470, and copped a new crip, but Jitt don't know where her new spot is. On da real, when we find her, we'll see how good she really eating. And when we done, I'ma make sure dat bitch never step foot in a courtroom," Crunch said.

Tank reached out for his boonk joint and took a pull, "Yo Crunch, I just got one question for you. When you held court in da streets, what wuz the verdict?" Tank laughed at him.

# Chapter 16

Finzi, Jada and the rest of his task force headed to North Dade. On the day Black swindled Jada, she had memorized the specialized license plate on his Jaguar, which read “BIG KID.” After they ran the tag, it was time to hit the address on the registration. The eight-car team slowly drove up the street, then, about five houses away from the address, they sped to the house, surrounding it from all angles.

Finzi stepped out of his car and was instantly disappointed. The residence was completely boarded up, obviously to prevent looting. Every inch of the home was deteriorating: rust corroded the metal poles supporting the carport, termites had done major damage to the wood siding, and the lawn was high enough to conceal a family of snakes.

“This dump looks like it’s been abandoned a couple years,” Finzi told Jada.

“Do you want me to put an A.P.B. out on his vehicle?” Jada asked.

“No, we’ll find ’em.”

Finzi hopped back into his car and lead his convoy back to the Federal Building to prepare around-the-clock surveillance on Victoria.

****

The next day was the day Victoria had waited for her entire life. All the time and energy that she had invested into her business was finally manifesting before her eyes: the grand opening of Diva’s & Don’s. The unisex salon was immaculate. Victoria had the 150-gallon aquarium installed inside the wall. Italian marble tile had been laid throughout the building, and what dazzled everyone was the lighting that shone from the beautiful crystal chandelier.

The turnout for the grand opening was bigger than Victoria had anticipated. Local radio 99 Jamz were doing such a wonderful job promoting Diva's & Don's that a few up-and-coming local celebrities and their entourages came through. Catering was done by Queen Spice It Up, and she definitely satisfied everyone's taste buds. By the time customers walked out of Diva's & Don's, they were promising to return because of the marvelous service. To Victoria's surprise, even Diaz made a rare appearance to show his support. To show her appreciation, she insisted he relax and get a massage. After the Jamaican masseuse completed Diaz's massage, Victoria gave Diaz a hug.

"Thank you so much, Diaz. All this is possible because of you. Words cannot express how grateful I am."

Diaz smiled and held Victoria's hand as he spoke. "I'm happy you've fulfilled your dream. After all you have been through, you deserve happiness."

"Excuse me?" Victoria responded with puzzlement.

"Before we met, I saw what happened to your brother and child on the news. Latricia and Tray came to my house the next day, and she explained to me that the story on the news was about her best friend's family. Of course, I never expected to meet you, but when Latricia told me you needed some help making a little money, I felt helping you was the least I could do."

"And I can't thank you enough for the help you gave me. Diaz, later tonight I really need to talk to you."

"I leave the country in three days. If it's truly important, perhaps we can speak privately in your office."

In truth, Victoria did not want to speak with Diaz about business now, but since she had opened the door, she led the way to her office. As they entered, Diaz admired the tasteful décor she'd chosen. Diaz took a seat in front of Victoria's computer desk.

"A'ight, Diaz, I've stressed numerous times how I appreciate what you've done for me. And I mean no disrespect, but I'm ready to retire from the drug game."

"Retire? You've just started seeing real money."

"You're right, and I don't wanna sell drugs until I get caught. This is all I wanted in life," she said, sweeping her hand around her office. "A legitimate business I can call my own. I will pay you for this building…"

Diaz waved her comment off. "Victoria, if I needed money, I could've easily sold this building. I gave it to you. It's yours with no strings attached."

"Although I want to go strictly legit, I have a friend that moves the majority of my product. And, with your permission, of course, I would like to introduce him to you."

"No, thank you. I'm not interested with any new distributors."

"With all due respect, to be honest, Diaz, it was him that made me and you money. I don't have a hustle game like my friend Black. My passion is in hair. Hustling is Black's life, not mine."

Diaz thought on what Victoria was telling him. He admired the way Victoria conducted her business, along with the degree of ambition she demonstrated to obtain what she wanted. And, if Victoria was not willing to move his kilos, perhaps Black could become a valuable asset.

"How long have you known this friend?" Diaz asked.

"Nearly all my life."

"And do you vouch for his loyalty?"

"Yes."

"Very well, I trust your judgement. I will return to the States by the middle of next week. Introduce me to your friend here. Let's say Thursday morning, one hour before the salon opens."

"You want to meet here?" she asked.

"Is there a problem?"

"No… No… No… There's no problem at all. First thing Thursday morning, he'll be here."

Diaz slapped both his thighs and rose to his feet. "Excellent. I will see you Thursday," he said, exiting the office.

Victoria could not find the courage to tell Diaz she did not want to conduct any illegal activities at the salon. Now, all she could do was hope that the salon wouldn't become a regular meeting spot. After Diaz left, Victoria switched back to playing the host and making sure all her customers were pleased with the quality of service. Every booth was occupied with a customer receiving either a hairdo, a pedicure, or a manicure. She even peeped inside the two massaged rooms and found they were full.

One of her female customers was enjoying a foot massage by a well-chiseled brother in a sleeveless shirt. Victoria smiled. She was unable to resist the temptation to show her hospitality.

"Well... well... well... It seems like you're enjoying dat much-needed foot massage."

The customer had her head leaned back and her eyes closed until she heard Victoria's voice.

"Victoria! Heeeeyy...! Gurl, how you and the boys doing?" Victoria's Aunt Tara asked, surprised.

"We've been just fine. How 'bout you? Looks like you're enjoying yourself."

"Gurl... this fine ass, sexy chocolate sculpture got me ready to take him home. Are you getting a massage?" she asked Victoria.

"No, I'm just making sure all my employees are satisfying my customers," Victoria said, rubbing her success in Tara's face.

"Your employees! What, you the manager or something?"

"Yeah... I'm something. Or you can say I'm the boss, owner, founder, or even the H.B.I.C., head bitch in charge. Whichever you see fit, I'm her."

"Owner? This your place?" Tara asked in disbelief.

"Yep! Thanks to you putting me out yo house when I was down, I had no other way to go but up. By allowing myself to be put in dat situation, it gave me the strength and motivation to accomplish all this," Victoria said, extending her hands to point out her achievements.

"Victoria, I hope you not mad still. I was upset about my jewelry being stolen. I work too hard for my things to come up missing and smile about it."

"Oh, no… Mad? Why would I still be mad? Had you not shown me your version of family love, there's no telling where I'd be or what I'd be doing. There's a good chance I would be broke and probably still doing hair at yo house. Aunt Tara, please don't think I'm mad. That is the last emotion I feel right now. Hey, why don't you and Tanika come to my house this weekend for dinner?"

"You still stay in the duplex?"

"I forgot to tell you, I moved. We live in Pembroke Pines now. I'll come and pick y'all up."

"Damn, Victoria, you sure is doing good. What kind of car you driving?"

"You see dat canary yellow Lexus out front?"

"That SUV?" Tara said, Jealous as she remembered the beautiful SUV parked next to the 99 Jamz promotional van.

"Yep, dat's mine."

"Who you sleeping with?"

"A cold pillow," Victoria told her. "I'm single."

"Ummmm… You doing something right. Well, it's good seeing you Victoria. I've got to get out of here. Tanika wants me to take her to a party," Tara lied. She reached into her purse to pay the male masseuse for her foot massage, but Victoria intervened.

"Dat was on da house," Victoria said, doing her best to kill Tara with kindness.

The massage room door opened, and Anna stuck her head in.

"Pardon me, Victoria. There's a guy in the waiting area that want to see you."

"OK, Anna, tell him one moment."

Victoria walked alongside Tara through the stained-glass door. The second she stepped into the waiting area, Victoria noticed Black standing at the receptionist desk, flirting with the very attractive receptionist.

"Leave dat gurl alone," Victoria said, playfully slapping him on the back of his neck.

"Why, when you got this beautiful eye candy needing my company? I gotta find somebody to love me. You won't," Black teased. "Damn, Victoria. I see you on some Beverly Hills type shit up in here."

Today was the first time Black had seen the salon complete. He turned in a circle, looking at the place, definitely impressed. As promised, he'd shown her his support.

Victoria gave him a hug. "Thanks for coming."

"Stop it. You know damn well I wouldn't miss it for the world. Ol' boy wit' da radio station want to holla at you," Black said, pointing to the radio DJ.

Victoria and Black walked outside towards the 99 Jamz promo van.

"Hey, everyone, I see the Diva herself," the DJ said. "Queen Victoria, get on over here. C'mon, tell the people what's so spectacular about Diva's & Don's." He held the mic towards Victoria.

She accepted the microphone and informed the crowd huddled around the van about the reasonable prices, friendly service, and how Diva's & Don's catered to all the customer's beauty needs. The crowd applauded, and Victoria thanked 99 Jamz for their assistance in making her grand opening a success. The positive energy she felt was overwhelming. After she passed the microphone back to the DJ, Victoria and Black went back inside the salon. They walked past the aquarium, and Victoria pulled Black by the sleeve. She leaned in and whispered in his ear. As he heard the good news, a smile appeared on his face.

Across the street from the salon, parked discreetly in the shopping plaza, Finzi, Jada, and part of his team sat in the disguised U-Haul truck. Finzi snapped photos of every person that stepped inside the salon.

Jada stared angrily at the still shot of Black on the camera LCD screen. She stood up and tightened the Velcro straps on her bulletproof vest. "What are we waiting for? Let's go and arrest the asshole that took our money."

"Patience, Jada. This is much bigger than that future convict. We have photos of Diaz, Victoria, and Black all in the same place. It's no coincidence all of them are here. We can't show our hand right now. Neither of them have committed a crime, besides Black swindling us out of our money. With that alone, he won't even get five years. Before we storm in, we need to see some duffel bags, briefcases, or something that resembles a transaction. In the meantime, we'll get a magistrate judge to rubber-stamp a search warrant, and, if nothing happens, we'll execute the warrant in ten days. I'm sure the judge will have no problem signing for another search warrant," Finzi said, zooming in on Black's motorcycle tag.

Ten minutes later, Black walked out of the salon, put on his helmet and hopped on his bike.

"Well, are we gonna at least tail him to see where he lives?" Jada asked.

Finzi turned his head and glanced at Jada, then focused back on Black. "Jada we're in a fucking U-Haul box truck. That bike is a Suzuki Hayabusa 1300. Even if we wanted to, without having a bird in the sky, he'd leave us like we were standing still. Like I said, have patience. After we show the grand jury Latricia Joyner's statements and get their indictments, I bet they will be begging us to let them cooperate for a time cut, including Diaz."

****

Meanwhile, inside her mother's bathroom, Latricia stood in front of the sink, looking at herself in the mirror. Stressed, depressed, and heartbroken about her situation, Latricia opened the medicine cabinet and scanned the labels of her mother's prescription pills. For several of the pill bottles, she had no idea if they were for high blood pressure or cholesterol. But she did know that too much of anything was bad for you. She removed five bottles of prescription pills. Several times throughout the day, she had held a razor to her wrist, contemplating whether she should slice side-to-side or diagonally. After much consideration of a bloody suicide, Latricia had had a change of heart, wanting to spare her mother a gruesome discovery. Her biggest stressor was the fact she'd signed an agreement obligating her to testify on Diaz and anyone else connected to him, including Victoria. The mere thought of sitting on the stand and betraying her best friend sickened her, even more so than the HIV flowing through her veins. To make matters worse, she had gone against her doctor's orders, never taking any of her medication. She wondered why it was necessary when there was no cure. Having knowledge of the deadly disease, and having to live with being responsible for Victoria receiving a lengthy prison sentence, weighed heavily on Latricia's mind. The weight had become unbearable, and she had decided to go to a better place.

Latricia filled the bathtub with cold water and placed each pill bottle on the rim of the tub. Through her teary red eyes, she looked at herself in the mirror one last time, then stripped off her clothing, leaving on her bra and panties. She eased into the bathtub, just as if taking a routine bath. Chill bumps flared on her skin as her body tried to adjust to the cold. She pressed down and twisted the child safety cap on each bottle, then, one by one, she poured the pills from each bottle into her hand and swallowed them, washing them down with water she drank from the tub. With each bottle empty, she waited. An hour passed before she started to feel any effect. She was unsure if her life was passing before her eyes, or if she was genuinely missing Tray. She started slipping out of consciousness. She had multiple flashbacks, from the days she'd first met Tray to the last time she'd seen him alive. Her eyes began to blink slowly as her body slouched lower and lower into the water. She sank low enough that the water was up to her chin. Her vision began to fade. Her eyes closed, then suddenly sprung open long enough for her to realize her vision was completely blurred. Once again, her eyes closed, but this time she drifted into darkness.

****

The following Thursday, Victoria turned into the Diva's & Don's parking lot two hours before the salon opened. She parked in her usual spot, went inside, and waited for Diaz and Black to show up. She kept the lights off and the Closed sign on the front door. Thirty minutes passed as she stared out the large picture window, watching the morning traffic go up and down Highway 441. She watched as workers arrived across the street at the shopping plaza. She looked at the time on her watch, then back across the street at the managers and employees unlocking the hurricane shutters on their businesses, preparing to open. She watched a U-Haul truck turn into the shopping plaza. Seconds later, Black pulled in on his motorcycle. He parked in the one spot designated for handicap parking.

Victoria opened the door for Black and rolled her eyes at his choice of parking.

Black stepped through the doorway and said, "What!" He looked in the direction of Victoria's gaze and smiled. "Stop lookin like that. You know damn well ain't no handicap people coming here this time of day."

She shook her head, "Anyway… Diaz not here yet. Give him a few minutes."

"Shhhhit, I'd give him a few days. This his tree. I'm jus' a squirrel tryin to get a nut."

Victoria sat on the sofa next to the window and glanced at the U-Haul truck, wondering whether anyone had got out.

"Black, before Diaz get here, do me a favor."

"C'mon, Victoria, you ain't even gotta ask. Just say it."

"Tell Diaz you prefer to meet at another location."

"Where?" Black asked.

"Anyplace but here. I don't want to start having meetings like this salon is a front for drug deals. That's all I ask."

"I got you. Don't worry 'bout it," Black said, then stared out the window. "Who da fuck is in dat raggedy ass truck?"

Victoria turned to see. "That is da man you've been waiting to meet."

"I want some birds, but not poultry," Black jokingly said, amused by Diaz's Chevy S-10 pickup.

She didn't reply to Black's wisecrack. When Diaz got within a couple of feet of the door, Victoria opened it to greet him. "*Buenos dias*, Señor Diaz."

"Ah... *buenos dias*," Diaz said, pleased that Victoria had greeted him in Spanish. "*¿Es estro tu amigo?*"

*Is that your friend?* Victoria mentally translated. "Si."

Diaz nodded his head at Black. "Can you remove your sunglasses for me?" Diaz asked, but in the tone of a demand.

Black did as Diaz asked, making eye contact with him.

"Diaz, this is my friend Black," said Victoria. "Black, this is Diaz, the man I've grown to love like a father."

The two shook hands firmly.

"Mister Diaz, it's a pleasure to finally meet you."

Diaz dug inside his breast pocket, retrieving a cigar, his concentration never wavering from Black.

"How long have you been trying to meet me?"

Black glanced at Victoria before answering. "Not long. When Victoria told me she wanted to quit hustling, I asked her for the opportunity to keep things going. I'm a business man, and business is booming."

Diaz and Black spoke for nearly an hour, discussing everything from Black's capabilities to his accomplishments. Their meeting went longer than Victoria had expected. She sat behind the receptionist desk until she saw a car pull into the parking lot.

She walked over and stood next to Black. "Excuse me, but one of my employees just arrived, and in a few minutes my clients will be here."

"Forgive me, Victoria. Business sometimes makes me lose track of time," Diaz told her, then rose to his feet. "Black, give me the address of where you sleep and one family member. This is simply to find you in case of an emergency."

Initially, Black was reluctant to comply with such a blatant request, but, in the pursuit of the almighty dollar, it was necessary to establish his trust. After giving Diaz the info he'd requested, Black followed him outside. They walked to the driver's side of Diaz's pickup truck.

As Diaz climbed behind the steering wheel, before closing the door, he looked Black in the eyes and said, "I must explain something to you. I am a very... very dangerous man. If you dream about playing with my money, I'll become your nightmare. If you believe you can run off and spit on my trust, I will hunt you down and show you horrifying images. And once your vision makes your heart skip a beat, I'll leave your ghost wondering how you died." Diaz smiled. "But of course, we don't have to worry about those terms?"

It was almost comical to Black to hear this threat come out of such a little man's mouth. But, to appease his new connect, he tucked away his pride.

"We won't have any problems."

"Good. Be home around four p.m.," Diaz said, then reversed and drove out of the parking lot.

Victoria stood at the door, watching as Diaz and Black drove off. She flipped the Closed sign around to Open, took a quick glimpse at the U-Haul truck across the street, and then proceeded with business as usual.

With a pair of military-issued binoculars pressed to his eyes, Finzi watched and recorded the brief exchange Diaz and Black had outside the salon. When Victoria went back inside and closed the door, Finzi put down the binoculars and got on the radio.

"Jada, where are you now?"

"I'm still trailing Diaz. We're just getting on the 836, heading west," she replied. "Hey, Finzi, either this guy is very cheap or very discreet. I never would've pictured him driving that piece of junk."

"One thing's for sure, he's not stupid, so maintain a safe distance."

Jada followed Diaz into Hialeah. It was relatively easy for Jada to keep up with Diaz's 45 miles per hour. Her original plan had been to trail Black, but because he was on his motorcycle, Finzi had reminded her not to waste time on the impossible. Fortunately for Jada, Diaz drove with an old gas stove in the bed of his truck. Had it not been for the stove blocking his rearview mirror, he might have spotted her.

She radioed in, "Finzi, Diaz just stopped at a residence off 104 St. in Hialeah."

"Good job, Jada. Watch the house, and, if he leaves, you make sure you're his new shadow. I'm gonna stick right here. I believe this salon is nothing more than a disguise to launder Diaz's drug money."

By 5:30 p.m., Victoria had cleaned up her booth, gathered her belongings, and headed out the door. She had to pick up P-Rock and Victor from Mrs. Knowles' house, so she left Anna in charge and jumped into her SUV. As Victoria threw the gear into reverse, she noticed the U-Haul truck still parked across the street. Oblivious to what it was that had caught her attention, she ignored the fact this was the first U-Haul she ever seen with tinted windows.

# Chapter 17

Sherman rolled up the sleeves of his sport shirt, pacing back and forth while he waited for Pig to come into the station. With ulterior motives, Sherman had called and explained to Pig that his signature was needed in order to honor his cooperation deal.

Pig was anxious to hear about his brother's status. He wasted no time racing to the police department. Pig walked into the lobby and told the white female officer at the desk that he had an appointment to speak with Detective Sherman. He was told to take a seat, and, two minutes later, Sherman stepped out of the elevator. Pig stood up and, when Sherman got closer, he could tell by the look in his eyes something was wrong.

"Let's go, Jarvis. We got some serious things to talk about," Sherman said in a cold tone.

"You sound like I did somethang wrong. I did what I was suppose to do, so wuz up wit' my brother?" Pig asked as they walked towards the elevator.

When they reached the elevator, Sherman pushed the up button, then spun to face Pig. "Newsflash, your drug-dealing brother is still fucked. The wire you wore was useless. Obviously, you gave him a signal in there."

"A signal! Man… dat's bullshit and you know it. Everything you wanted me to do, I did it. Now I gotta walk these streets with my face dirty."

The elevator door opened.

"You leaked," Sherman said, stepping inside the elevator.

Pig didn't move. "I ain't leak shit. You wasn't in there. Crunch was about to kill my ass."

Sherman put his hand on the side of the elevator door, preventing it from closing. "Look here, you gave us nothing, you get nothing. And, unless you can convince me otherwise, your brother's going to be in prison a long time. Now get in this elevator."

Pig still didn't budge. "I ain't going nowhere. I'm outta here."

Pig turned and walked towards the exit. Sherman stepped out of the elevator and followed him. Outside, Pig dug in his pocket, pulled out a pack of Newports and his lighter, and lit a cigarette, exhaling smoke and a piece of stress.

"Let me bum one of those," Sherman said behind Pig.

Pig shook his head while giving Sherman a cigarette and the lighter. But, instead of lighting the cigarette, Sherman put the lighter in his pocket.

"C'mon, Jarvis. Let's go upstairs. I got some questions you need to answer."

"Fuck you and your questions. I'm out," Pig said, walking away.

Sherman followed, coming abreast. "Alright, tough guy. I may have used a poor choice of words. The audio from the wire you wore wasn't completely useless. Crunch did implicate you in an armed robbery that resulted in an innocent citizen being shot in his ass." Sherman patted his pocket. "I'm gonna hang on to this lighter. I think this is a key piece of evidence that will tie you to the crime. And you do know, for a crime of that magnitude, here in Florida it falls under the 10-20-Life guideline. Which one you think you fall under? I'll give you a hint, it damn sure ain't ten. You can bet on that."

Sherman could see the guilt written on Pig's face. But, sadly, as much as he wanted to, Sherman did not have enough to arrest Pig.

Pig avoided Sherman's eyes. "I don't know what you're talking bout'. I bought that lighter from Walgreens." He walked a little faster, putting distance between himself and Sherman.

Sherman stopped following Pig and yelled at him as he walked away. "We'll be in touch real soon, so don't go too far!" He stood in front of the station, watching Pig until he drove away.

****

Crunch punched the steering wheel, thinking about Pig's betrayal. Parked on the side of the county jail, Crunch daydreamed about Pig as he waited for inmates to be released. Peanut's bail had been taken care of. Peanut's mom had reached out to Crunch to thank him and to confirm the approximate time of Peanut's release. He patiently watched as several newly released inmates raced out of the jail, running to the property window, all except one.

Peanut stuck out like a sore thumb. Unlike the rest, he strolled from the door without a care in the world. He heard a horn honk and glanced in the direction it had come from, and his face lit up seeing Crunch. He jogged over to the car, jumped in, and gave Crunch dap.

"It ain't too many people that are men of their word. I gotta admit, I didn't have no faith you was gonna come through for me. When dem people told me to pack my shit, I was like, ol' boy the real one.'

Crunch waited for traffic to pass, then drove off. "I stop playing games when I turned seven. I'm 'bout handling business. If you 'bout getting yo paper right, then you da kinda people we have on our team, paper chasers."

"Dat's what I'm 'bout, getting dat bread day or night. Shit, I don't give a fuck if a muthafucka young or old, male or female. When it come down to it, anybody can get it if dey stand in my way," Peanut said.

"I hear dat big boy shit, but you gotta show and prove to impress me. If you really 'bout dat life, we'll see. I only fuck pussy, I don't hang out with it," Crunch said firmly.

"So, wuz up, you want me to do something like an initiation?"

"Dis ain't no gang, Jitt, but to ride wit' us, you gotta be cold-blooded. You can say anything wit' ya mouth. Have you ever killed a man?"

"I don't know, I've been in some shit where muthafuckas got wet," Peanut said, trying to understand the direction Crunch was taking their conversation. He listened to how casually Crunch spoke about doing malicious acts. "I heard you say ride wit' us. Who's us?"

"Me and my mans, but right now he ain't tryin to meet nobody, because of this problem I got." Crunch looked over at Peanut. "How you feel about snitches?"

"I can't stand a muthafucka dat can't hold his own. Dem da kinda people dat need a bullet for breakfast."

"Dat's da kinda shit I'm talking bout, Jitt!" Crunch said excitedly. "You straight Jitt, you need sumpin?"

Peanut was seconds away from answering out of pride, but seeing Crunch pull out a wad of cash, he nodded and watched Crunch count out thirty twenty-dollar bills.

Before Crunch had gone to the county jail, Tank had explained to him how to get Peanut comfortable, dependent, and, in the end, dedicated. Crunch stuck to the plan and was doing all of the above.

"So wuz up, Jitt, you tryin to go fuck sumpin?"

"I gotta go by the bail bondsman before I do anything. After I leave there, shit, I don't give a fuck, I'm down for whatever. I'ma ride."

"You a rider, huh? I guess we'll see."

Crunch drove to Helping Hand Bail Bondsmen Inc. He reversed into a parking spot next to a minivan, and Peanut hopped out and walked inside. When he got back into the passenger seat twenty minutes later, he noticed for the first time that there were no keys in the ignition.

"Yo, you pick me up in a splack?"

Crunch started the Pontiac Grand Prix with a flat head screwdriver and said, "This the true meaning of down for whatever." He reached under his seat, retrieving a MAC-10 submachine gun, and passed it to Peanut.

Peanut accepted the deadly weapon. He admired the MAC-10 as if he had a fetish for guns. Gently rubbing his fingers over the extended clip, Peanut said, "Damn, you wild as fuck. First you pick me up in this hot ass car, then you riding wit' this gun like this shit legal."

"I know I'm wild. How wild are you?" Crunch asked, turning onto a street in the Cloverleaf neighborhood. He slowed down. "You see dat blue Honda Civic right da're? Dat's where that snitching muthafucka live dat set me up."

"Who?" Peanut foolishly asked.

Peanut's question irritated Crunch. He mashed the brake pedal a little harder than necessary. "Look, Jitt, all dat gangsta talk you did in da county, don't tell me that shit was a show?"

"Naw."

"You just said snitches need a bullet for breakfast. So let's feed dat muthafucka!"

Crunch drove past Pig's house, hating the fact Pig was still breathing. Involving Peanut when he handled Pig wasn't originally in his plan. But Tank refused to take Pig out because, after they'd robbed Tray, Crunch had pleaded with him not to kill Pig and leave his body in the van. Crunch's sympathy had turned around and cursed him.

"Jitt, there's 'bout $30,000 or more up in da're, plus some work. You do his bitch ass, we split da change and the work is yours."

The pay enticed Peanut. He looked down at the MAC-10 and said, "Say no mo', but how do I catch him slipping? Do he got a gun in da're?"

"Hell, naw, his soft ass ain't got no gun," Crunch convincingly lied. "Dis all you gotta do." Crunch began explaining his master plan.

Inside Pig's two-bedroom townhouse, to relieve some stress, he was in the middle of entertaining the neighborhood hoe. Her name was Diamond Head, a name she'd rightfully earned by the way she'd polish a dick to a spit shine. Diamond Head normally turned tricks for cash, but when Pig had let her sample the raw cocaine they'd taken from Tray, the high she had was better than money. And as long as Pig continued shoveling coke up her nose, she was happy to do whatever it took to keep her high. Diamond Head was an attractive light-skinned woman; had it not been for her coke addiction, a woman with her looks would have never gotten involved with Pig, especially sexually.

Pig relaxed on his back while Diamond Head sucked his shaft like she was competing in a marathon. His toes curled into a fist, then his stomach jiggled, and he did the unmistakable jerk. Using his shaft as a straw, she sucked every drop of protein that his testicles could produce. Finally, she rose to her knees, licking her lips seductively.

"Ummmm.... ummm... Big Daddy, you taste so good," she said, stroking his ego to manipulate more coke from him.

"You ready for round two?" Pig asked, sprinkling a line of coke on his shaft.

Diamond Head gave Pig a big smile, then dropped her head in his lap, snorting all the white powder off his shaft. She rose up, rubbing her index finger over her gums, giving herself a freeze. Then, just as she put all five inches of him in her mouth and watched him close his eyes, she was abruptly interrupted.

*BONK... BONK... BONK... BONK...* Pig's car alarm went off.

Pig pushed Diamond Head to the side, jumped out of bed naked, and darted to the window. He snatched back the curtains and was instantly infuriated by the sight of his passenger window smashed. The neighborhood Pig stayed in had a high rate of auto thefts, and, though his car wasn't worth stealing, Pig assumed the thieves weren't discriminating. Assuming Crunch was still in jail, he felt no fear when he saw a teenage limping away, only anger. Pig scrambled from the window, threw on his pants, and raced out of the bedroom. He charged from the front door, running towards the unrecognizable teenager.

"Hey, muthafucka!" Pig screamed, nearly out of breath.

When Pig got within ten feet of what appeared to be an injured teen, he was greeted with a MAC-10.

"Wuz up, fat boy! Nice and slow, let's go back in yo crib and get them car keys," Peanut aggressively commanded.

For the moment, Pig was somewhat relieved all the kid wanted was his keys. He backed towards his house, holding his hands up and trying to smooth-talk Peanut, praying he'd make the mistake of coming within his reach and allowing him to wrestle the gun away, unaware of Crunch standing at the side of the house.

"You got too much heart to be around here wasting yo time stealing little bullshit cars like mine. You should be out making some real paper. I can put you down on getting some real bread, if you put that gun down," Pig said in a weak attempt to get in Peanut's head. He was so focused on Peanut and the barrel of the MAC-10 that he was oblivious to Crunch creeping behind him.

"Yo, homeboy, I thought we was bred from a finer cloth than dat," Crunch casually said. Pig spun around at the sound of Crunch's voice.

Pig's eyes stretched as wide as a meth addict's when he came eye-to-eye with Crunch.

"Crunch… Man, dat bullshit wasn't suppose to go down like dat," Pig said, trembling at the cold stare in Crunch's eyes.

"Tell me how it was supposed to happen." Crunch grabbed Pig by the back of his head, pushing him forward. "Tell me all about it inside!"

Pig looked over his shoulder at Crunch. "I got company."

"You think I give a fuck about yo company?" Crunch yelled, then punched Pig in the mouth.

Pig fell to the ground and rolled on his back. With tears forming in his eyes, he cried out, "Please don't kill me Crunch, please!"

Crunch laughed. "You think I'm here to kill you? Naw, homey, I want dat work back and come up off that piece of change."

"Damn, man, you go' rob me?"

Crunch kicked Pig in the ribs. "Get yo bitch ass up! You betta be glad you still breathing. Didn't I say get the fuck up?" Crunch kicked him again, making Pig backpedal through the front door. As soon as they stepped inside, Crunch punched Pig in his bloody mouth again.

In Pig's bedroom, Diamond Head was high and horny. While Pig was gone, she was sneaking bumps of coke, then placing the coke sack exactly how he'd left it. She lay back on the bed and began enjoying her own body. She rubbed her nipples and stuck her index and middle fingers inside her love box, stroking her fingers in and out. She slowly pulled her fingers out and tasted her own juices. She got so into masturbating that she let out loud moans, trying to get Pig's attention.

"It sound like two people back da're," Peanut said, easing towards the moans.

"How many people back da're?" Crunch asked Pig.

"It's just one broad."

"Let me hold da fiya, and go check dat shit out," Crunch ordered.

Peanut gave Crunch the MAC-10, then walked to the bedroom. The door was cracked open, so he peeked inside before easing the door wider. He saw Diamond Head completely nude, grinding her hips as she rapidly rubbed her clit. Enjoying the show, Peanut instantly got an erection. He crept into the room and was surprised when she was unfazed by his presence.

"Hey, gurl, you in here making all dat noise by yourself?"

"Umm… hmmm…" she moaned seductively, nodding her head. "What's your name?"

"Does it matter?" Peanut asked, grabbing his crotch.

Diamond Head's eyes went down to his hand. "Don't touch it if you not gon' use it."

The amount of cocaine she'd snorted had her open. On her hands and knees, she crawled on the bed towards Peanut. He took a step closer and stood at the edge of the bed, looking down as Diamond Head unzipped his pants. Peanut was thinking with the wrong head and allowed her to give him a blow job. Even though this was far from his purpose of coming in the bedroom, after all the days he'd spent in county jail, he felt a little head was due.

"Yo, Jitt!" Crunch shouted. "Wuz going on back da're?"

Pig was on his knees, still pleading, "Crunch! Believe me, man, dem police was already outside. I swear to God on my son life, I didn't know that shit was gon' happen."

Peanut came jogging out of the bedroom with his pants unbuckled.

"Goddamn, Crunch, you gotta go back da're. Dat bitch an animal on the dick."

"We ain't come here for no pussy, and da bitch done seen yo face."

Crunch's last comment terrified Pig. If Crunch only wanted to rob him, his words sure didn't reflect that.

"Crunch, da money is under my mattress, and da work is in the top of da closet," Pig confessed, hoping that would satisfy Crunch.

"Go check it out, Jitt," Crunch said to Peanut.

Peanut trotted back to the bedroom and burst through the door, catching Diamond Head in the act of snorting coke out of Pig's private bag. Unconcerned with her devious deeds, Peanut walked to the closet, looked up, and pulled out the partially open kilo.

He then turned towards the bed and yelled, "A, bitch! Get yo ass up!"

"Ah… ah… Who da fuck you talkin to like that?"

Not in the mood for any lip, Peanut shoved her off the bed. She fell flat on her back. He yanked the mattress up with both hands. As his eyes glanced across the money lying on the box spring, Diamond grabbed the partially open kilo and chucked it at him. It connected with the side of his face. Angered, he released the mattress. Diamond started screaming and cursing at him. Peanut charged and tackled her to the floor. He sat on her chest and began punching her in the face. He stood with saliva dripping from his mouth and stomped her uncontrollably. She screamed and cried out in pain as Peanut kicked two of her bottom teeth out.

Hearing the agony Diamond was in, Pig looked up at Crunch. "What he doing back da're?"

"I don't give uh fuck!"

Diamond was once again moaning, only this time it was not from the pain of pleasure. Peanut was satisfied she would not cause him any more trouble. Pissed, he flipped the mattress onto her. He picked up a pillow off the floor and snatched off the pillowcase, then hurriedly gathered all the cash and coke, throwing everything into the pillowcase.

Peanut returned to the living room where Crunch and Pig waited.

"What da fuck happened to you?" Crunch asked, noticing that the side of Peanut's head was covered with white powdery residue.

"Dat crazy bitch started trippin. I had to put her in her place."

"You couldn't have put her in her place, because I can still hear da bitch moaning," Crunch said, giving Peanut a cold stare.

Pig wasn't the sharpest tool in the shed, but he wasn't slow, and he immediately realized what was about to take place. With firsthand knowledge of Crunch's deadly habits, Pig understood that now was his only chance to act. In a fraction of a second, Pig made a bold attempt to run for the front door while Crunch chastised Peanut. To no avail. Unfortunately for Pig, unlike in Crunch's apartment, Crunch did not chase him. Instead, he raised the MAC-10 and let a bullet catch him. The bullet ricocheted off Pig's spine and pierced his carotid artery. Pig's body collapsed to the floor, and he laid paralyzed. Crunch then faced Peanut and passed him the MAC-10.

"Time to show how you get down, handle yo business," Crunch said.

Without hesitation, Peanut walked over to Pig's motionless body, aimed the MAC-10 at the back of his head, and squeezed a single round through Pig's skull, killing him instantly.

"Dat's not da business I was talking about." Crunch looked in the direction of the bedroom.

Peanut understood. With his adrenaline level at its peak, Peanut returned to the bedroom. Crunch peeped out the living room window to see if any witnesses were lurking around. The next moment, he heard a terrified scream followed by two shots. Peanut came back around the corner, noticing Crunch digging through Pig's pockets.

"We got all his money. Let's get da fuck outta here."

"I'm not lookin for no damn money. We need his car keys," Crunch said, coming up empty-handed. He scanned left, then right, spotting the car key on the kitchen counter. "Now let's get da fuck outta here."

****

One hour later, two unmarked Crown Victorias and a marked patrol car pulled up in front of Pig's house. Inside the first Crown Vic were Sherman and Menendez, followed by a pair of Miami Beach Robbery detectives.

Looking at Pig's driveway, Menendez said, "Fat bastard probably got the hell out of town."

Sherman and Menendez stayed in their vehicle while the Miami Beach detectives went to knock on the front door. The detectives made a sudden stop, quickly looking back at Sherman and Menendez, who both observed this bizarre behavior. When the detectives unholstered their firearms, Sherman and Menendez realized something was wrong. With guns in hand, they jumped out of their vehicle and rushed to assist the other two detectives. The uniformed officer ducked into his patrol car, retrieving his 12-gauge shotgun.

One of the Miami Beach detectives, without saying a word, pointed down at a bloody shoe print.

"Menendez, you and Detective Ryan take the rear. We'll take the front," Sherman said, then crept within inches of the front door. "We enter on three."

Preparing to kick the door in, Sherman instinctively twisted the doorknob first, and to his surprise the door was unlocked. Sherman eased it open, noticing a puddle of blood congealing at the base of the door. Standing with his firearm aimed through the crack, he continued to slowly push the door wider until an object prevented it from opening any further. Sherman could feel, through the door, that the object was soft and heavy. From his experience, he knew it could only be one thing.

"We got a body," Sherman advised the detectives.

The MBPD detective followed Sherman to the rear of the house. Menendez was peeping in a window when they came around the corner.

"Looks like the house had been ransacked from what I can see," Menendez said.

"We got a body on the inside blocking the door. To prevent disturbing the crime scene, we're gonna have to enter through the back door," Sherman explained. "Menendez, call it in."

Sherman twisted the rear doorknob. Unlike the front, it was locked. He used his pocketknife to jimmy back the latch on the doorknob. He cautiously entered. And almost immediately noticed Pig's corpse lying in a massive pool of blood.

MBPD Detective Ryan stood beside Sherman and said, "Is that our suspect?"

Sherman nodded.

They searched the rest of the house together. As they stepped into Pig's bedroom, Sherman recognized the feet of a female sticking out from under the flipped mattress. "Jesus, what happened in here?"

Menendez returned from radioing in for back-up. He looked around the bedroom, then at Sherman. "I hate to admit it, but we might be a little responsible for this."

Sherman inhaled a deep breath and exhaled, "Get the forensic team down here to get us some evidence. That sonofabitch is going down."

****

In Opa-Locka, Tank was laying low in a rooming house. He had isolated himself from the rest of the tenants. He only left in the daytime when it was an extreme emergency, and only opened the door for Crunch. For the past two hours, he'd been sleeping off and on. It wasn't until the siren from a passing firetruck woke him that he got out of bed. Out of habit, he looked out the window, then headed towards the bathroom. Scratching his crotch as he walked, Tank saw two shadows suddenly appear under the door. As a precaution, he grabbed his black .357, cocked back the hammer and stood by the door listening. He waited to hear voices, then discreetly looked through the peephole. Luckily for his visitors, he recognized Crunch standing alongside a young stranger.

Tank swung the door open and put the barrel of the .357 to Peanut's forehead. "Who da fuck is this?" he yelled, knowing the answer.

"Chill out, Tank. Jitt a soulja. He exterminated dat problem and got da change back."

Tank removed the barrel from Peanut's forehead. "Oh, yeah? Dis muthafucka don't look much like no soulja." He looked him over. "So you a soulja, Jitt?"

"Damn right I am."

"Shit, I hope yo don't think I'm impressed cause you handled dat bitch ass, fat muthafucka. He was a straight pussy."

"Gangstas can get it too!" Peanut spat back.

Tank smirked at Peanut's confidence. "Time will tell."

Crunch tapped Peanut's shoulder with the back of his hand. "Tell my man 'bout this Black dat you told me about."

"Like I said earlier, Black been eating long before Victoria. I use to work for him at his detail shop. Dat shit got closed down cause we use to sell mo' dope than cars washed. And I know where he live at."

"Y'all still cool? Can you call him, or go by his crib and cop some work?"

"I don't know," Peanut replied. "We was alright, but, if he found out I broke in Victoria's place, it's no telling how he'll feel 'bout me."

"If you show up at his crib, will he let you in?" Tank inquired, digging for more details.

"I can't just show up knocking on his front door."

"Why not?" Crunch asked.

"For one, dem big ass dogs he got won't let me in the yard, and two, Black stay strapped. If he gets a bad vibe, he bustin first and asking questions later."

"From what you saying, dat shit sound sweet. Two dogs, no goons. Unless them dogs can shoot a gun, fuck 'em."

Crunch nodded his head, picturing the same scenario as Tank.

"Dat bitch is really eating like that?" Tank asked.

"I can't say what she working wit', cause I don't know. All I can say is, she pushing keys, and be breaking Black off proper."

Peanut continued going over Victoria's transformation; he even went so far as to explain the time she rode the city bus with him.

"Tank, dat's who we need to handle first. She's the one making power moves, and keep in mind dat bitch top priority," Crunch said.

"Naw, Crunch, if Black got it like Jitt say he do, we handle his ass first, because after we take care of dat broad, I'm through wit' Miami." Tank looked at Peanut and tossed him his phone. "Call yo' boy, see if he'll let you spend some money wit 'em."

Peanut pushed *67 to block the phone number, but to no avail; each call went to voicemail. For the next couple of hours, though Peanut was determined to reach Black, he was still unable.

"Damn, his phone battery must be dead," Peanut concluded.

"Try again first thing in the morning. If the calls still keep going to voicemail, fuck it, we'll go for what we know. We muthafuckin Jack Boys," Tank said, pounding fists with Crunch.

The three of them smoked boonk joints all night. Tank and Crunch listened to Peanut brag about the money he had run through in his 18 years, seven of which he'd spent in the game. Then he repeated Black's story, adding a few more details. By three in the morning, Peanut and Crunch had fallen asleep.

Tank stood gazing out the window, collecting his thoughts while they slept. These were the moments when he thought best. He was planning the best way to catch Black at his most vulnerable. He glanced back as Peanut rolled over in his sleep. Tank took to Peanut far better than he'd done with Pig. But he refused to let history repeat itself. Once they'd robbed Black and handled Victoria, Peanut would no longer be needed. Even though Peanut had no knowledge of their history, Tank had no intentions of allowing Peanut to see his $19^{th}$ birthday.

The following day, Tank, Crunch and Peanut drove past Black's house. They circled the neighborhood twice to get a feel of the front and back of the house. As they passed for the second time, Peanut pointed at the two bull mastiffs lying underneath a palm tree.

From the backseat, Tank said, “Crunch, drive around the back one more time. I want to see something.”

Tank observed the backyard, examining the sliding backdoor. Seeing what he needed to, Tank was satisfied there were no security bars anywhere on the house.

“Jitt, you think he up in da’re?” Crunch asked.

“I don’t know. His Jaguar and Chevy can fit in the garage. He could be on his bike, or he could be in da’re.”

“Let’s get up out of here. Dis how we gonna do this shit.”

Peanut and Crunch listened as the plan was devised.

# Chapter 18

Black anticipated hearing from Diaz by four in the afternoon. He paced in front of his picture window until he heard his guard dogs aggressively bark, as they always did when an intruder was near. Black stared out the window, watching suspiciously as a produce box truck parked in his driveway. He could tell the driver was not Diaz, nor did he look Spanish. The bull mastiffs continued barking at the truck. Black watched as the driver put a cell phone to his ear. Black's phone rang in his pocket.

"Who dis?"

"Señor, I would ring your doorbell, but I do not believe your dogs will allow me to do that," the caller said.

"I got'cha… Hold up," Black replied excitedly, pumping his fist in the air. He opened his garage door. "Cash, Lady, c'mere."

The two bull mastiffs obediently ran to their master. Black lowered his garage door, locking the two ferocious dogs inside, then walked out to greet the driver. The driver's African American complexion confused Black, but the moment he spoke with his heavy Spanish accent, it wasn't hard to tell he was a Latin male. The driver and Black shook hands.

"I thought Diaz was coming?"

"No… No… I make all deliveries for Señor Diaz. Now, come. I need help with these bags."

"What the hell is he talking about?" Black wondered, but, rather than question him, he helped carry four fifty-pound sacks of potatoes. As they walked toward his front door, Black looked at the Ginuwine look-alike, wondering what his position was. After they brought the sacks of potatoes inside the living room, Black stepped back as the driver laid one of the sacks in the middle of the floor, removed a knife from his pocket, and split the sack down the center. He pushed several potatoes to the side and removed a sack of cloth camouflaged to resemble the texture of the potatoes' skin. Four kilos were concealed in the sack.

Black looked into one of the other sacks to see if he could tell the kilos were inside. Not only were they not visible, the cloth blended in perfectly. The potatoes were tightly compressed around the kilos, preventing any movement. It was hard for Black to believe that each sack contained four kilos.

"The agreement you and Señor Diaz made was for 15 kilos, so be grateful there's a bonus one also."

"Tell Diaz thanks, I'll have his money A.S.A.P., and, when he see how I get down, he gotta up the ante."

"I will deliver your message." From his pocket, he pulled out a card with his number on it. "Call this number when you're ready, and say nothing more than, 'I slept good.' And then hang up."

Black put the card in his back pocket, then walked Diaz's associate to his truck. Black gave him a salute as he reversed down the driveway, then jogged back inside.

Unbeknown to Black, parked inconspicuously down the street, Tank, Crunch and Peanut observed the delivery from beginning to end. Though unsure what was in the four sacks, Tank knew one thing for sure: they were going to find out.

Black unwrapped one of the kilos, preparing to see how good the coke was. He gathered all his utensils, digital scale and baking soda, then set everything on his kitchen counter alongside the microwave to begin his magic.

Outside no traffic was passing, nor was anyone standing in their yard. The only movement was Tank and his crew, driving past Black's house one last time. Assuring themselves that the coast was clear, they proceeded with the plan Tank had laid out.

"A'ight, Jitt, now remember, the moment he take his eyes off you, put dat pistol in his face. That will distract him long enough until I come and take control of the situation. Can you handle dat?" Tank asked.

"I got it, but you gotta be sure to kill him when we get inside."

"You just do your part, and I'ma handle mine."

Peanut assured Tank he could do his part. Now he had to reassure himself that he was up to the task. Doing Pig had been easy. Black, on the other hand, might not go down without a fight, and truthfully that scared the shit out of Peanut. The time arrived, and Peanut had to put aside all his edgy feelings. Tank got out and snuck into Black's next-door neighbor's backyard, watching as Peanut stood in front of Black's fence, shouting for him to come outside.

Looking out his kitchen window, Black said to himself. "What the fuck he doing out da're?" He stormed out the front door, charging straight at Peanut.

"Wuz up, Black?"

Black had an enraged look as he approached the fence. "What da fuck suppose to be up?"

"Huh?" Peanut nervously replied.

"'Huh.' Muthafucka, you ain't dumb. What da fuck you doing at my house? You tryin to break in my house too?" Black yelled.

"Hell naw, Black. C'mon, man, you know me better than that. I ain't break up in nobody shit. Them folks locked me up for being at the wrong place at the wrong time," Peanut lied, nervously gazing at the gun grip sticking out of Black's waistband.

Black took a step closer to the fence. "You gon' bring yo ass to my house uninvited, then gon' try and play with my intelligence like I don't know what time it is? You broke in Victoria's place. Matter fact, I'ma call her right now." Black reached into his pocket to get his cell phone.

As Black took his eyes off Peanut, Peanut took a quick glance down the street to see if Crunch was waiting by the stop sign. With his confidence barely built up, he snatched the .357 from underneath his shirt and pointed the barrel at Black's chest, catching him completely off guard.

"So, this is how I die, by the hands of you? 'Cause you and me both know you're gonna have to."

Peanut was speechless. He simply stood there aiming at Black's chest, the gun shaking in his hands.

Suddenly a voice came from behind Black. "He might not, but I'll blow your muthafuckin head off if you make a wrong move."

Peanut hurried inside the fence and disarmed Black. The sound of an engine accelerating could be heard as Crunch pulled up in front of the house and jumped out to assist Tank.

"Let's go get dem sacks, gangster."

Black did as his captors commanded. The second he walked through the doorway, Crunch struck him in the back of his head with his gun. The blow knocked Black to his knees. This was a tactic Crunch enjoyed using to intimidate his victims.

"Bruh, you ain't even gotta do all dat. I don't disrespect no Jacks," Black said, rubbing the back of his head. "Gon' ahead and get da work. It's in the kitchen."

Peanut ran to the kitchen and returned with four kilos.

"C'mon, big timer," Tank calmly said. "I know a baller like you got more than four of dem thangs. Where the rest of dem, and where dat bread at? You say you don't disrespect no Jack. Dat's good because I don't ask twice."

"Dat lil' backstabber got da work. My change is in there," Black told Tank, pointing at the door Crunch was standing next to. "Look inside the mini-fridge."

Crunch didn't hesitate. He swung the door open in search of the mini-fridge. The door led out to the garage. Crunch went down the two steps, immediately locating the mini-fridge in the far corner next to the Jaguar. Crunch rushed over, dropped to one knee, and opened the mini-fridge, paying no mind to his surroundings. By the time he noticed the two 165-pound bull mastiffs, it was too late. Crunch had no time to react before the dogs attacked.

One of the enormous dogs locked onto his calf, and the other bit into his forearm, jarring the gun from his hand.

"Ahhhh…!" Crunch screamed out.

Tank and Peanut's attention was abruptly drawn to Crunch's screams. Black had been anticipating either a scream or gunshots; either way, it was the little distraction he was waiting for to make a run for it. With Tank focused on the garage door, Black sprung to his feet and dashed towards the front door. Tank quickly swung the barrel of his gun at Black, releasing two rounds, just missing him.

Black went to the ground as he dove out of the door. Scrambling to his feet, he ran left, diving again as he reached the corner of his house. Without delay, Black sprinted as fast as he could, hurdling over the rear chain-link fence and running to the next street.

Back inside, Tank decided to help Crunch instead of chasing Black. He ran into the garage and was stunned to see Crunch being mauled by the bull mastiffs.

"Get 'em off me! Get 'em off me!" Crunch screamed when he saw Tank's face.

Tank walked up close to one of the mastiffs and fired a round into the dog's ribs. The mastiff was unfazed by the bullet, refusing to release Crunch's calf. Tank shot the dog again. This time, the mastiff relented. He then shot the other mastiff, firing three rounds into the dog. It instantly collapsed. During all the excitement, Peanut stood at the top step, watching.

"Jitt, get yo ass over here and help me get him to the car."

"I can make it. Get the work so we can get the hell out of here," Crunch said, slowly rising to his feet.

Peanut grabbed the four kilos and started to run out the door.

"Get da muthafuckin sacks!" Tank shouted, slinging two of the 50-pound sacks onto his shoulders.

Peanut struggled with the last sack, dropping the four kilos in his attempt to imitate the way Tank slung them onto his shoulders. Once secured, Peanut ran out of the house with the sack on his shoulder, making it to the car at the same time as Tank.

Tank threw his sacks into the backseat and helped Crunch get in the rear also. He ran to the driver's side and got behind the wheel. "Jitt, hurry up and get yo ass in!" Tank yelled, slamming the gear into drive.

As Tank mashed the gas pedal to flee the scene, Peanut literally had to dive into the moving car.

"Damn, dem dogs fucked me up bad," Crunch said, feeling blood leak from his wounds. "Look at my arm." Crunch's forearm had ripped muscle tissue exposed and barely clinging to his skin. The more he examined his wounds, the more concerned he became. "Fuck! My arm won't stop bleeding. Take me to Jimmy's," Crunch mumbled through the pain.

Jimmy Mitchell was a former surgeon who had lost his license after a malpractice lawsuit in which the hospital's Board of Administration had discovered that Jimmy had an addiction to crack cocaine. After doing three years in prison for practicing medical procedures without a license, Jimmy had turned into a full-fledged junkie.

Tank sped to Jimmy's mother house off County Line Road and parked in front of the old motor home where Jimmy slept.

"We here, homeboy," Tank said, but his words landed on deaf ears because Crunch was passed out from blood loss in the backseat.

Tank and Peanut carried Crunch inside the rusty motor home. Tank pounded on the door, startling Jimmy, who was scraping residue out of an old TV antenna that he had converted to a homemade crack pipe. Jimmy opened his door and had to step to the side as Tank stormed in with Crunch. Without asking Jimmy where to lay Crunch, Tank took it upon himself to lay him on a foul looking twin mattress that Jimmy used for sex with his lady friends in exchange for hits of crack.

Peanut stared at the dingy man and the terrible condition of the motor home. He wondered what on earth Jimmy could possibly do for Crunch.

Jimmy was still standing by the wide-open door. He was in his normal attire: blue slacks, a white dress shirt, and a tie. The downside was, this had been his outfit for the past nine days.

"Jimmy, don't just stand da're. Get over here and fix him."

"Hey, man, I need a wake-up. You come in here with a body, all this friggin blood and shit, I can't focus without a hit," Jimmy said.

"Muthafucka, fix 'em!" Tank shouted, pulling his gun out.

"Hey, bro, don't shoot me. Jesus! Will you look at my hands? They're shaking like this because I need a hit."

Tank rubbed beads of sweat off his forehead, then tucked his gun back into his waistband.

"Jimmy, you know I got you. Do something for my homey and I'll give you your own coke to cook up, or do whatever you want to with it, but for right now FIX 'EM!"

Jimmy was still nervous after seeing Tank's gun. He tried to control his shakes, but his fingers wouldn't stop shivering. He looked at Crunch, then at his hands. Finally, taking a deep breath, he got to work. Fortunately for Crunch, Jimmy had enough medical supplies on hand to conduct a minor operation. Tank and Peanut watched as Jimmy stitched Crunch's wounds and gave him a tetanus shot.

Crunch rolled over and stared at the needle Jimmy had used. "Dat bet not be one of yo old heroin needles," he said in a low tone.

"Don't insult my character. I may smoke a little crack here and there, but I've never done heroin. I don't have a lot, but I do have some standards."

Tank laughed at Jimmy, then pulled five hundred dollars from his pocket and threw it on the table. "There you go, Jimmy. Don't spend it all in one place."

Jimmy snatched the money off the table as if it was about to run away. Despite his crack habit, Jimmy took pride in the medical procedures he performed. And as long as he was passionate about what he did, criminals always had their own doctor to remove bullets and stitch up lacerations, the same as the doctors in the emergency room. Minus the need to report their condition to the police.

Crunch slowly limped to the car and paused, looking at the blood in the backseat.

"Tank, did you kill dat muthafucka?" Crunch asked.

"No."

"I want to see Black again, and, when I do, it ain't to rob him."

****

Just an hour after Black had escaped with his life, he returned home. Surprisingly, his neighbors hadn't called the police. He hid inside a neighbor's toolshed until he assumed his attackers were gone. When he stepped through his doorway, the first thing he noticed was that the potato sacks were gone. He didn't make a sound; his anger silenced his words. Beside his leather sofa, he spotted the four kilos on the floor. Black's thought's flashed back to the robbery, and he ran to the garage.

Inside Diva's and Don's, Victoria was putting one of her clients under the dryer when Kim came and told her she had a call.

"Hello."

"Victoria, you need to get to my house right now!" Black said.

"I can't right now. I'm in the middle of doing my client's hair."

"This ain't no social call. Get here now!" Black demanded. "I been robbed!"

Black's news took Victoria's breath away. Her heart pounded in her chest. Black hung up, and Victoria stood motionless, holding the phone against her breast. There was no doubt she needed to leave and get to Black's house. Since running out on a client was so unprofessional, Victoria told her client that an emergency had come up, Kim would finish her hair, and the hairdo was on the house.

Victoria raced to Black's house. Her SUV kicked up gravel as she slid to a stop. By the time she had hopped out and reached the fence, Black was standing in the open doorway with a Mini-14. Victoria stared at the assault rifle and the drum clip attached to it. Not only was she nervous seeing the weapon in his hand, she was also worried seeing Black's T-shirt covered in blood.

She entered his yard. "Black, are you hurt?"

"Yeah," Black responded. "They killed my dogs."

"Who?"

"Uh dead man. Peanut and some mo' muthafuckas got the jump on me. And what's fucked up, dey took the work Diaz gave me. The crazy shit is, I didn't have da work twenty minutes before Peanut and dem fools show up. I'm not slow. Either dat's some hellafied coincidence, or Diaz just did some real bullshit."

"Black, don't talk like that."

"You really think I'm gonna pay him for some shit I ain't have long enough to even open? My house never got broken in, and I never got robbed. Now, remember, he was da one who wanted to meet here at precisely four o'clock. Then he don't even show up, some other muthafucka come to my crib, and you know I don't like people coming here. And another thing, how did dey know to take da sacks da work was in? Nobody just gonna take some fucking bags of potatoes unless dey knew what was in them."

"Black, what you need to do is calm down."

"Fuck calming down!" Black shouted. "Then, to make shit even more suspicious, why the fuck would dey leave four bricks, like I'm supposed to grind dat shit and pay Diaz $192,000?"

"I vouched for you. You gotta pay him."

"I ain't paying him shit! He gotta holla at me. Dis shit bigger than Diaz's money. Dem fools tried to kill me!" Black said angrily. "Either Diaz set me up, or dat pussy ass hoe Latricia."

"Damn, Black, I'm out the game, and now look how I'm dead in the middle of this bullshit. Is this what I get for tryin to help you out? If you step to Diaz on some personal shit that got nothing to do with him, there's no telling what he might do."

"It's only one way to find out. First, I'ma find Peanut, and, before I kill him, if he tell me anybody with an accent told him to rob me, Diaz gon' see I got killers too!"

****

In Victoria's quick departure from the salon, she paid no attention to the navy-blue Ford Taurus that followed her to Black's house. Finzi had had an eight-car apprehension team trailing Victoria's every move for the past couple of days. And now, finally, after several hours invested in surveillance and manpower, Finzi's diligence had paid off. He had the location of Black's residence.

Finzi blew a kiss at Victoria's SUV as she left Black's house. "Thanks, sweetheart," he said with a smile. "Alright, Jada, it's time to serve some indictments."

"I bet Diaz flip on everybody first," Jada said.

"Twenty bucks."

"Deal."

Finzi put together a 20-count indictment. Along with several local police departments, they formed a task force to conduct major drug sweeps, using the acronym O.G.O. for Operation Game Over.

Two days had passed since Black was robbed. For the entire 48 hours, he had driven around Miami searching for Peanut. He'd combed several night clubs, hotels, and old neighborhoods Peanut hung in. Black's rage never decreased, nor did his thoughts change about what he was going to do when he found Peanut.

The unique Miami weather was humid and foggy around six in the morning. After hours of hunting for Peanut, Black decided it was time to head home. He made a right turn onto his street but had to slam on the brakes as a Ford Taurus nearly collided into him head-on. Two more cars sped up behind him, sliding to a tire-screeching stop. A fourth car block him in, leaving no way to open his door. With handguns and rifles drawn, officers and agents surrounded Black's car, making escape impossible.

With his gun aimed at Black's head, Finzi shouted, "Nice and slow, climb out the window with your hands up!"

Following Finzi orders, Black climbed out of the driver's-side window and was immediately slammed down by an officer the size of the professional wrestler the Undertaker. Black's face hit the asphalt first. Then a knee was dropped on his back, and his wrist were handcuffed.

"You have the right to remain silent. Anything you say can reduce your sentence if you don't say enough, it can be used against you in a court of law. The choice is yours," Finzi said, standing over Black.

Black was pulled by his arms off the ground, and, once he stood straight up, he laid eyes on a familiar face.

"Hello, Black. I hope you still got my money."

Black stared in Jada's eyes with pure disgust. He spit on the ground, then was escorted to an awaiting paddy wagon. Finzi shoved him inside and slammed the steel door. Black looked at the four faces inside: two he recognized, two he didn't. The two he knew were Jay and Country.

"Damn, Black, dey got you too?"

"Dem folks rolled up on me so fast, I ain't know what the fuck was happening. One thang fo 'sho, that bitch Latricia workin wit' dem folks," Black told Jay.

"I didn't never fuck wit' Latricia."

"Right now, I don't know what da fuck's going on. But I do know dis much, dat's da feds, and if you know like I know, you'll shut da fuck up before you get another co-defendant."

****

At 7:30 that same morning, Victoria dropped P-Rock off at school and took Victor to daycare. Then she headed to the salon. With the kids gone, her mind drifted to Black. She hated to know it, but there was no doubt in her mind he was going to kill Peanut when he found him. She was more concerned about what might happen when Black and Diaz met again.

She made it to the salon. The parking lot was completely empty but for her ride. Victoria got out and started unlocking the hurricane shutters. The next thing she knew, the parking lot was swarming with unmarked cars. Dozens of agents and officers raced towards Victoria, pointing several different types of guns at her, from riot pumps to handguns. They came to arrest Victoria as if she was armed and dangerous and a threat to national security.

"Victoria Cole, we have a warrant for your arrest, and a search warrant for these premises," Finzi said.

"For what?" Victoria asked in confusion.

"Conspiracy to distribute cocaine."

Victoria's heart did not stop, but it definitely accelerated. Tears poured down her face before Jada could place her in handcuffs. At that moment, everything appeared to be moving in slow motion. She gazed at the number of officers who had come for her. As she was placed in the backseat of a Crown Vic with a prisoner cage, Victoria wished this reality could simply be one of the many nightmares she'd had of this day, and that she'd wake up any minute. But this was no dream, and no matter how many times she closed her eyes, when she open them, she'd witness firsthand PART OF THE GAME.

From the backseat, she watched as the task force stormed inside her salon. For over 90 minutes, they searched every inch of the salon. Finzi went as far as slicing the sofa cushions open. Despite all his affords, Finzi was quite disappointed when they came up empty-handed. He walked out of the salon and looked at the Crown Vic Victoria was in, then went over to have a word with her.

Finzi opened the rear door. "Ms. Cole, where are the drugs?"

"I don't know nothing 'bout no damn drugs!"

"That's cute, sweetheart, but you and me both know it's a lie. I hope you're not getting your hopes up because we were unable to find anything. Just so you know, we're going to both of your homes. Yes, we know about the duplex and your pretty little hideout in Pembroke Pines. Yessiree… I can't wait to slam a sledgehammer into your walls. We will find your drugs and money, and that's a promise."

With all the confusion of the entire ordeal, Victoria was more worried about picking her kids up than about Finzi stumbling across any incriminating evidence at either of her houses. No more time was wasted at Diva's and Don's. Finzi and the task force cleared out of the parking lot and drove to the duplex.

Before stepping out of the vehicle, Finzi turned around to speak with Victoria. "OK, Ms. Cole, you can save yourself the headache and trouble if you go ahead and be truthful about what's inside there."

Victoria did not answer Finzi. Unconsciously, she rocked back and forth, her kids we're heavily on her mind.

"Suit yourself. We'll do it the hard way," Finzi said, hopping out from behind the steering wheel. He looked at Jada in the passenger seat, and said, "Bring Ms. Cole inside so she can enjoy the show."

Inside, the task force were ransacking the duplex no differently than burglars. Finzi, Jada, and two other agents were searching Crow's old bedroom. It wasn't until one of the officers hollered like a cowboy that Victoria remembered the guns and counterfeit cash. Finzi walked out of the bedroom with an AK-47 in one hand and a Python .357 in the other.

"Mrs. Cole, do you care to explain the purpose for this much firepower? What are you protecting, and please don't say your family."

"Why don't you fingerprint them? You will see I never touched them things. They belonged to my brother. I didn't even know they were in there," Victoria lied, finding no reason at that moment to be honest.

Finzi thought about what Victoria had said, and, without a doubt, he was sure that, unless she pleaded to the weapons, a jury would never convict her on weapon charges. But along with drug charges, once Victoria pleaded guilty, he was certain the U.S.D.A would enhance her sentence with the AK alone.

A Metro Dade Narcotic officer, part of the task force, came in from outside with a message for Finzi. He spoke low so Victoria couldn't hear. Finzi nodded, then went outside. He was gone roughly five minutes before returning with a message from Mrs. Knowles.

"Unlike their mother, your kids have a decent godmother. She wants me to tell you, if you need her to pick up your boys, she'll get a ride to get your oldest son, but you'll need to call the daycare for your youngest and give them permission to release him in her care," Finzi said, then walked over and sat on the couch next to Victoria. "I'm willing to allow this to show you, in good faith, I'm not such a bad guy, but I got a job to do. And giving me the silent treatment is not helping your situation. Technically, protocol is for me to immediately notify the Department of Children Services."

Those was the right words to start Victoria crying again.

Trying to influence Victoria to cooperate, he continued, "I'm not going to make that call. You can arrange with the daycare for your son to be released in his godmother's care. Just don't forget my kind gesture."

"Can I use the phone?" Victoria said in a soft tone.

"Absolutely." Finzi removed the handcuffs from her wrists and allowed her to use the phone.

Victoria told the coordinator at Victor's daycare that a family emergency had come up and gave approval for Victor to be released to Mrs. Knowles. The moment Victoria hung up was the very moment her reality became unbearable. Her tears no longer poured out in silence; she let out a scream, and cried harder than she had ever cried before. This was the part of the game she had done her best to avoid. Despite the fact she was no longer in the game, the bad part had a way of finding you.

Still sitting next to Victoria, Finzi let her troubles sink in, then began trying to get information out of her. "Ms. Cole, this does not have to be as bad as you think. Do you think I want to send you to prison? I know what happened to your brother, and I can't imagine what you went through when your child was shot. I don't want you, I want Diaz. We tried to arrest him before we came for you, but somehow, he just vanished. Now, I know you can serve him to me on a silver platter. This is your last chance to ride this boat, because once it leaves shore, I promise the next time you see your kids, your grandkids will be your age."

Victoria heard every word Finzi said. However, her mind was elsewhere. She watched as Jada and the other officers walked out of Crow's bedroom with nothing else in hand. Victoria said to herself there was no way they could have found the guns and not the counterfeit money that had been hidden in the same place. Only two people knew where the money and guns were: P-Rock and…

# Chapter 19

Lying in a hospital bed, shivering in the chilly room, Latricia finally woke from the coma she had arrived in. Her entire body was in pain. She slowly tried to rise from the bed, but couldn't.

*Clink... Clink...!*

Latricia looked down at her wrist, found that a pair of stainless-steel handcuffs prevented her from leaving the bed. She swept her eyes across the room. There was no telephone, TV, or anything else electrical. She thought back to what she'd done; what she couldn't remember was what had gone wrong. What Latricia was oblivious to was the fact she'd taken the cocktail of medication on an empty stomach, causing her to vomit the pills that weren't fully digested. Her mother discovered her unconscious but still breathing. When the paramedics arrived, Latricia was on the bathroom floor. Now, because of her ill-advised stunt, Latricia's bond had been revoked, and she was to remain in the custody of the U.S. Marshals until her day in court.

"Why didn't they just let me die? I'm dying anyway!" Latricia cried, prompting the Marshal on duty to peep in and check on her well-being.

The Marshal didn't interrupt her moment of sorrow. He simply observed her through the small square window in the center of the door, then sat back down to resume reading his newspaper.

****

Meanwhile, Sherman sat at his desk, skimming a copy of the latest report Internal Affairs had delivered to his captain. His desk phone rang, and he answered on the second ring. The call was from the forensic lab in reference to the evidence collected at Pig's house. He immediately rushed to the lab.

"Sherman, we have some astounding results for you. The evidence shows the female victim engaged in oral sex with the male victim," the female forensic technician said.

"Doc, that's a little too much useless information, don't you think? You could've spared me that thought."

"If you would let me finish, as I was saying, the female victim had small traces of semen under her tongue. I have conducted a deoxyribonucleic acid test—"

"In English, Doc!" Sherman said.

"The male victim's DNA matches the semen found her mouth. But we found more semen on the side of her cheek, and it does not match your chubby friend."

Sherman's eyes widened. "Wait a minute. Are you telling me the suspect left DNA?"

"Better, he left a match. The DNA goes back to a rape suspect who eluded prosecution when the victim recanted her story, admitting she lied. But, as with all suspects, his DNA was kept on file, giving you your prime suspect. Marcus Robertson."

"Thanks, Doc. What would I do without you?" Sherman gave her a kiss on the forehead.

Sherman returned to his desk, and quickly typed the suspect's name. A mug shot appeared on the computer monitor.

"Marcus Robertson, 5'8", 145 pounds, and one extensive rap sheet. Goes by the alias Peanut," Sherman mumbled to himself, then read Peanut's criminal history. "What do we have here? Currently incarcerated at Dade County Jail."

Sherman called Menendez and relayed the new information. Overcome with excitement, Menendez rushed to Sherman's cubicle.

"What are we waiting for? Let's go get 'em," Menendez said, dangling the car keys.

Sherman logged off his computer, and they headed to the County Jail. By the time they made it there, both Sherman and Menendez were full of anticipation. Sherman approach the front desk and flashed his credentials to the duty officer. He told her what their business was and gave her Peanut's name. Sherman rapidly tapped his fingers on the desk, waiting for her to give him Peanut's whereabouts.

"Ahhh… No wonder I couldn't find him. I'm sorry, Detective. Marcus Robertson was released a couple of days ago."

"Are you sure?" Sherman asked.

"Positive," she replied, then twisted the monitor around. "See for yourself. He was released on bond the tenth of this month."

"The tenth! Menendez, that's the same day Jarvis was murdered."

"Now that's original. This guy makes bond and commits a double murder hours after he's released. Sounds like ol' Marcus had a score to settle," Menendez speculated. "Sherman, I could be wrong, but this just doesn't feel right. What bothers me is the fact that Jarvis never mentioned Marcus's name to us, nor was Jarvis responsible for his incarceration, so why go after him so vengeful?"

"We can't always connect all the dots, but we can follow the evidence, and it leads to this guy. When we find him, you can ask him." Sherman turned his attention back to the duty officer. "Do you have an address for Marcus?"

The duty officer typed a few keys, then nodded and gave Sherman the address of Peanut's mother's house.

"Well, that's a start. But, before we put all our eggs in one basket, can you tell us which bonding company he used?" Sherman asked her.

When they arrived at Helping Hand Bail Bondsmen Inc., they walked in and shook hands with the company's bounty hunter and part-owner, Big Jim

Big Jim stood six-seven and weighed 290 pounds. He was a former UFC fighter who retired after his arm was broken when he stubbornly refused to tap out. A year into retirement, he used most of his prize money to become a partner in the bonding company.

“I didn’t do it; I swear to God I was home last night.” Big Jim put his hands in the air. ‘Hey, Sherman, you still hanging with this Mexican?”

“I’m Cuban, you washed-up loser,” Menendez humorously spat back.

Big Jim laughed, then clapped his hands. “OK, what can I do for you fellas?”

“A few days ago, March tenth to be exact, your company bailed out a Marcus Robertson, a.k.a. Peanut. We have evidence linking him to a double murder. We just went to the county jail hoping to interrogate him, then discovered he was released through you guys. We’re gonna need all the addresses he used for references.”

“That’ll be no problem. Just let me go get his file,” Big Jim said, walking off. It took him a few seconds to search through the file cabinet and retrieve Peanut’s folder. He called Sherman and Menendez over to his desk to review Peanut’s paperwork.

Sherman chose not to sit; he stood next to the edge of Big Jim's desk reading the file. “Marcus’s mother is the one who paid his bond. Nothing unusual there,” Sherman said, closing the folder. “Well, it looks like his mother’s residence is our next stop.”

As Sherman and Menendez were heading towards the exit, Big Jim said. “Hey, Sherman, you guys gonna question him or arrest him?”

“An arrest warrant hasn’t been issued yet. And if we reach Marcus and he has a logical explanation, which I strongly doubt he do, then we’re back to ground zero. But I’m following my gut on this one, and, once we catch up with Mr. Marcus Robertson, he’ll be charged, then convicted for murder.”

“Makes no difference to me. If you guys do arrest him, I don’t have to worry about him skipping bail,” Big Jim said.

Sherman thanked Big Jim for his assistance. Menendez tapped on the wall three times, demonstrating what Big Jim should have done before sustaining his career-ending injury. After leaving Helping Hand Bondsmen, they drove to Peanut’s mother’s house.

The residence was located in the Parkway neighborhood. The home was in desperate need of major renovations. Sherman looked at the peeling paint on the exterior and the non-operational Ford Tempo that appeared to be sinking into the ground, under a large mango tree. As they knocked on the front door, Sherman kept his eyes trained on the peephole, concentrating to see any movement on the opposite side of the door.

The clear white reflection vanished from the peephole, immediately followed by a question.

What the hell y'all want?"

"We're the police, ma'am. We need to have a word with you pertaining to your son Marcus."

Peanut's mother opened the door, looking more like his older sister than his biological mother. At thirty-five, 5'7", firm and dressed in a mini-skirt as if she was in her late teens, it was hard to believe that she had an 18-year-old son.

"Sorry to bother you, ma'am. I'm Detective Sherman, and this is my partner, Detective Menendez. Is your son Marcus Robertson home?"

"I haven't seen dat boy in a couple of days. What y'all want him fo' anyway?"

"Marcus is a person of interest in a double murder we're investigating."

"DOUBLE MURDER!" she yelled, appalled. "My son just got out of jail da other day. Y'all got the wrong person. My son don't know nothing 'bout no murder!"

"Ma'am, we're aware of the time Marcus has been in jail. We're also aware that you posted his bail the same day the murders were committed. It's imperative that we speak with Marcus. It's in his best interest that he finds us before we find him. Things may not turn out good if that happens."

"Did you just make a threat on my son's life?"

"Oh, no, ma'am. But, as his mother, I hope you make the right choice for you son."

"Well, I can't help you. Like I said, I haven't seen my son since the day he got out. He didn't stay here ten minutes before he was gone again."

"Did he say where he was going?"

"I ain't ask and he ain't say."

"Alright, ma'am. Here's my card. If Marcus calls or comes back home, advise him it is urgent for him to get in contact with me. If he chooses not to, then, for his sakes, I hope you do."

"For his sakes! What's dat, another threat?" she asked with her hands on her hips.

"You have a good day, ma'am, and think about it," Sherman said, frustrated.

As they drove off, Menendez inquired what their next move was.

"C'mon Sherman, run me by the station, so I can put together a warrant. It's time to get this dirt bag off the streets."

"You're right, and, while you're handling the warrant, I'm gonna try and locate Victoria Cole. She needs to positively identify Curtis Hayes as the shooter."

Sherman repeatedly called the house phone at Victoria's duplex. He even drove to the duplex and was quickly disappointed. There were no signs of Victoria. Still, he stood on the porch, called the number again, and listened as the phone simply rang.

As with all of Victoria's visitors, Mrs., Knowles watched Sherman's every move from her kitchen window until he returned in his vehicle and drove away.

Once he returned to the station to pick Menendez up, Sherman explained he'd had no luck finding Victoria.

"Don't worry, we'll find her," Menendez said, waving an arrest warrant. "What do you say about a full-fledged manhunt for Marcus?"

Sherman glared at Menendez and said three words.

"Let's do it."

****

Driving another rental, Tank, Crunch and Peanut passed Diva's and Don's for the fifth time. Peanut had asked around and learned about Victoria's salon. After learning the address, Tank decided to scope the salon to establish a plan. The salon was open, so they patiently waited for Victoria's SUV to arrive, but it never did. Tank even called inside and was told Victoria was not in.

"Dat bitch still ain't come to work. I don't think she working today. The salon opens in the morning. We'll come back then," Tank suggested.

"Yo, Tank, drive by dat muthafucka Black's crib. I wanna check something out," Crunch said, rubbing his forearm.

"Nah, now is not da time to handle dat shit. You know dat's a rookie move. Personal beef always comes after business. We ain't putting nothing in front of our priorities. And right now, I don't know nothing more important than finding dat bitch Victoria."

Crunch heard what Tank was saying, but he wished he'd been driving; then there would have been no way Tank could have stopped him from passing Black's house. Yet now, to prevent a no-win battle with his friend, Crunch sat back thinking on what he'd do the moment he met with Black again.

****

*Ring... Ring...* The telephone suddenly rang.

"Sherman here."

"How's it going, Sherman? You ready to pay your debt?" Finzi said.

"Not really, but nonetheless what can I do for you?"

"It has come to my attention that you've been working a case involving a major drug suspect we have in custody, by the name of Victoria Cole."

Sherman dropped his pen on his desk. "A major drug suspect! Finzi, don't tell me the D.E.A. is now desperate enough to arrest a single mother whose only crime is being related to a drug dealer."

"Come again?" Finzi replied.

"Were you guys investigating her brother?"

"No, we're investigating her, but I do know about her brother, and he was small-time compared to her."

"Well, I don't know where you got your information from, but I can assure you, Victoria Cole is definitely not a major drug dealer."

"Obliviously we can't be talking about the same person. The Victoria Cole I have in custody has statements wrote on her, and one of our registered C.I.'s gave us a detailed debriefing on her involvement in the drug trade. I'm expecting any minute for her to start cooperating," Finzi told Sherman.

"So, Finzi, what is it actually you need my help with?"

"Securing a conviction, for start, but apparently you got a soft spot for this drug dealer."

"Finzi, that girl's been through hell. Her only sibling was murdered, her youngest child nearly lost his life, and I still have not brought her any justice. And now the one thing you want me to do is to help you get her a prison sentence? You sure know how to pick a favor," Sherman said, with no remorse.

"Look, Sherman, all I need to know is, have you noticed anything suspicious at her residence?"

Sherman did not have to think long. The second Finzi asked his question, it triggered thoughts of the moment he smelt the heavy cocaine scent inside the duplex.

"No!" Sherman lied. He no longer wanted to play games with Finzi. Being a senior detective, Sherman understood Finzi was doing what law enforcement called a fishing expedition. "Finzi, let me tell you something. The only thing I saw was a young woman doing her best to cope with the traumatic events of the gruesome night her brother was murdered and her child shot. I am willing to put the relatively small amount of information I have on record, if need be."

"Jesus, Sherman, what happened to a little professional courtesy?"

"What happen to arresting the real problem, instead of targeting single mothers whose lives are already hard enough? Finzi, you've sunk to an all-time low. When you need help moving a sofa or need a ride, let me know. Until then, don't ask me for any favors." Sherman slammed the phone on its base. After he took a moment to think, things finally made sense. "Damn! No wonder I couldn't find her."

Sherman drifted into a temporary daze. He stared at his wall, pondering what Victoria could have possibly done to get herself in such a predicament. Snapping back to reality, he sat up and logged onto the D.E.A. database to review Victoria's charges.

"WHAT THE HELL! Conspiracy to distribute five kilos or more, conspiracy to distribute 50 grams or more of cocaine base, and possession of illegal firearms. This is ridiculous. Finzi oughta be ashamed of himself," Sherman said out loud.

While Sherman was focusing on Victoria's charges, Menendez approached his desk, noticing Victoria's mug shot on Sherman's monitor.

"Is that—?"

"Yeah, it's her," Sherman said, cutting Menendez's question short.

"Well, fill me in later. Right now we gotta roll. Big Jim left a message to call him, so I did. He told me he did a follow-up on Marcus and went out to his mother's house, and, sure enough, Marcus was there briefly with another guy. Now, here's where things get interesting. Guess who the other guy was."

"I'm really not in a guessing mood."

"I faxed Big Jim a photo of Tank and Crunch, and it turns out Marcus and Crunch roll together. He said the other guy was definitely Crunch."

"So, do you got the warrants?"

"Signed and ready to execute. I've passed out copies of Marcus's mug shot to a few of the boys. The only thing left to do now is get our asses in the car and arrest this garbage."

"I guess it's time to take out the trash." Sherman said, chambering a round in his firearm.

# Chapter 20

One o'clock the following Tuesday.

Victoria was seated in the Federal Courthouse, shackled and listening to the U.S. Attorney describe her as a monster. She could not believe a total stranger could say such horrible things about her with such conviction.

"…And furthermore, your Honor, in a separate matter, Ms. Cole placed her children in harm's way by keeping them in a known drug house, causing one of the children to be put in a position where the child was left clinging to life after becoming the poor victim of a drug-related shooting."

"THAT'S A LIE!" Victoria yelled.

"Order… Order…! Ms. Cole, this is a courtroom. You may not simply cause a disturbance at your convenience," The judge said. "If you have anything to say, channel it through your attorney."

Victoria looked at her court-appointed attorney and chose to say nothing further.

"Your Honor, please excuse my client. It's just that these absurd allegations have no merit. Yet the government continues to suggest to the court that my client is the next kingpin. Defense pleads with the court for a lenient bond. Ms. Cole's kids need her. She is not a flight risk, and she's also a first-time offender. She has a reputable business to run, and, above all, she's innocent of these superficial charges."

"If that is all, counselor, and the government has nothing further, bail is set at $200,000. This court is adjourned." The judge banged his mallet.

Victoria was led out of the courtroom. Outside in the corridor, as the U.S. Marshals walked her to the elevator, she noticed Finzi in a heated discussion with Sherman. They both stopped talking as Victoria was led passed, Sherman's only gesture was a shake of his head, showing Victoria an expression of disappointment.

****

Earlier in the same courtroom, Black had been set a $350,000 bond. After his mother put up his house for collateral and 15% cash with a bonding company, he anxiously waited to hear his name called. Pacing back and forth, even with his federal case pending, Black's sole focus was finding Peanut. The moment he got released, he planned to continue his quest of vengeance.

Black and Jay were in the same cell block. Bond was denied for Jay due to an attempted murder charge pending in Macon, Georgia. It hadn't been hard for Finzi to persuade Country to reap the benefits of being the first to cooperate. By the time Finzi finished with Country, there was a strong probability that Jay would never see the streets again.

Jay saw Black pacing, then walked over to him.

"Dis shit fuck up. You know what my pussy ass cousin said? Country told my brother he don't love me enough to do time for me. This muthafucka gon' say some shit like that when I shot dem fools in Georgia over him. Fuck it, I ain't got shit to lose, I'ma still go to trial. What about you?"

"Trial! Fuck, no! These folks got dudes on standby, ready to testify to whatever the prosecutor want them to say. People you ain't see in five years liable to be trying to get a time cut off you..."

The C.O. shouted Black's legal name and told him to pack up. Black snatched his sheets and blanket off the bed, stuffing them in his net bag. Jay walked with Black to the door, they gave each other dap, and Black followed the C.O., never looking back.

Finally, back in the comfort of his own home, Black looked around at the mess left by the task force. He went into his bedroom and couldn't believe what a shamble it was left in. He walked to the foot of his bed and smirked because the carpet underneath was intact. Despite the task force's vigorous search for evidence, they had overlooked the floor safe, which contained his money and four kilos.

It was the sight of the four kilos that brought Black to the conclusion it was time to call Diaz. He dug in his dirty clothes, found the card Diaz's associate had given him, and dialed the number.

"Hey, I need to talk to Diaz!"

"This is Ramon. Can I help you?"

"Hell, naw! You can't help me with shit. Put Diaz on the phone."

"I am sorry. Señor Diaz is unavailable," Ramon said, then paused. "Wait a minute. Is this Black?"

"Are you dat muthafucka dat came to my house? 'Cause some fucked up shit went down!"

"Is there a problem with the merchandise?"

"Man, look! I ain't got time to talk to da help. Somebody set me up, and yo ass could've been the one behind dat shit!"

"Ha... Ha... Ha... You African Americans are so funny. I do many things, but stealing isn't one of them."

"Right now, I ain't tryin to hear shit you gotta say. Matter fact, I believe you was behind it, and, if I find out you did, I'm coming to see you, and you won't see me coming."

"Black, declaring war with me is not wise."

"Thinking I'm something to fuck wit' ain't neither! See you when I see you!" Black barked, ending their discussion.

****

Victoria blinked as her eyes adjusted to the rays of the sun. She stepped out of the F.D.C. relieved to know that Mrs. Knowles had come through once again for her. P-Rock and Victor were watching from the backseat as their mother came out of the building. When she got close to the car, Victor ran into her arms.

"Hey, mama little man!" She greeted Victor with much excitement, wrapping him in her arms. "I missed y'all so much."

"Ma, why were you in jail?" P-Rock bluntly asked.

Victoria was going to wait and explain everything once they got home, but with P-Rock's unexpected inquiry, she laid everything out once they had all climbed into the car.

As they stopped at a red traffic light, Mrs. Knowles said, "Victoria, you know your business is your business, but, chile, it will be devastating on these children if something was to happen to you. Right now ain't the time to think about yourself. Think about yo kids' future, or what their lives would be like wit' out you in it."

"Mrs. Knowles, my life revolves around my kids. Every single move I make is to prevent them from having to struggle like I did."

"Lord knows what kinda trouble lies ahead. Do you honestly feel like you have secured their future?"

Victoria held her hand up. "Mrs. Knowles, please, not right now. This is not a good time for a lecture. There is just too much on my mind. I appreciate everything you've done for me, just please not now." Victoria put her left hand to her forehead. "Mrs. Knowles, can you swing me by the salon?"

"Sure," Mrs. Knowles answered, and said no more as she headed to the salon.

When Mrs. Knowles pulled into Diva's and Don's parking lot, Victoria noticed Anna's car and a few regular customers' vehicles. She left P-Rock and Victor in the car with Mrs. Knowles. When she walked into the salon, almost immediately all eyes were on her. She simply waved to all the clients in the waiting area as she headed into the back.

As soon as Victoria stepped into the work area, Anna stopped talking mid-sentence and rushed over, giving Victoria a hug.

"Oh my god… I'm so glad you're alright. Do you need me to do anything?"

"No, I'm fine. I need to talk to you."

Anna nodded, and they causally strolled out of everyone's presence. Victoria could feel the energy of everyone's eyes boring into the back of her head. Feeling both embarrassed and irritated, she remained quiet and simply walked into her office and closed the door.

"Victoria, an agent came by here yesterday and delivered this envelope," Anna quickly explained, then walked to the top desk drawer to retrieve the envelope. "Here you go."

Victoria ripped it open, and read the contents, then flung the letter into the air.

"Damn! The government has put a lien on the building."

"What! Can they just do that?"

"They did dat. Anna, did you tell yo grandfather I got arrested?"

"Of course. They tried to arrest him the same day. He's out of their reach now. He will be glad to know you're out."

"Tell him to call me on your phone," Victoria said.

"No problem." Anna reached into her pocket and handed Victoria her phone.

"Thanks, Anna. I got my kids outside. I gotta get home. Call me."

Victoria walked out her office, giving everyone a meaningless wave, and stood in the salon entrance doorway. She watched as the unique Miami weather produced one of its usual 15-minute sunshowers. She waited a few seconds, then dashed to the car. Jumping back in the passenger seat, Victoria grabbed a brown towel Mrs. Knowles had on the front seat and dried her hair. She bent down, drying her neck, as Mrs. Knowles pulled into traffic.

****

"I'm tellin y'all, dat wuz her," Peanut said, watching the taillights as the car drove down Highway 441.

"How da hell you know? Dat bitch had her head down," Tank said, as he too looked at the receding car.

"A'ight, follow dem. I bet dat's her."

"I know how she look, and dat bitch didn't look like her. I'm not about to follow dat raggedy ass Hyundai. If she getting money like you say, what da fuck she riding in that muthafucka for? We gon' wait right here, and wait fo' dat Lexus to show up. And if it don't, we do the same thing tomorrow."

****

Black patiently waited for Diaz's call. One loyal customer after another called his phone trying to re-up, but handling business was not on his agenda. He looked at his watch and called his brother-in-law.

"We still good, right?" Black asked, referring to his brother-in-law's Monte Carlo.

"Hell, yeah, we good, fam. C'mon and swing by. I just got off from work."

Black told him he was on his way. He hopped on his bike and sped to his sister and brother-in-law's house. He drove up the sidewalk, parking on the porch.

Black's sister stormed out the door. "Boy, why you park that thing right there, making all that damn noise!"

"Gurl, quit trippin. Yo man wanna hold my bike. Tell him where to park it."

She frowned. "Oh, really? Where he think he going on that thing?"

Black's sister bolted back inside faster than she'd come out. Black could hear her arguing with her husband. A few seconds later, his brother-in-law stepped out the door and tossed him his car keys, and Black tossed the keys to his bike. As he walked towards the Monte Carlo, Black could hear his sister still raising hell. Now in a discreet vehicle, Black returned home, ready to go hunting. He checked the time again, then went into his backyard, lifted the doghouse, and pulled out a black trash bag with his .223 sniper rifle inside. When he got arrested, his twin Glocks had been seized, so earlier Black had had to buy a hot 9mm Browning semi-automatic. With his rifle under his arm and the nine at his waist, Black hopped back into the Monte Carlo. He laid the rifle on the backseat and covered it with a Miami Hurricanes jacket his brother-in-law had left in the car. After double-checking whether a round was chambered in the Browning, Black headed to the house of the one person who could get in contact with Peanut.

"Knock…knock…"

"Hello, Ms. Robertson."

"Hey, Black. I haven't seen you in a while. C'mon in," Peanut's mom flirtatiously said, stepping to the side.

Black walked inside, quickly scanning the living room for Peanut. "Ms. Robertson, have you seen Peanut today?" I got some money I promised him." He pulled out five hundred dollars.

Ms. Roberson's eyes were glued to the money, and they stuck to the wad as he put it back in his pocket. "Peanut came by yesterday. I told him da police came here looking fo' his ass. He went in his room and got some clothes. Just when he was walking out the door, he bumped into a big ass white guy from the bonding company. I don't know what they talked about, but Peanut got back in the car with some guy. Dat was the last time I seen him."

"Well, can you call him and tell 'em to come home? I wanna be here and give him the money myself. And do me a favor, don't tell him I'm here. I wanna surprise him. I know he think I forgot about 'em."

"OK, I do dat fo' you, Black." She smiled provocatively. "I am kinda lonely here all day by myself."

Peanut's mom had always been infatuated with Black's swagger. For years, she'd made several attempts to come on to Black; unfortunately, each of her advances had been timed wrong and interrupted by Peanut. Now she finally had Black the way she wanted, all to herself. She didn't want history to repeat itself, so, instead of calling Peanut like she said she would, she pretended to call and told Black he did not answer.

From the kitchen, she asked, "Black, are you hungry?"

"I was hoping you'll give me something to eat," he said, licking his lips, doing his best LL Cool J impersonation.

Peanut's mom was instantly turned on. "Look at you, acting like you know how to use dat tongue."

"Ms. Robertson…"

"Black, please quit making me feel old. Call me Erica. I'm only a few years older than you." She sat down on the sofa.

"A'ight, Erica. You said another guy was with Peanut. What did he look like?"

"I don't really know. He never got out the car. You know, Black, you can sit down next to me. I'm not gon' bite you, unless you want me to."

Black moved closer to the sofa. He didn't sit down; instead, he stood in front of her, looking into her eyes. "Actually, I'm into biting… licking… and sucking."

Black laid his charm on, telling Erica the right things to get her nipples aroused and panties wet. He stepped closer and grabbed her hand, gently rubbing circles on the back of her hand.

"Ummmm…! Boy, you betta stop before you start something you can't finish," she whispered in a seductive warning.

Finally, he sat on the sofa next to her. He wrapped his arms around her waist, delivering gentle kisses to her earlobe. Unable to resist, she let out a sensual moan. Black's true intentions were not to have sex with her; he merely wanted her open enough to unknowingly assist in his plan. What he didn't predict was how aggressive she would become.

She stared into his eyes. Passion circulated through her veins as she watched his crotch rise. She ran her hand lightly up his thigh until she felt his manhood pulsating. With pure lust controlling her actions, Erica massaged his shaft, feeling Black's full erection through his R.L. jeans.

"I wanna taste it," she said, tugging on his zipper.

Black assisted her with the zipper on his jeans. Caught up in the moment, he pulled his shaft out and watched as her lips wrapped around it and disappeared down her throat. He tilted his head back as she gently massaged his testicles. Ready to release his hot load, Black palmed the back of her head, firmly gripping her hair to make sure she didn't lose a drop of his protein.

"Ummm… You must drink a lot of pineapple juice, 'cause you taste too sweet." She smacked her lips, still holding his shaft. "Feel like my friend is getting soft. Mama can fix dat."

Black took extraordinary pleasure cumming in Erica's mouth. In his mind, it was the ultimate disrespect to Peanut, and would also be the last thing he told him before putting three bullets in his head.

"Hang on a sec, Erica. I need to handle some business. I'll be back in 20 minutes, I promise," Black lied. "If Peanut call before I get back, don't tell him I came by. I wanna surprise him."

"You just hurry back," she said, patting Black on his ass.

Thirty minutes passed, then an hour, and another. Erica kept staring out her bedroom window, hoping to see Black pull into the driveway. Three hours passed before it actually sank in that, to her disappointment, Black was not returning. The moment they'd shared was now a memory. Accepting the reality, Erica laid back in her bed and fantasized about the next time she would be back in Black's arms.

In the meantime, the night air filled Black's lungs as he prepared to get in position. Three houses down from Erica's, Black climbed an enormous mango tree with his .223 rifle. Approximately sixteen feet up, he found the perfect branch, giving him an excellent vantage point. Although comfort was impossible, another branch did offer a little back support. He unsnapped the lens cover of the rifle scope, aimed, and put Peanut's mom's house in the crosshairs.

Black patiently waited in the tree, tracking every car that passed. As the hours of the night closed in on dawn, Black's spot became irritatingly uncomfortable. No matter which way he positioned his body, soreness started to take its toll. But, like a professional assassin, he endured whatever life threw his way.

Another hour ticked away. Black had the will and patience to tolerate the stationary positioning needed for this type of attack, but not the necessary supplies. Cars began passing more frequently. There was now less than an hour before the sun would rise. Black considered staying in the tree another hour; however, there was the risk of a nosey neighbor spotting him and calling the cops. So, without further delay, he decided to climb down while darkness was still on his side.

Black dangled his feet from the tree and tried to jump down, but the strap on his rifle got caught on a branch. Suddenly, a pair of headlights came up the street. Unable to jump without his rifle,

Black broke the branch and crashed to the ground. The approaching car came to a tire-screeching stop. Black squinted his eyes, trying to see past the bright headlights. Unable to tell if the car was driven by a regular motorist or a police officer, he concealed his rifle behind the bark of the mango tree. With his Browning nine-millimeter snug against his back, Black stood his ground, waiting for the vehicle to pass or make its next move. It was impossible to see through the windshield, and, by the time Black realized the windows were rolling down, it was too late.

Multiple rounds were fired from the driver's and passenger sides of the car. The assailant's vehicle sped off in reverse, did a remarkable three-point turn, and made a clean getaway without any witnesses.

Black was on the ground, shot but not fatally wounded. He'd been hit three times, twice in the left leg, once in the right shoulder. He managed to pull himself painfully off the ground, using his rifle as a crutch. The porch lights came on at the house Black was in front of. He limped faster to the Monte Carlo, leaving a trail of blood.

"Ahhh..." Black cried out in pain as he plopped down in the driver seat.

His left leg was completely numb. Black brought the supercharged engine to life. More porch lights came on, and he mashed the gas pedal. He glanced at his leg and could see blood gushing out of his wounds. Though he needed to take himself to the hospital, instead he sped home to stash his guns. Despite the amount of blood he lost, he remained conscious. Almost home and determined to stay alert, Black gunned the accelerator and accidentally crashed into his mailbox. He parked diagonally in his driveway.

Slowly opening the car door, Black fell out, landing directly on his wounded shoulder. He let out an excruciated scream. The agony grew unbearable as he lay on his back. Fatigued and dizzy, Black began wishing someone would come to his aid. His eyelids were becoming too heavy to keep open. His vision blurred, but just as his eyes were closing, his prayers were answered.

Help arrived. Black was hoisted off the ground. His blurred vision made it impossible to focus on the man who helped him into his house.

"Thank you… Thank you…" Black said, out of breath and through his pain.

Placed on his Italian leather sectional, Black squirmed as his shoulder hit the cushion. He rubbed his left hand above the bullet wounds on his leg. He then felt the bulge of his house keys in his pocket. Though his awareness had been slack, Black's attention was suddenly drawn to the fact his front door had been unlocked.

"How da fuck my door get open?" Black asked.

His question landed on deaf ears. The man that helped Black inside was unresponsive to his question. He simply stood behind Black and put one hand on his shoulder.

Black inhaled his last breath as he looked up, and locked eyes with the same man that dropped off the potato sacks. Just as Black was about to say something, he felt the cold steel of a razor go across his throat.

# Chapter 21

"I know I hit Black at least five times!" Peanut exaggerated to Tank back at the rooming house.

Since Black had literally fallen out a tree, Peanut's head had been gassed up. He talked non-stop about seeing his bullets penetrate Black's chest.

"Damn, Jitt, you bust on ya ol' homeboy like dat?" Tank asked, grinning.

"Fuck dat, I'm on a paper chase. If you ain't helping me eat, then you food," Peanut replied, real cocky.

Tank laughed, then said, "Jitt, you hanging around dis muthafucka too long. You starting to sound like him." Tank nodded at Crunch. "Keep dat heart, 'cause when we roll up in ol' gurl spot, you gon' need it."

"Shit… Like I said, I'm down fo' whatever until my heart stop."

For the rest of the night, Tank and his crew followed their normal routine: they rolled boonk joints and got high. The room could easily have been mistaken for being on fire, from the amount of smoke that loomed in the air. Once their smoke feast was over, one by one they fell asleep. A couple of hours later, Tank was wakened by the rays of the sun shining through the window. He hopped up and realized they'd overslept. The plan had been to be at Diva's and Don's when it opened, but they were an hour behind.

"Fuck!" Tank yelled, waking Crunch and Peanut. He grabbed his cell phone and dialed a number. "Shhh… Y'all hold it down."

"Good morning, Diva's & Don's."

"Yeah, is Victoria in?" Tank asked.

"Yes, she is. Can I ask who's calling?"

"I'm selling movies, CDs, and…"

"Sorry no soliciting."

"Oh, a'ight." Tank ended the call. "Yo, let's ride. She da're. Crunch, remember, when we get da're, wait on Jitt to lay da witnesses down. Then find dat bitch and bring her ass out back. I'm gon' tie her up, throw her ass in da trunk, then we gon' get da fuck out of da're and see if she's a diva with a don money."

****

Victoria sat in her office with the door closed all day. Too emotionally distraught to work properly, she cancelled all her appointments for the entire week. Five minutes earlier, her court-appointed attorney had explained that the government's case against her was strong. Her only option to avoid spending twenty years or more in prison was to cooperate and assist in securing a conviction on Diaz.

Victoria had never smoked a cigarette in her life, but, due to the stress and pressure of her dilemma, she'd started doing several things that deviated from her norm. Trying to ease her mind the night before, Victoria had gone out to the club with Anna and Kim. After passing her limit on drinks, she'd found herself having to live with the regret of a one-night stand with a guy who name she couldn't remember.

With a Newport in hand, Victoria shook her head at what she'd done, and at the fact she'd slapped P-Rock this morning for referring to one of his classmates as a stanking bitch. Victoria took a drag on the Newport and rode her emotional rollercoaster with no direction or destination. A knock on the door snapped her back to reality.

"Come in," Victoria shouted.

Anna entered Victoria's office, noticing the lit cigarette. Without commenting on Victoria's new habit, Anna told her she had two visitors outside.

Victoria tapped ash into the ashtray. "Whoever it is, tell 'em I'm not here."

"Sorry, I can't do that."

Victoria exhaled a cloud of smoke. "Why not?"

"Because I already told them you were here. It's the police."

"I ain't got shit to say to da police. Tell them to talk wit' my lawyer."

Out in the lobby, Sherman and Menendez stood in front of the receptionist desk, waiting to speak with Victoria. Sherman still needed her to positively I.D. Crunch as the suspect that had shot her child. Also, he had to give her some troubling news.

Anna returned in the lobby and relayed Victoria's blunt message. Sherman refused to leave without speaking with Victoria. He took it upon himself to storm through the door Anna had come through. He walked to the work area and looked around at the employees and customers. Then he turned and caught a glimpse of Victoria through her office window. Without knocking, he barged right inside.

"Look, Ms. Cole, I'm not here to harass you, and I'm not going through no damn attorney to say what I gotta say. I'm trying to give you justice for what happen to your brother and child. Because you made yourself impossible to reach, we had to release one of the suspects." Sherman pulled Crunch's mug shot from the folder under his arm. He slammed the photo onto her desk. "Is this the guy that shot your child?"

Victoria immediately recognized Crunch's face and confirmed with a nod of her head.

Sherman raised his fist in triumph. "We're gonna get his ass off the street today. Thank you. Now, before I leave, I'm not sure if you've heard already, but one of your co-defendants was found dead in his home. He was known in the streets as Black."

Victoria hands sprung over her mouth.

"He was found this morning by his brother-in-law, and his murder was not a robbery gone wrong. This was a professional hit. He was shot several times, and had his throat sliced. Robbery is excluded as motive because he had $2,600 still in his pocket. They found dried blood in his garage. It is believed to have been there several days. His murder could have been a retaliation for whatever took place in that garage. Do you know anything about that?"

Victoria was speechless. Tears rolled down her cheeks.

"I know you and Black were involved in illegal activities. Now, what I don't know, and hopefully you will shed some light on, is who did Black have beef with."

****

Tank drove pass Diva's & Don's confused. He scanned the parking lot, but there was no sign of Victoria's Lexus SUV. To cure his curiosity, Tank called the salon again.

"Diva's & Don's, how can I help you?" the receptionist said.

"I need to make an appointment with Victoria. Is she in?"

"Yes, she is, but I will need to take a message."

The call went dead after Tank received the information he needed.

"Y'all ready? Dat bitch up in da're. She must be pushing another whip. Peep game, you two go up in d'are. I'm gonna be parked right in the back. Jitt, you just make sure to have Crunch back. If anyone play hero, pop dey ass."

Tank dropped Crunch and Peanut off on the side of the salon. He then drove to the rear of the building.

In the lobby, Menendez was standing in the corner next to the aquarium, flipping through a Sports Illustrated magazine. He started reading the feature story about the beautiful swimsuit model on the cover. Sitting on the couch was three female customers; two were also reading magazines they'd got from the coffee table, and one was talking on her cell phone.

Menendez was so busy gawking at the swimsuit model, he was unaware of Crunch and Peanut strolling in the salon. Oblivious to Menendez's presence, Crunch walked around the receptionist desk, ignoring her inquiry about who he wanted to see. Peanut gazed across the couch at the three customers. Menendez raised his head just as Crunch opened the glass door behind the receptionist desk and stepped through. Menendez flung the magazine aside, unholstered his firearm, and began to follow Crunch. Until…

"All you muthafuckas get da fuck on the floor!" Peanut shouted, pulling out his massive .357 from underneath his shirt.

Everyone quickly did as Peanut ordered—all except Menendez. With his gun already drawn, Menendez double-tapped Peanut in the chest. The .357 sounded like a dumbbell hitting the floor, followed by Peanut's body. Drowning in his own blood with every breath, Peanut could only look at Menendez's feet as he ran over and kicked the .357 from his reach.

In the rear of the building, Crunch heard the gunshots, and so did everyone else back in the work area.

"Stay down!" Sherman yelled to Victoria, pulling his Glock 40 from his holster. He eased out of Victoria's office, crouching low, moving with his shoulder against the wall. He quickly glanced at the few employees and customers hiding behind whatever shelter they could find.

Crunch initially thought Peanut had started shooting prematurely, but when he rushed back through the glass door and saw Menendez standing over Peanut's body, he realized court was in session and it was time to plead his case. Menendez never saw him come from the rear. Crunch aimed his gun sideways and released five rounds into Menendez's back.

The three petrified customers screamed at the sight of Menendez's chest exploding, the bullets annihilating several vital organs.

Since joining Robbery-Homicide, Menendez had stopped wearing his bulletproof vest. As his body collapsed directly on top of Peanut's, Crunch walked over and stood next to it. Unsure whether Menendez was wearing a vest, Crunch fired two additional rounds into his head. Suddenly the glass door burst open. Crunch's reflexes spun him in the direction of the door. The moment he turned, Crunch looked right into the barrel of Sherman's gun.

*POP!*

Sherman said nothing, and gave Crunch no time to think of dropping his gun. He hit Crunch point blank in the forehead, killing him instantly.

Outside, in the rear of the salon, Tank heard shots. Sensing a bad vibe about the outcome, Tank dropped the gear into drive and sped around to the front of the building. He jammed on the brakes, barely avoiding two women running out of the salon. More people spilled out. Peering through the entrance into the chaotic scene, Tank could see Peanut's and Menendez's bodies. Having seen enough, he cruised out of the Diva's & Don's parking lot, never looking back.

Victoria was still in her office, too frightened to come out. The salon had fallen into an eerie silence. Tiptoeing, she opened her office door, peering in all directions before taking a step. She continued tiptoeing to the front of the salon, and, as she stepped through the glass door, she walked into a room of horror. She screamed at the top of her lungs at the sight of the three dead bodies.

Sherman was outside trying to gather witnesses when he heard Victoria scream. He raced back inside the salon, aiming his firearm.

"It's over, Ms. Cole," Sherman said, holstering his weapon. "C'mon outside with everyone else." He went to her side and placed his arm around her shoulder. Guiding her towards the door, he felt her body tense up as they passed Crunch's lifeless body.

Walking past Menendez's bullet-riddled body, Victoria stopped, seeing Peanut's body underneath.

"Do you recognize that suspect?" Sherman asked her.

She nodded. "He's the guy that broke in my house."

"Was he involved in your brother's death?"

"I… I don't know," she stuttered. "I'm sure the other guy is the one that shot my child."

Back outside with the rest of the crew, Anna saw Sherman walk out of the salon with Victoria. She rushed over and hugged Victoria. Sherman took his arm from around Victoria and carefully scanned the crowd in the parking lot. Unfortunately, there was no sign of the one person he was looking for.

"Damn..." He sighed in disappointment.

Police cruisers blocked Highway 441, the Metro-Dade PD had a helicopter in the sky, and, in the distance, sirens could be heard from the ambulance rapidly approaching. On their arrival, the paramedics stormed into the salon, pushing a stretcher. Their speed was in vain.

On his knees in tears, Sherman looked up at the medics with an expression that said it all: Menendez was dead on arrival. Nevertheless, Sherman was moved aside, and the medics tried to revive Menendez. Even after their failed efforts, since Menendez was a cop, his body was hoisted onto the stretcher, placed in the rear of the ambulance, and rushed away from the scene.

Metro-Dade investigators arrived on the scene. They walked under the crime scene tape, having full jurisdiction. The media arrived, swarming onto the scene in a frenzy. Cameramen and field reporters scrambled to broadcast exclusive details and video images of the suspects' bodies before the coroner removed them. After all the drama, if anyone had missed the grand opening of Diva's & Don's, or had simply never heard of the salon, by six o'clock, practically everyone in Dade and Broward County with a radio or television set had heard about the deadly shootout that left two suspects and one police officer dead.

The next morning during the police briefing, an all-out manhunt was initiated for Tank. Three local networks repeatedly interrupted their regularly scheduled programs to display Tank's mug shot. On the front page of both the Miami Herald and the Sun Sentinel was a photo of a younger Menendez, smiling after graduating from the police academy. Also, a small corner photo of Menendez's wife and two daughters crying.

Tank watched the news all night and morning, seeing the police spokesman stand at a podium, and say into several microphones that law enforcement would not rest until they had apprehended Tank. Without wasting another moment, Tank packed all the money and drugs they'd accumulated during their paper chase into a large black Nike gym bag. Before walking out the door, Tank turned and double-checked the room, making sure he'd left nothing before his departure from the States. Now, thanks to the coverage CNN had plastered across millions of television sets nationwide, Tank was quickly becoming one of the most recognizable faces in America. Ready to head for Canada, he grabbed his suitcase that concealed his AK-47, then strapped the gym bag to his back. Moving stealthily, Tank stuck his head out the door and looked both ways before exiting.

He threw his luggage in the trunk, hopped behind the wheel, and headed toward I-95 north. The morning traffic was congested as he drove through West Palm Beach. Even with the 5% tints on his windows, Tank drove with the seat leaned back to prevent detection. Eventually, the traffic thinned out, and Tank was able to drive the speed limit.

Tank reached North Florida without stopping. After almost five hours, and despite the fact the gas needle was on E, he drove until the ambercolored fuel light activated. He spotted a blue advertisement sign for Waffle House, Subway, and a B.P. gas station and got off the interstate. He stopped at a red light with the gas station to his right, and the very second his eyes rested on the parking lot, his heart skipped a beat. Two County Sheriff patrol cars were parked side by side next to the vacuum and air pump.

Though his car was literally riding on fumes, the minute the traffic light turned green, Tank drove straight and hopped back onto the interstate. Traveling another three miles, he came across a sign that read, "Snacks, Gas and Clean Bathrooms Only Six Miles Away." Hoping to preserve as much fuel as possible, Tank maintained a speed of 65 miles per hour. Now only two miles from the exit ramp, the car stalled. Tank was no longer riding on fumes; he was out of gas. He let the car cruise to a rolling stop. He turned the ignition switch, but the engine wouldn't start. Enraged with not only the car but himself, Tank jumped out and slammed the door with both hands. He walked towards the exit ramp. The temperature was ninety degrees, and it did not take long for Tank to start perspiring. Frustrated and uncommonly miserable, he made it to his destination, a secluded Exxon gas station.

Behind the counter was a young white male who studied Tank the moment he walked in. He wasn't aware that Tank was a wanted man; his suspicion was due more to fear of being alone in the store with a strange black man.

Tank paid the clerk no mind, and walked over to where the gas cans were sold. He picked up a two-gallon can and turned towards the clerk, whose heart trembled as Tank approached the counter. Tank handed the nervous clerk a twenty-dollar bill.

"Put the change on pump one," Tank said, then walked out the door.

Tank filled the gas can, then headed back. Finally returning to his car, he felt a sense of relief. Just as he began pouring in the gas, his relief turned into unease as a Florida Highway Patrolman pulled up behind his car. The vehicle's insignias identified it as a K-9 unit. The six-foot, 200-pound trooper resembled the actor Tommy Lee Jones.

'Good afternoon. Having a little car trouble?" the trooper said, immediately looking through the window at the interior of the car.

"No, sir. I just ran out of gas," Tank explained, hoping to get rid of the trooper.

The trooper glanced at Tank, then gazed back in the vehicle. "That's good. Glad to hear your car problems are minor. I-95 can be a dangerous highway. We've been having major problems with certain motorists trafficking drugs, guns and all sort of illegal contraband up and down this highway. You wouldn't happen to have any of those things in your vehicle, would you?"

"No, sir," Tank answered, regretting that his 9mm was under the driver's seat, while everything else the trooper had described could be found in the trunk.

"That's great. Then you wouldn't mind if I took a peep in your vehicle, just to make sure?'

"I was just stopped an hour ago, and, if you don't mind, I'm in a rush to pick up my girlfriend."

"Well, sir, under Florida law, I am allowed to walk my dog around your vehicle, and, if he alerts me that contraband is present, that'll give me probable cause to conduct a search of your vehicle."

As the trooper spoke with Tank, the same two county sheriffs from the B.P. gas station pulled onto the scene. Already perspiring from the heat, Tank had no control over the sweat that began heavily pouring down his face. The trooper greeted the sheriffs both with a handshake, then explained the situation. He asked the sheriffs to keep an eye on Tank while he retrieved his K-9. From the back of his squad car, the trooper released a large Belgian Malinois. He also grabbed a small toy clown that the dog used to chew on.

Returning to Tank's vehicle with his K-9 in tow, the trooper began conducting an exterior search. As soon as the K-9 swept his nose around the trunk, he sat down.

"Good boy! That's a good boy!" the trooper said, dropping the toy clown at the K-9's feet as his reward.

Tank watched as the K-9 sealed his fate, all for the pleasure of chewing on a toy. With limited options, Tank only saw two ways of escaping. Either unlock the car with the remote and hope he could reach his 9mm and shoot them before they shot him, or make a run for the woods. While the trooper was placing the K-9 back in his squad car, the sheriffs were busy staring at the trunk. Noting their lack of concentration, Tank bolted towards the woods. Hurtling over the four-foot barbwire fence, Tank sprinted through the trees. The sheriffs quickly gave chase, and the trooper grabbed his K-9 by the leash and followed.

Tank refused to let the two out-of-shape sheriffs apprehend him. He raced past trees with remarkable speed, ignoring the cuts and bruises from the sharp branches. Tank could hear the K-9 barking. He looked back to see how far behind the sheriffs were, but never stopped running. He could not see them, but the K-9's barks were getting louder and closer.

Running off his leash, the K-9 ran past the two sheriffs and had Tank in his sight.

Tank ran on, hoping to outrun fate. Pumping his legs as fast as he could, he finally saw a road 20 yards ahead. He ran faster than he had ever run in his entire life. With adrenaline fueling his determination, Tank reached the road, making a sliding stop.

Standing in the middle of the road was a police officer, who spotted Tank and immediately ran towards him.

"Get down on the ground!" the officer screamed, charging at Tank with his firearm aimed.

Tank backpedaled a few steps to retreat back into the woods and turned directly into the jaws of the K-9. The 85-pound Belgian Malinois tackled Tank to the ground, clamping down on his arm. The police officer, sheriffs, and trooper caught up and surrounded Tank, but allowed the K-9 to continue biting his arm. Once the K-9 released Tank's arm and went for his legs, the trooper restrained the dog while the officer put his knee in Tank's back and placed him in cuffs. More officers appeared, delivering a couple of unwarranted kicks; then there were high fives and smiles all around as they learned they'd apprehend the most wanted man in Miami.

****

Tank was taken to the Palm Coast Sheriff's Department. Though exhausted, he lay in a holding cell at emotional peace. As he relaxed with his feet propped up against the wall, and using his interlocked fingers as a pillow, his cell door open, and two D.E.A. agents from the Jacksonville office stepped in.

"Hey, seen you got a lot of people looking for you in Miami," the lead agent said. "What I can't understand is, what were you thinking riding around with all that money, drugs and firepower in your trunk. The friggin whole state of Florida looking for you, and your stupid ass run outta gas on the side of the road The more brazen you criminals get, the dumber you get. Those guys in Miami may need to go back and get retrained after letting your dumb ass get away. I hope you got yourself some pussy last night, because it will be the last piece you ever get."

Sherman could not persuade the State Attorney to automatically charge Tank in connection with Menendez's murder. At this early stage of the investigation, there just wasn't adequate evidence. Yet, when Sherman was notified of Tank's arrest, he immediately put in for Tank to be extradited. But because of the drugs and guns, the Feds had jurisdiction, and Sherman would have to wait until they were done with Tank before he got his turn. That small defeat didn't stop Sherman from arranging a face-to-face meeting.

The next morning, Sherman drove to Flagler County Jail. He hoped Tank wasn't going to exercise his Miranda rights and want his lawyer present. Sherman identified himself at the desk and was led to a room. He waited about 15 minutes, sitting at a table with four chairs around it. Then the door opened, and Tank was escorted in. He was dressed in an orange jumpsuit. He had shackles around his ankles and handcuffs on his wrists. He was seated across from Sherman.

Sherman looked at Tank with a cold hard stare, appearing to see into his soul.

"So how long did you think you could run before we caught you?"

Tank gave no reply; he merely looked at Sherman with the same cold stare. The only difference Tank's cold-hearted stare could be seen in the hatred in his eyes.

"You don't have to talk. Just sit there and listen. I know you were involved in the death of my partner. I also know you played a major role in a double murder and attempted murder of a toddler. You killed your own cousin, and, if you weren't stopped, you probably was going to kill your ex-girlfriend too, you sick sonofabitch. But we got you, and it's just a matter of time before you're strapped down on a table, preparing to receive lethal injection. So please do me a favor and keep that same weak ass stare on your face. I'm sure the jury will find it real intimidating, you fucking faggot!" Sherman taunted, trying to goad a reaction out of Tank.

Tank took a deep breath and exhaled as if he was bored. "Are you done?"

"Far from it, but what's left of your pathetic life is, just like your friend. I wish you could've seen the look in his eyes when I put a bullet in his brain. It was priceless. Too bad you missed it. But one thing you won't miss is me sitting in the front row the day of your execution. I'll be right there, watching that syringe get injected into your vein," Sherman said in a calm tone.

Tank smiled. "You know what? I got a few things to say too. Remember you and the wetback was parked at my dog crib? Both of you muthafuckas lives were in my hand. When I pulled up and blocked y'all in, all I had to do was squeeze. My only regret is not pulling the trigger. You should be thanking me for sparing you and yo' partner's lives. Too bad he still ate a bullet like yo wife eat a dick," he boldly said, then spat on the floor.

Sherman's smirk disappeared after Tank's comment. He suddenly, lunged across the table, wrapping both hands around Tank's neck. He squeezed so hard, Tank couldn't even scream.

The correction officers standing outside the door heard the commotion and burst inside the room. They had to wrestle Sherman off Tank.

"Uggh… peeew…" Tank brought up all the mucus he could and hawked it in Sherman's face. "Fuck you!"

Sherman lunged for Tank again, but was quickly restrained by the correction officers. Tank was rushed out the room, and then Sherman was released. He knew he would be reprimanded, but he didn't care. Sherman pounded his fist on the wall and kicked his chair clear across the room.

Several months later, Tank pled guilty to possession with intent to distribute five or more kilograms of cocaine, and due to his criminal history, he was charged as an armed career criminal. At his sentencing, Tank said nothing on his own behalf. And although he was never officially charged in the death of Menendez, the judge showed no mercy. Tank received a mandatory sentence of 360 months, and he still got the double murder case pending

Because of Tank's immediate acceptance of guilt, his conviction and sentencing were handled quickly. The judge recommended he be placed in a facility near Miami. For security purposes, he was transferred to the Duval County Jail until the U.S. Marshals took him to the Federal Detention Center in Tallahassee, Florida. Making this his last stop before being transferred to a United States Penitentiary.

# Chapter 22

Victoria had been advised by her court-appointed attorney to come into his office so they could discuss her legal options. After waiting for him to finish a phone call, she was finally led in. Victoria sat in one of the brown leather chairs in front of his desk and listened as he went over the benefits of pleading guilty.

"The U.S. Attorney is willing to give you a sentence of 120 months, but you will need to take the deal today," her attorney said, showing her a copy of the plea agreement. "I will go over the stipulations with you, but we must do this today, before the government seeks other enhancements."

"Enhancements!" Victoria screamed. "You call me in here like you had good news, and the only thing came out your mouth is fucked up news. I got two kids I'm raising on my own. I can't do no ten years."

"Ms. Cole, the agent overseeing your case was outraged when he heard about this plea deal. If you do not sign and obligate the government to honor this deal, I'm sorry to say you're gonna do a hell of a lot more than ten years."

Victoria shook her head. "So, you telling me if I don't hurry up and plead guilty, they gon' give me more time, just like that."

"Look Ms. Cole, they have three witnesses ready to take the stand on you. That alone is enough to start your sentence at a mandatory twenty years. I strongly advise that you take this deal. It is your best option. At this moment, the government is not upset with you, but, when you reject this deal, it's going to be like spitting in their face."

"I'm not taking no plea for ten years." Tears formed in Victoria's eyes. "I'm going to trial."

"And you will lose," he quickly replied. "Ms. Cole, please don't make the same mistake as so many others, believing that, since they were caught with no drugs, the government's case was weak. I swear, this conversation is like déjà vu. Three months ago, I had a client of mine and his girlfriend sitting right in that same chair you're in. I explained to the girlfriend that she'd been implicated with her boyfriend and was facing the same charge as him. But because of her stubbornness she received a 22-year sentence when she was just looking at seven. I implore you, please don't make the same decision she did. Consider the plea agreement before it's too late."

Victoria tilted her head up at the ceiling, then gazed out the window. And, just as clearly as if they were standing outside, P-Rock's and Victor's faces were all she could see. Victoria pulled her purse strap onto her shoulder and stood up.

"I've decided it's time I find myself a new lawyer. You have a good day." She walked out of his office.

Anna was parked out front. As Victoria walked down the stairs, Anna could see the tears in her eyes. When Victoria climbed inside her Volvo, she silently looked at Victoria as she let it all out.

"I need another lawyer!"

"What happened? I thought he had good news."

"If me doing ten years is good news, I hate to hear the bad."

"I can call my grandfather's lawyer. He's a close friend of our family, and considered one of the best in the state."

"Please give him a call. And speaking of your grandfather, where is he?"

"Let's just say he's far away and safe," Anna answered. "You know what? You can give the lawyer a call. He might ask questions that only you can answer. Here's his number. His name is Mike Carson.

Anna drove Victoria to Mrs. Knowles' house. During the ride, Victoria briefly spoke with Mike Carson. Carson could sell milk to a cow, and, as always, he sold himself to Victoria. He convinced her he was the right lawyer to handle her case, and she made an appointment to see him at nine in the morning. When

Anna pulled up in front of Mrs. Knowles' house, Victoria noticed Victor outside playing in the sprinklers, while as usual Mrs. Knowles sat on the porch talking on the phone. Victoria thanked Anna for the ride, and they said their good-byes.

Mrs. Knowles ended her call and met Victoria halfway. "Victoria, that boy of yours gon' be good and tired tonight. He's been up all day running and playing. Oh, and I let P-Rock go down the street wit' dem Wilson children."

Victor ran into Victoria's arms, getting water on her blouse.

"Boy, you done got me soakin wet," Victoria said, hugging Victor.

"So, how did things go wit' your lawyer?" Mrs. Knowles asked.

"I don't have a lawyer, and I don't think I ever did. Tomorrow I have an appointment wit' another one. I gotta be at his office in the morning. Mrs. Knowles, if it's alright with you, we're gonna stay here tonight."

"Of course. Now, y'all c'mon inside so you two can dry off."

Later that night, after P-Rock and Victor were fast asleep, Victoria went outside, sat on the porch, and looked at the stars. She was outside for about twenty minutes, then Mrs. Knowles joined he.

"Can't sleep?" Mrs. Knowles asked.

"Even if I lay in the bed, with so much on my mind, there's no way I'm getting any sleep."

Victoria and Mrs. Knowles talked about what the lawyer had said earlier. By the time Victoria explained how much time she was facing, her tears were pouring down her face again.

"Victoria, maybe taking that plea agreement is not such a bad idea. You can still have a life after ten years, but, if you go to trial and get a life sentence, Lord knows dem children won't be able to handle that."

"Mrs. Knowles, you talking like if I go to trial, I'm gonna lose fa'sho."

"Dem people got a 98% conviction rate. They don't lose often."

"The only thing they have is three statements from some snitches that don't know what the hell they're talking about. I don't even sell drugs no more. Black's dead, Peanut's dead and…" Victoria paused and, at that very moment, simply dropped her head. "Latricia may have wrote statements on me."

"What make you say that?"

"Awhile back, I went over to Latricia mom's house. She told me she had some minor legal problems, and I haven't seen her since. Damn! I should've seen the signs. They were right in my face." Victoria shook her head at the thought of Latricia's betrayal.

"Victoria, that's another reason not to go to trial. You friend get on that stand and testify on you, chile, you'll be nothing more than an addition to that 98% conviction rate."

"It's not a hundred," Victoria replied softly.

"If you make dem have to call people to the stand, you will lose. I tell you what, go ahead and talk to that lawyer tomorrow. If he's talking like your last lawyer, you truly need to consider that plea agreement."

The following morning, Mrs. Knowles drove Victoria to the law office of Mike Carson. Victoria walked inside the two-story building and introduced herself to Carson's secretary.

"Good morning, Ms. Cole. I'll let Mr. Carson know you're here," the secretary said, then made a call.

Moments later, an average-size white male, mid-forties, full head of hair, and dressed in gray slacks, white dress shirt, and a vest the same color as his slacks, stepped out of the elevator and approached Victoria with his hand extended.

"Morning, Ms. Cole. I'm Mike Carson. It's a pleasure to meet you. Why don't we go in my office to discuss your case?"

Victoria walked alongside Carson as he led her to the elevator. They rode to the second floor, and, after stepping out of the elevator, Carson opened his door, allowing Victoria into his lovely spacious office. She sat in one of the two chairs facing his mahogany desk. Carson walked around and sat behind his desk. He typed for a moment on his keyboard, then noticed Victoria observing a few paintings from his art collection.

"I see you're admiring my paintings. Those are just a couple pieces I collected on a trip I took to Chartres."

"Where's that?" she asked.

"It's a small town southwest of Paris. Now, as much as I love indulging in conversation about French art, I'm sure that is not the subject you are here to discuss. So please, tell me about your case. Start from the beginning."

Victoria left out no detail. She described everything from the moment she arrived at the salon to the second she was taken into the D.E.A. headquarters. Carson gave Victoria his undivided attention. Once she finished, he gave her his evaluation of her options. Victoria's story was one of many he'd heard before. Carson went straight to what he considered the worst-case scenario. He spoke bluntly and firmly as he estimated the likelihood of Victoria going to prison for the allegations the government had against her.

"Ms. Cole, as I advise all my clients, my ethics speak for themselves. If you decide to retain me, I can't and won't promise your trial will end in your favor. The U.S.D.A. stacks the deck against any defendant who challenges the government. If you choose to plead guilty, I can promise you I will get you the lowest sentence possible, and that I can guarantee."

"Mr. Carson, I came here because I'm not trying to go to prison. Please tell me what I can do to prevent going to prison?"

"Well, I would advise cooperation, but you still may go to prison." Carson stopped and let that choice linger in the air, then continued. "The government does not give out probation on the type of charges you face. Going to trial and prevailing is basically the only avenue you have. The government do not drop charges unless there's a stronger charge to take its place."

"How much will you charge me to retain your services?"

"Ms. Cole, if you were to plead guilty and I was to negotiate a plea deal, I would file every motion possible to make sure you receive every downward departure you're entitled to, and frankly you fit the criteria for several. My fee would normally be $15,000. However, I will only charge you $10,000."

"Ten thousand dollars and I'm still going to prison?" Victoria said in disbelief. "I could've kept my court-appointed attorney for that."

"Ms. Cole, I've laid out my work ethics. I'm not a magician. I've dealt with many cases identical to yours, and the results never change. Either you do a little time or a lot. That's a choice you're going to have to make yourself, because you're the one who's going to have to do the time. But if you want to take a chance and fight, well, goddammit, we'll fight! My fee for trials starts at $50,000, plus expenses."

Victoria didn't frown nor blink at his price.

He continued, "Will we win? I don't know. But, Ms. Cole, I'm not some half-assed attorney. What you will be getting is one of the best attorneys money can buy," Carson assured her in a stern tone to get his point across.

After he finished, Victoria looked him directly in the eyes, smiled and said two words.

"Let's fight!"

****

Mike Carson and his team of paralegals had gone over every inch of Victoria's discovery. Before the trial date, they'd searched meticulously for any loopholes in her case. The day had come for Victoria's pre-trial conference. For this particular hearing, there was no need for Victoria to be present. Mike Carson battled strenuously with the U.S.D.A. During the hearing, Carson was given the names of government witnesses and the statements that were going to be used against Victoria.

Carson had no knowledge of the witnesses' relations with Victoria, but, after skimming over their statements, he was well aware their comments would be extremely damaging to her case. After the pre-trial conference, Carson returned to his office, removed his jacket, loosened his tie, and plopped down behind his desk. His secretary called and relayed all his messages over the intercom. She mentioned one particular name, making Carson sit straight up in his chair. He thanked her and quickly returned the most important call.

"Señor Carson."

"Sorry I missed your call, Mr. Diaz. How's everything going?"

"You have to tell me."

"Certainly, on the issue we discussed, surprisingly, even facing so much time, she's still holding strong. We're preparing to go to trial soon. There are some very harmful statements made against her, but don't worry. I should be able to undercut the witnesses' credibility. Well… all except for one."

"One!'

"Yes, a very close friend. She may be a problem."

"All problems can be solved, with the right solution," Diaz said.

"Not this one. It will do more harm than good. Right now, Victoria is demonstrating that loyalty does still exist. Let me deal with the government witnesses. You just keep doing what you're doing." They ended their call. Immediately after, he called Victoria to give her the latest developments in her case. "…Ms. Cole, I've tussled back and forth with the U.S Attorney over your case. As of now, he's confident that, with the charges pending against you, he'll get a conviction."

"Will he?" she asked.

"I told you, I never promise the outcome of a verdict. He asked the judge to set a trial date. But, thankfully, the Judge understood that, with your case and my Post Office murder case, I need more time. So, during this extension, we will need to go over these statements that the government plans to use against you. It's not mandatory that you come in, but I figured you would like to know who has betrayed you. From my experience, most of them I will be able to discredit in cross-examination. The only one that's troubling me is this close friend of yours. She is really hurting your case."

"I know who she is Mr. Carson. I really don't care to see what she said about me."

"I understand, Ms. Cole. Well, if you can think of anything that may help, let me know. By next week, we will need to prep you, just in case you will need to take the stand. Normally I would never put a client on the stand, but, if these witnesses testify and you say nothing, the jury will see that as guilt."

"OK, Mr. Carson, if I can think of anything, I'll give you a call. Bye!"

Victoria could not hide her anger. Her eyebrows arched, and images of Latricia flashed through her mind, which made her even madder. Only one thing could pacify her anger, and that was answers. She gathered her kids and asked Mrs. Knowles to take her to Latricia's mom's house.

For the entire ride, they rode in silence. Victoria reminisced on childhood memories. Good and bad thoughts danced through her mind until Mrs. Knowles pulled up in front of the all-too-familiar home of Latricia's mom. Victoria's disgust at Latricia's betrayal returned with a vengeance. She quickly got out of the car, angrily stomped her way to the porch, and banged on the door.

The door opened, and Latricia's mom greeted Victoria with a warm smile. "Hey, Victoria, how've you been doing?" she asked, holding the door open so Victoria could come inside.

"I'm fine, Mrs. Lawrence. I won't be here long, I wanted to have a word with Latricia. Is she here?"

"Sorry, Victoria, Latricia hasn't been here in a while. Latricia is in jail."

"Jail! What did she do?" Victoria inquired, wanting as many details as possible.

Mrs. Lawrence stepped out on the porch with Victoria and broke down all Latricia's problems. She told Victoria about the counterfeit and drug case, dealing with HIV, and Latricia attempt on her own life. The emotional stress caused by Latricia's reckless behavior had started taking a toll on Mrs. Lawrence. Victoria's presence was much needed. She poured out her heart and soul, confirming her pain with tears of sorrow.

Trying to imagine what Latricia had been going through left Victoria with mixed emotions. But the fact Latricia had stolen the counterfeit money and was the government's number one witness outweighed any pity Victoria felt.

Seeing Mrs. Lawrence in tears weighed heavily on her heart. Victoria gave her a hug and said she'd call her later, then slowly walked back to the car with an unmistakable expression of sadness.

Mrs. Knowles looked over at her and said, "You might want to consider that plea."

****

The weeks rapidly passed to the day of Victoria's trial. The night prior, Victoria had a case of insomnia. She tossed and turned all through the night, seeing visions of twelve strangers with her life in their hands. The time had finally come, Victoria arrived at the downtown federal courthouse alone. Mrs. Knowles had explained she would be unable to accompany her due to a morning doctor's appointment. Victoria found the courtroom her trial was being held in after nervously browsing through the docket sheet. Then, from a distance, she heard someone call her name.

"Good morning, Ms. Cole," Mike Carson said.

"Believe me, there's nothing good about this one."

"I can see the nervousness written all over your face. Just relax and let me throw the punches. If we're lucky, I might even throw a knockout. And don't forget, if I need you to get on the stand, remember everything I taught you, try not to pause as you give your answers, and make them brief and straight to the point."

"Is there anything else?"

"Yes, there is. Speaking in my second-rate urban dialect, I want you to know I'm a ride'a," Carson jokingly said, bringing a smile to Victoria's face.

Victoria and Carson entered the courtroom together. A chill went through Victoria's spine as she looked at the massive size of the judge's bench and the heavy presence of the U.S. Marshals. She sat in the last row while Mike Carson exchanged handshakes with other defense attorneys and members of the court staff. After what seemed like the longest ten minutes of Victoria's life, the bailiff entered the courtroom from a door near the judge's bench and loudly advised everyone to rise for the Honorable Martha Cowart.

"You all may be seated," The judge said as she sat down. "Mr. Stevens, please call the first case."

The court clerk, Mr. Stevens, rose with a piece of paper in his hand. "Yes, your Honor. The court calls the case of United States of America versus Victoria Cole."

The clerk's very words, 'United States of America versus Victoria Cole' turned the butterflies in her stomach into falcons, ripping at her gut with their talons. Victoria walked to the front table and sat next to Mike Carson. The judge addressed a question to Victoria, then had to repeat herself because of Victoria's unresponsiveness.

"…Ms. Cole, are you under the influence of any type of alcohol or narcotics, legal or illegal?"

"No, Your Honor," Victoria answered.

"Very well. The government may proceed."

The first two hours of Victoria's trial went relatively well. The government only called one witness, D.E.A. Special Agent Finzi. Finzi gave the court flawless testimony on Victoria's participation in the drug operation. Mike Carson scribbled down several notes on his legal pad, and patiently waited to cross-examine Finzi, hoping to capitalize on contradictions.

U.S. Attorney Rawls looked towards the judge. "I have nothing further, Your Honor."

And, as usual, Mike Carson wasted no time. "Good morning, Agent Finzi. Excuse me if I'm brusque. But, as the records reflects, you testified under oath that your investigation on Ms. Cole surpassed twelve months. Is that correct?"

"Yes, sir," Finzi replied.

Carson walked closer to Finzi. "During the beginning stage of your investigation, what incriminating acts, if any, did you witness Ms. Cole commit to further extend your surveillance?"

"In our initial investigation, we had no knowledge of Ms. Cole. Harold Cole Jr., also known as Crow, was our primary target. Because of the violence surrounding the drug trade, Harold

Cole lost his life during a drug deal gone wrong. Also, Harold Cole was Victoria Cole's brother.

"So, Ms. Cole was not even on your agenda?" Carson asked.

Finzi gave Carson a self-asserting grin. "Like I said, not initially. But through our confidential informant, it was brought to our attention that Harold Cole or Crow left Ms. Cole with several kilos of cocaine."

Victoria listened to Finzi's testimony, and his words made her fingers tremble. She began getting worried as she wondered what else Finzi knew.

"Our C.I. has been reporting directly to me on a regular basis. If I may refer to my notes," Finzi said without giving Carson the chance to answer. "The month of last November, Ms. Cole along with a Latricia Joyner cooked several ounces of cocaine, turning it into crack. She'd done this at least six times that month. Then she arranged meetings to distribute her drugs to other members of her organization."

Carson saw right through Finzi's intentions. Finzi's goal was to paint a vivid picture to the jury that Victoria was far from innocent. Carson cut Finzi's cross-examination short.

"That will be all, Agent Finzi." Carson returned to his seat next to Victoria. He watched as Finzi stepped down, looked over at the jury and gave them a nod. "What the fuck was that?" Carson whispered.

"Do you think you won that round?" Victoria asked.

"I don't know, but it sure would've been nice to have your friend Latricia Joyner on the stand to discredit that garbage."

Victoria turned and gave Carson a puzzling look. "Latricia is a government witness."

Without even glancing at his copy of the witness list, Carson replied, "No, she's not."

"Yes. she is. That's my close friend you were talking about."

"Ms. Cole, I do this for a living," Carson whispered. "Believe me, Latricia Joyner's name is nowhere on the list. Even if it was, the person we need to be worried about is the C.I…"

"Your Honor, if the court is ready, I'd like to introduce my next witness," U.S. Attorney Rawls said. "We call Mrs. Monica Knowles."

The name Monica Knowles echoed in Victoria's ears as if the prosecutor were repeating it over and over. She watched in total disbelief as Mrs. Knowles walked into the courtroom.

Mrs. Knowles looked straight toward the judge's bench as she strolled down the center of the courtroom. She dared not look in Victoria's direction. Instead, she focused solely on U.S. Attorney Rawls. He gave a smile, then led her to the stand. As Mrs. Knowles was seated, the bailiff told her to state her full name and raise her right hand to be sworn in.

Victoria leaned over and whispered in Carson's ear. "Why didn't you tell me she was testifying against me?"

"I told you to come view the statements. You said you knew who she was." Carson whispered. "Apparently, you were wrong."

U.S. Attorney Rawls stood between the jury and Mrs. Knowles. "Good morning, Mrs. Knowles. We've met several times, correct?"

"Yes, on many different occasions."

"If you will, Mrs. Knowles, please tell the court what your relationship is with the Drug Enforcement Administration."

"For the past five years, I've been cooperating with the D.E.A and Agent Finzi as a registered confidential informant."

"And what is your reason for cooperating with Agent Finzi? Have you been arrested?"

"I've seen too many killings behind drug wars, and I wanted to make a difference."

Rawls smiled. "Well, aren't you the model citizen," he said, getting a few chuckles out of the jury.

As Mrs. Knowles continued to help U.S. Attorney Rawls secure a conviction, Victoria pitifully looked on with red teary eyes, hurt by the betrayal of the woman she had viewed as a mother figure. Victoria looked over, noticing that Carson was jotting down numerous remarks Mrs. Knowles was making.

"Now, Mrs. Knowles, what has the defendant Victoria Cole done with the cocaine her brother left for her?" Rawls asked.

"OBJECTION!" Mike Carson jumped up and shouted. "He's leading the witness, Your Honor."

"Overruled," the judge spat back.

"Victoria came over to my house and asked me to hide some drugs while she and her friend cooked up the rest."

"What do you mean, 'cooked'?"

"Crack. She cooked the coke to crack," Mrs. Knowles answered.

"Then what happened?"

"All of a sudden, people started coming by her duplex all through the night. Sometimes Victoria paid me to clean her house, and while I was there, I would see her give people small and large amounts of coke and crack. Then there were times she would have me to hide thousands of dollars for her."

"Did Ms. Cole ever commit any violent acts due to her participation in the drug trade?"

"Yes. Her friend Latricia's husband sent a threat for Victoria to collect the money he owed in blood, and one of her workers, Black, kept asking her to let him kill her husband,"

In a compassionate tone, Rawls asked Mrs. Knowles, "What order did Victoria give Black?"

"She said not yet, he's going to get his."

"And where is Latricia's husband now?" Rawls softly asked.

"He's dead. He was tortured, then murdered. It was all over the news."

"OBJECTION!' Mike Carson sprung to his feet, yelling once again.

"Overruled," the judge said, glancing at Carson.

Carson plopped down in his seat and, under his breath, said, "I'm gonna eat that old bitch alive."

As Mrs. Knowles testified, Victoria studied the jurors' faces to see their expressions. One by one, Victoria observed some members of the jury shake their heads, while others listened to Mrs. Knowles and showed no emotion.

"Just one more question," Rawls said. "What would you say was the most drugs you've seen in Ms. Cole's possession at one time?"

"On four different occasions, I witnessed two suitcases filled with dozens of kilos."

"No further questions, Your Honor."

Mike Carson glanced over at Victoria and winked his left eye before rising to his feet. And he wasted no time, hitting Mrs. Knowles with a barrage of questions.

"How are you, Mrs. Knowles?"

"Blessed," she replied.

"That's nice," Carson said, not bothering to hide his sarcasm. "I was listening to you testify against Ms. Cole. Now, since you're under oath, I want to be very clear and make sure you understand that, by lying under oath, you could be charged with perjury."

"I have no reason to lie."

"Great! Earlier, you gave a very detailed testimony about drugs and killings. And, as you did so, you told this court that you wanted to make a difference in your community. That is your sole reason for your cooperation, correct?"

"Yes, it is."

"Do you feel all drug dealers destroy communities?" Carson asked.

"Of course."

"Mrs. Knowles, during your five years of cooperating with the DEA, has your husband benefited and received time off his sentence?"

Rawls hadn't prepped Mrs. Knowles for that question. She sat on the stand speechless, then nodded her head.

"I'm sorry, you're going to have to verbally answer for the record."

"Yes! I am doing a third party for my husband," she said firmly.

"And what kind of charge is your husband serving time for?"

"OBJECTION!" Mrs. Knowles' husband is not on trial," Rawls blasted.

"Overruled," the judge said, then looked at Carson. "This is a warning, counsellor. Tread lightly."

Carson nodded. "Yes, Your Honor. Can the witness now answer the question?"

Mrs. Knowles waited until the judge told her to answer the question. "My husband has drug charges."

"Drug charges! Please explain to the court how you can truly be making a difference if your real motive for testifying is to get your drug-dealing husband out of prison. And this guy is a heavy hitter, he was known in the streets as the real deal. Why would you want this drug dealer back on the streets when he poisoned so many communities?"

"Because he's my husband!"

Rawls dropped his head.

Carson smiled and went in for the kill. "Mrs. Knowles remember what I said about lying under oath. Other than cooperating with the D.E.A. to get your husband's sentence reduced, have you ever assisted in any type of law enforcement without looking for something in return?"

"No."

"Each time you testify or help with an arrest, it is for the sole purpose of your drug-dealing husband?"

Rawls jumped to his feet. "Your Honor, I object, and Carson's line of questioning is out of order!"

The judge banged her mallet and pointed her index finger at U.S. Attorney Rawls. "Counselor, you do not tell me what is out of order in my courtroom. I tell you. And the witness will answer the question."

Rawls quickly returned to his seat.

Carson turned back towards Mrs. Knowles and repeated his question. "Have you ever assisted the D.E.A. without your husband benefiting from your cooperation?"

"No."

"You certainly are the model citizen," Carson said, cutting his eyes at Rawls.

Mrs. Knowles desperately wanted to get down from the stand, but Carson continued drilling her.

"Do you have any substantial proof, confession, or any kind of evidence that Ms. Cole orchestrated the death of Latricia's husband, Tray Joyner?"

"No."

"I'm through with this liar. Nothing further!"

"OBJECTION!" Rawls jumped up screaming as Carson walked back to his seat. "Your Honor, the counselor is belittling my witness."

"The jury will scratch that last comment made by defense counsel," The judge said, then stared at Carson. "No more warnings, counselor. Do I make myself clear?"

"Yes, Your Honor."

Now that Carson was finished with Mrs. Knowles, she practically ran out of the courtroom.

U.S. Attorney Rawls then called Taj, and then Country, to the stand. And Mike Carson destroyed the testimony of each. By the time the Rawls presented his closing argument, Carson was quite pleased with the direction in which the trial was going. Several times, Carson glanced over at the jury with an "I know you're not buying that" expression on his face.

After Rawls delivered an impressive closing argument, Carson gave his. He spoke passionately to the jury, using Victoria's tragedies as leverage to their hearts. He hand-fed the jury with truth and capitalized on the government's witnesses' contradictions. Then the jury was given their instructions by the judge, and finally they rose and left the courtroom to deliberate.

Most people in the courtroom cleared out after the jury left. Victoria sat in the lobby alone, overcome with grief from Mrs. Knowles' testimony. Taj and Country taking the stand wasn't much of a surprise, but Mrs. Knowles…

Victoria was allowed to go home. Before leaving, Carson strongly advised Victoria to go nowhere near Mrs. Knowles' house. She caught a cab to Pembroke Pines and had Anna drop her kids off, and she stayed there for the rest of the night.

Bright and early the following morning, Anna rang the doorbell, ready to pick up P-Rock and Victor. Anna wanted to support Victoria and come to court with her, but Victoria wouldn't allow her, especially with no one else to trust with her boys. They all climbed into Anna's car, Victoria made arrangements with Pam, Crow's daughter mother to look after her boys. After dropping off P-Rock and Victor, Anna drove to the courthouse.

In the lobby, Carson told Victoria the jury had not reached a verdict. Hours passed, and Carson came back and forth, checking on Victoria. While Carson was talking to Victoria trying to lift her spirits, two U.S. Marshals approached and informed Carson that the jury had returned from deliberation. Victoria's body got a jolt from those words. Carson stood and led the way back to the courtroom. Victoria walked behind him, slow and nervous. She sat in the same seat next to him. Minutes later, the jury entered the courtroom.

Everyone settled into their seats, and the Judge asked the foreman if they'd reached a verdict. The suspense was extremely intense, and, in Victoria's mind, all eyes were on her. The foreman stood up and passed the judge Victoria's fate, then put on his glasses and read.

Victoria closed her eyes as if she didn't want to see the words.

The foreman said, "In the case of Victoria Cole, we the jury could not reach a unanimous verdict."

The judge glared at the foreman. "Do you think, with more time, a verdict could be reached?

"No, Your Honor. Several members of the jury are steadfast in their decision."

"Very well," the judge replied.

Victoria's case had a hung jury.

Rawls rose and took a couple of steps towards the judge's bench. "Your Honor, the government will be retrying Ms. Cole as soon as possible."

Confused, Victoria leaned over and whispered in Carson's ear, "What do he mean by 'retry'?"

Carson patted Victoria on the shoulder. “Don’t worry about his temper tantrum right now. What we accomplished today rarely happens in this courtroom. Enjoy this moment. With what I did to the government witnesses, and once I get your trial transcripts, when the time come, if Rawls pushes for another trial, the words you will hear will be ‘not guilty.’ Now, let’s get out of here. Go home and take pleasure in being able to hug your kids.”

Victoria and Carson stood up and she gave him a hug, then he led her out the courtroom. Outside she, hugged Carson again before they went their separate ways. Victoria was truly happy not to be going to prison, but her happiness was short-lived with the thought of Mrs. Knowles’ betrayal weighing heavily on her mind.

# Epilogue

The following week, Latricia was sentenced as a first-time offender. Because of her lack of cooperation against Victoria, the U.S. Attorney used all her prior statements against her. During her sentencing, Taj testified, and due to his testimony, Latricia's sentence was enhanced. Her possession of a combination of more than 50 grams of crack and ten kilos of cocaine put her guideline range from 188 to 260 months. After all the court's formalities, and Latricia's mother's pleas for leniency, the judge sentenced her to 240 months, demonstrating to Latricia the truth of an old saying that circulates throughout the Federal Bureau of Prisons: "There's only two kinds of people in the Feds, the ones that told and the ones that wish they told."

****

It didn't take long for Tank to adjust to everyday life in a Federal U.S.P. Over three months had passed since his arrival, and, in such little time, Tank had already been in two fights. Yet, thanks to the code true convicts followed in the pen, none of the staff members were aware of any of Tank's beefs.

Victims that had been robbed by Tank in the streets plotted and did their best to put a rusty piece of steel between his ribs, but, in each failed attempt, Tank's assailants learned the hard way how vigilant Tank truly was. He kept two six-inch shanks of his own on him at all times. Unfortunately, that was life in the pen; you either set an example or got made an example of. Tank knew all too well what it took to survive in the belly of the beast.

One mid-afternoon much like any other, Tank was waiting in line to use the phone. Once his turn came and a phone was free, just as Tank walked towards the phone, a tall skinny guy from D.C. rushed in front of him. Instantly feeling violated and disrespected, Tank stormed over and quickly got into an argument. The rapid escalation was mere seconds away from bloodshed. Tank was looking at the guy's neck preparing to stab him, when suddenly he was approached by an older inmate.

"Youngblood, let dat shit go."

"Fuck dat! This bitch ass muthafucka must think I give a fuck 'bout him or his boys," Tank said, peering around with a fierce look on his face.

"C'mon, not over no phone. Save dat frustration for someone dat deserve it."

The D.C. guy gave the same stare back to Tank. "Cold, you betta get his pussy ass from 'round here, before he leave in a bag!"

Tank frowned and attempted to rush the guy, but the older inmate held him back.

"Not like this. You gotta handle dat shit another time. C'mon upstairs. Look like you could use a drink. I got some of dat white lightning."

Had it not been for the fact the older inmate was from Miami (and, in prison, this made him a homeboy), Tank never would have agreed to end the confrontation peacefully. Instead, he followed the other inmate upstairs. Tank entered his cell and, as usual, kept his guard up. He cautiously watched as the older inmate slowly got on his knees and began shifting his boots and sneakers around.

"What dey call you, Youngblood?"

"Tee!" Tank replied.

"Everybody call me Cold." he said, then pulled out a batch of prison wine from underneath his bed. He untied at least eight plastic bags from the wine, which was a way to prevent the scent from being detected. "Yeah, Tee, dis shit here dat gas. Made it myself."

Tank hadn't move since he'd stepped into the cell and stood next to the sink and toilet.

"Here you go." Cold passed Tank a cup of the hooch.

Tank accepted the cup and guzzled the contents.

ɪn, Tee, you drunk dat shit like water. Lem'me fill you ,

'Nah, I'm good," Tank said.

"Drink up, man. Don't tease yo'self. I can't drink all this by myself anyway." He poured Tank another cup and another. The white lightening started to affect Tank's behavior.

He started talking more than usual. He began reminiscing about the many different strippers he'd been with. "Shhhhhit… I use to run through all dem hoes at Coco's and the Rolex. It was one bitch from Alabama, she got away. I ain't never get to fuck her."

Cold listened and let Tank have the floor. He handed Tank another cup. Tank was unaware how much alcohol he'd consumed. Cold was babysitting his cup while Tank drank until he was intoxicated.

"You good people, Cold. I would've fuck wit's you on da bricks," Tank slurred. "I should've been hanging around some ol' gees."

Cold peeped into Tank's cup, making sure it didn't stay empty long.

Seeing someone pass the door for the second time, Tank took a couple of steps and looked through the rectangular glass window, but no one was there. He stared out the window a few seconds, turned, and noticed the photos Cold had taped to his wall. Tank's eyes went from picture to picture. Suddenly they were glued to a photo of Victoria. He then noticed a photo of Crow smiling with P-Rock and Victor. Out of his peripheral vision, Tank caught a glimpse of movement at the door. He turned and looked directly into the eyes of the D.C. guy he'd had problems with.

"What da fuck you…!" Tanks words were interrupted. The only sound escaping his mouth were painful grunts from the ten-inch ice pick-like shank Cold repeatedly stabbed him with.

"My name is not Cold like the temperature. It's Cole, as in the father of Victoria Cole." He whispered in Tank's ear as he pushed his shank into his ribs. "The grandfather of the child you shot." He stabbed him again. "And the mad muthafucka whose

COMING SOON...

# PART OF THE GAME
# II
# JACK BOYS... R.P.S. (THE ROSE PETAL STRANGLER)